DEMONS IN THE TALL GRASS

DEMONS
IN THE TALL GRASS

James Tipper

Edited by Elaine Partnow
Cover art by John Pelico, Jr.

A Waxlight Press Book
LOS ANGELES

Library of Congress Control Number: 2015947345
ISBN: 978-0-9882433-6-1

Text set in Papyrus and Constantia

For Jim and Margaret Ann

Your boy has slain his demons.

ACKNOWLEDGMENTS

Nobody writes a long novel without help. Many thanks to Darcy Lindner for her knowledge of the funereal arts, to Dave DiGregorio of the West Hollywood Sheriff's Department for his procedural help, to Peter Glawatz for his first hand experience in small town Nebraska, as well as for his patience and support, and to Elaine Partnow and Cristal Brawley for their keen editing.

Though the characters and events in this book may bear a resemblance to people and events in your own town, this story is a work of fiction.

Chapter 1

The Antique

It was just another day in June when Linda Vanderboom realized she might be a "hoarder." She narrowed her eyes at the shrink on the television and stopped chewing. It had been only moments ago that she had a harmless passion for collecting antiques, but now...

"Hoarder..." she grumbled to herself, one hand buried in a bag of baked potato chips--the kind that are supposed to make you thinner. She figured they just might, mostly because the chips tasted like shit and she found little pleasure in eating them. Morosely, she popped another chip into her mouth anyway. She plucked a crumb from her powder blue house dress, lodged between two rolls of her stomach. Nope, the chips were definitely not working.

On the television, the snot-nosed shrink--a pretty boy with teeth that were far too white to be fooling anybody--was still spouting his theories.

"Oh, so I'm crazy now?" Linda asked the tube, wrinkling her nose. Yet, she began wondering exactly when it was that she had first started collecting things. She had never really thought about it before. She glanced around her darkened room, a small den lit only by the meager offering coming from the fringed shade of a single Tiffany lamp on an end table. She frowned. She was pretty sure she knew when.

It all started when her husband died. Sure, she had always liked collecting things, but maybe she had gone just a tad overboard after Roger kicked the bucket--because finally she could, because finally nobody was holding her reins. After years of poverty and neglect she figured she deserved whatever she wanted. Roger never wanted her to work. "I'm the old-fashioned type," he used to say.

That was harmlessly folksy in those early days of their courtship, but once the knot was tied the terms of their arrangement quickly changed. The wine and roses dried up.

Roger's son Lance from a previous marriage was in junior high when Linda met Roger. Linda was given an allowance, and most of it went to supporting the boy. Roger was even known to tally the receipts that littered their old oaken, roll-top desk. As for the rest of the cash he managed to net from his auto body shop in downtown Dawson, he pissed it away at the track.

Roger Vanderboom's horse never came in, but Linda's finally did. Roger dropped dead three months ago, at the age of 68, after ignoring his rotten liver. There was precious little money left to pass on to her or to Lance, so Linda eventually had to get a part-time job at the bakery down the street. She worked the graveyard shift, as all bakers do, spending the small hours unattended in a kitchen full of frying dough. In two and a half months she gained thirty pounds.

In a lachrymose whisper, the pretty boy shrink on the television informed the mousy girl with the wet eyes across from him that she hoards because her nest is empty. "The kids are all grown and gone away," he says. "Collecting is an obsession, an attempt to acquire what you have lost," he says.

"Bullshit..." Linda muttered through a mouthful of chips conspicuously free of everything that makes a chip good: fat, salt and flavor. "When did everything become a fucking problem? Why can't it just be a hobby? Who am I hurting?"

She realized that she had been directing these questions at a soapstone seal that shared the coffee table with no less than twenty other oddities. Among them: a turtle lamp--not plugged in, a black pickaninny doll with red lips and impossibly black felt skin, and a miniature carousel horse with a hand-painted bridle.

After sixty-two years of avoiding any diagnosis of mental illness--and probably just barely, she would concede--the loose-lipped T.V. shrink had twisted the one comfort in her life into a "potentially serious condition."

With a flourish of disgust, Linda flipped the bag of baked potato chips off of her hand and headed for the kitchen for some real food.

Pinned to the refrigerator under a magnet shaped like a square of Hershey's chocolate, was the flyer for the monthly Lincoln, Nebraska Swap Meet and Flea Market. She made a mental note to replace that magnet with something else. Fake chocolate at eye level was just masochistic.

The phone rang and Linda jumped.

It was Sylvia Blair, it had to be. No one but Sylvia called her anymore. Linda wondered if Sylvia knew that she too was crazy. After all, she hoarded--maybe even more so than Linda.

Linda's cell phone was lost within the piles of collectables on the breakfast bar. She spotted the phone and, reaching for it, knocked a mint condition Mr. Potato Head to the floor. She swore and jabbed at the talk button on the phone, "Yeah."

"Afternoon, honeybunch," came the raspy voice of Sylvia Blair. "What kind of trouble are you getting into, young lady?"

Linda only grunted a reply, bending to pick up the Mr. Potato Head. The packaging was dented. She winced.

"Well, you sound as fun as an infection," said Sylvia Blair, coughing out a smoker's laugh. "You think you got it bad? You should try my world. They keep dropping like flies."

"You still at work?" Linda asked. She could hear Sylvia drawing on a cigarette, and even after years of knowing the woman, Linda still couldn't believe that a mortician would so blatantly tease a co-worker like Death with such an overt act of defiance.

Sylvia Blair exhaled, slow and steady, her breath chugging through her lips with derisive puffs. "Ann Klimpton took everything I had to make her look good."

The potato chips in Linda's stomach kicked and tumbled. She had no idea how the Blair family did it--generation after generation-- putting make-up on dead bodies. Just hearing about it made Linda queasy, always had.

"She was never that great looking in life," Sylvia continued conspiratorially, "so I had my work cut out for me. I kind of think she looks like Ronald McDonald in a prom dress. Not my finest hour, but a vast improvement over how she normally looked. Her husband will be absolutely delighted. He will think she looks like a Vargas girl. After all, we're talking about Ralphy Klimpton, the poor son of a bitch. He had shit taste to begin with."

Linda said nothing.

"You okay, hon?" Sylvia asked.

"This shrink on the tube..." Linda began with a sigh. "Did you know we were crazy because we collect things? Yeah, it's called hoarding. We are hoarders..."

"I've heard all about it. I couldn't give two shits."

"It's the first I've heard of it."

"Well," Sylvia said with a contemplative exhalation of smoke, "what are you prepared to do about it?"

"They guy says I'm trying to replace what I've lost."

"What have you lost other than Roger? And really, you haven't lost him. We know exactly where he is." Sylvia barked out another of her notorious laughs and Linda waited patiently for it to evolve inevitably into a coughing spasm.

Sylvia continued, "You can't be trying to replace Roger with objects. That makes zero sense. You hated Roger. You were just waiting for him to die. He kept you under his thumb, gave you nothing, let you do nothing, and you're telling me that you're filling a void because he's gone? He was the void, honeybunch. So you want some material things now. Christ, everyone else does."

Linda listened to the crackle of a cigarette being dragged on before Sylvia continued, "Screw that shrink. Who knows if they even need a license to run their mouths on television? Do what makes you happy. If it's crazy, then be bat shit bonkers and own it. And...that's the name of that tune, honeybunch."

"I guess," Linda said. She wished Sylvia didn't say "and that's the name of that tune" all the time. It referenced a game show that hadn't been on for 30 years. It bugged the shit out of her, plus, it made her feel older than dirt. She could've also have done without "honeybunch."

Again, Sylvia lowered her voice to the conspiratorial whisper, "I think what you're doing is the best revenge. The ultimate."

"So, why do you hoard stuff?" Linda interrupted, regretting the question instantly. It might push a button with Sylvia, make her get dark. Linda didn't like the dark Sylvia, didn't like it at all in fact. Yet, her need to commiserate on this issue was great. She was convinced that if anyone had a problem with hoarding, it had to be Sylvia. She didn't even collect pretty things. Well, some pretty things, but mostly Sylvia liked dead things: stuffed birds, animal heads, furs, skins--and then there was the old man in the wheelchair that showed up a few months ago; the most horrible thing of all. Sylvia said the life-sized dummy was a prop from some Hollywood splatter movie. Linda would never consider buying a piece like that, keeping such a thing in her house. She couldn't even bear to look at the damned thing.

"Why do I hoard?" Sylvia repeated the question, chewing it with mock deliberation, "Because I'm crazy, too!" She laughed a booming gritty laugh that made Linda smile and cringe at the same time, like when a funhouse fright gets you and gets you good.

But Linda's smile wilted fast. This was all small talk. She knew why Sylvia was really calling. Linda promised, during one of her weaker moments, to help Sylvia set up her stall at the swap meet and flea market in Lincoln this weekend. Suddenly Linda's mind was twisting, searching for an excuse as to why she wouldn't be able to make it. It was unlikely that she could come up with something that would hold water. Sylvia knew her too well. She knew her schedule, knew she didn't have much of a life. With her husband dead and Lance married with his own family, Linda had nobody to hide behind. Nothing was going to get her out of her loose-lipped commitment. A chill began to crawl its way down her spine.

The old man in the wheelchair was going to be there.

It was Sylvia's favorite piece lately, her big draw. Passersby were almost incapable of ignoring her stall when the figure was placed at its entrance. But the nightmares it gave Linda were bad--like the kind of nightmares she had as a child--the kind that made her wake up screaming.

Linda remembered the first time Sylvia presented the figure in Omaha—a much bigger flea market where pickers from all over the country converge to find Midwestern and pioneer treasures. What you don't often see in Nebraska is movie memorabilia, and Sylvia had her fair share: gowns from period movies, little models from the days of stop motion, and props of all kinds that made her stall a popular one. But the old man in the wheelchair got the most attention at that Omaha show. No one bought it, but Sylvia didn't care. It stopped people in their tracks.

Linda wouldn't get near the thing though, wouldn't even look at it. Sure, she helped Sylvia set up her double stall, but that was the extent of it. Linda stayed well clear of the old man in the wheelchair despite the fact that the dummy enjoyed pride of place at the entrance to Sylvia's stall, right in between an early American roll-top desk and a fiberglass cowboy from an old torn down roadside concession that once served barbecue to truckers along I-80. There the dummy had sat, slumped in the wheelchair, as if sleeping and waiting for a nurse to rouse him with a teaspoon of medicine.

Linda recalled a fascinated young couple standing before it, staring, not daring to get too close. The figure was startlingly lifelike: an old man of indeterminate age slumped so that his chin rested on his chest, his eyes closed. He wore a blue wool sweater with a white shirt underneath, the collar frayed and yellowed. His pants were khaki. Pinned to the back of the simple, metal wheelchair was a sign:

"Don't touch me."

The old man's skin was so realistic that the staring young couple could not help but begin to lean forward for a closer look.

Linda had watched from a good distance away, ignoring a woman who was staring right at her and holding up a glassy-eyed doll in a summer frock.

"Excuse me?" the woman had asked. "Do you work here?"

Sylvia came to the rescue. "Ten dollars."

Linda jumped and Sylvia had leveled a loaded look at her before breezing by to intercept the couple who were staring at the old man.

"A movie prop," Sylvia said, parking beside the young couple and cocking a hand onto her hip. "Pretty realistic, huh? He looks good, doesn't he?"

The young couple had turned numbly to Sylvia. Linda could still see the identical weak smiles smeared across their faces.

"Do you want to take him home?" Sylvia had asked.

"No," the girl replied too quickly, gripping her boyfriend's hand before she could offer a recuperative smile. "I mean, no, thank you. It's really something else. Very realistic."

"You can even see the veins," the boyfriend said, waving vaguely at the old man's hands, which were folded limply atop his legs.

"The magic of Hollywood," Sylvia had said. "Lots of talent went into it. Well, please feel free to look around."

The young couple nodded and tentatively entered the shadows of the stall as Sylvia returned to Linda's side. "He sure gets 'em in the door. I don't think he's going to sell any time soon, but you never know. You just never know..."

"You there?" Sylvia prodded, wondering at the long silence.

"Yeah..." Linda said, realizing she'd been lost in thought.

"So, I'll meet you at the fairgrounds. Inside the south entrance by the hotdog stand, just like last time. Okay?"

"Sure," Linda said. She wanted to say more, maybe try one of the excuses she had loaded onto the tip of her tongue, but her mouth had gone dry.

The old man in the wheelchair was sitting in her dining room.

She stood frozen, staring across the kitchen into the little darkened space that lay just beyond, a room just big enough for her small dinette. She blinked, but still he sat there, bellied up to the wrought iron table in his wheelchair as if waiting to be served. His eyes were closed. No, not just closed; they were stitched closed, stitched closed...

So they wouldn't pop open.

His head was slumped at an angle that only the dead could manage, his chin resting on his chest against the blue knit sweater draped over his bony shoulders.

Linda was barely aware of Sylvia's voice coming from the phone that was still pressed to her ear. "...and don't worry about being crazy...you deserve to have what you've always wanted..."

The phone slipped from Linda's ear and from her hand at her side. Her arm had filled with jelly. She could still hear Sylvia's voice rattling in the phone like some far away radio station.

"...he's probably..."

"... just hungry."

Keeping an eye on the hunched figure in the dark, Linda jerked the phone back to her ear.

"WHAT!? What did you just say...?"

But there was no one there. With a trembling hand she lowered the phone and placed it on the breakfast bar. It rang again and she jumped. Her panic flared. She had taken her eyes off the old man for only an instant, but when she flicked them back toward the dining room, he was gone.

"Linda?" came Sylvia's voice. "What happened? I lost you."

"Yeah...I'm here..." Linda replied weakly.

"Shit," Sylvia hissed, "they can send a man to the moon, but I can't have a conversation with a friend a few blocks away, for chrissakes. And you wonder why America is spiraling down the crapper. So, see you at the show?"

"Yeah, sure..." Linda hung up, still shaking. She chanced a final look into the dining room, but there was nothing there, nothing but shadows. She yanked open the freezer and grabbed a pint of ice cream. She opened a kitchen drawer to get a teaspoon, thought better of it, and snatched up a tablespoon instead.

#

It was a good turnout at the Lincoln show. It always was. There seemed to be an inexhaustible supply of people looking for bargains who didn't mind sifting through someone else's abandoned treasures.

"One man's garbage..." Linda mumbled as she parked, threw on a pair of gold-rimmed, oversized Chanel knock-off sunglasses, and made her way onto the fairgrounds. She glanced down at her pass, hoping for a short walk: Stall 31.

Not bad, she thought.

Moreover, the day was mild, the humidity low. That meant she would not be bathed in sweat from the walk. Sometimes things just went your way.

Long before she spotted the stall number Linda spotted Sylvia, who was in front of her cavernous, double-wide space, bent over in front of a chest of drawers of knotty pine, her wine-colored spandex pants stretched across her considerable ass.

Sylvia righted herself and spun around, a wadded-up dust rag in her hand, her tight grey curls wobbling atop her head, her dry and deeply lined face cracking into a smile. She stretched her arms wide as Linda approached.

"You're a sight for sore eyes, Thanks for coming, honeybunch." The two kissed, Linda wrinkling her nose at the fumes coming from Sylvia's ashtray mouth. "You're just in time. The boys just unloaded the last of it."

The "boys" Linda knew to be Jimbo and Dylan, two high school seniors who often did Sylvia's grunt work, and with all the "dead weight" at the funeral home--a joke that never got old with the boys--there was always plenty of it to be had. They certainly had no problem moving Sylvia's antiques into place on a Saturday morning for money they could blow on weed that night.

Sylvia cut their embrace short. "They're just about to open the gates."

Linda followed Sylvia into the shade of the stall. In the gloom, her eyes darted up, down and around at the myriad junk: lamps, furniture, a card table full of vinyl records, a stack of books, and of course, a few of Sylvia's more imperfect examples of taxidermy – always keeping the good stuff in her house back in Dawson.

With a shudder, Linda avoided the glassy stare of a ratty great horned owl. Thankfully there was no sign of the old man in the wheelchair. Relief flooded through her. Maybe Sylvia had lost her fascination with the damned thing, finally catching a clue: no one was going to buy that lifelike rubbery old doll. Mercifully, Sylvia had left it at home, or in the basement, or buried in a landfill where it belonged.

But then she saw it.

It was sitting across the stall, his skeletal form pressed against the antique wheelchair's metal slats. He was facing away, at the far corner of Sylvia's glut of antiques and oddities, positioned strategically at a junction. Patrons were just starting to pour down the fairground's narrow market alleys and already the old man was drawing anxious glances, slowing the pace of those who had the misfortune of crossing his path.

Linda kept staring across the stall, between the pile of books on the card table and a pair of lamps with thick resin bases and missing shades. She wanted to take her eyes off the old man, but she couldn't. He sat, slumped sickeningly in his wheelchair between two whitewashed children's bookcases decorated with faded blue decoupage flowers. All she could see of the man was his back: a spray of white hair, shoulder blades hunched like a vulture's, and draped with that pilly, blue wool.

"I see you've spotted your friend," Sylvia said, coming up beside Linda.

"No friend of mine," Linda replied absently, finally looking away.

"No?" Sylvia cooed and then laughed, leaning in to whisper into Linda's ear, her breath thick and almost sticky with old smoke. "You never liked him, I know. But, when he sells—which I'm feeling good about today—when he sells, then we can throw a party and he will foot the bill. Won't that be the cat's meow?"

A woman's voice interrupted them from behind, "Excuse me. I don't see a tag on this."

Sylvia turned to see a woman hefting a tarnished bronze doorstop of an English bulldog in one limp-wristed hand. Turning back to Linda with a tight smile, Sylvia said, "Gotta run," before flitting cordially toward the woman to haggle.

In spite of her best intentions, in spite of every instinct not to do so, Linda's head slowly turned back to look at the old man in the wheelchair. He had already drawn a crowd: a pair of women in jeans and sunglasses and a little girl, her eyes wide with terror, clinging to the hem of an old woman's skirt. A big man in his late twenties-- undoubtedly the father of the little girl and probably the son of the old woman—was staring at the motionless figure with a crooked smile frozen to his face. He was intrigued. He leaned forward, staring intently at it, scanning the thing with eyes that were bright with morbid curiosity.

As Linda watched from across the stall, she saw something that made her veins ice up, something that squeezed the breath from her lungs: the big man had turned white. He had turned white and the smile on his face had died a sudden death. He had just seen something terrible. Or worse...

He had just figured something out.

Linda could feel the man's dread, feel it crawling on her as it dawned across his face like a black sun. The big man began to back away from the old man in the chair, his haunted eyes twitching, searching for his family who had long since moved on.

What the big man had seen, whatever horrible revelation had bleached his face, had been bad. And, it might still be there. It probably was. Linda found herself walking through the shadows of the stall toward the old man, walking with slow, dragging steps, not taking her eyes from the hunched-over thing.

A new crowd formed briefly around the dummy, but they peeled themselves away in the usual manner: quickly and with cartoonish grimaces twisting their faces. They weren't looking close enough. That was all. The big man had looked closely, much more closely than most people had the stomach to look, and whatever he had seen had killed the man's smile, killed it and buried it where he wouldn't find it for a very long time.

Stop walking, Linda thought. Turn and run.

She didn't want to know, but her eyes were still hopelessly locked onto the back of the old man's slumped head. She hoped her feet would have mercy on her and fail her, simply refuse to take another step. She didn't need to look that thing in the face again. She already knew it too well: the skin wrinkled like a dry, yellow onion, the thin, bloodless lips pressed together like a fingernail scratched across a cantaloupe, the eyes stitched closed like two sutured scars.

Stop walking. Just stop walking. Who cares what the big man had seen?

It had smiled, hadn't it? Its lips had peeled back and it had smiled.

Suddenly, she wanted to be far away. She wanted to go home. She wanted to scream.

Or maybe it had been his eyes. The eyes had popped their stitches. That was it. The eyes had ripped open.

"It's fake..." Linda muttered to herself dismally, "...from the movies..." But her voice was thin and weak and entirely unconvincing, like a little girl being picked on. She puffed out her cheeks and blinked hard.

Sylvia had bought an ugly, horrible, morbid dummy from some prop house. That's all. It's not like it was going to...

Bite.

Of course not. It was full of wax or silicon or straw for all she knew. It couldn't...

Get her.

Linda flashed on the shrink from the television. Maybe the guy had been right. This was crazy. Who would want such a thing? Who would even go near such a thing?

But she had gotten nearer to it. Her feet had betrayed her; they had kept shuffling forward after all, and now she was close enough to see the hand-scrawled sign that was pinned to the old man's sweater:

"Don't touch me."

She moved forward, staring, and rounded the dummy's profile to its front. A quick pant of relief puffed through her lips. It was ugly, it was disturbing, but it looked no different than usual.

A voice screeched beside her, "What is THAT? Is that real?"

Linda jumped.

A young man, effeminate and wide-eyed, was staring at the thing, his hand clasped to his mouth.

"No," Linda replied, "it's from some movie..."

"What movie?"

"Don't remember...the owner is over there," Linda said, cocking a thumb vaguely behind her.

"It's weird," said the young man lifting the hand from his mouth just long enough to speak. He shook his head and quit the patch of sunlight beyond the shadows of the stall, walking away briskly.

"Yes," Linda said to nobody, "it is...weird."

She was about to turn away when she noticed something out of the corner of her eye. Her breath caught. A confused little sound escaped her. She gripped the edge of one of the children's bookcases and leaned forward slowly. As if swallowing some foul brew, she winced and made herself look closely at the bleached and wrinkled face of the old man.

The post meridiem sun had crawled into the stall just enough to splash a small finger of light across one of the old man's cheeks. Shifting her weight, Linda saw the tiniest glint of metal. It was coming from one of the eyes. Something was wrong with one of the eyes.

She emitted another sound, but this one was a rusty pop, as if some gear deep inside her mind had snapped a spring. She clapped a hand over her mouth.

One of the eyes was half open. It was not stitched closed anymore. But they had never been stitched closed after all. No. They had been stapled. And the staples on the eyelids of the right eye, those that had been holding the old man's eye closed, had come away from the skull. But it hadn't just been holding the eye closed. It looked like...

"Gross, huh?" said a man as he breezed by. "Who would buy that?"

Linda did not respond, could not move. The papery skin around the old man's ocular bone was loose and puffing out freakishly as if it were an exit wound from a gunshot. Yet it wasn't until she saw the subtle bunching of skin around the neck, the finely torn, ragged edge that had worked its way out of the old man's yellowed collar, which she knew what she was really seeing.

"A mask..." she said, her words far away.

And it was no rubber mask. Somehow she knew that, as clearly as she knew anything. Maybe it was the color, which was the color of starved human tissue that only registers on some primal level, the fragility that crinkles and ravages dead skin when it is no longer being nourished by flowing blood. No, this was no Halloween mask. It was...

Oh, God.

It was someone else's face, peeled off them and attached to this dummy's head.

With staples.

Linda backed up, stumbling over an early American watering can with a clang. She regained her balance and kept backing away. "Why..." she said, the word leaking from her like a wound. She backed into a woman, knocking a bottle of water from her hand.

"Thanks a lot," the woman snapped, but Linda was already leaving, retreating into the shadows of the stall, panic beating at her ribcage with an icy fist. She began to run, her breath coming in shallow rasps, her hands groping the air.

Suddenly, Sylvia was gripping her by the arm, "And where are you going?"

"Away..."

"Oh, no you're not, honeybunch. Not now. We have a big problem. He's showing through isn't he? Why didn't you tell me he was showing through? We've got to get him out of sight. Jimbo and Dylan aren't coming back until the end of the show and I can't move him alone."

"Showing through?" Linda whined. "Showing through?"

"What has gotten into you?" Sylvia spat. Her eyes narrowed. "You were going to take off weren't you?"

"Who..." Linda asked weakly, "who is showing through?"

"You were going to take off!" Sylvia said, her eyes steely and accusing. She tugged Linda into the stall by the elbow, "Get in here and help. This wheelchair doesn't move for shit. It's rusted up. We have to pick it up and hide it until I can fix his face. Someone was touching it. The staples are coming out!"

Linda was frozen. Sylvia tugged her arm again but she wouldn't move, wouldn't blink. Sylvia glanced around to see if anyone was watching and then slapped Linda across the face--slapped her hard. "Don't pussy out on me now, Linda! Don't you dare! You hear me? After all I did for you!"

Linda rubbed her cheek dreamily and turned her wet eyes beseechingly to Sylvia, "Who? Who is showing through?"

"Have you lost your mind?" Sylvia scolded, tugging Linda vainly toward the old man in the chair. "What do you mean who? It's Roger. It's your husband. Who do you think? And everyone is going to know that if his mask falls off! There are people here who might recognize him! If that happens...don't think it's just me who is going to be up the creek, honeybunch. You're going down with me! And that's the name of that tune!"

"Whose face is that?" Linda began to cry pitifully, "that he's...wearing?"

Sylvia shook her. "Look, if you don't help me NOW we are both going to be neck deep in shit."

Sylvia crouched between the two whitewashed bookshelves and began to tug at the back of the wheelchair.

"How much is this?" a woman asked from behind. Both Sylvia and Linda jumped.

"We're closed!" Sylvia snapped, not bothering to turn around. "Fuck off!"

Linda was still crying. Her hands were gripping her head as if trying to keep her mind from leaking out. Sylvia stopped tugging on the wheelchair and grabbed her by the shoulders, shaking her again. "Snap out of it!" Then she lowered her voice to a menacing whisper trained directly into Linda's ear, "I swear to Christ, if you fall apart on me now..."

"Roger?"

"Yes. Roger."

"Then...whose face?" Linda asked, her voice barely a whisper.

"We've gone over this, Linda. Haven't we gone over this? I've heard of denial, but this is fucking ridiculous. Are you blanking on all of this? Really?"

Linda only stared at Sylvia catatonically. "Whose...face?"

"Who gives a good goddamn?" Sylvia fumed. "What? You want a name? I just helped myself to a few parts at the funeral home before sending a body to the crisper. YOU were the one who thought it was smart. 'People know Roger,' you said. 'People will recognize him', you said. Is any of this ringing your bells?" Sylvia tapped a finger on Linda's forehead.

Linda stared, unblinking.

"Are you telling me you don't remember any of this? How you went on and on about how Roger gave Lance the auto body shop free and clear, but didn't give you shit. It was all your idea, Linda."

"No..." Linda whined.

"Oh, yes," Sylvia hissed into her ear, "you said, 'Sylvia, I have an idea. You should embalm him and sell him at a flea market, sell him alongside all of your other stuffed things.' Remember? We laughed long and hard about it. You said 'It would be the ultimate revenge, the ultimate.' If he was nothing but a worthless bum, then maybe his body could bring in a few bucks. He would end up providing for you whether he liked it or not."

"I WAS KIDDING!" Linda screamed.

"Keep your voice down, goddammit!" Sylvia warned.

A family walking by the stall hand and hand had slowed to stare at them.

Sylvia glared at them until they moved on. She turned back to Linda who was covering her face and moaning into her hands.

Sylvia's raspy voice, still in Linda's ear, purred with syrupy calm, "You can say 'no' until the cows come home, honeybunch, but it won't change a thing. Now listen...you need to put on your big girl pants, snap out of it and help me move this thing..."

"We're crazy..." Linda howled. "We're crazy, we're crazy..."

"Keep your voice down!" Sylvia warned again, pressing a palm over Linda's mouth. Linda stared back at her, her eyes as big as fried eggs.

"Calm down...just calm down..." Sylvia said through gritted, nicotine stained teeth, teeth that now looked feral to Linda. "Just for one teeny-weeny second. Pretty please? With sugar on top?"

Linda's eyes relaxed a little. Another gaggle of shoppers were staring at them now and again Sylvia dispersed them with a withering glance. Tentatively, she removed her hand from Linda's mouth.

"They're going to know..." Linda said miserably. "I was kidding...I was kidding...I don't even remember..."

But she did remember. It was all coming back. It was all saturating her mind, slowly filling in the grey spaces like some ghastly image blooming on a sheet of old Polaroid film.

"Ew!" a little girl yelled from outside the stall, pointing. "Look, Mama! His face is coming off!"

Sylvia dropped to a crouch again and tugged at the wheelchair. "Go away!"

The little girl flinched and ran off. Sylvia kept tugging. With a groan, the wheelchair rolled back a little, the slumped old man wobbling like a bobble head. Linda watched stupidly as Sylvia sprang to her feet and ran to the other side of her stall, snatching a Navajo area rug hanging from the aluminum frame. When she returned, she threw the blanket over the old man's head, then turned to Linda, breathless. "Help me!" she commanded.

Numbly, Linda began to move. She grabbed one of the handles of the wheelchair. Sylvia grabbed the other. They tugged. The chair rolled from between the bookcases. Sylvia panted out a relieved laugh. "That's it! Keep going!"

They tugged some more, the chair jerking backwards. With a gritty whisper, the Navajo rug slid from the old man's head and into his lap, the nap of the rug dragging the torn face off of his skull. Linda screamed.

The stranger's tattered face was still stapled to the chin of its host, hanging at Roger's throat like a lobster bib with eyeholes. Linda stared at her husband. His revealed eyes, milky and accusing, fixed on her.

She screamed.

She was on her back now. A smudgy man was standing over her, maybe floating over her. He was saying something. With effort she held her runaway breath for a moment to listen.

"Forty ccs of Diazepam, stat," said the man.

A pair of fingers wrenched open Linda's eye and her vision filled with light. A woman's voice said, "Pupils are reactive."

Something pinched Linda's arm. Warmth flooded through her. Her breathing calmed. A room came into focus: a single high transom window, minty green walls. She made a final attempt to tug at her restraints and then surrendered to the rush that made her heavy head slump back onto her pillow. Through half-open lids she watched the man and the woman walk toward the propped open door and into the fluorescent lights of the hall beyond.

"Her episodes are violent," whispered the woman to the man as they walked out of the room.

Linda watched dreamily from her bed. The nurse had been holding a folder at her side, which she now placed on the wall beside Linda's door before reaching into the room to switch off the overhead light and kick up the rubber stop on the heavy door. The two disappeared from sight.

Linda's eyelids felt like sandbags. She could hear her breath, slow and steady, and the sound of the heavy door as it slowly hissed closed on its hydraulic hinge before clanging shut.

Her husband was standing behind the door.

Linda tried to scream, but...

...the...

...drugs...

Her throat only gurgled.

Roger's human mask was still stapled to his chin, hanging at his throat. His cracked and rotting lips pulled back from his teeth in a wolfish grin. "Nighty-night," he croaked.

Linda wiggled vainly against the straps. Darkness was swallowing her.

"Sweet dreams, darling," the thing in the pilly blue sweater said as it began to wobble its way toward her bed.

Chapter 2

The House on Second Street

The house on Second Street was not the biggest in Dawson, Nebraska, though if pressed to think about the old Victorian mansion more than they wanted to, the townsfolk would certainly consider it the most looming. Most could not tell you why this was or what specifically would distinguish a large house from a looming one. Perhaps it was the fact that one could never really get a good look at it through its shroud of oak and hickory trees, tricking the eye and mind into thinking it was bigger than it was. Or maybe it was that when the sun hit it just right – which it rarely did –one could see that it was bigger than one thought, and did, indeed, loom--if any house was ever said to loom.

Its stately sprawl of dark wood rose to a single dormer window, a Cyclopean eye that peered past the peaks of its roof and just above the treetops to silently watch the street below. Some who passed would swear that they saw things in those high windows when the light was just right, which again, it seldom ever was.

Richard Penny's twin boys said they once saw a gorilla. When asked what kind of gorilla, they said "a big black one." It had been standing in the window, they said, not moving, just looking down at them, its narrowed eyes yellow and unblinking. The younger Penny boy had pissed his corduroys that day – a disappointment for the entire Penny family, as they had been sure that Todd had outgrown such forms of expression.

Others saw things, too, but one had to be about a half-block down Second Street to spot the window at just the right angle between the trees, and when one did, one might even see something quite impossible. Take Tania Kinders' claim to her parents over one Sunday dinner that she had seen a black swan reflected in the glass of that dormer window, gliding on a body of water that didn't exist on Second Street or anywhere else within the Dawson city limits.

But such tales were to be expected, for the one who lived in this house had always been the object of hushed conjecture, and hushed conjecture was one thing that Dawson did just about better than anywhere else. For the townsfolk, the mortician's house had always been the perfect depository for all of their fears and anxieties. It was a big, looming treasure chest of them. A passerby could flick any of these from their minds at the structure and leave them behind to be absorbed and consumed by its dark Victorian wood.

Sylvia Blair knew all of this, and she liked it just fine. Kids crossed the street rather than walk too near her house. Cars might slow a bit, and then think better of their pernicious curiosity and drive away with a hasty grumble of exhaust. But no one treated Sylvia Blair any differently than anyone else in public--people rarely did in Dawson--and if they needed a target for their gossip, she figured she was the most equipped to handle it. The Blair family had been handling it for generations.

So let them talk in their backyards, with the chiggers jumping up their socks as they sit on their patio gliders, beer koozies in hand, speculating endlessly in salacious whispers but never knowing anything for sure. Yes, that was how Sylvia liked it.

A small town like Dawson (population: 7,000 on a healthy day) had the kind of elbow room that would make an actual controversy awkward for everyone. But the fabricated kind, the kind that provided fertility to long-dulled imaginations, was the best prescription for a healthy community--plenty to talk about and no polluting reality to clean up. Sylvia Blair and the Blair Funeral Home were just as good and as likely a target as one could find within the five miles that made up the town's borders.

To Sylvia, the best part about being The Weirdo was the space it afforded her. Oh, sure, kids came to the door to sell candy, but not often. They came to get their candy back on Halloween, but not often. And better yet, the JoHos never came by to talk to her about their version of God's plan. The only Bible thumpers with the boulders to approach her door had been a pair of squeaky-clean teenage boys in short-sleeved white shirts and ties. That had been a year ago.

Everyone knew everyone in Dawson, and Sylvia hadn't seen the Mormon boys before. It was obvious that they had been shuttled in and told to stay until they had met their quota of souls. That hadn't stopped Sylvia from asking the question anyway, "You two sweet things are from out of town, aren't you? And you don't know me at all, do you?"

The boys on the porch shook their heads. Sylvia was about to close the door when one of them blurted out, "No, ma'am, we're from Lincoln. We are from the Church of Jesus Christ of Latter Day Saints."

"Mormons!" Sylvia had cried in mock surprise, clapping a hand to her cheek before using it to brush the sleeve of her black and pink house dress up her arm so she could snuff out her cigarette at the side table by the screen door. Her pink painted lips pulled back into the pantomime of a warm smile that didn't include a bit of her flinty, keen eyes.

The boys hadn't noticed the lack of sincerity in that smile though. Their goal was to talk her off her spiritual ledge and they were oblivious to all other concerns, and just like any vampire would have to, they were about to ask if they could come in.

Sylvia Blair didn't like company; it never led to anything good. Usually the rare and chatty visitor, after standing on her porch without the expected invitation to enter the house, would end up hugging themselves or glancing up at the sky during the inevitable pregnant lull in conversation. Sylvia would just let them twist there like a wind sock in a gale. It served them right. Everyone was so curious. Everyone wanted a tour of the house so that they could report back to the gossips at the Corner Café instead of walking away like they should.

That was when Sylvia Blair might just give them what they thought they wanted. Like a cat's heavy paw lifted briefly from a squirming mouse, once in a great while she would invite the caller in from the snow or the soaking heat. But once they were in, there was nowhere for them to go. Her house was full of the things she had collected, all five thousand square feet of it – including the full attic.

Nothing was displayed in any deliberate fashion either. There were no lovingly dusted curio cases, no pedestals or spotlights. Her collection of things was packed into any space she could find. Some of her items were innocuous and familiar to first time callers, but the majority of her treasures certainly were not.

It was the taxidermy more than anything that wiped the smiles from the faces of her visitors. The stuffed dead things were everywhere, peering through the darkness at her guests with dull, black eyes. In short order, the caller would forget how to breathe; they would sweat and lose their penchant for chatter, their original purpose for visiting suddenly replaced by the pressing need to escape with a socially acceptable amount of haste.

Be careful what you wish for, Sylvia would think to herself with a grin. In fact, she thought that sentiment should be etched into a welcome mat and slapped down on her porch.

But last year's squeaky-clean Mormon boys had hung in there for an impressively long time. Sylvia figured they were dim as bricks or just had big ol' balls packed into those dime store, black rayon church pants. The boys were both the same age, or close to it, maybe sixteen. It had been the one with the angry zit on his nose and the ginger tinge to his hair that had spoken once she had let them into the house, "We won't take up much of your time, ma'am."

"Let me guess," Sylvia had said, "you want to talk about God with me, don't you?"

The boys had nodded eagerly.

"There is no God," Sylvia had said, her black and pink house dress billowing clerically as she pressed in on them. "We die and we get eaten by worms. The adults are bullshitting you so they can control your mind and take your money, you sweet things. And you believe them don't you? That's adorable! Stupid, but adorable."

Though they had gone wide-eyed, the boys held their ground admirably; their church shoes steady on the planks of Sylvia Blair's hardwood floor. This part wasn't in their script, but they could overcome it. Sure they could. They were sixteen after all, with big ol' balls packed into their black rayon church pants.

But one discerning look at the plump and wrinkled gypsy of a woman in the black and pink house dress, one look unencumbered by the all-consuming optimism of youth should have told those boys that getting Sylvia Blair into a church, any church, was just about the most foolish use of their limited time on earth.

So Sylvia Blair had humored them, humored them until she could watch the birth of what were to be their constant companions throughout the remainder of their grueling and bewildering lives: Fear and Doubt. Sylvia loved being midwife to such watershed moments, and as far as she was concerned, it wasn't until the birth of those twin demons that a human life truly began.

She remembered quite clearly that it had been in the spring when the Mormon boys had visited. She knew this because when she read in the Dawson Independent that the boys had gone missing, presumably somewhere between Lincoln and Dawson, there had been baby birds chirping in her hickory tree. It was funny how one remembered such things.

There had been no solicitors since.

So when there was a knock on her door on the Tuesday afternoon following the big swap meet weekend in Lincoln, Sylvia looked up from the stuffed coyote she was grooming with a wire brush and raised an eyebrow.

The front door had been barricaded; the foyer finally succumbing to her endless purchases of oddities not long after the Mormon boys had darkened its porch last year. Now, if a stranger knocked at the big front door they would have to endure some rather uncomfortable minutes standing alone on her grand and creaky wraparound porch, the wind whispering the bushes against the dark wooden face of the house. The caller would be left to stare up at the windows with their velvety drapes forever drawn, or up at the dark eye of the dormer window beyond the eaves, or ahead at the weathered iron gargoyle with the knocker in its teeth.

But this knock was coming from the side door by the kitchen. This meant it was someone she knew. It was the only door she used now; the only door she could use. And really, to Sylvia, it was her last egress to the brightly lit world beyond her domain, a world that served as nothing more than the garish tunnel connecting her house to the funeral home across town that bore her family's name.

She could hear the aluminum screen rattle in its frame with the next knock. Then came the voice, "Sylvia! You home?"

It was a man.

Sylvia dropped her silver brush and waddled through the only path that was clear of oddities in the house: from the couch where she slept in the parlor, past the powder room, through the kitchen and to the side door.

It was Sheriff Bob Lutz. She could see his hat in the fan of the Irish window. She narrowed her eyes. She figured he might show up. Though she wasn't the social type and had never been a fixture on Main Street, Sylvia had little trouble imagining the conjecture that must be bouncing off the walls of The Corner Café the last couple of days along with the cigarette smoke and mayflies.

This had to be about Linda Vanderboom.

She patted the tight, grey curls around her head. In lieu of stretch pants, today she had worn a florid housedress embroidered with tropical flowers, and she gathered its hem as she made for the door. She passed a round, antiqued mirror hanging on the hall wall, no bigger than a ship's porthole, and paused at it as she passed, leaning into it to give her pink coated lips a restorative smack before pulling open the door, the little blinds hanging across its Irish window clacking against the panes.

"Hi, honeybunch," she said, her voice smoky sweet. "What can I do you for?"

Physically, Sheriff Lutz was as close to the male analogue of Sylvia Blair as one was likely to find in the town of Dawson. Also in his early sixties, short and round, his face weathered, he had his own set of gray curls cropped close. As similar as their age and looks were, an observer might think he and Blair had been long married and maybe in another life they might have been, had Sylvia any interest in men at all. The biggest difference between them was that the sheriff's face always seemed to be red around Sylvia, because, unlike the mortician's macabre preoccupations, Bob Lutz's interests were baser and far more carnal.

Sheriff Lutz was in full uniform, and just beyond his shoulder, Sylvia saw his squad car parked in the shade of her oak tree. The radio on Bob Lutz's belt squawked and Sylvia's eyes flicked toward the sound.

Lutz was used to the random noise and generally tuned it out unless dispatch was emphatic, so he took Sylvia's downward glance as a sizing up rather than the moment of simple curiosity that it was. Sylvia knew it the moment it happened, too, and she almost pitied the man for the ridiculous conceit that followed. The sheriff tugged at his gun belt with both hands and stood up just a bit straighter. He gave Sylvia a pursed lip smile that acknowledged her perceived hunger.

Sylvia's stomach flipped, but she returned the smile. Already, her paw had lit on the squirming mouse—only the mouse didn't know it.

It was certainly not the first go-round for these two, and if Sylvia had her way it would be the last, but she needed this to go well today and she had every confidence that it would. Soon enough, Sheriff Lutz's short and pudgy cock would be down her throat again and the world would be right as rain. But it was the pageantry of it all that she could do without: the confident shine in his piggy little eyes, the thought in his head – even for a moment – that she wanted it as badly as he did.

"How ya' been, Sylvia?"

Sylvia's smile was easy, and she even managed to tinge it with bashfulness. I should win some kind of fucking prize for this performance, she thought.

"I actually have to talk to you about something today," Lutz continued gravely, offering Sylvia an apologetic pout that he hoped would take the sting out of her certain disappointment. After all, he was the sheriff and he had a job to do. "It won't take but a few minutes," he added. "Do you mind if I come in?"

"Sure, honeybunch," Sylvia said, brightening as best as she could. "Christ, you poor thing, it's hotter than the devil's nut sack out there. Come in off the porch and let me fix you some lemonade."

"Don't go to any trouble," Lutz said.

"No trouble," Sylvia assured him, holding open the screen door for him as he passed. She watched him head toward the living room, down the only path clear of antiques, piles of flea market acquisitions and taxidermies. She watched him lower his girth onto one of the only two available chairs cleared of junk before she headed for the kitchen.

She poured him some lemonade from a carton that had been in her squat refrigerator for longer than she could remember, sneaking a sip first to make sure it wasn't spoiled. That would just anger him, and there were many reasons why she wanted him to leave her house happy and satisfied today. With the sleeve of her flowery house dress she wiped the smudge of pink lipstick from the rim and flitted breezily into the parlor, "So, what's on your mind?" She took a seat demurely across from him on an overstuffed armchair covered with shawls, "You seem so business-y today."

"You were at the big swap meet in Lincoln over the weekend with Linda Vanderboom," declared the sheriff, watching her over the rim of his glass of lemonade.

Sylvia produced a pack of American Spirit 100s from within the folds of her housedress. "Yep. What a shame that was." With the flick of her wrist she made one of the cigarettes almost jump out of the soft pack. She grabbed it with her lips. "Mind if I smoke?"

Without waiting for an answer, and without taking her eyes off Sherriff Bob Lutz, Sylvia grabbed a black Zippo with a grinning skull etched onto its case from the end table. With another flick of her wrist, the lighter flew open and roared with flame. She touched it to the tip of her smoke. Clicking the lighter shut, she inhaled deeply and said, with a sigh and a puff of smoke, "Poor girl."

"The way she told it to her nurse," said Lutz, taking another sip of lemonade, "you were selling a dead body on the open market."

Sylvia's laugh barked from her in a cloud of smoke, degenerating into a cough. Flapping away the smoke with a convulsive hand she said, "I don't mean to laugh, really. It's a terrible thing, Bob, losing your mind like that. I don't think she was ever really the same after Roger kicked the bucket. You catch my drift? You know...a couple sandwiches short of a picnic? It's sad as all get out. I tried to do what I could..."

"What was she doing at the fair?" asked Lutz.

"Helping me," said Blair, "that's all. I thought she needed to get out of the house. I mean, all she does is sit and watch these crappy talk shows with people flapping their gums about a lot of nothing. Plus, she needed some exercise, for chrissake. Her heart's going to explode. She's a big girl, Bob."

"Well, it did," said Lutz, slugging the last of his lemonade, "last night."

Sylvia stared back at him, frozen, the tip of her cigarette fuming at the end of her arm.

The sheriff could read nothing in Sylvia's expression. It was blank. Not an eyebrow twitched, and her mouth, with its starburst of fine wrinkles radiating from the pink, painted lips, neither frowned nor curled upward.

"She had been under psychiatric observation at Lincoln General since Sunday," Lutz continued. "She died early this morning. The cause of death was cardiac arrest, but she was clearly a very disturbed woman. She had almost clawed her own face off."

From the shadows of Sylvia's parlor a Bavarian cuckoo clock struck the hour and they both flicked their eyes to where the little wooden bird was erupting from its miniature chalet.

Sylvia coolly tipped her long ash into a tarnished silver ashtray and let out a sigh.

For a moment neither of them spoke.

"She had quite a story about you," said the sheriff, picking up his glass again and sucking the last traces of juice from an ice cube. "One hell of a story…"

"More lemonade?" Sylvia asked.

"No, thank you. I had an opportunity to read the report. Evidently, Linda had some kind of breakdown at the fair? All she could say to the responding officer was that you two were both crazy."

"Well, I won't deny that!" Sylvia said with her widest and most charming grin.

Bob Lutz only stared at her, Sylvia's grin wilting to solemnity.

Lutz went on, "She said you were trying to sell Roger's corpse."

"I know," Sylvia said. "It's so sad."

"A witness did see an old man in a wheelchair," said Lutz, "The witness said the face of the old man was coming off, said it had been stapled onto the skull."

"An old movie prop, Bob," Sylvia said wearily. "She was not a well woman. She swore up and down that it was Roger. She must have been hallucinating. Crazy people do that. Maybe she was on drugs, or meds, or whatever. Was she? Christ, she must have been. She just went bat shit on me. Lost her fucking marbles right there in the tent in front of everybody. It was embarrassing, if you want to know the truth."

"What about this stapled on face the witness was talking about?"

"The dummy was a piece of shit, Bob. It was coming apart. It was from some B-movie horror flick. It was from this guy who gets me movie stuff from L.A. He lives out there, said it was in the back of a prop house at a place called Gower Studios somewhere in Hollywood. It was a steal so I picked it up. I mean, if you haven't noticed, I have a bit of a thing for collecting. Linda never liked that piece. Hell, I never really liked it much either, but that Hollywood shit really sells around here."

"Who sold it to you?"

"I don't know his name, Bob. I think it's Max? Matt? Something like that? I run into him at shows: older guy, glasses, funny walk, prostate problems maybe. What does he have to do with Linda flipping her lid?"

"Where is the dummy now?"

"Sold it. Not long after Linda lost her shit and fair security took her into some holding cell. Then they came and told me that Linda was going for a ride. They asked me if I knew where she had parked her car."

"Who did you sell the dummy to?"

"Shit. Who knows?" Sylvia produced her pack of cigarettes again, flipped them around in her hands, and put them away. "It was some guy. He paid cash. I don't know who these people are. It's a swap meet. Merch changes hands all day long. What difference does it make? I mean, you don't think I was selling Roger Vanderboom's corpse in broad daylight at the Lincoln swap meet do you? I mean, for fuck's sake, Bob."

Lutz said nothing. He picked up his empty glass, sucked another ice cube, let it clatter back into the glass, and then leaned forward. "It's my job, Sylvia – gotta follow up on everything. You'd be surprised at how loose ends can unravel the whole bolt."

"Keep in mind," Sylvia said with an accusatory frown, "I just found out that my friend died. I'm feeling a little down in the dumps about it."

"Sorry," said Lutz, "you're right. Maybe you need some time?"

"Maybe a little, for chrissake. Her body isn't even cold yet."

"Of course I don't think it was a real body," Lutz said, "much less that of Roger Vanderboom. I've never heard of such a thing and don't know what the point of it would be. Anyway, you have the records of his cremation at the home, right? He was cremated, correct?"

Sylvia nodded, "Yep. And his ashes are in the wall at the mausoleum at Parkland, safe and sound. Is police work always this pointless? I mean, following up on every delusion that happens to crawl into your ear from the mouths of nut balls? That's got to be exhausting."

"Can be," said Lutz. "Sometimes it sure can be..."

Another silence bloomed between them.

Sylvia spoke first: "Did she really claw her own face off?"

"If not off," said the sheriff, "then damned close to it. Autopsy isn't back yet, but from the looks of her fingernails she might have done it herself. Then again, they could be defensive wounds."

"Huh," Sylvia pondered. "You know, I know a few things about autopsies. Generally, you don't do one when the Jane Doe is under a doctor's care."

"And generally that would be true," said Lutz, "but this was violent. And although it looks clear-cut--like I said before--her torn fingernails could have been defensive wounds. We've gotta wait for the pathology on this one."

"That's one for the fuckin' books, I tells ya," Sylvia muttered.

The silence resumed, sober and contemplative, as the cuckoo clock ticked diligently in the shadows. Lutz craned his neck to look around. "You do have a lot of stuffed road kill in here. Gives me the creeps. What do you see in it?"

"I've always been fascinated with the art," she replied. "That's why I took up the family business, I guess. Preserving things gives me a feeling of power. I cheat the worms out of a decent meal. I cheat the soil out of absorbing every last bit of energy from a once living thing. It's beautiful to me. There's power in preservation. It's unnatural, and going against nature is locking horns with the most powerful force we know. So she really clawed her own face off?"

Bob Lutz pursed his lips and nodded gravely.

"You poor dear man," said Sylvia. "The things you see. And poor Linda, too...Jee-zuss. That old girl was just plain off her goddamned rocker, wasn't she? You always hear about that kind of thing happening to people, but you never really see it happen. But I saw it. I was there at the moment her guitar broke a string."

"And that's exactly why," Lutz began, "the Lincoln P.D. will probably have more questions for you. Just so you know."

"But you," Sylvia went on, "you deal with this kind of thing all the time: married couples beating the shit out of each other, kids wrapping their cars around power poles on prom night. It's got to be stressful."

"Can be," Lutz said.

"I know, honeybunch," Sylvia said, standing and reaching for the clasp on her housedress. "Maybe it's time to relax?"

Sylvia's cell phone began to vibrate and skitter across the glass top of the coffee table between them. She frowned, yanked it up and glanced at the I.D.

C. BRIGGLE

Shit, she thought. What in hell does he want?

She glanced up at Bob Lutz. His mouth was half open, his eyes wide. He looked like a kid holding his breath the moment before tearing open a Christmas present.

"You...have to take that?" said Lutz, his voice thick with disappointment.

"It'll be quick," Sylvia said curtly, redoing the clasp on her housedress and marching from the room.

Entering the kitchen, she looked back. Lutz sat impassive, his back to her. She hurried to the back corner of the kitchen, opened the door of the guest powder room just around the corner and closed it gently before stabbing the answer button on the phone.

"It's me," the voice panted into her ear. "It's Clayton Briggle."

"I know, you idiot," Sylvia hissed. "I have caller I.D. like every-fucking-body else since the 1990s. What are you calling me for? And why from your own phone?"

"I didn't want to call from my dad's phone."

"Then get a disposable, like I told you."

Clayton cut her off. "Did you hear that? That's dad. All he does is moan. It's driving me nuts. I thought about waiting, but I'm going to do it tonight. I might as well, he's almost dead anyway."

"Are you listening to me?" Sylvia said through her teeth. "You were supposed to buy a disposable phone."

"I'm going to do it tonight. Just wanted you to know."

"Fine," Sylvia shot back. "Is that all? I'm a little preoccupied."

"I'm going to do it tonight," said Clayton.

"You said that already. And why, for the love of Christ, do you feel compelled to call my home, not my office but my home, and announce this over the phone?"

"Just want to make sure we still have a deal."

"Why wouldn't we. Nothing has changed. I'm hanging up."

"Twenty percent of the hundred thousand," Clayton said.

"And you're reiterating that over an unsecure line?" Sylvia switched the phone to her other ear, lowering her voice to a growl. "You're such a fucking idiot, Clayton Briggle." Sylvia opened the bathroom door a crack, listened, and closed it softly again. "Are we through?"

"Did you call me an idiot?" Clayton asked. "Look, I don't need this shit. I'm nervous enough as it is. You get ten percent of the inheritance, but only if your funeral home can smooth things over with the hospital in Colorado Springs and get a clean death cert. Any problems and the deal is off."

"You're losing it," said Sylvia, "I'm not going over this again."

"So it's a deal, right?"

"Yeah, that's the deal, just like it was yesterday, and the day before that. How about you pull yourself together, figure out what you want to do and get the fuck off my line. I do this shit all the time. That's why it isn't costing you much. So do your job and I'll do mine and we'll both be so happy we'll be shitting glitter. I'm hanging up now, Briggle."

"Shit! Okay...wait!"

Sylvia did.

"I might be there really early in the morning," said Clayton. "It might be, like, three or four."

"I don't give a flying fuck what time you get here," Sylvia snapped.

"I just wanted to make sure we still had a deal. That's all"

"I'm hanging up now, Clayton."

She did, and screwing on an easy smile, she returned to her parlor.

"Business?" asked the sheriff.

"Yes," Sylvia said. She was about to put the phone down on the coffee table again, thought better of it, and swiveled to place it on the end table near her own chair. It seemed she would be needing Sheriff Lutz more than ever in the coming days and that meant she had to get to work.

Bob Lutz watched as Sylvia Blair let her housedress fall into a flowery puddle at her feet. She wore a black bra and panties, the former doing an insufficient job of containing her fat which blossomed over the sides of its straps like rising dough.

Bob Lutz didn't care though, and neither did his prick, which began to stiffen. Beggars certainly couldn't be choosers. Bob remembered being a beat cop back in Omaha, fresh out of the academy. Omaha didn't have many beggars, but the ones the city did have were certainly not choosers. They smoked discarded cigarette butts, and they ate food right out of the trash.

What stood before him now was an old cigarette butt, a wad of cold and greasy fries in the bottom of a crumpled McDonald's bag, but boy, could she suck a dick: that tongue hammering action she had, the lack of a gag reflex, the fact that she swallowed him, all of him. Just thinking about it made his cock buck in his pants.

"Is business time over?" Sylvia purred as she dropped to her knees in front of his chair.

Sheriff Bob Lutz could only smile his reply.

Chapter 3

The Ghost You Never Hear

The hardest part of dealing with a dead body is the weight. At least, that's what Clayton Briggle figured. During those long months of contemplating this moment, he had tried to anticipate everything that could possibly go wrong. He knew he was no criminal mastermind, and this made his task all the more difficult. Failure meant being dragged back to L.A., possibly to the Twin Towers Correctional Facility for a long stint of getting his pooper poked by men with empty eyes and even emptier heads, men as big as major appliances.

Of course, back then, during those months of plotting and scheming, this particular problem was luxuriously rhetorical. What is the cleanest way to kill your father? It was a harmless meditation back then, back when he could just hang up on the threatening phone calls, back before said phone calls became the total destruction of his rat-hole apartment in Hollywood.

He had to stay here in Colorado Springs until the job was done. Going back to L.A. was not an option. His creditors were possessed of that particular brand of tenacity that only exists when a denizen of the underworld gets royally screwed by a nobody like Clayton Briggle. He had pleaded; he had sworn up and down that he hadn't stolen the dope. He had been robbed. But there were no misunderstandings in the world into which he had entered. There were only consequences. He was now on the hook for twenty large or the equivalent in black tar heroin, and Clayton figured it would take just about a thousand years of gigging in pay-to-play clubs on the Sunset Strip with his now middle-aged band, Kribdeth, to shit that kind of coin.

His decision had been made for him. Time was up. He had to kill his stroke-ravaged father and collect what money he could from his meager inheritance.

Euthanasia, he believed it was called.

Or murder, he reminded himself: murder one. They would also call it that. You bet your ass they would.

And he had to kill the old man sooner than later, before the money was pissed away on round-the-clock Filipino nurses. Then, as if that weren't enough, he also had to somehow get the body across the state of Nebraska to his estranged birthplace of Dawson, and into the grimy hands of a local mortician named Sylvia Blair.

He fucking knew it. There had always been something shady about Sylvia Blair. Scratch that – everything had been shady about her. Even as a kid, Clayton knew it. Hell, everyone knew at the very least that Sylvia Blair was a grade-A weirdo. He and his pals would unconsciously cross the street on their way home from school, even into oncoming traffic, rather than pass her house on Second Street. But Clayton still could never have imagined what the Witch of Dawson had proposed when he had called her to see if there was a space left for pops near his grandparents in the Dawson Cemetery.

The plan had been hatched a week ago when Clayton had called the Blair Funeral Home from L.A., where he had been lying low with the lights out and the curtains drawn at his bass player's house, hoping his pursuers wouldn't track him down before he could blow town. Casually, he had fished for information on procedure if his father were to succumb to his stroke and die. Although he couldn't remember exactly how, at some point in the conversation he must have let it slip about his money problems because Blair, as if by some kind of predatory telepathy, and as if she had cut this particular kind of deal many times before, was the first to mention the word "euthanasia."

"I mean, if you're tired of waiting, that is," she had added.

Blair then went on to assure him that if he could get the body to her without being tailed, she would take it from there: make it disappear, and arrange for a clean death certificate. Of course, she would want a cut of the estate, not too big a cut, but she would need to get her beak wet, and she hoped he understood. "High risk," she had called it, "but not hard for a seasoned professional like herself." So Clayton had agreed, and by doing so had consigned himself to crawling into bed with the Witch of Dawson--his childhood boogeyman, or boogeywoman, as the case was.

It would cost him twenty percent of the estate--take it or leave it--and according to Clayton's projections, that would be close to twenty grand. Either that or he could try his luck reasoning with the Mexicans who had fronted him the half-key of now-vanished heroin.

He took the deal.

His life now revolved around the logistics of killing his father, and yep, the weight was going to be a problem.

Clayton Briggle was a big guy, but over the years he had gone soft in the middle, and he didn't have the strongest back. Not that the body beneath the yellowed sheet that he stood over now weighed much. It had been eleven months since the stroke had taken all of the piss and vinegar out of the old man, and what lay before him now was a breathing husk that looked more like a rubber doll from a haunted house than the right-wing Alpha male that used to backhand the glass of milk out of Clayton's hand in grade school for "having the fucking balls to roll his eyes at him."

He wondered if the old bastard could even tip the scales at a hundred and a quarter at this point. Still, when the time came it was going to be dead weight. That's what they called it: dead weight.

Clayton laughed dully, "Ain't that the fucking truth."

All Clayton hoped for now was that old Foster "You Don't Know What Hard Work Is, What Real Pain Is" Briggle would check out au naturel, that the merciful hand of God would come and squeeze the remaining breath from the rag doll wheezing on the soiled sheets before him and do them both a favor. Not that Clayton had ever believed in such mercies, but maybe that was what praying was all about: winning the lottery with The Big Guy. You can't win if you don't play. Isn't that what they say? Isn't that the mantra of the perpetual loser?

Wait. Had he actually been praying out loud?

He had.

"Please end this shit," were the whispered words still hanging in the air. Suddenly he felt stupid and ashamed for mumbling magic spells, believing he had super powers like he had imagined when he was little. He remembered those wishful incantations of his youth, how if he concentrated in just the right way he could make people he didn't like eat shit on the monkey bars and break a tooth, or make himself fly by affixing a dish towel around his neck, or how he could somehow now save himself from becoming the Angel of Death in a dingy trailer in Colorado Springs.

The worst of it was that he was pretty sure that swearing when praying was frowned upon. Maybe "please end this shit" hadn't been the right tact. Great. He had already fucked up. He muttered the word "sorry" into the gloom.

Hoping his sudden penitence had restored the potency of his prayer, Clayton looked up from the breathing, rasping form below him expectantly. He wasn't sure what he thought would happen. Would Jesus be standing there shouting "Move!"and waving him away like some irritated IT guy summoned by an idiot to fix their hopelessly clogged email account?

But nothing happened.

For his efforts the room only got darker and more forsaken as the weak sun beyond the trailer's grimy window succumbed to a bank of bruised clouds.

Was the old man asleep? Or was he awake? His breathing sounded like snoring and his snoring sounded like his breathing. His eyes were blind and always half-opened so there was really no way to tell. Not like it mattered. It was unlikely the old man even knew the difference between being asleep and being awake. His circuits were too gummed up. How would he know, and at this point, why would he care? Clayton chewed a cuticle, his eyes glazing over as he listened to the tick of his father's cheap bedside clock. To Clayton, it sounded a lot like the ticking of a bomb.

Yes, he was definitely more concerned with the weight than any nightmares that might come to him later. That was, if he could bring himself to go through with the deed. He tilted his head and sized up the situation afresh, as he had done a hundred times already. He regarded his father dispassionately, as a logistical issue, the way one might stare at a dresser and wonder how it was going to fit through a bedroom door. He didn't have to be that careful. Weird ol' Sylvia Blair told him that much.

An autopsy was not going to be an issue since the body would disappear, and even an inquiry was unlikely. Severe stroke victims dying after a year didn't raise many eyebrows. This theory was also corroborated by a young, black nurse at the Greenfield Rehabilitation Center where his father had been lying in a semi-vegetative state for months.

"I want to release him, but what if he dies under my care?" Clayton had asked. "I mean, I guess he's going to. He has to, eventually, right? That's expected, right?" Keeping his head down and sorrowful, he had flicked his eyes toward the young nurse as she folded a sheet at the vacant bed beside his father.

"Don't worry yourself sick, honey," the girl had said. "No one does an autopsy on someone in this condition if they have been under a doctor's care in the last six months,"

Clayton had looked up slowly, catching the girl's eye. Her eyes were set deep in her black face, the whites the color of her uniform, and they had pierced him to his chair. He remembered how his breath had caught at that moment. The nurse's lips were pressed together grimly, and Clayton would be goddamned if the girl hadn't raised her eyebrows ever so slightly, offering him a faint, tight smile before returning to folding her sheet.

She knew. She knew exactly what he was thinking of doing, and it probably wasn't the first time she had handed out advice of this nature in her line of work. It also seemed clear that she didn't care. "Ain't none of my business, Mr. Slick," that smile had said, "you do what you gotta do and leave me the hell out of it."

But was she right? Was he going to risk everything on her knowledge of criminal procedure? Of course, he double-checked with the internet, but surprisingly it didn't have much to say. It did seem that the death of an emaciated stroke victim shouldn't raise suspicion if it was clean and bloodless.

Emboldened, Clayton had then insisted to the staff that his father be checked out under Clayton's own care, to be "surrounded by a familiar environment for his final days. Turns out, this was not an unusual thing to ask and the request was granted.

But the real reason the request was granted was because it was inevitable that Foster Briggle was going to lose his bed. Insurance doesn't pay to store vegetables. They would rather he just die and save them some money. Once a patient was deemed to be unsalvageable, it was only a matter of time before they were out on their ass and burning through the family fortune until they qualified for welfare. And in the case of Clayton's father, the writing was on the wall and everyone knew it, including Blue Cross. Insurance had paid one hundred percent at the rehabilitation center during the first six months after the stroke, when hope of rehabilitation still existed; but Foster Briggle was broken bad. Now, insurance was only shelling out fifty percent, which amounted to tens of thousands of dollars in the last five months.

Clayton had stepped in just in time. Or at least, he hoped.

Clayton realized he was staring out of the trailer's window. The clouds were eating up what was left of the day's sun and they were stacked high, threatening a summer storm.

He returned his focus to the problem at hand, sizing up his father yet again. There was one piece of good news: the old man didn't have to haul around the Briggle Beer Belly anymore. Eating nothing but Ensure and sugar water through a tube had taken care of that. In fact, according to countless doctors, Foster "Music Isn't A Real Job, Cut Your Hair You Fucking Hippy, You Haven't Worked An Honest Day In Your Life" Briggle wasn't going to haul around shit anymore. His honest day's work from now on would be to lie on death's doorstep until someone answered the door. And who knew that death's doorstep would be a mobile home in Meadowlark Trailer Park in Colorado Springs, Colorado?

Who was he kidding? He couldn't do this. Hell, he didn't even like the old man well enough to assume this kind of risk.

Fuck him.

Yeah, fuck him. This whole situation was utter bullshit. Let nature take its course. He didn't need the money that bad.

Oh, but you do, he thought. Why else would you be sweating bullets in this trailer a thousand miles away?

There was no way around it. The expedited death of Foster "I've Got One Hundred Grand With Your Name On It If You Let Me Chew Your Ass Out Four Times A Year When I Call" Briggle was going to have to happen and Clayton had to go it alone. Seeing how his mother had left long ago and couldn't give a pair of shits about the welfare of his father – whom she now undoubtedly flippantly referred to from behind a champagne flute at one of her rich-bitch cocktail parties as "her ex" – and seeing as how he was the only child, it looked like his old man's treasure was his to lose. That is if you could call a hundred grand, give or take, earned from forty years of repairing airplane seats a treasure. And Clayton could.

Oh yes, at this point, he most certainly could.

Maybe his father should have shut his trap about his ducats. Maybe then Clayton wouldn't have been so gung-ho on turning him into fertilizer. He would have just let the old man suffer in the rehab center for God knows how long and let whatever petty cash he thought his father had spiral down the crapper.

But wait. It was actually working out well for both of them, wasn't it? If you really looked at it, the old man was actually paying Clayton for the hit. The dad gets some much needed mercy, and the dutiful, long-suffering son gets a little coin to get him out of hot water with some pissed off cholos back home.

Everybody wins.

So why didn't Clayton feel like a winner? He turned to leave the bedroom. Behind him, his father gagged violently. Clayton stiffened and stopped in his tracks. After a moment, the old man resumed that incessant, rattling breathing. Clayton continued walking away from the dark bedroom, wiping sweat from his forehead.

It was stifling in the trailer, and the humidity was high. The small air conditioner was valiantly grinding away, but it was old, its filters undoubtedly clogged, and it did little to cleave the trailer's soupy air. Clayton peered into the mirror above the television. His beard was getting gray, his bald head was sanguine and slicked with sweat, and his belly had just recently started to hang over the waist of his jeans.

"Are you really going to do this?" he mumbled to his reflection. Haunted eyes stared back at him, offering no resolve.

He turned into the small galley kitchen and grabbed a can of beer from the squat fridge. It was time to stop thinking about it for a few blessed moments, time to call John Supernau, let him know he was close and should be arriving soon at his house in good ol' Dawson. Supernau might be putting him up, but he wasn't in the know and wasn't going to be. This was just to be a social call, two old friends catching up, and before he got any dumb-ass ideas about confiding in Supernau about what he was planning on doing just because they'd been friends since childhood, Clayton took his last completely sober moment to vow himself to secrecy again. No matter how insecure or freaked out he got, no one was to know about this.

Well, except for Sylvia Blair. That was bad enough, but it had to end there.

Clayton was looking forward to this call. He needed to hear a familiar voice, to calm his nerves, and to prove that life was still normal beyond this godforsaken trailer, and he was almost relieved to tears when his old friend answered on the second ring.

"My Dad keeps it so dark in here," Clayton said, expertly cracking the pull tab of the beer with his free hand and sitting down hard in the recliner. "It's so fucking gloomy."

"When did you get there" John Supernau asked thickly.

Probably fresh-baked, Clayton thought with envy, and as if to confirm his suspicion, the sizzle of a joint being pulled on was followed by a stifled cough.

"Five days ago," Clayton replied, "It's a long fucking drive, brother."

Supernau grunted his condolences, "So what's the sitch?"

"It's not one of the nicer units," Clayton said, "Some people make the best of living in these trailer parks: little yards in front, lawn ornaments, wind chimes. Not Dad. He doesn't give a flying fuck. It's bare bones in here, bro. He's got a recliner and a couch and an old tube television in the living room. A tube...television. That's just wrong in so many ways. But the fucker works; I tried it. And there's a mirror above the T.V., I guess so he can see what's going on out the window behind him, and really, that's about it.

"The kitchen is a joke: formica peeling off the side of the counter. There's nothing in the cupboards except dusty glasses and a couple grimy plates. I tried using the microwave last night to nuke some Chinese food, and that didn't go well at all. It looks like a fucking science experiment in there. You know, these Filipino home care nurses are getting seven grand a month. You would think they would use one of those sponges they wash my dad with and clean this place a little. It pisses me off. And I thought my place was a shithole.

"Wait. Wait. Listen. Can you hear dad? Can you hear that? He's moaning. He does it all the time. Dude, I've spent four very long nights here. He does it in the middle of the night. He sounds like a fucking ghost. He's not even dead yet and he sounds like a fucking ghost. It scares the shit out of me. As I said, it's gloomy in here already. At night it's even worse. When he does that shit at three in the morning, I'm telling you, bro, it makes my balls crawl into my stomach."

Clayton took a long slug of the beer, his Adam's apple pumping like a piston, and wiped his mouth with the back of his hand before going on, "When I first got here I couldn't believe how bad he looked when I saw him at that rehab center. He's home now and I got the two Filipino nurses to take care of him so at least I don't have to do the dirty work, but I still haven't got used to the sight of him."

"Why didn't you just leave him where he was?" Supernau asked.

Because I can't kill him there, Clayton thought.

"Because I should take care of this. It really is my responsibility. Besides, I kind of feel sorry for the old guy. He has no friends, no family except for me."

"That's because he's a dick," said Supernau. "I thought you guys weren't very tight. I thought you pretty much hated him."

"I don't hate him," Clayton protested. "I just....well, I guess I kind of do. But what am I supposed to do? I'm telling you, Supe, I know there's a lot of ways to buy the farm, but having a stroke as bad as this one is seriously fucked up. Not even he deserves this. It's got to be one of the worst things that could happen to you."

Supernau grunted, conceding that at least a modicum of moral conflict was in order; then the two of them fell into a contemplative silence.

"You know the thing that gets me," Clayton said, "is that I never know if he really knows I'm there. His eyes are always half open. Sometimes his moaning seems to correspond to things I say, sometimes it doesn't. I don't know if he's in agony or if he's just trying to tell me something. The moans are garbled with gunk from his throat – which he doesn't have working muscles to clear. He has no control over his tongue. I swear to fucking God, Supe...this is a nightmare.

"So, I tell him to hang in there. I tell him everything is going to be okay. I actually said that to him. But nothing is going to be okay. Every doctor he has seen has said as much. Sure, there are a bunch of shysters who will take his last dime. A bunch of hippies have already come out of the woodwork offering oxygen therapy and some other holistic crap. I looked it all up, and of course it's all bullshit. No, there's nothing to be done. Bottom line, it's 'round-the-clock care for the guy for as long as his heart keeps beating. And there's nothing wrong with his heart. He's only 75. He could live another decade in this bed, in this grimy trailer, with a catheter jammed up his rod.

"And that's another thing, Supe. That just might be the worst part of it. In fact, I don't even like talking about it, about how he keeps ripping out his catheter. His arms work a bit, and so do his hands a little, so that's what he does all day. It bugged him from the very beginning, so now he has ripped it out so many times that it hurts like hell when the Filipinos put it back in. I know this because he moans and pulls it out again within minutes. I also know this because I was in the room when the two girls put it back in once, and it was like jamming a knitting needle into the bloody eye of a dead snake. I almost lost my lunch. See, I can't even talk about it..."

On the other end of the phone, John Supernau writhed audibly.

"The two Filipino nurses finally devised a plan," Clayton continued. "They put pants on him backwards, tucked his night shirt into the pants, and ran the catheter's tube down his leg and out of the cuff. Now, he can't get it out. He's too weak to do anything about it. Oh, believe me, he tries, but his hands just kind of paw at his crotch and they finally fall at his sides after a few seconds. Then he'll get another burst of energy and fumble at it again. He does it all...day...long."

Queasy and flushed, Clayton polished off his beer, crushed the can into jagged points and let it drop onto the brown carpet.

On the other end of the phone, John Supernau let out a long, commiserating breath.

"One of the Filipino nurses arrives at 8:00 in the morning," Clayton went on, "the other at 2:00 in the afternoon. They overlap for just long enough to do things that might require both of them, like lift Dad out of the bed to change sheets, diapers, or whatever, and then the first nurse takes off. The second nurse stays until about 8:oo at night. Of course, I call them nurses, but I don't think they are in any official way. Really, they are just two sisters, immigrants with a limited vocabulary, who are willing to deal with this kind of shit for money. Going after that American dream, right?"

Supernau emitted a slight chuckle.

"Eh...whatever. Dad doesn't actually require a nurse at this point anyway. Nurses help you get better, and he has no chance of getting better. No, Dad is a piece of furniture at this point, a piece of furniture that has one tube that takes in liquid and one tube that drains it out, a piece of furniture that starts moaning in the middle of the night just like a fucking ghost."

John Supernau said nothing.

"You there, Supe?"

"Barely."

"Here's the thing, dude..." Clayton said, gripping his cell phone tighter and lowering his voice as if it mattered to do so, as if what he was about to impart had to be handled with care, like something volatile, like nitroglycerin, like something that just might explode in the middle of John Supernau's mind like it had in the middle of Clayton's own."You never really hear that moaning ghost from the movies, Supe. You know? The one we have all heard in Scooby Doo cartoons or in haunted houses. You never really hear that in real life. But I've heard it every night I've stayed here, heard it cut right through the thin walls of this horrible cracker box and come straight for me in my dreams. I don't think you can ever un-hear it, and I know I'm going to hear it in my nightmares. I'm going to hear it for the rest of my..."

Clayton stopped short.

His father was laughing.

Clayton jerked the phone away from his ear and turned his head to look toward the bedroom door, his veins icing up.

The laugh came again, slow, malevolent, and rumbling toward him down the hall's dark throat.

It was a knowing laugh, Clayton thought, the worst kind.

"I know what you're up to, son," said the laugh, "You're a bad boy. You're a very bad boy, but I bet you can't do it. I bet you a nickel and a fishhook that you don't have the boulders, you devious little shit stain. Your plan is never going to work and you're never going to get a dime from me. I'm going to just lay here forever and moan like a rusty door hinge through your sleepless nights while you watch my money burn through the hands of those Filipino vultures. And even if you did try what you're thinking, everyone would know what you did. You know why? Because you're a fuck-up, Clayton..."

"You all right, dude?" Supernau said, his voice far away, "Where'd you go?"

It hadn't been a laugh. No, it had just sounded like it. It had been another one of his dad's slow, percolating coughs, the kind where he ended up choking on his own sputum. Still, Clayton stared down the dark hallway toward the bedroom. Then he glanced down in wonder at the gooseflesh stippling his arm. If he was losing his shit now, what chance did he have of pulling this thing off? He swallowed the lump in his throat. He needed another beer. He sprang to his feet and headed for the kitchen.

Supernau tried again: "You there?"

"Sorry," Clayton said, "yeah...hold on." The cold beer in his hand fortified him and he returned to the recliner and renewed his vow not to fall to his knees and plead for help, though he never wanted to spill a secret so bad in his life. He managed to mutter "Okay, I'm here" before collapsing back on the recliner.

"How long do you have to stay there?" Supernau asked.

Just until I kill him...

"Not much longer," Clayton replied dreamily. "I might even be at your place tomorrow. I mean, if that's cool..."

"Sure. You're welcome any time," Supernau said. "If you show up and I'm at work, just come down to the office and hang out."

"Thanks, man. I really appreciate it."

Then Clayton and John talked about other things, they talked about Dawson, about who had gone nuts, and about who still looked hot and who didn't, but Clayton's mind was on what he had to do tonight. He didn't really remember saying goodbye to John Supernau, but at some point their call had ended because a dial tone was now humming him out of his reverie.

He glanced at his watch.

9:36

The last nurse had been gone for over an hour. Now was the time. He looked at the door at the end of the hall. It was still ajar. Faintly, he could hear the rasp of the old man's breathing.

Clayton blinked hard. He was losing his shit alright. His heart was hammering in his chest. He puffed out his cheeks, took a bracing breath, drained the rest of the beer, dropped the can onto the carpet, and with both hands lifted his body out of the recliner, a body as heavy as wet sand, and with his fists balled at his sides, he headed for the open bedroom door.

It was time to put them both out of their misery.

Chapter 4

Upside Down from Now On

Clayton stood looking down at his father, the pillow clenched in his hands. He was shaking. Sweat poured from his brow into his beard and his breath chugged like a steam engine. His eyes were wide, just like his father's, as they stared at one another. But Foster Briggle's was the fixed and bloodshot stare of a strangled man while Clayton's was of the twitching, thousand-yard variety, the kind of stare alive with the shine of many things: disbelief, fatigue--and horror.

The old man had put up more of a fight than Clayton had thought possible. The emaciated body with the stick figure limbs that lay beneath the yellowing sheet had flailed and kicked through the excruciatingly long amount of time it took to smother him. But Clayton had kept the pillow firmly over his father's face, pushing down harder, riding the bucking form like some ghoulish cowboy until the flailing finally slowed. That took four and a half minutes. It took another thirty seconds until all movement had stopped completely and Clayton had dared to back off, slowly at first, and then completely to witness the result of his considerable labor. He was exhausted. The movies he had seen where the process took a matter of seconds had all been make believe, just an effort for filmmakers to get the point across without dedicating five minutes of film to the gruesome process of squeezing the life from a grown man.

And that's what it had been: gruesome.

Clayton didn't really know what he had expected. Did he think that the old man was going to sleep through the whole thing? That his father would have just welcomed it?

Yes, that is what Clayton had thought might happen; that maybe--though he couldn't articulate it in any way--his father, through all those burps and gurgles, had been sending him a telepathic message, the kind that only your kin can receive on some exclusive frequency. Surely, his father had wanted an end to it all, to pawing at his crotch to pull out the catheter from his livid and cored-out urethra, to put an end to having Ensure poured down his gullet and his diapers changed by a bunch of strange women--Orientals he would have called them if his tongue had only been able to work.

But instead, the old man had gone kicking and screaming. He had fought like hell, and the only way Clayton had been able to go on was by forcing himself to repeat the same mantra that had enabled him to drag himself into the bedroom with pillow in hand in the first place: this is mercy...this is mercy...It's only mercy.

As he stood there feeling small and alone in that trailer on the edge of Colorado Springs, for the first time in his life he was no longer the fat kid, the loner, the guy who could never quite accomplish what he had set his mind to. Now he was the bully, the monster in the shadows, the murderer.

Clayton's eyes erupted in hot tears, and they ran down his already glistening face. He still couldn't catch his breath. It was so hot. The humid air seemed to coagulate on his skin like candle wax. His heart was racing. He felt his carotid arteries beating a tattoo in his neck.

Was he going to have a heart attack? Wouldn't that be the perfect end? After years of drive-thru burgers, to pick this moment to kick his ass? How long would it take the detectives to figure that one out: Briggle, the younger, with an exploded heart lying atop the corpse of his strangled father.

All at once all of these thoughts ceased, as if exploding apart in his mind. Something amazing was happening before Clayton's eyes, something amazing and horrifying: his father's jaw was slowly yawning open, the milky eyes with their bloody starbursts of shattered veins still fixed on Clayton's own. Incrementally, as if in slow motion, the mouth gaped ever wider, revealing the toothless gums and raw throat. Finally the bottom jaw reached the breastbone and settled there like a nesting cat.

Foster Briggle was staring at his son and silently screaming at him. It was as if the old man's soul had finally ripped away from the corpse, releasing the last bit of tension in that husk of a body, before being vacuumed away to whatever oblivion awaited.

Clayton pressed the pillow to his face and screamed into it.

A full minute passed before he could get himself to stop. When he did, his tears refracted the terrible image before him into the surreal ghastliness of a funhouse mirror.

"Daddy..." Clayton wept, clutching the moist pillow to his chest. "Oh God...I'm sorry, Daddy. I hope you're okay now. I hope you're oh...kay..."

Clayton backed away from the body until he smacked into the bedroom wall. There he sank to his knees and again screamed into the murder weapon.

He flashed on his childhood, those few precious years when he and his father connected in brief, watercolor moments now endowed with the charity that memory affords. There were some good times back in ol' Dawson, Nebraska when the corn was taller than he was. Back before the messiest divorce that his mother and father could have managed, with no regard for him and how, for years, he would struggle to pick out something good to remember between the flying cookware, splintering doors and curses volleyed over his head at ear-shattering volume.

He sat slumped against the wall in his father's death room, his eyes squeezed shut and pouring tears, remembering the Christmas when his dad gave him a set of honest to God professional drums: Ludwig. They were the kind with tom-toms that sounded like H-bombs. Clayton had been 11 years old.

He remembered the bonding that took place over those skins, how they laughed and made noise together in the garage with its space heater and frosted panes of glass along the panel door as his father tried to teach him how the contraption worked, making an unholy racket, and occasionally letting a drumstick squirt from between his fingers to clatter to the cement floor. His dad had done this with a comical frown and knitted brow that was hilarious to them both. It didn't take young Clayton long to realize that, after years of tapping out his anxieties on anything he could get his hands on, he could instantly produce solid, syncopated rhythms. Clayton remembered how his father looked amazed at his boy's intuitive skill as Clayton launched into Led Zeppelin's "When the Levee Breaks."

(ratatat tat...arata...tat...tat)

Clayton would never forget how his father had stared at him with awe, and with something else that Clayton thought he would never see in his father's eyes: pride. Alone in the cozy warmth of that long-ago garage, with the snow gently falling beyond the windows, covering all that was soiled in the world beyond the two of them, for the first and probably the last time, his father had been proud of him.

(ratatat tat...arata...tat...tat)

He could still hear the drumbeat as his father's pride, like warm syrup, soothed the cold places within him.

(ratatat tat...arata..tat...)

Suddenly he realized someone was knocking on the trailer door.

(rata tat tat)

Clayton held his breath. There was another knock, louder this time, and then came the cheap and tinny sing-song of the doorbell.

Clayton jumped to his rubbery feet, stumbled, threw himself through the bedroom's threshold, smacked into the hallway wall, and then ran toward the front door.

This made no sense. It was late. Who could it possibly be? His father had no friends. Clayton had made sure of that. He had specifically asked the Filipino nurses, "Does anyone ever come by?" "Not that I've seen," one of the nurses had assured him, "He has a friend he talks to on the phone, but Mr. Foster didn't like company."

That's what the Filipino nurses had told him and he had believed them. So what the fuck? This plan wasn't going to work if neighbors were bringing over fresh baked pies at 10 o'clock at night.

Frantically, Clayton reviewed what he knew: dad's two best cronies--the guys he used to work with in the maintenance department of the now defunct Western Airlines--were no longer a problem. One died a year ago and the other had retired to Florida. As for the guy who his father "talked to on the phone," Clayton was stumped--could be anybody. Maybe that was him at the door?

He skidded to a halt in the living room just as a key was being fitted into the lock of the front door. He backed away and his fevered mind had only seconds to answer what suddenly became the most important question of his life: Who had a key to the front door?

The key found the lock and turned. The sweat covering Clayton's body instantly turned to a sheet of ice.

The dead body in the bedroom with the bloodshot eyes, the silently screaming face and the blue skin with the bruises around the mouth and nose looked a long way from having died of natural causes. Whoever was about to come in the front door would surely lose their shit when they saw that, and probably scream, as Clayton had. That scream would tear through these crappy, pressboard walls. And then the neighbors would come. Or, just as bad: the intruder would want to help, to commiserate, to stay with Clayton until the authorities came so he wouldn't be alone. And that could not happen. The authorities would spot the signs of a strangled victim within seconds. And if for some reason the responding officer was not the brightest star in the C.S.P.D constellation and didn't arrest Clayton immediately, the coroner would still have all the above indications of murder, plus scads of time to find the carbon dioxide in the old man's lungs.

The front door opened.

Mirasol, the swing-shift nurse let out a yelp and clapped a hand to her mouth when she saw Clayton. "Oh, I'm sorry, Mr. Clayton. I ring the bell. I hope you not sleeping!"

"In the bathroom..." Clayton managed.

"Sorry?"

"I was in the bathroom," Clayton said again. His tongue felt heavy, his lips numb and as blubbery as slugs. What in the hell was she doing here? Suddenly, Clayton wanted to slap the shit out of her and push her out the door.

"I don't mean to bother," pleaded Mirasol. She was short, plump and her long, dark hair was pulled back under a light blue baseball cap that said "Pikes Peak" within a glittery line drawing of the famous mountain. "I just come for my phone. I think I leave it somewhere."

"It's a little late," Clayton seethed.

"I so sorry! I no work here for four more days. Remember? I leaving early to Omaha to see my cousin. Long drive. You was sleeping?"

Long drive, Clayton thought. You're not kidding. I got one ahead of me, too, and I certainly don't need this shit right now.

"No..." Clayton moved back a little more to block the hallway entrance. "Not sleeping."

"You not look good, Mr. Clayton," Mirasol said, closing the door behind her and stepping into the room. "You okay?"

"Bad food I think," was all Clayton could manage. Once he said it though, it sounded good to his ears and he embraced the lie, his brain beginning to work again in earnest, "Yes. I don't know what it was. I ate at Chicken Delivery and...I don't know, maybe the coleslaw..."

"You be okay?"

"Yes. I'll be okay. Thank you."

If you'd get the fuck out of here I would be fine and dandy, Clayton thought.

Mirasol and her analogue, Riza, who worked the morning shift, had been told to take a hike for four days, ostensibly so Clayton could have some quality time with his father. The girls had not been happy. In fact, they had been belligerent about leaving. Clayton knew they needed the money, but he was surprised how ballsy they had been about their "valuable time" and their "bills that needed paying." Clayton had heard somewhere that you could catch more bees with honey, so he had resorted to his puppy dog face and an apologetic tact. They reluctantly consented and Clayton swallowed his resentment whole with a big chaser of relief.

As far as the two girls would know, Foster Briggle would pass away peacefully during their hiatus and would receive a call from a bereft Clayton thanking them and telling them their services would no longer be needed. They were certainly going to flip out at the news, but for purely self-serving reasons that would be short lived. Since the two girls had been referred by the Greenview Rehabilitation Center, there was no reason to think that they wouldn't hastily wash their hands of this job and return to sniffing around Greenview for another gig, giving the Briggle family and their misfortune nary a second thought.

Mirasol finished glancing around the end tables in the small living room and started heading toward Clayton, toward the hallway and the bedroom beyond.

"Wait!" Clayton snapped, his palm jerking up reflexively to slow her. "I mean...he's...sleeping," he whispered. "I finally got him to relax. He needs his rest, y'know? I'll look in the bedroom for you. You look in the kitchen."

Mirasol pursed her lips disconsolately, then shrugged and turned around. Clayton watched her go and then hustled back to the bedroom. He didn't plan on letting Mirasol anywhere near this bedroom, but just in case, he reached out and turned the old man's head away from the door and pulled the sheet up. With a wince he closed the glaring eyes with his index finger. The pillow he had used was lying near the wall. He tossed it onto the bed, turned to go, and saw Mirasol standing at the end of the hall.

"Nothing," Clayton said quickly and far too loudly. "I looked everywhere. No phone. Did you find it?"

Mirasol held up her phone with a weak smile.

The relief that flooded Clayton almost swept him off his feet. He rode the wave of euphoria and realized he was locking eyes with the woman and not saying anything. An awkward silence was blooming.

"Good," Clayton said, "Great! Congratulations! You must feel better now, right?" He came up beside her, put a hand on her shoulder and nudged her toward the door.

"You should drink lot of water," Mirasol said, frowning.

"I will. Promise."

"Mr. Foster be okay? You can lift him okay by yourself?"

I guess we're about to find out, Clayton thought.

"Sure," Clayton said. "It's a little awkward, but I'll get better at it."

Mirasol's face relaxed as Clayton opened the door. He forced an easy smile.

"Sorry to bother again," she said.

"No worries," Clayton said, and watched her descend the two porch steps, walk down the short path, and yank open the door of a truly beat-to-shit 1990s Nissan Pathfinder. She waved. He waved. As calmly as he could, he shut the front door with a soft click.

"Ho…leee…SHIT!" he panted down the front of his shirt.

Staggering, he lurched toward the kitchen and its purring little refrigerator. There was one beer left, lying on its side, still attached to the yoke. He grabbed it, popped it open, and threw its contents down the back of his throat. With a trembling hand he wiped the froth from his lips.

At this point, drunk driving was the least of his worries. The dead body that was about to take a ride with him was far more concerning.

The galley kitchen had a side door to the carport, and through this door's grimy mini-blinds, Clayton saw the bulk of his '03 Dodge Ram 1500 parked like a cruise ship just a few feet from the window. Night had fallen, the summer sun finally dying somewhere over the Rockies, leaving Clayton and the darkened trailer park to bake in the aftermath of its belligerent efforts.

It was 10:14 p.m.

Spreading the mini-blinds apart with thumb and index finger, Clayton scanned left and right, though there was hardly any sightline beyond the looming gray side panel of his truck--The Beast, he sometimes called it. The truck sure looked less conspicuous here in Colorado than it did back home, lumbering down the streets of Hollywood. Of course, when you're in a band and can't afford roadies, giving up your ability to ever park again in L.A. without cursing through your teeth was simply the entrance fee to the Land of Living Your Dreams. Clayton slugged the last of his beer.

He opened the kitchen's side door and stepped onto the porch step. The outside air was a bit cooler than that inside. It even smelled like rain. A large bug fluttered dumbly at his ear and he waved a convulsive hand at it. He quit the porch step and walked to the truck's tailgate, quietly unlatching it and trying to picture how he would drag the body around to the back and somehow lift it into the truck.

For almost three months after he had bought The Beast, Clayton could still smell weed in the cab, though the guy he had bought it from--a friend of a friend and a dope dealer known around Hollywood as Bear, for obvious reasons--had assured him that the dope Bear used to smuggle from Humboldt County down to the San Fernando Valley had never ridden in the cab. The goodies had always been packed into the massive Delta Champion chest toolbox in the truck's bed. Bear claimed it was just as secure and airtight as a car's trunk, but psychologically less conspicuous, sitting out in the open as it did.

From the outside, the chest was nothing but your typical, albeit large, aluminum toolbox, but inside it had been gutted. The provided separators had all been removed leaving a cavity just about five feet in length, two feet wide and a foot deep with an extra six inches of clearance in the lid. Not very comfortable for the living, but for the dead--especially the dead who had not managed to eat much for six months--it would be positively roomy.

A perfect coffin.

Clayton craned his neck to the side of the tailgate to gain sight of the street, but nobody was out and all he could hear was the ubiquitous yapping of small dogs somewhere at the other side of the trailer park.

Foster Briggle's private carport was just wide enough to receive the big truck, its roof a corrugated plastic overhang and its side a wooden fence, the barrier between him and the next trailer. The fence was painted red and topped with more yellow, corrugated plastic panels that shone sickly under June's feverish half moon. Beyond the fence, the neighboring trailer was dark and quiet. Behind the trailer, the small lot backed onto a creek shrouded with thickets of bramble and Morning Glory.

Clayton climbed into the bed of the truck, removed the toolbox key from his pocket and unlocked the chest. The cavity within was empty except for two lengths of rope which Clayton looped loosely around his neck before crawling backwards out of the truck's bed. Then, he turned and went back through the kitchen door into the hot air of the trailer, sparing a moment as he passed the laboring air conditioner to flip it the bird.

Entering the bedroom, Clayton balled his fists and took three deep breaths. The old man's head was facing away, just like Clayton had staged it in those panicked moments when Mirasol was prowling the other room for her lost phone, and this was fortunate. Clayton knew that if he had been greeted with that hanging face with the silent scream, he might have lost his nerve as well as his mind.

With one last deep breath, and with a swift and deliberate motion, Clayton lifted the corpse's midsection and dragged it to the floor. He was startled as one of the limp arms grazed the end table and upset the cheap alarm clock, knocking it to the floor.

Now it read ten to four.

Panting, Clayton stared at it uncomprehendingly.

"Upside down," he muttered finally. Wasn't that the truth. Everything in his life was upside down now, and if he hadn't known it before, he was sure of it now: it always had been and it always would be.

He caught his breath and studied the results of his effort. The method of pulling the body off the bed from the middle had worked: the corpse landed wrapped in a tidy burrito of bed sheet, except for one bony leg.

And one staring eye.

Somehow the eye had come open again and it watched Clayton standing there and catching his breath.

Clayton had to look away. Another sickening image was worming its way into his mind, something he had seen on television about a guy who went around the world eating the grossest food he could get his hands on. Clayton remembered one particular episode where the guy ate something called a balut egg, a developing duck embryo that is boiled alive and eaten in the shell. The guy had cracked it open to show the viewer just what was in store for their taste buds should they choose to meet the challenge: a yellowish, white gelatinous goop shocked with bright red veins running through it. Clayton thought it might even have been a dish from the Philippines. Did Mirasol eat shit like that? Clayton shuddered at the thought. But that's what the eye looked like: a cracked open balut egg.

Clayton's stomach roiled. He stooped and quickly tugged the sheet up over the eye and tucked the exposed leg into the swaddling.

Next, he removed the two lengths of rope from around his neck. He fiddled with the sheet, moving the body this way and that until the corpse was well-centered before he twisted the material near the feet and tied it fast. He did the same at the head, twisting the sheet and this time, tying it so that a good amount of lead rope was available for tugging.

He took a moment to right the alarm clock and then stepped over the body and into the hall where the pocket door to the linen closet stood open. He removed a replacement sheet, returned to the bedroom, whipped the sheet open and let it flutter onto the bed. Then he bunched it and swept it back on one side before returning his attention to the dingy white cocoon at his feet.

The path to the truck and its toolbox was clear. Now, all he needed was strength and a prayer that his back wouldn't go out in the middle of his task. With both hands he tugged the rope at the head, swiveling the bundle around. He dragged it through the door. It wasn't that difficult, moving the body by tugging on the rope. It whispered easily over the low nape of the trailer's rug. He rounded the hallway, headed through the living room and into the kitchen. Here, he took a moment to catch his breath and rub his hands together. He stared at them, flexing his flushed fingers and rope-burned palms. With another heave, the body slid easily over the kitchen's greasy linoleum floor.

Clayton brushed the sweat out of his eyes, stuck his head out the kitchen door, and peered toward the end of the short driveway. Across the little trailer park street was the edge of a pond where ducks usually glided across its green and glassy surface, but now the water was black, silent and still. Beyond that, the amber porch light of another trailer lit a cloud of insects. The yappy dog in the distance had stopped its barking.

Clayton swiveled the body so it pointed headfirst at the porch step. There were only three feet between the porch step and the truck and this was the only stretch of his mission where the suspicious bundle could possibly be seen by anyone who happened by at the end of the driveway. With one tug he would have to make the sharp turn and get the body to the foot of the open tailgate as quick and as silently as he could. Crouching and grabbing the rope with both hands he tugged, backed into the truck's side panel, and, using the momentum, swung the body left. With shuffling steps, as silent as he could make them, he dragged the bundle over the concrete and toward the back of the truck.

He was halfway there, but the hard part was next. Now, he had to lift the dead weight onto the truck bed and then again into the toolbox. According to the medical chart at Greenview Rehab, his father's height was five feet, ten inches. The length of the toolbox was five feet, and since rigor mortis wasn't going to set in until well after the old man was in the box, with legs bent at the knee and doubled underneath, this would allow plenty of room for the body. God knew the width or height wasn't going to be a problem after his father's very effective diet. Clayton figured that if he grabbed the waist of the body with both hands, with a little effort, he could...

Footsteps were coming.

Clayton dropped to his knees fast. When he realized that one of them was planted firmly on his father's ribcage, he jerked it away.

The crunch and scrape of footsteps came closer. Clayton held his breath. He listened.

They were not coming toward him, they were coming from across the little street, at the side of the lake and headed laterally. As the carport was in total darkness, he dared to peek around the side of the truck. It was a woman, a younger woman, out to piss her dog. It was a little dog, maybe even the yappy dog that was melting down earlier. The dog paused for a moment, and Clayton would be good-goddamned if the thing didn't look directly at him. He jerked his head back.

Maybe it could smell death.

The terrier leveled a brief, gurgling growl, but the woman holding its leash was not interested in anything but getting her nightly slog over with and getting back to her Jimmy Fallon.

"Knock it off, Misty," the woman's voice said dispassionately. The dog lurched forward as the woman tugged the leash, but not before the animal shot Clayton one more distrustful glance over its shoulder.

"Of course," Clayton muttered, "fucking of course that would happen." His adrenaline was so sickening, it blurred his vision. He listened and waited until their footsteps had faded from hearing.

Quickly, he shoved his hands under the body, got his legs under him, and, like an Olympian performing a deadlift, heaved the body onto the tailgate. Then he climbed on and tugged the body across the fluted bed and toward the yawning toolbox. He paused. He waited. He listened. He had made some noise, but not much. Only the neighbors beyond the red fence at his right could have heard anything. But no one stirred. No porch light popped on.

One more deadlift and the body tumbled into the toolbox. It tumbled in perfectly, the legs folding just so. Clayton's eyes welled with tears, tears for the reprehensible thing he had done and tears of relief. How many times had he rehearsed this on the seemingly endless drive from L.A.? A hundred, maybe? But the nerves he had fought had come mostly from one fact alone: in the end, it was always the unforeseen that gets you. He knew this now better than ever, especially now that he was on the run from a botched drug deal. Sure, there had been a few hiccups tonight, but he had done it. His cargo was aboard.

He jumped out of the truck's bed, ran into the kitchen, and yanked open the freezer compartment of the little fridge. Grabbing the two bags of ice he had stashed there for this occasion, he returned to the toolbox and threw them atop the body before locking the toolbox's lid with his key. He didn't know how long a body took to smell and he didn't want to find out. On his seven hour road trip he would have to stop for gas once and he didn't want anything to happen that might attract unwanted attention. He wanted to be just another pick-up truck chugging its way through the night on I-80.

After retracing his steps several times Clayton locked up his father's trailer, jumped into the truck's cab, and gripped the wheel. He stared out at the edge of the dark pond at the end of the drive for a moment before he jammed the key into the ignition and the engine roared to life.

It was going to be a long night.

"It doesn't matter what time you show up, honeybunch," Sylvia Blair had assured him. "I'll take care of everything. Everything will be just fine."

Clayton hoped to God she was right.

Chapter 5

The Butterfly Effect

Now that she was middle aged, with plenty of cash and time on her hands, Ruby Wegner accepted that she had officially become a career student. She hadn't set out to become such a thing: when she began her studies at Dawson's Concordia University the distraction that came with thinking of things other than why her family had disintegrated had simply enabled her to go on. She relished taking courses like Chaos Theory and Predictability. She wanted to know why everything happened or why it didn't. But knowledge quickly went from being a distraction to being a comfort. With any luck, she hoped it would eventually become a catharsis.

As of late, she had started gravitating toward science and physics rather than the straight philosophy and existentialism of her last few years of study. It was less poetic, but more concrete, relying less on conjecture. The scientific process could be illustrated mathematically and that felt tangible and good. Plus, it had a familiarity to it. There had been scientists in her family once upon a time.

While Ruby buried herself in her studies, she was not concerned with garnering a degree: she was too old now to show off for employers half her age, had been through too much to think that such status was relevant, and perhaps most importantly, had the luxury of independent wealth. So she simply audited whatever course might help her understand her world. Though she did not show up for tests, she never stopped turning over in her head the concepts and theories she learned.

Chaos theory, she thought, pulling on her jogging shorts, exactly the type of thing she wanted to drown in and not come up for air: nature's random cruelty, its violence and its uncertainty. These were the things she had to understand, and she would spend the rest of her life trying.

Every morning she allowed herself a couple of hours before her summer course to not think of such things. She gave herself that. In spite of her will to the contrary she refused to become a complete robot. So she had developed a morning routine, her one chance a day to get some air, and the first stop was always a place of light and community. In Dawson, that place was the Corner Café.

The café was in the ground floor of a two-story brick building on the corner of the leafy square in the center of town. She always got there early, usually around 7:30, for a light breakfast before her morning jog and before the summer heat started to thicken and claw at the town. Peggy Jones, the proprietor, always had her yogurt parfait and coffee waiting.

As she scanned the Dawson Independent spread before her on her café table, she began to suspect that her 44-year-old eyes might soon have to suffer the indignity of reading glasses.

Most would consider Ruby pretty, though she held a weariness in her eyes that wasn't from lack of sleep or her inability to read the paper as easily as she used to; it was more the slow erosion of her spirit. She hardly ever wore makeup, and today was no different. As always when she stopped in the Corner Café, she wore a tank top and jogging shorts, her auburn ponytail riding high out of the adjustable band of her baseball cap, her freckled face screwed up at the newspaper's headlines.

"Linda Vanderboom," she said at the paper. "That's Lance's mom."

From over Ruby's shoulder, Peggy Jones, at the counter polishing smudges from her coffee pot, said, "It's a shame. That kid has lost both of his parents this year." Peggy clicked off a tsk-tsk.

Lance Vanderboom--or "that kid," as Peggy had called him--was forty-seven now. He had graduated St. Mark in 1986, the same year as Ruby's brother Scott. But to the venerable Peggy Jones, who had watched them all grow up, most in town were still kids to her and always would be.

"Losing both your parents," Peggy repeated, "can you imagine?"

Of course Ruby could. Everyone knew Ruby didn't have to imagine such a thing, but Ruby was beyond bristling at Peggy's faux pas. After all, it had been a harmless oversight, just a thing to say.

Still, Peggy caught herself and was opening her mouth to backpedal when John Supernau walked in, the little bell on the café's door tinkling.

"Morning, Ruby," John said as he passed her table heading for Peggy's carafe of coffee, though he didn't really need to come here to buy it. He managed the Pak N' Save in town and its deli always had fresh brewed joe all day. But visiting Peggy and the Corner Café was a habit that he thought he might never break, nor did he want to. There was something calming about taking a moment before a long day's work to sip coffee and sit by one of Peggy's windows with their lemon yellow Provençal curtains bunched with pale blue tiebacks. There was always someone around to shoot the shit with if he wanted. Even better, sometimes he would just stare out of the window and watch the light spread across the town square.

John grabbed his mug of coffee, sat at a table in line with Ruby's, and watched a pair of finches hop across the top of the bandshell. Independence Day was coming, he thought. Soon the bandshell would be thrumming, the square full of food booths. Hell, the whole town would be overrun. But for now all was quiet, like it usually was, the way he liked it.

"How about some coffee cake, you two," Peggy called from the counter. "Just made it this morning. This time I tried it with raisins."

"No thanks, Peggy," Ruby answered.

John took the offer and hopped up to the counter to receive the extended saucer. "That's a new clock!" he exclaimed on his way back to his table.

Indeed, there was a new clock on the brick wall across from the windows. It hung just where the old one had: to the left of the Nebraska Cornhuskers pennant and to the right of the pennant for the Concordia Bulldogs. Its round face glowed with a thin strip of blue neon.

"Fancy," John added.

"Isn't it just?" Peggy said. "Sandy Kawolski gave it to me. You know Sandy...looks after the yarn store? Barb's girl? Said she had it in her attic for years and was never going to use it."

"Did you hear?" Ruby said to John. "You know, about Lance's mom?"

"I did," John said soberly. He got up and swung around his table to join Ruby.

"All it says," Ruby said, scanning the page of the Independent, "is that she was hospitalized after attending the Lincoln Swap Meet and then she died of cardiac arrest overnight at General." Ruby looked up and added under her breath, "I guess she was pretty big...fat, I mean."

John only smiled at her.

Ruby had always had a crush on John, and his proximity still flushed her. If pressed, she would blame his hair. Unlike every other boy in Nebraska who seemed to cut theirs with a weed-whacker, his was naturally thick, blond, wavy and fell right, always had. It had style. She had always wanted to run her hands through it. He'd always had a mustache, too, ever since high school. Ruby figured this was because he was the only boy who could grow one as a teenager without it looking like a tattered anchovy affixed itself to his upper lip. The mustache was blond, too, and Ruby had never seen him without it--couldn't imagine him without it. Back in high school, it had made him look so much older than anyone else. More perilously, in the '80s a mustache had been an anachronism, tantamount to a top hat, but John had still gone with it. Somehow, what could have been ridiculous with anyone else became sexy in John's hands.

But three years in age made a big difference back in high school, and now John was married. Ruby had never had a chance with anyone from her brother's peer group. Along with her brother, Scotty, the group had consisted of John Supernau, Lance Vanderboom, Paul Neumann-- "spelled differently" than that of the famous actor he would have to say his entire life--and Clayton Briggle. The Fearsome Five, they had called themselves, though the only thing fearsome about them had been their penchant for nonsensical alliteration. Ruby would freely admit that she had a crush on each of them at one time or another, but as Scotty's little sister, her infatuations had always remained unrequited.

Ruby hadn't seen Paul and Clayton for a long time, but so far, John Supernau had turned out to be the best catch. He had become a local celebrity of sorts. As of last November, he had become the mayor's son, after a landslide election, thanks to Hal Supernau's sunny disposition and a very catchy campaign slogan: "We Need Hal Supernau Now!"

"His stepmom," John corrected.

"Huh?" said Ruby.

"Linda was his stepmom," said John, leaning toward Ruby, his eyes as green as a pond, "Remember?"

Ruby glanced down at the newspaper, forgetting briefly what they had been talking about. That's right, she remembered. Lance's real mom left Roger when Lance was a tyke, and Lance himself had told Ruby that he and Linda never really saw eye to eye.

"Still," John continued, "you should talk to Lance. He would appreciate it. It's got to smart."

John took a bite of his coffee cake and studied Ruby, wondering if she was listening. She was staring somewhere between her newspaper and the trunks of the oaks beyond the window.

"You're the only one who knows how it feels," John continued gently, following Ruby's gaze as it lifted across the town's square to the hopping finches. "In fact, I'm beginning to think we are at the age now where we are all going to know how it feels sooner than we think. And you know what?"

John craned his neck to Peggy for a moment, "I like it with the raisins."

Peggy smiled and John turned back to Ruby, "It means we're next in line. That blows my mind, you know? After our parents are gone, we're the next in line. I mean, I still think of your brother and me smoking that weed we found growing along the Blue River in the bowling alley bathroom at the Christmas party during freshman year, trying to blow the smoke out of that transom window before anyone came in. And do you remember old George Lockhart came in and found us and thought a skunk had gotten loose in the building? He told everyone to use the girl's bathroom until he could find the critter and then..." John laughed, blowing crumbs of coffee cake, "he went into the bathroom with a broom!"

Ruby cracked a smile and then laughed, a hand to her mouth.

The two sighed and fell into silence.

Ruby gazed out the window, biting her lower lip. The sun was now starting to bake the brick faces of the two august banking institutions that faced each other across the square: Jones and Cattle National Banks.

"I'll see how Lance is doing," Ruby said. "I can pass his shop on my run. I don't know what to say though. I'm no expert on moving on."

"I think you're amazing at it," John said, "absolutely amazing."

Ruby flushed, hiding behind her last sip of coffee.

"Clayton Briggle may be in the same situation soon," John added. "I just spoke to him last night. His dad is pretty sick. He's helping out his dad in Colorado, and then he's going to come by for a visit, hang out at my place for a bit."

Ruby brightened. Clayton was another of her brother's friends she had always adored. She thought him so talented. He lived in Hollywood, after all. She didn't know anybody who lived in Hollywood. And he had made it in the music business, or so everyone said. Ruby didn't listen to the kind of music Clayton played, but she bet he was good at it--as far as that kind of music went.

"He's coming from California?" she asked.

"He sure is," John confirmed. "But he had to go to Colorado to take care of his dad who had a stroke. Clayton said the old guy didn't seem long for this world. You remember Foster Briggle, don't you?"

"Sure," said Ruby. "I didn't see him much--kept to himself mostly, didn't he?"

John nodded.

"So when is Clay coming?" Ruby prodded.

"I think he said in a day or two." John polished off his last sip of coffee. "Well..." he stood up, "into the box."

Ruby understood "the box" to be Pak N' Save where John managed the day shift. They both said their goodbyes to Peggy and went their separate ways, Ruby heading to a park bench at the edge of the square to stretch her tendons before her run.

#

Completing her circuit through the town and out of breath, Ruby gained Second Street and slowed to a brisk walk. Stewing in both guilt and relief, she noted that she never made it to Roger Vanderboom's auto body shop--now Lance's auto body shop--on her run. She wondered if she ever would. Could she comfort someone else? Was there really comfort in anything?

Chaos, she reviewed, is sensitivity to initial conditions. The randomness of nature can be determinate.

Maybe she should take the test on chaos theory. She wasn't grasping it as firmly as she would have liked, and she needed to.

She looked up and stopped walking. For some reason, there was a police car across the street from her house, parked in front of Sylvia Blair's place.

Slowly, Ruby walked by the Victorian mansion. Under the pretense of working out a kink in her neck, she trained a peek at Blair's windows. As usual, the house divulged no secret. It only stared back, quiet and shrouded with its heavy curtains and branches.

What was the sheriff doing at the witch house? Maybe it was nothing. Or maybe it was a whole lot of something. Was Blair okay? Ruby might have cared once, but not anymore. Really, other people's affairs made little difference to her. She had been through the wringer already. Maybe the wringer had tired of her and the wringer was just on to somebody else.

Sensitivity to initial conditions, she continued reviewing in her head, is sometimes known as the "butterfly effect," so called because of a published paper in 1972 entitled: Predictability: Does the Flap of a Butterfly's Wings in Brazil set off a Tornado in Texas? The flapping wing represents a small change in the initial condition of the system, which causes a chain of events leading to large-scale phenomena. Had the butterfly not flapped its wings, the trajectory of the system might have been vastly different.

Might have been, she reminded herself.

Somewhere along the way, something had flapped its big, dark wings and now she lived with its effect, lived with it every day.

Her father, Dr. Peter Wegner, had not died suddenly, at least not in the eyes of those who followed his decline, but her mother had decided to guard Ruby and her brother from his illness, maintaining that it seemed like the right thing to do. They were so young back then, back when they still lived in Chicago--Scotty was nine and Ruby only six. Yet, on the day when the truth could no longer be bridled, the truth had come with a regrettable cruelty.

After being called into their mother's room they had climbed up on the creaking end of her mattress. They looked up at her swollen eyes and her makeup-smeared face and had no comprehension of the choked words she spit at them through her sobs. She might as well have told them the most absurd thing that she could imagine: that they were all giraffes, or that they would all be moving to the bottom of the sea. Not only did her news make little sense, but the state of their mother's being had compounded their bewilderment: her eyes not able to focus, her shoulders rounded, and her back hunched with an unbearable weight. She looked broken inside.

Their strident, confident mother, the one who never took any shit from anyone, who had been the paradigm of the liberated 1970s woman, and who taught classes at Chicago's John Adams High School in a whirlwind of geeky and infectious energy, had broken. This day was to be one of Ruby's earliest and most indelible memories. Sitting with her brother on the edge of that bed, in that darkened bedroom, they had twisted inside, suspended in an eternal moment as in the angst-riddled interim before a magician deigned to restore a vanished object with a rectifying wave of the hand. When that moment never came, the two children tried their best to grasp that their father was gone forever.

Dr. Wegner's friends and colleagues--of which there were many--used colorful words and phrases at his funeral, words like: "irascible," "stubborn" and "brilliant"; phrases like: "would give you the shirt off his back," "was there when you needed him," "knew what he liked and knew what he didn't," and "was a family man before being a scientist."

The procession had moved from the church to nearby Graceland Cemetery in the Lakeview neighborhood of Chicago, lit that day by a kind, crisp autumn sun. The mourners followed a meandering path lined with thick stands of oak and hickory trees, the changing leaves still clinging to their branches like forks of golden fire. Ruby would never forget the glossy casket sitting beside the black hole of fertile earth. She had thought that the ground looked somehow hungry, ready to swallow her father whole.

Alice Wegner had thrown the first fistful of dirt onto her husband's casket, Scotty and Ruby stiffly following suit before being reabsorbed into the gathered throng of strangers. Scotty, in his ill-fitting suit, kicked at the ground absently, sending chunks of sod spiraling into the hole before him. Ruby gripped her mother's hand as if the planet were spinning out of control.

The encomium that appeared in the Tribune was an exercise in praise tempered with solemnity and included eighteen inches of print with a photo of Dr. Wegner in cerebral tweed and black-rimmed glasses. "Pioneer" and "innovator" were peppered throughout the article along with a detailed history of how he had come to found Wegner Electronics.

Peter Wegner prized his children above all else, and the feeling was mutual with Scott and Ruby. The kids had been willing ears whenever the detailed explanations of their father's life work and passion for physics and alternative, untapped power sources came in exuberant gushes.

Occasionally, the kids could visit Wegner Electronics in Evanston, and when they did, one of their favorite illustrative tools was a miniature solar-powered helicopter that sat on the broad sill in the window of Peter's private office, gathering light through the diamond-paned window for its next flight. The kids would ask excitedly if the tiny solar panels on the plastic rotors were full of enough sun to schedule another whispery flight over the beds of perennials and flowering shrubs surrounding the company campus.

"In the long run," their father had once said, placing the helicopter gingerly in the center of the birch quadrangle behind his office, "mankind will have no choice but to turn to the power of the sun if it wants to survive."

The drama of this preamble made the wobbly liftoff a thing of consequence. The 'copter gained altitude and rode thermals around the yard, threatening kamikaze maneuvers into one of the stately oaks surrounding the property before crashing indelicately back to earth.

"Eventually, solar cells will be able to provide all the electrical power this country needs. Imagine..." Dr. Wegner had said, bending over with a grunt to scoop up the drained toy, "every rooftop in every town and city drinking in the sun."

He fascinated Scott and Ruby. Their father had been their hero. He talked to them as if they could understand anything he was saying, and only later, when they remembered him, did this touch them profoundly.

"Did you know," their father had told them, "that most of the communication satellites floating around the earth right now have solar panels manufactured by Wegner Electronics? And I just sold this company! I'm going on to something else, something even bigger!"

What that was going to be, Scott and Ruby would never know.

After their father's death, nine-year-old Scotty wanted details, and after a period of halfhearted evasion from his mother, he discovered that it had been a brain tumor that had killed their father. He reported this to his sister--though she didn't seem to require a reason for his death as the end result was the same. Yet, they both did feel a particular injustice in the bitterly ironic cause of death. If the brain, the tool that had carried him to glory and success, could kill a man as smart as their father, then danger and absurdity were everywhere, nothing was absolute and nothing could be trusted. There was no permanence, no safety. That greedy tumor had not only robbed them of a dad, but had cracked the fragile shell surrounding the only insular sanctuary they would ever know: the great, too short daydream of childhood.

As soon as she could get her wits about her, Alice put the family home up for sale and moved them all from the site of their pain and back to her hometown of Dawson, Nebraska. Dawson reminded her of simpler times, of her own childhood, which had been particularly good, all things considered. Maybe there they could start again.

Upon arriving in Nebraska, the only thing good for the Wegners had been money. They had more than enough for where they were going to now live. Compared to Chicago, everything in Nebraska was practically free. With that kind of independence, Alice could bring some stability to their lives again. She never threw money around. Really, there was nowhere to do so, and that was just as well since ostentation in the small town wouldn't have garnered her many friends.

Alice had needed a new car, though, and for some reason, buying a classic American car in the Midwest is a forgivable sin. So she went for the ride she had pined for as a teenager, but had been refused by her parents: a '68 Chrysler Imperial.

The Imperial had a horizontal bar grille with ends that wrapped around the sides of the front fenders, and at the center of the grille appeared the Imperial Eagle, mimicking a similar emblem at the rear. It was a Crown Coupe, painted in rich burgundy, and it was like riding a cloud. Of course this would be her fair weather car, and a new Chevy Blazer would have to do the dirty work in the harsh Nebraska winters.

And so the three of them lived and healed in Dawson for over a decade, their mother's inexplicable strength preventing a total collapse of the family. Alice found a teaching job, and both kids had their mother as their teacher when they passed through seventh grade. The kids went to school at St. Mark Lutheran--not that they were Lutherans or even particularly religious, but because it was walking distance from their house and the school's reputation was good. Both kids garnered respectable grades--Ruby's a bit better than Scotty's. The three of them went to church every Sunday--again just for the sake of community-- and the three of them became well-regarded as a kind, handsome and remarkably well-adjusted family.

One October, when seventeen-year-old Ruby was spending the long Columbus Day weekend with a friend and twenty-year-old Scotty was on a weekend trip to Kansas City with his fellow frat boys, Alice decided to get out of town herself. She would take a road trip in her Imperial to go and see her old friend Dolly Featherstone in Highland Park, just outside of Chicago. It would be an eight hour drive, but she looked forward to the time alone. After teaching junior high, a few hundred miles of tall grass and big sky had sounded just fine.

On the third day of her trip, Columbus Day, she had stayed at Dolly's well into the afternoon, longer than she had wanted to, allowing time for the rain to stop falling in exchange for a drive in the dark. A bone-chilling wind blew from the northeast across Lake Michigan that day, and as she began her trip home there were periods of hail. The dropping temperature threatened snow by sundown.

The police report stated that the markings left by the wheels of Alice Wegner's car on a lightly traveled stretch of Lake Cook Road that cut through a forest preserve indicated that the vehicle braked suddenly. A streak of blood was found on the chrome of the overturned car's grille and the conclusion was that a deer had broken cover, ran across the slick road, and had been struck with a glancing blow. The deer had disappeared, perhaps mortally wounded, into the forest lining one side of the road.

On the other side of the highway ran a shallow river masked by reeds. The car had maneuvered evasively, hit a patch of black ice, drove into a furrow and flipped, landing upside-down in the creek. The head injuries sustained by impact with the steering wheel were enough to render Alice unconscious. However, the head trauma was not determined to be the cause of death. Snow had begun to fall by the time emergency vehicles reached her, shrouding the wreck from view. The coroner determined the cause of death to be asphyxia and hypothermia.

"It's unimaginable," said St. Mark's principal, Don Creech, at a school assembly days later. "It's absolutely tragic. Mrs. Wegner was a gifted educator, a good person and an invaluable addition to this school." Wiping away a tear, Principal Creech had replaced his glasses above his push broom mustache before he was able to continue. "Both Ruby and Scott Wegner will need our support through this. As you all know, Scott is finishing his degree this year at Concordia--I know you see him in town all the time--and Ruby is in her senior year here. Let them both know they are loved. That is what the St. Mark community is all about. That is what Dawson is about. With our support I know Scott and Ruby will get through this."

And just like that, Scott and Ruby Wegner had become orphans. Together, they continued to live in the modest house on Second Street that their mother had bought when they moved to escape the pain of their father's death. Scott was old enough to assume custody for Ruby's last year of childhood. Given their paternal grandparents in South Dakota had never been overly concerned with them, and given their maternal grandparents resided in Dusseldorf, Germany, it was the only sound choice. So they remained living together in Dawson.

But their parents were never far from their thoughts: Alice Wegner's picture never gathered dust where it sat on the fireplace mantel, nor did Peter Wegner's solar helicopter which sat right beside it.

#

Finished with her morning jog, Ruby tugged the keys out of the front door of the house with her mail under her arm and called for her brother.

She found him sitting in the dark, in front of the fireplace.

"Are you going to move from that chair?" Ruby scolded."You really should come out into the garden. It's beautiful today. It's not too hot." With her hands on her hips, she waited for an answer. When Scotty didn't give one, she started to sort the mail, "So, by the way, there's a police car out in front of Blair's."

"They're fucking," Scotty said simply.

Ruby started, turned and gaped at her brother. "Wait...what?"

"Sheriff Lutz and Sylvia Blair...they're fucking."

"Oh, come on! How would you know that, Scotty?"

"Just do," Scotty muttered. "I know a lot of things."

"Well, be that as it may...that wasn't what I wanted to talk to you about," Ruby said, "What I wanted to tell you was that Lance Vanderboom's mom died."

"Linda wasn't his mom," Scotty corrected.

"Whatever," Ruby said peevishly, "that's neither here nor there. The point is: she's dead. That was little Luke's grandma, and Lance has to be a little hurt about it, what with his father dying a few months ago and all. It's a lot to take. Lance has no parents at all now...just like us. I figured you'd want to know since he's your friend."

It was rare for Scotty to be seen in the living room. He usually kept to the upper floor, and whenever he did make it downstairs, and especially whenever he was sitting before his mother's portrait and his father's helicopter, he was always particularly moody. So when Scotty didn't respond, Ruby was not too surprised. She cursed herself for saying "he has no parents; he's just like us now." That had been careless. Neither of them needed to be reminded of that.

But then Scotty said, "That's sad. Tell Lance I feel for him."

"I wish you could tell him yourself," Ruby said, but she knew that would never happen. Scotty had no intention of ever leaving the house or saying anything to anyone but her. He had told her as much.

Ruby paused a moment to look at him, to think of how she could help him. Even in his dark stoicism, he was strikingly handsome: his cheekbones high, his auburn hair piled in thick waves, his eyes big and emerald green, and his skin--which had not seen the sun in a great many years--was flawless and white, almost vampiric.

Scott caught her eye and he smiled tightly. "There's nothing I can do, Rubes. It's beyond me. Lance was much closer to his father and he got over that somehow. He'll be fine."

"Still," said Ruby, "it's going to be hard."

Scotty peeled his eyes from the fireplace mantel and looked at his sister, "It's always hard, Ruby. That's all I would tell him anyway. It's always going to be hard."

A butterfly floating just beyond the dining room window arrested Ruby's attention. Beating its wings, it tossed its way toward her bed of petunias in crazy loops before it rose and disappeared from sight.

"Yeah," Ruby said absently, "you're probably right about that."

Chapter 6

The Long Drive

Clayton Briggle swung his truck onto I-70, his knuckles white upon the steering wheel. He figured the next time he would breathe would be after Denver. There was a lot that could go wrong, passing through a big city--fender benders, checkpoints, speed traps--though the latter was not his biggest concern. He could make good time at a reasonable speed at this time of night if he just didn't push it. He could cut the eight hour drive to six-and-a-half by flirting with 80 mph on the stretch between cities, but he would have to play it cool through Denver and as he got closer to Lincoln. Near these cities would be the biggest police presence. There would be restless, graveyard-shift State 'P' who would be looking for anything to get themselves promoted or break up the monotony of their long night.

Slow and steady, Clayton thought.

"It's done," he said to his reflection in the windshield. "Call it what you want--murder, mercy killing, whatever...but it's done. So deal with it."

He wished the light would change and that his reflection would go away. He looked haunted, and his greatest fear was that he always would be.

After a half hour on the highway he thought he could hear the body rolling around in the tool box in the bed of his truck. But that was impossible. The body was in there too tight to roll around. Wasn't it?

But he kept hearing it.

Light rain began to patter on the windshield. He drove, tensed, both hands on the wheel. New emotions flared in his head, all of them as unique and as molten hot as freshly fired bits of blown glass and he recognized none of them. Was that fear mixed with relief? Was that hope, denial and self-loathing in one fiery belch of conscience?

"It's done," he said again, flatly. He wasn't sure why he kept saying it aloud, but it helped, somehow it helped the disbelief of it all.

After a while of repeating it over and over, though, it began to backfire, reminding him of an obvious and horrific fact: it could not be undone. Clayton had no certainty that he wouldn't wake up someday and regret his decision more than all of the other regrettable decisions he had made, and when he did, he knew he would wake up screaming.

"Fuck," he muttered, and he cried. He cried for everything he had lost and everything he never had. And he cried for his father rolling around in the tool box...

Not rolling, he assured himself with desperate insistence. He can't roll. He's wrapped in that dirty sheet and packed in there so tight I might even have broken something...maybe an arm? A few fingers at least.

He wiped his eyes peevishly with his shirtsleeve. If he was crying for all he had lost and all he had never had, then wasn't that body in the toolbox the very incarnation of that lamentation? Just like his mother, his father had checked out at some point. He had washed his hands of what it meant to be part of a family. Why? Because he thought his son was a lost cause? Because he thought he was a lost cause himself? Their love for each other had slowly atrophied like an unused muscle, leaving the "why" and the "when" of it all to the haze of time.

He blamed his mother for all of it. She had left his father and hadn't bothered to look back. Never mind that her son was going through puberty at the time and already confused as hell. Obviously, she had been cheating on his father for some time since, after just a few months, she remarried a rich douche bag named Trevor and thereafter led a life of vapid excess and emotional unavailability.

After that, Clayton couldn't look at her anymore, couldn't carry on a conversation with her anymore. She used words like "Dahling!" and "Delish!"--words that real people didn't use. The mother he once known had been consumed by this new and alien personality. Clayton could simply have labeled her piteously nouveau riche if he had only known what the term meant, and it would have been easier for him to dismiss her as the tragic cliché that she had become rather than think it had something to do with him. Yet, that didn't happen. Instead, he had taken it personally. He had been crushed by it.

The most unforgivable part of the whole thing was that the marriage to Trevor the Turd had been misinterpreted by his mother as a total relief of motherhood, a lotto ticket that she had no intention of sharing for fear that it would jinx her improbable good fortune.

Granted, his father had been no prize, but Clayton thought the old man had actually loved her once. He must have, but looking back on it all, Clayton wondered how he was ever conceived and how they ever could have stayed together as long as they had. In a way, Clayton figured that although miracles had been rare in his own life, he was living proof that they did exist.

He wiped the final tear from his face and steeled himself into a phlegmatic ball of will. He was on his own, always had been. But the good news was that he had passed through Denver. Yep, he had. The long black ribbon of I-80 that would take him to Dawson now stretched before him. The whole time he had been trying to make sense out of where he'd come from, he'd been conquering a major obstacle in his way: Denver was behind him, the road ahead was clear, and all at once, he didn't care anymore about the past. The wind was at his back. His eyes were already getting heavy, but he stared ahead at the open road, leaving Colorado's foothills to fade into the horizon in his rearview mirror.

#

A few hours later, as he passed the sign that welcomed him and his dead father to "The Good Life" of Nebraska, thunder clapped and lightning forked into the endless corn fields that rolled to the horizon.

Just like a horror movie, Clayton thought. Of course, there had to be thunder and lighting.

The night was dark, the moon still new, and the summer storm splashed erratic patterns of rain on the windshield. He glanced at the truck's clock: 2:04 AM.

The click-clack of the highway beneath him now threatened to lull him to sleep. He cranked up the air conditioner. There was nobody on the road ahead of him, save for the distant taillights of a truck at the horizon. He checked the rearview.

Clayton screamed.

His father was standing in the bed of the truck, glaring back at him, wind whipping the corpse's hair into dancing white spires as he rocked back and forth with the movement of the truck. The jaw still hung down to the thing's chest, the yawning dark hole of a mouth wet with black, viscous goo as it chewed the air, reaching for Clayton.

Clayton swerved the truck across the slow lane to the shoulder of the road. In the rearview mirror the corpse scowled, teetering in and out of view, its eyes now blazing with hate. Clayton saw it begin to rip the dirty sheet off of its body with one bony hand. With the other, it reached out and clawed at the cab's back window. The glass shrieked under its yellowed fingernails.

Clayton screamed again and sent the truck screeching back toward the median. The tires skittered over the highway's rumble strips, filling the cab with a cacophony of sound before he could straighten the truck into the fast lane. He flicked his eyes back to the rearview mirror.

Nothing.

"What the fuck?" Clayton panted, his heart thudding, his vision swimming. "What the...fuck!?"

He couldn't catch his breath. He looked into the mirror again, but only saw his own wild eyes shaking in their sockets and headlights in the slow lane approaching about a mile back. Gripping the seat behind him, he craned his neck to check the lid on the toolbox. It was closed. It was secure.

Slow down, he cursed himself. Did you fall asleep you fucking idiot? Did you really fall asleep? Straighten up. Check your speed. Good. Fine. Everything is fine now.

Unless the car about to crawl up your ass is a cop.

Is it?

A man in a white Cadillac sedan pulled up next to Clayton and glanced at him with a disapproving look before speeding up and passing him in the slow lane.

"Yeah, fine," Clayton spat, shaking with adrenaline. "Fuck off."

Relief felt its way into his veins and his breath came back to him. His hands steadied. Clayton goosed the truck up to the speed limit. Going too slow was no good either. Now he was fine: driving straight. Good speed. He panted a laugh at the rain-speckled windshield.

He watched the Cadillac fade away ahead of him and watched it signal its way back into the fast lane well ahead of him. Checking the rearview, he saw a semi approaching beside him in the slow lane now and another one a couple of miles back.

Lincoln was coming up. Undoubtedly, that was where Mr. Cadillac was headed, or maybe beyond to Omaha where all of the insurance money allowed for a few fancy cars now and then. Clayton's optimism returned. Lincoln would be his last major obstacle and he felt more up to the challenge now than he had before. That scare had really sharpened his senses. The last vestiges of adrenaline were still pricking his extremities, but rather than making him feel like he wanted to throw up, as it had a mile back, it was now invigorating him.

According to the odometer, Lincoln was still a few hours away. Mr. Cadillac was far from home. Shit, so was everyone out here on I-80. There was nothing in every direction: tall grass prairies and fields of feed corn that would look golden and prosperous in the sun, but at night had just become one immense, black blanket tucked into the curve of the earth.

Clayton squinted. Taillights were clustering in the distance.

"No," he muttered, "what's this?"

There was a slow down. Clayton hissed through his teeth. Checkpoint? For what? He glanced at the clock: 3:38 AM.

It wouldn't be a sobriety checkpoint. Fourth of July wasn't until next week. Was it a weigh station? He doubted there would be any out here in the flats, and there were no grades that would require a big rig to get weight-checked. It was a wreck. It had to be.

The next fifteen minutes of stop-and-go traffic dragged and stretched until the answer appeared in the form of several sheets of aluminum siding littering the highway. Clayton skirted the debris. Thankfully, it had been a fresh payload dump and the Nebraska State Patrol was not yet on the scene. He sighed with relief. The four or five cars and big rigs that constituted the slow down all dispersed quickly and Clayton was back up to his cruising speed of 75 mph in a matter of minutes.

Three more hours went by, and Clayton was getting very tired now, and though the A/C howled valiantly into his face, his eyes were still heavy. Lincoln was not coming as fast as he would have hoped. The odometer portended close to two more hours of driving. This was going to put him in Dawson between five and six in the morning, give or take. He couldn't remember the last time he had pulled an all-nighter without drugs. He had thought about bringing a huge cup of coffee but that stuff always sat in his stomach like battery acid, especially when he drank a lot of it. Funny, he could do enough coke and acid to kill a horse, but Folgers kicked his ass. Go figure. He had to gas up though. Maybe he would grab a cup when he did and risk the shits for the caffeine buzz.

The thunder rolled across the sky again and lightning forked into the horizon. He was following the storm. At least the rain was light, he thought, but what about twisters? That was a possibility, wasn't it? This was definitely twister season. One could be touching down in the darkness in any direction and he wouldn't know it until it was well up his ass.

"You've been in California too long," he told his reflection in the rearview mirror. He was looking better. Tired, but better.

His radio had been on, mostly as background noise, mindlessly pumping out classic rock hits that Clayton had heard a thousand times apiece. He switched to AM and fumbled through the dial until he found "Traffic and Weather on the Fives." The inexplicably perky jock--given that it was pushing four in the morning--advised him that there was nothing much to report, nothing to worry about. The storm was moving toward Eastern Nebraska with "just some light rain in Lincoln for your morning commute."

Clayton saw a small pool of civilization ahead under blue LED lights: a service station, time to gas up. Cutting his speed he eased the truck off the highway onto the exit ramp, down the access road and through a washed-out dip in the road that sent a rooster tail of mud spraying from his back tires. The truck bounced out of the gulley, back onto the pavement and rolled up to one of the three gas pumps. No one was around. This was good. He climbed out of the cab and let the light rain piss into his face as he stretched. It was cool, yesterday's humidity swallowed handily by the long night's dark gullet.

His ass was asleep, sure, but it was his back that ached more than anything. Lifting that dead weight had not been easy and his vertebrae were reminding him of that fact in petulant little spasms that Clayton tried to twist away as he pumped his gas. Thankfully, it was a fresh injury in a different place than where he had hurt it on that part-time construction job, which he never should have taken. Just because the band had been going through a slump didn't mean he could hop right into blue collar work. You had to be in shape for that sort of thing.

Standing in the glow of the service station lights, he leaned forward, hands on hips. The last thing he needed was a re-injury and to go back to chewing up Percocet like they were Altoids. It had taken years to get that deranged monkey off his shattered back. Clayton wasn't proud of much these days, but he was proud that, against all odds, he'd nipped that particular addiction. Shit, there was hope for him. That proved it. He gritted his teeth and moaned. The stretching was already helping his range of motion return.

The store didn't look open. No coffee. That was just as well. He slid his credit card through the pump's pay station, walked into the tall grass beside the station to take a leak, and climbed back into the truck feeling far more awake than when he pulled up.

About a half-hour passed. He was back on FM. Aerosmith was on. Steven Tyler was singing "Dream On" and Clayton wondered just how many times he had heard that particular song. A thousand? Two thousand? He would have changed the station, but it would have done no good. It was country music or nothing out here in the sticks, and even suffering through "Dream On" for the billionth time was better than hearing some corporately-fabricated "cowboy" whining in a farcical Southern accent about how much pussy and beer he would like to obtain this weekend given that he had just got paid.

A new pair of headlights caught Clayton's eye in the rearview mirror. Mr. Cadillac was back. Clayton's brow furrowed, wondering how he had gotten in front of him again. Mr. Cadillac must have stopped for a while, too. But now there he was, about a quarter-mile back. Yep, Clayton could see its white hood and its...

Wait.

It wasn't a Cadillac at all, and before Clayton could register that it was a Crown Victoria, the state patrolman lit his cherry.

Clayton's heart iced over.

"Oh, fuck no," he yelped.

His mind started racing, his hands numb on the wheel. That fucker had come out of the blue, right out of the fucking blue. Had he fallen asleep again? He didn't even know anymore.

The cop pulled up behind Clayton and chirped the siren.

What had he done? He'd done nothing. He was sure of it. How could they know about the body?

They couldn't, Clayton thought. Not this soon, at least. There was no way, so get a hold of yourself.

But he didn't believe his own counsel, didn't believe it a bit. Obviously, he had done something. Maybe it was something simple. Taillight? Maybe. Speeding? He wasn't speeding, he knew that for sure. Then what?

"Ah, fucking shit," he moaned. His voice was miles away. This was it. This was it. This was fucking it. And the fact he didn't know what he had done made it so much worse. That meant it could be anything.

(Did you know that your toolbox is open, sir, and some old man is trying to climb out of it?)

Clayton was shaking now. There was nowhere to pull over. To his right, running along the slow lane, where there was usually a shoulder, was only a recently eroded ditch abutting a field of feed corn. Only a thin strip of soil served as a shoulder. He slowed, pulled over as best as he could, and cut the engine.

"Oh, fuck me," he whined into his lap. He shoved his shaking hands under his thighs and pressed on them. He had a few moments to get his breathing under control, to get his story under control. He pressed his legs down on his hands to stop them from shaking. He looked into his rearview again just as the state trooper was pulling in behind him, his headlights trained on him, trained directly on the tool box.

No, he assured himself, the lights are not trained on the toolbox. The toolbox is just there. The lights are on it because the car is behind you, that's all. It's in the way. It's just between you and the headlights. The guy's not lighting it up on purpose. If you keep thinking like this you're going to crack. Pull your shit together. If you were being popped because the police had somehow figured out what you had done, then this guy would be rolling with backup. So be cool, because if you're not, this guy is going to ask you to step out of the car, and then you're fucked. Your job now is to avoid probable cause. You've been around the block. You know this shit. You just have to avoid probable cause...

Breathe.

So Clayton, with every nerve tensed, sat and he waited. He sat listening to the tick of the radiator cool and the tick of small droplets of rain hitting the windshield. A semi passed with a whoosh, rocking the truck, and then the silence in the cab bloomed once again, seeming to go on forever until finally Clayton could see the patrolman approaching in his side mirror.

Clayton eased a hand out from under his thigh. He watched his white finger float to the window button and press it down. Now he could hear clearly the crunch of the officer's boots approaching on the wet asphalt until finally a hand lit on his doorframe and a voice said, "Good morning."

A young man leaned down to peer into Clayton's window. He was in his late twenties, was wearing a state patrolman's hat, and was carrying a flashlight which he lifted and trained on Clayton.

Clayton blinked against the light. He could hair the rain pelting the fabric of the man's hat. The cop had said good morning. That meant it was Clayton's turn to talk. This was the test. Could he say "good morning" without sounding drunk, crazy or scared out of his fucking mind, which of course he was?

"Morning." The word fell out of Clayton's mouth, and though it didn't sound like his voice necessarily, it sounded fine. At least it sounded normal and coherent. Now, should he follow up with the expected "what seems to be the problem, officer" bit? Did he even have the balls to try that? Or should he keep his mouth shut, leave well enough alone? Because what if the answer to that question was: The trouble, sir? Well, the trouble is that we have reason to believe you have your father's dead body in that toolbox back there. Yes, we know the whole story thanks to that ditzy Filipino bitch back in Colorado Springs. She was pretty chapped that you put her and her sister on permanent vacation. Boy, did she give us an earful...

Clayton could feel the blood leaving his head. Was he going to pass out? Could you pass out sitting down?

"Two numbers on your license plate are obscured," the officer said.

"Huh?"

"By mud," the officer added. "You've got to keep an eye on that."

Now Clayton was dizzy with disbelief. He almost felt like laughing. Mud? On the license plate? It had been that shit road in front of the gas station. That's why he got popped? He could feel his jaw starting to hang open.

The officer took a step back from the truck, looking it up and down.

Clayton clamped his mouth shut, holding his breath.

"Also," the officer said, "it looks like you have a flat."

"Flat?" Clayton said dumbly, his voice small and a thousand miles away.

"Your back left. It's not running on the rim yet, you probably would have felt that. It's got a slow leak though. You got a spare back there?"

To Clayton's horror, the young cop waved his flashlight vaguely at the bed of the truck.

"No," Clayton said too fast, his heart hammering. "I mean, I used to, but...don't now."

The trooper took another step back from the truck and shined his light at the back tire. "Where you headed?"

"Lincoln," Clayton said thickly.

"Well, I'll tell you what," said the officer, "there's a turn-off about three miles ahead with a service station. Take the Pioneer Street exit. I'll be following so..."

The patrolman's head suddenly snapped right, his eyes wide, his hands raised in protection. With a boom like a cannon shot, a semi slammed into the cop, roaring by just inches from Clayton's face, shearing off his side mirror in a spray of metal and glass. Clayton screamed, pulling away as far as his seatbelt would allow, the belt cutting into his chest. The roaring wall of steel screamed as it rushed passed his open window, its brakes now fully engaged, the wind from its sheer mass filling the cab with a cyclone of hot wind. Clayton's Ram 1500 rocked violently as the semi's back bumper clipped the front panel as it headed for the cornfield, its brakes still shrieking. The giant truck drilled its nose into the cornstalks and then finally came to a halt.

A final piece of metal fell from Clayton's side mirror before silence came, thick and complete.

The patrol car's headlights behind still flooded the cab of Clayton's truck as he sat hyperventilating. Before him, the semi's taillights burned for another few seconds and then went dark. That was when Clayton lost track of time. How long he sat frozen, his eyes fixed forward, he didn't know. At one point he was vaguely aware of a car rubbernecking, passing slower than the speed limit. His mind was swimming through a dream state where he could remember the sight of the young patrolman disappearing from beside his door. He could still hear the sound of it, could still feel the hot wind of it. Where the kid had gone, Clayton didn't know.

Clayton blinked hard when he thought he heard the 18-wheeler's door open deep in the corn field ahead of him.

It had.

A man appeared beside the massive truck, slogging toward Clayton through the corn field, his hand steadying himself along its side panels until he finally gained the asphalt, squinting into the beam of Clayton's headlight. He was older with a grey mustache, and a pot belly hanging over his belt. He looked like he had just woken up. He also looked terrified.

Clayton and the trucker stared at one another for a long time. Clayton's window was still open, but neither man spoke. Both men were calculating, eyes moving ever so slightly in different directions, before re-locking with each other's. Clayton, somewhere deep behind his fear and panic, felt wonder in the amount of information he and this stranger conveyed without uttering a single word. It was an intricate communication, a marvel of the unspoken. On the surface, it appeared the trucker was the only one in real trouble, and once Clayton sensed this conclusion between them, he endeavored that their strange telepathy not betray that fallacy. For all the trucker knew, Clayton had only been popped for a fix-it ticket--which happened to be the absurd truth.

As the trucker stood in the light rain, frozen in Clayton's headlights, he stretched his neck to look past Clayton at the cruiser. Then slowly he looked down to see the trooper's hat--soaked, but otherwise in mint condition--lying on the asphalt in a pool of headlights as if it was the prestige of a vanishing trick from some cabaret magic show. Clayton watched the horror dawn across the man's face like a dark sun. There were no body parts, no blood. The cop had completely disappeared. The man turned to look over his shoulder, looked down at the hat again, and then lifted his head to look at Clayton through the windshield.

Clayton nodded. Yes, his eyes said, you killed him. He's lying dead in the cornfield.

The trucker only stared wide-eyed.

With a sharp nod of his head Clayton gave the man his blessing. Go, he tried to convey, his eyes burning with urgency. Get out of here. Nobody on the highway saw this happen. You got to go now.

The trucker turned and started walking back to the truck.

Clayton didn't know if his own truck would start. He had been clipped hard. He also didn't know if the toolbox was secure. He craned his neck around. It looked fine, but he wasn't about to get out and check it in front of the police cruiser's dash cam. That would not be an easy thing to explain later, and there certainly would be a later. He fired up the truck. It turned over and roared to life.

A car passed slowly and then moved on. At least, Clayton thought, he was pretty sure no one had actually seen the wreck, but once it was determined that an officer was down, all hell would break loose. I-80 would be flooded with troopers in both directions heading for the scene. How long did he have before that determination was made? How far was he from Lincoln?

The odometer promised 40 miles to Lincoln. Now he would speed. He had to. He had to cut the time it would take to get to the interchange that would take him off the major highway and onto the relative obscurity of Highway 34 to Dawson. Without looking like he was fleeing the scene of a disaster, he could make Lincoln in 20 to 30 minutes going 85 to 90, then it would be another 20 minutes to his hometown and to safety.

Quickly, he fumbled for the door handle, threw open his door and threw up--half on his running board and half on the wet asphalt. He slammed the door, put the truck into gear and pulled back onto the highway. He spared a look at the semi's cab as he passed to see the old trucker gripping the wheel and staring straight out to the horizon.

QUALITY FOODS were the words emblazoned on the side of the truck.

Poor son of a bitch, Clayton thought. That'll teach you not to avoid some good amphetamines on a long haul turn around.

Clayton thanked God that there still wasn't much traffic, even with the few gawkers that had slowed to look, but it would sure as shit pick up around Lincoln. Sunrise was coming and so was rush hour.

5:27 AM

Clayton wanted to barf again, but he gritted his teeth instead. There was no time. The rain had stopped. At the horizon purple thunderheads were still piled, but now pale indigo leaked from between them. He had to get out of here now.

Clayton pulled into the fast lane and floored it. His mind raced. It was possible for him to get out of this unscathed. It was very possible. He had been pulled over for something irrelevant, nothing illegal.

That poor patrolman, Clayton thought. He couldn't have been 30 years old. Didn't he say one of the tires was going flat? Clayton could feel the tire now. Was it going to make it another hour? It had to. There was no other choice. He should have checked it when he gassed up. How did it happen? That aluminum siding in the road a few hours back? Probably, but it didn't matter. Even if he had showers of sparks spitting out of all four fenders, he wouldn't stop. He was so close.

But even if he did make it to Dawson and got the body out of the toolbox, they would still have questions: why had he not called an ambulance or even look for the body of the officer? Okay. Well, his phone...yes, his phone. He would just say that his phone had been out of juice. So why didn't he look for the body or offer assistance? Because the cop had been hit by a goddamned eighteen-wheeler at full speed, that's why. Really, what could he have done?

He was running home to call for help. That would be his story. It had some holes, sure. He could have just waved down another motorist, but again, he was panicked--shaken to his core. Maybe they would buy it, maybe they wouldn't when he was eventually questioned--and that was certainly going to happen since his license plate was undoubtedly clearly on video. But he has still done nothing illegal. The dash cam would show that.

He decided he would call when he got to Supernau's house and cover his ass. No problem. He would feel a whole lot better and far more eager about being a witness when he wasn't sleep deprived and didn't have the corpse of his murdered father stowed away in his goddamned toolbox.

Yes, he could do this. He was only forty-five minutes away. He was forty-five minutes away from Dawson, the Blair Funeral Home, and the end of one hell of a bad dream.

Chapter 7

Sex in the Age of Luke

Sheriff Bob Lutz informed Lance Vanderboom of his stepmother's death at 7 AM on Sunday morning, June 19th, four hours after the estimated time of death. Lance's wife Laurie and their six-year-old son Luke slept through the doorbell's chime and Lance had padded to the front door alone and shirtless, his dark hair sticking up in tufts and his morning erection deflating in his boxer shorts, to receive the sheriff.

Lance had been a good-looking raven-haired boy, but had become a rather plain middle-aged man. Love handles were starting to bloom like rising dough at the band of his underwear, his trunk-like body pasty and amorphous, his only muscle tone of note being in his forearms from years of working a socket wrench at his father's garage, the garage he now owned.

After his father had died, he had toyed briefly with changing its name from Midwest Automotive to something more personal and snappy, but Vanderboom wasn't exactly the best name for a business of any kind and he knew it. Even Lance's Garage sounded corny, so once again he shelved his creative pangs. Creativity was not really his thing. He was technically-minded and generally disdained imagination, dismissing it as needless fancy.

Besides, Linda Vanderboom had meted out rations of shit for even thinking of renaming the garage. Lance suspected she didn't want him to change the name because it was a trusted brand more than for any sentimental reason. The garage brought in decent money and she must have thought its profits would somehow filter her way, but Lance was willed the garage free and clear--mostly because Linda always resented the time it required of his father and she had made that clear for years. Her sudden interest in its success once his old man had bought the farm did not convince Lance that her intentions were any less selfless. It was always about the bottom line with Linda, always had been. Still, her admonitions on messing with success were probably right.

As Lance stood at the front door processing Bob Lutz's hangdog frown and hat in hand, it was becoming clearer by the moment that he wouldn't ever have to listen to Linda's opinion on anything ever again. But Lance figured he needed to give the news of her death a little gravitas, just so he didn't come off as a complete dick. He was a Christian after all. Plus, Luke had just lost a grandma and the kid wouldn't be happy about that. Oddly, Linda had been good to Luke, and for all Lance knew, Luke had been the only person in the world that Linda had ever really liked.

Lance stood motionless in the doorway, his groggy head trying to fully process one of these thoughts before finally his eyelids, gritty with morning crust, fluttered and he showed the sheriff in for coffee. He and Lutz would be undisturbed in the kitchen. Luke could wake up any minute, but Laurie wouldn't be up for another half-hour. Lance figured he would let Laurie sleep and tell her the news later. He didn't need her comfort on this one. After weathering the seismic news of his dad's death a couple of months ago, this would be just an aftershock.

Well, except for one thing: although Linda's primary cause of death was being ruled a cardiac arrest, Lutz mentioned--as artfully as Lance supposed Bob Lutz could manage--there had been some additional details that Lance should probably know about.

"Clawed off?" Lance asked as the coffee belched and perked on the counter behind him. "Really?"

Lutz nodded gravely, and then amended, "Well, not off, off...but there were claw marks on her face."

Lance propped his elbows on the dinette and ran his hands through his hair. "And how did this happen while she was under observation? Fuckin'-a...was she totally nuts?"

"Was she?" Lutz asked. "Did she have a history of mental illness? She wasn't under the care of any psychiatrist that we know of, at least not here in Dawson."

"No. I mean, yes. I mean, she was a little off since dad died, but..."

"You don't have to talk about this right now if you don't want to, Lance."

"Why would she do that? Claw at her face? Was it a seizure? Was it bad medication? I mean...shit."

"An autopsy and toxicology report has been ordered," said Lutz. "It's a little early for anyone to know the sequence of events that led to her death with absolute certainty. You'll be the first to know."

They sat in silence, Lance staring down at the table, and Bob Lutz letting him, saying nothing more. Finally, Lance continued in a mumble, recounting the last twenty-four hours methodically:

"I got a call yesterday from Lincoln General. They had gotten my number out of Linda. They told me that she had been checked in, maybe for heat exhaustion or a...what did they call it? Nervous episode. Is that even a thing? It sounded like they didn't really know what was wrong, but she was losing her shit about something. They were going to keep her under observation, give her fluids, and try to get her to calm down. They didn't really tell me much more than that."

"She had become convinced," Sheriff Lutz amended, "that your father, Roger, was at the swap meet."

"Dad? What, his ghost? He's been dead for months. Was he selling spark plugs?" Lance laughed and shook his head. "You know...that's funny because, living or dead, that's the last place he would ever show up: at a swap meet or flea market where Linda was buying more shit to stack around the house for him to trip on." Lance pushed his chair back and stalked over to the coffee pot, slammed down two mugs and filled them. He thrust one at Sheriff Lutz. "I knew it. I always knew something was off about her. How dad lived with it..."

"I'm sorry, Lance," said the sheriff. "It's a lot to take in, I know. I've already spoken with Sylvia Blair. She was with Linda at the swap meet. She saw Linda's...well...breakdown."

"Sylvia Blair?" Lance spat. "She's crazier than anybody."

"What do you mean?" asked Lutz.

"Nothing..." Lance trailed off, and then added with desperation, "Come on, Bob. She's a kook--the freakin' Witch of Dawson. Of course she's going to be a part of something no one can explain. So what did she have to say?"

"Not much," said Lutz.

Lance darkened, "Figures."

"But," Lutz continued, "it was only the first of several conversations I plan on having with her." He pushed his chair back and stood. "Thanks for the coffee, Lance, and again, I'm sorry. Please don't hesitate to call the station if you think of any other details that might help us make sense of this--especially any erratic behavior you may have noticed recently in your mom...I mean, Linda. Anything...."

"Yeah..." Lance said, faintly. "Thanks."

"Are you going to be alright?" Lutz asked.

"Fine," said Lance, straightening his shoulders and putting his coffee down on the counter. "I'll be just fine. The good Lord has gotten me through worse. I'll be in church in a couple of hours and I'll pray for her soul. I'll pray for all of our souls."

Lance saw the sheriff out and spent the next half hour at the dinette table reviewing his life. For most, being awakened from REM sleep by a death announcement at your front door would be the preoccupying issue of the day, but not for Lance. Lance had just had a very interesting Saturday night. It was his wife that was concerning him more than a dead stepmother who had only tolerated him because he'd been bundled in a package deal with his father. No, what had happened last night on his computer was far more important to him. Linda clawing her face off after an apparent psychotic episode and then croaking would have to enter his Hot 100 Shit He Has to Deal with Chart at #2.

What happened last night was still #1--with a bullet, and as Lance held his mug of coffee to his lips with both hands he tried yet again to figure out how last night had come to be.

At forty-seven, Lance would be the first to admit that he didn't have the sex drive that he used to have, but he still required it once in a while. Laurie did not, not anymore. Sex used to be pretty good with

Laurie, not great, but perfectly fine. What Laurie had lacked in lustiness, she had always made up for in eagerness, and that had been a sweet turn-on.

They had never intended on having a kid so late in life, but Laurie had dropped the ball just long enough to punch little Luke's ticket to Earth. Lance didn't think she had missed pills on purpose as some of his friends had speculated. After all, Laurie was a known ditz-- the paradigm of the dumb blonde--and it probably hadn't been more nefarious than that. Still, the pregnancy had been a shock. Abortion was unthinkable for a Lutheran--at least as real and devout a Lutheran as Lance prided himself on being. Some would probably have called their nuptials a shotgun wedding, but now that Luke was here to stay, Lance could never imagine life without the boy.

Post-partum depression had killed Laurie's sex drive. Lance couldn't say much about that without looking like a monster. But the drought never really ended. That was when Lance began his speculations. Was Laurie scared of having another baby? She certainly wasn't of child-bearing stock and the nine pound, six ounce Luke had torn her up.

"What about...you know...some oral stuff?" Lance had ventured one day, thinking he had expertly threaded the ol' needle--sidestepping her fears.

But that didn't work either. Laurie gagged just brushing her teeth, and Lance knew it.

Laurie then assured him that she had no worries about having another kid, pointing out that she wasn't as ditzy as she used to be and there were to be no further surprises unless they were to plan something together.

So, in Lance's mind, that left only one reason why she offered him a cold shoulder more often than not: she wasn't into him anymore.

Still, he tried. He would walk up behind her while she was doing the dishes and kiss her neck, working his way to her earlobe. She had always liked that. When Luke was on a play date, he would take it further. He would slide his arms around to her breasts and lock his lips onto her ear, gently nibbling at it while his cock grew and pushed at her ass.

"Lance!" she would scold, "What are you doing?"

"Ready for dessert," he would say. Maybe it wasn't the best line, but it was good enough, he thought. He wasn't saying it to be cheesy. He wasn't saying it to be threatening. It was playful. Wasn't it? He became self-conscious. What was he supposed to say?

"Not now," she would insist, "I'm doing the dishes."

He knew she was doing the dishes. He could see her doing the dishes. He didn't give a fuck that there were dishes to be done. He wanted to take his wife right there in the kitchen before his balls exploded. He wanted to lay her on the veneered dinette and fuck her brains out until she spoke Chinese. Why not? Was that a bad thing?

But what he got instead was a look over her shoulder that said, "Are you serious? You're making a fool of yourself."

He would then storm off and not talk to her for a long time until she finally asked what was wrong. He would tell her, then there would be an excuse as to why she had rebuffed him: "Tired today" or "A lot of crap at work" or "I feel nauseous."

Lance didn't believe any of these. He used to, but not anymore.

"What's wrong with me?" he asked her one night, regretting instantly that he had exposed such vulnerability.

"Nothing," she assured him, "You're my Lancy-pants. You know that."

He wanted to believe that. He really did.

"Then why don't you want to smoosh?" he asked her.

That's what they called sex, smooshing, derived in a slow evolution from the word "smooching," but neither of them would be able to tell you when the word had morphed. Neither could either of them tell you when the smooshing or smooching had come to an end. Had it been because of the baby? That was six years ago. They'd had sex since then, of course, but before long once every two weeks tapered to once every two months. Lance couldn't accept that.

His friends sympathized, reminding him that having a toddler around is not good for romance, and this logic held him for awhile until that particular excuse also wore thin. Sure, Luke needed a lot of attention, but he also went to bed early and slept deep once he had turned three years old, and while there was always the chance of a bad dream and the potential for coitus interruptus, he had figured out this problem a year ago by putting a simple push lock on their bedroom door. But the lock had turned out to be nothing but manifest optimism.

It was not only the lack of sex that was making him crazy, it was the psychology of it. Very slowly, year after year, it was making him feel less of a man, and less loved. He never thought that would be the case. Like a lot of men, he had never attached love to sex as much as women often did. Sex was like eating: it was necessary and primal. Hell, he could fuck a thousand women without ever loving them. But he loved this woman, he loved Laurie, the mother of his son, and she had little interest in him.

How long had it been since he had a blowjob? Six months? He was beginning to think that was never going to happen again and that meant he would cheat. He would have to. He couldn't go the rest of his life without another hummer. That was crazy, and it was crazy of her to expect him to remain faithful. God would have to understand. God had given him the hunger, and God had also provided a bounty to be had, so wouldn't he be nothing more than a fool for not feeding himself?

But that would break up his family, and that he could not do. Logistically, it wasn't realistic either. Dawson was too small a place. He would have to go to Lincoln to pull something like that off, and there was little excuse to go to the capital for long periods of time.

He was stumped.

The worst part of his insecurity was that it perpetuated her sexual abandonment of him. He knew that the more insecure he was, the more unattractive that would make him to Laurie, to any woman. So he had tried a different tact: ambivalence.

He felt good about the plan at first. He went to church every Sunday at St. Mark and prayed for strength. After a while though, he would fall apart. She could outlast him. It seemed she could go indefinitely without sex and it didn't bother her in the least. So he always ended up cracking first and succumbing to insecurity by asking her, once again, why she didn't like him in that way anymore, showing weakness, and compounding his problem afresh.

Maybe he cared too much about it. Maybe there was something wrong with him? Was he a sex addict? Was he a pervert? He had reasons to suspect that he was. If he was supposed to have outgrown it, it hadn't happened yet. He prayed, and for a while patience won the day as he held to the notion that one day soon he would be released from this hunger.

But then, over lunch one day, John Supernau--who was just as old as he--let slip that he and Kat still did it once a week.

Again, he was stumped.

Damn it, why couldn't he just let it go? He supposed it was the principle of the thing. He didn't want to slide into his grave without ever getting his knob bobbed again or without consistently losing one inside a hot blonde--which he still considered Laurie to be. Like most men, he still pictured himself as he had when he was in his late 20s: a raven-haired jock who deserved to be an object of desire, and he was pretty sure that even on his deathbed he would be staring at his nurse's ass.

He decided he would just have to make adjustments. What those adjustments might be, he hadn't decided yet, but they would have to be made...and soon.

His wife was standing in the doorway to the kitchen in a nightshirt and panties. Lance had been so lost in his reverie that he didn't know just how long she had been there.

"You're up early," Laurie said, breezing past him to the coffee maker.

I am up early, he thought before he could remember why. That's right. He still had to tell Laurie and Luke the news about Linda. He would wait on that. Now, it was more important that he studied Laurie to see if she suspected anything regarding what had happened last night on the computer.

"Luke up?" Lance asked.

"Yeah..." she replied absently, "in the potty."

Then Luke yelled from upstairs, "Momma! Can you help me?"

Laurie sighed, finished stirring her coffee and threw the spoon in the sink with a clatter.

"Mommy!" Luke yelled again.

Laurie passed Lance as she headed for the hall and said with a smirk, "Did he fall in?"

Lance smiled back.

Nothing.

She was the same old Laurie this morning. She didn't suspect a thing about last night.

While she was upstairs, Lance spun the whole scenario through his head one more time. He had to. It was just so hard to believe.

There were two computers in the house and only one was mobile: Lance's. The other was a PC in the downstairs office off of the kitchen--the one that Laurie used. Lance never touched it.

Laurie stayed up later than Lance did. He opened his garage at 8:00 in the morning and was usually dead to the world by 10 p.m. Laurie worked nights at the local movie theater--The Rivoli--punching tickets and popping corn. Saturday nights were a big night for her and she would often come home around 10:30 too wired to sleep right away. Lance would always hear her come in "like a hurricane," as he would always say, and it would be a good hour before she slid into bed beside him. By that point, Lance was always too groggy to care.

But two weeks ago Luke had a really bad fever and had woken up screaming. The kid's cry had been blood-curdling. Lance had sat bolt upright in bed, eyes wide, just in time to hear Laurie pounding up the stairs, passing their bedroom, and heading for Luke. Not to be derelict in his duties as a parent, Lance helped out by going downstairs to get some frozen peas from the freezer for Luke's head. On his way back upstairs he heard their cat, Raisin, sharpening her claws on the upholstered chair in Laurie's little office.

(pop, pop, pop)

Lance had taken two menacing, clomping steps into Laurie's office, hissing at the cat, which bolted from the room in a blur of black fur. Turning, Lance saw Laurie's computer screen. The screensaver had yet to activate and Lance could see the desktop's wallpaper. It was the Dawson bandshell in the snow. Below that, in the taskbar, was a minimized browser tab. It read: cupidsarrow.com

Cupid's arrow? Lance knitted his brow and paused, the sack of frozen peas draped over his hand. Maybe it was a greeting card company or something? Sounded like it.

Upstairs, Luke was still crying, but softer now.

Lance reached out for the mouse and maximized the tab.

What he saw made a noise escape him that he didn't recognize and couldn't ever repeat voluntarily. It was part moan, part gasp, and part surprise.

Cupid's Arrow was a porn site. Along the edges of the window there were pictures of both women and men. The women were in lingerie. The men were shirtless. There was a dialog box active in the center of the screen and he read it, his mouth gaping.

So no, it wasn't a porn site exactly.

It was a dating site.

"Welcome SEXYSADIE," it said in the window's upper right corner near "My Account."

In the active dialogue box in the center, the last three sentences were:

HORNYBOYFLA: "Do you like doing it in public?"

SEXYSADIE: "Sure. What do you have in mind?"

SEXYSADIE: "BRB"

BRB, Lance thought. She even knew the lingo. She had written "be right back" because her son, her sick son, had screamed for her.

Sexy Sadie?

Lance felt numb, as if an epidural had been shoved into his spine.

Sexy Sadie was a Beatles song, but it was also Jodie Foster's license plate in an old movie called "The Accused"--a movie about a girl who gets raped and testifies against her assailants. Laurie had always been a Jodie Foster fan. But who the fuck was she talking to? And about "doing it in public"? He had to read the conversation three times to believe what he was seeing.

His head swam.

Upstairs, Laurie called his name sharply, insistently.

Lance minimized the tab and ran upstairs.

For two weeks afterwards that night had tormented him. It seemed his wife was a bit more interested in sex than he had been led to believe. He couldn't bring it up though. He had spied. He had to eat it. He also had to admit that he looked at porn, too. But the difference was that he was willing to put out anytime. She was not, and that sucked. The other big fucking difference was that he didn't cyber with real people. That was bullshit.

So he had been right. She had lost interest in him. She didn't love him anymore--at least not in that way.

A week went by and the thoughts needling his brain became unbearable. He couldn't beg for sex because it was unattractive to do so. He could not abstain completely because he still wanted to. And he could not talk about how he knew she still had a sex drive without looking like a spy. There seemed to be no way out. That was when he decided he would trick her into having sex with him, the kind of sex that a married couple with a kid would probably never have: filthy, nasty sex.

Last night, after a week of planning and waiting for the right moment, he had finally gone for it.

Laurie had come home from The Rivoli at 10:30. She logged onto Cupid's Arrow just before 11. Lance knew this because he had signed up to the site himself, sitting on the toilet in the upstairs bathroom, in the dark, with his tablet, logged in as a name he had just pulled out of his ass: NYSTUD007.

The site had a searchable database for members and so it hadn't taken him long to find SEXYSADIE. All he had to do was wait until the icon that signaled whether a member was online or not lit up before going in for the kill.

Her icon lit, and he tried starting a chat session with her.

NYSTUD007 wants to chat.

She accepted.

"You live in New York?" asked Sadie.

Lance flinched. Maybe he shouldn't have used NY in his avatar. He knew nothing about New York. He had never been. He just figured Laurie would find it exotic. Evidently, she had.

"Yeah," Lance wrote, "I'm from New York. Where you from?"

"A small town in Nebraska," came her reply.

"Oh. Farm girl?"

"Yes."

Yes? Right, Lance thought. The closest Laurie had gotten to a farm was visiting her long-dead grandparents' place in Goehner where they grew some vegetables for personal use. She was no 4-H girl. She had tried de-tasseling corn one summer for some extra cash and she lasted about a week.

"What do you look like?" Sexy Sady asked. "Have any pics?"

He did. They were not of him. He had done an image search and acquired some random shots of a guy using a simple image search for "naked men." He found a guy who kind of looked like him. The model had dark hair--because that's what Laurie liked, but he was younger and had a much better body. He also had a bigger dong--thicker at least. He figured Laurie might like that, too.

Then came the point where Lance asked for her to reciprocate with a picture of her own. He waited for her reply, his stomach cramping. His pictures were graphic, and he wondered if that was the right thing to have done. Was he supposed to have sent a picture in a suit or something? He didn't know. He hoped he hadn't spooked her.

Several minutes passed without a reply.

He glanced at her online icon. It was still lit.

If she did send a picture it certainly wouldn't be graphic. Only guys did that kind of thing, and Laurie was especially demure when it came to such things. He bet he knew what picture she would use: probably that one in her bikini that she took when she went down to the Gulf coast to see her brother and his kids. She looked good in that one. She had been nervous about going to a beach and wearing a bikini.

She had fretted about it for a month ahead of the trip, dieting and even joining Ruby Wegner on her morning runs through town.

With a soft chime, a reply came through. Lance clicked on the picture.

He almost dropped his tablet on the bathroom floor. Laurie was naked and holding her tits. She was wearing sunglasses. She was standing in the little office off the kitchen. Lance could tell because a corner of the landscape painting that hung behind her desk was visible.

Two words leaked slowly from between Lance's lips: "Holy shit." To his bewilderment and total amazement, Lance was having cyber-sex with his own wife.

Then the rage came. It boiled up from depths he didn't know he had, racing up to the top of his head where it flushed him with needles of prickly heat. For all his wife knew, he was a stranger, just some guy in New York. He stared at the picture, her tits as white as two frog bellies and pressed together like some whore in Hustler magazine, a sexy pout offered below her sunglasses--sunglasses he had bought her on a birthday shopping spree at Sunglass Hut in Lincoln: two-hundred-dollar sunglasses.

And how many times had she sent this picture out? To how many people?

His fingers were shaking so badly that he had to retype his next sentence three times before he could send it: If she was going to act like a slut, he would treat her like one.

He wrote: "How many guys have you fucked at once?"

"Five," was her reply.

It was a lie. It couldn't be true. He knew Laurie better than anyone. At least he thought he did. Either way, there was no way that she could have ever done anything like that. She had no opportunity. She never left Dawson, had never left for college. A gangbang involving Laurie Hessler would have been a town scandal.

She wants to be bad after all, Lance thought. Fine. Let's see how bad.

"Finger bang yourself," Lance wrote, "and send me a picture."

Lance pushed "send," his heart racing, and held his breath. He was sitting in the bathroom, in the dark, cheating on his wife with...

Well...with her.

She wasn't responding. Maybe he had gone too far.

He waited.

A full five minutes passed before his lap chimed again. Her reply had come through. There was also another picture. He clicked on it, gasping as it popped onto the screen as if he had been hit with a pail of ice water.

Her legs were spread, her hand buried in her pussy, the pointer and index fingers spread into a peace sign.

Lance's mouth went dry. All he could think of was that his son, their son, had come into the world down that road and she was shooting pictures of it into space, to NYSTUD007.

He stood up on shaky legs, pacing around the bathroom in the dark before sitting on the toilet again and giving the picture a second look, marveling at the balls she had by sending it, marveling at how garish the image looked on his tablet, lit as if it were on a movie screen, marveling that he had a semi in his boxers.

Wait, was he turned on? He was turned on that his wife was betraying him?

No, he was turned on because she was horny. She was still horny. Maybe only in this fucked up way, but she was still interested in sex. She wanted it. He just had to speak her language. She hadn't actually cheated on him. He knew that. He didn't know why he knew it, but he just knew it. So the best thing he could do now was to keep this in perspective. If he went too far with his indignation it could cause an even bigger problem than this was. He was good to her. He provided for her, and other than not screwing as often as he would like, they were relatively happy. This was just some kink she had, a kink he never in a million years would have suspected.

#

Lance was still staring into his coffee cup when Laurie came down the stairs with Luke in tow.

"Good morning, Daddy," said Luke.

"Mornin', tiger," Lance said, blinking hard.

"You want Cheerios?" asked Laurie.

"Donuts!" Luke attempted.

"We don't have donuts," Laurie said. "You're going to have to wait until after church for those."

As he watched his son belly up to the dinette table, the little guy's head barely clearing its oil cloth cover, Lance vowed that he would never break up this family. With the Lord's help he would be strong.

Laurie looked serene as she served the boy his breakfast. She hadn't suspected a thing about last night. That was good, Lance thought, because he had something to tell them.

"Did you two hear the doorbell this morning?" Lance asked his family.

They stared blankly at him.

"Well," he continued, "It was Sheriff Bob Lutz. I have some bad news."

Chapter 8

Homecoming

Though the majority of its inhabitants are conservative in almost every sense of the word, the residents of Dawson, Nebraska don't care to be brazen about their views. Most people in town would rather avoid conflict and controversy than invite discordance with any untoward stridency.

Well, most of the time.

As Clayton Briggle's Ram 1500 rattled down Highway 34 toward Dawson in the early hours of Monday, June 24th, its flat tire now flapping a bit, he passed a barn with "JESUS SAVES" emblazoned on its red roof in white paint, reminding Clayton just how far he was from California.

The Midwest was funny that way: full of quiet and hospitable souls often encumbered by generations of unyielding anachronistic dogma. Sure, news cycles blew through the town in occasional squalls from the coasts, carried by the big networks, challenging Dawson's conservative sensibilities with the latest liberal revelations, but they seldom enticed the townsfolk into public debate. For most cultural growing pains, venting a peevish grumble around the dinner table would usually suffice. There was little need to kick and scream about what the blue states were doing since most in Dawson were in accord, and those who were not had left town as soon as they were able.

As a result, the dark and strange side of the world didn't affect Dawson's citizens all that much. For the most part, they had little reason to suspect that an anomalous nature would exist among them, and though gossip was a favored pastime among many, the favorite themes of conversation around Peggy Jones' Corner Café skewed catty rather than being those of real consequence. Confrontation was the enemy of the Midwest lifestyle, and if something more serious were to arise, there was trust that their churches were well-attended and that the objectionable would find little oxygen amidst the candle smoke of their altars.

Alcoholism was about the worst vice to which one would admit, but it wasn't considered the greatest transgression. After all, there wasn't a whole hell of a lot to do with only a single-screen movie theater in town to pair with its bowling alley.

But what Dawson lacked in big city entertainment, it made up for in charm. Clay soil along the town's Big Blue River and Plum Creek made good bricks, so the downtown area and older, upper-class homes were constructed of brick early on, as were the downtown streets-- unusual in prairie towns of the time. It was these brick streets that chewed up what was left of Clayton Briggle's shattered tire when he finally made it to Main Street.

Against all odds, Clayton was minutes from the Blair Funeral Home. He was feeling safe now Dawson felt like an island thousands of miles away from the horrors of last night. The town might be surrounded by tall grass and fields of corn for as far as one could see, but as remote as it felt to him now, Clayton knew that it really wasn't, nor had it ever been since it was platted back in 1865. In those days it had been the end of the line for the railroad, but now Dawson sat at the junction of US 34 and Nebraska 15, so if the police were looking for him, Clayton knew they would hardly need a 4-wheel-drive truck to find him.

In its early days, the positioning of the town had made Dawson a good place to start a business. At one point it had five grocery stores, three drug stores, two furniture stores (that also made caskets), three blacksmith shops, five auto garages, three grain elevators, two alfalfa mills, two flour mills, two lumberyards, four clothing stores, four dry goods stores, two cigar factories, a soda bottling factory and Kroeger's, which had been the oldest shoe store in Nebraska until it recently closed.

There were also big companies on the outskirts of town. Nearly every kid who had grown up in Dawson, including Clayton, had at one point worked at the Walker Muffler plant, Hughes Brothers (a manufacturer of cross-arms and telephone poles) or "de-tasseling" entire fields of corn on early summer mornings, allowing the strains to

cross-pollinate correctly, for one of the three seed corn companies--
Dekalb, Cargill, or Pioneer. As for education in town, you were bound to
be labeled either Public or a Mark-er, for those who attended St. Mark.
The latter institution was a private, Missouri Synod Lutheran school in
the middle of town, and though Missouri Synod was reputedly the most
conservative brand of Lutheranism, Clayton didn't think he wore as
many mental scars as a couple of his old Catholic friends had reported
suffering.

Clayton's truck limped past the school, riding on a rim flapping
bits of rubber, its sheared-off mirror evident by its absence. Clayton
marveled at how unchanged it all was.

He passed Concordia College, where Ruby Wegner may take
every course they offer by the time she is done with her quest for
knowledge. He passed the bandshell and the town square. Every
building held a memory: there was where he had his first fist fight in
elementary school, and there was where old Mr. Knorr had fallen and
cracked his head. Clayton had stayed with him until help came. That
was in middle school. And there, on the corner by Cattle Bank, was
where he had stolen his first kiss from Becky Blaha--not the best name
in the world, he conceded, but even in eighth grade she possessed a set
of knockers that could make any boy cry like a newborn calf.

No, nothing much had changed. Every building looked the same,
although some of the signs on them were different now: Hinky Dinky
had become Sun Mart, the barber shop was now called Hair Trix instead
of His N' Hairs and the Gas N' Shop had turned into Git N' Split.

Shit, Clayton thought. He had to cut the sightseeing short. He
was heading straight for the sheriff's station, unless it had moved in the
last ten years since he'd been back, but he doubted it. He was tired,
bone tired, and he had drifted into reverie in the final stretch. This was
no time to catch up on old times. He needed to pull his head out of his
ass, circle around the edge of town and creep over to the Blair Funeral
Home on back roads. Hopefully, that hadn't moved either. He jerked
the truck off of Main and onto Columbia. Before too long he hit
Pinewood.

Pinewood had once been the northernmost street in town. Not
anymore. When Clayton was in grade school some developer decided
that they'd make some money with some bigger lots along Pinewood's

hilly rise overlooking a grassy valley. Almost every doctor and high-level businessman in town bought a lot there, each trying to outdo the other: a gabled traditional, a brick and shake-shingled Cape Cod, a timbered Tudor, a diagonal-sided ultra-modern--and Clayton knew everyone who lived in each one; at least he used to.

Oddly, the three richest families in town never lived on the newly christened Snob Hill. Their money was older. Tommy Wake, the patriarch of the Jones Bank family, owned the castle-like turreted Victorian on Columbia. John Cattle, Sr., whose equally popular bank sat on the opposite corner of the town square, across from the bandshell, lived in an ivy-coated storybook Tudor on Fifth, where the lots were deep and the pin oaks shaded the quiet street.

Then there was Jack Graff. Jack and Imo ("Lovey") Graff lived in a salmon-colored brick manse on Columbia, in the oldest part of town, near Tommy Wake. Jack Graff had been the most ostentatious rich man that Clayton had ever seen before or since, the kind they didn't make anymore. Jack Graff carried a cane, wore cravats, and always tipped his hat to the ladies. When he was a kid, Clayton thought Jack Graff looked a lot like the Monopoly man.

Clayton often wondered if he had left Dawson for Hollywood's promise of fame and fortune because of Jack Graff. The man had made quite an impression. Clayton remembered how the Monopoly man and his wife, Imo--who had a penchant for anachronistic feathered hats-- would float around town on the buoyant suspension of a maroon Cadillac bearing the license plate "A-1."

The Cadillac had been grand enough, but it was nothing compared to the Graff's mysterious second car. Everyone had heard the rumors that the other car hiding within Jack's rear-facing, two-car garage was a Rolls-Royce. What's more, the rumor had it that Rolls-Royce had shipped Jack the car on a boat from England, then on a train, packed in a box, so that there would be no miles on the car when Jack took delivery in Omaha. No one had ever seen the Rolls, but they were all sure it was there. For years after, every head that passed the salmon colored brick mansion on Columbia Avenue turned for the chance to glimpse the town's phantom car with the appropriate model name, Silver Ghost.

It was oddly sad being back, Clayton thought, probably because he was not returning triumphantly as the new rock n' roll Monopoly man, as he'd long ago hoped. Far from it, his life had gone wrong since leaving this quiet, idyllic little town and there was no one to blame but himself. He couldn't even blame the old sonofabitch packed into his toolbox. To be fair, Foster "I Told You So" Briggle had told him so.

Clayton realized that if the folks here knew his story, knew why he was on the run--if they would even believe him--they would surely stare at him as if he were a complete stranger, and with disappointment, just as he stared at himself now in his visor mirror. He could have stayed in Dawson and had a decent life. Instead, he had chased a dream, and in the process, had run so far away from who he'd been that he didn't know if he could ever find his way back. Someday he would let his story out, maybe even to one of his old friends here. Maybe then the old familiar breezes, the ones that came in from the fields and rattled the cornstalks like bones, would blow on his wounds and turn his own skeletons to dust.

But he couldn't spare another thought for romanticized notions of salvation now. No, that kind of bullshit would have to wait. Right now, he had to get the dead body out of his truck and into the crisper before he did twenty-five to life.

He pulled up to the Blair Funeral Home at 6:30 AM--an impressive time considering that clusterfuck scene on the highway, he thought, and considering he was running on three tires.

Sylvia Blair wasn't going to be waiting for him inside. He was supposed to have called her so she could meet him here, but a groggy trucker on I-80, back from a West Coast turnaround and in need of a map or some good uppers, had fucked up that game plan, along with Christmas for some state patrolman's family. Clayton knew if he wasn't so numb and tired he would be in tears for that kid. The cop had been so young, his big patrolman's hat falling over his eyes, making his uniform just about as convincing as a Halloween costume.

There was nothing he could have done for that kid, Clayton had to remind himself. All he could do now was concentrate on getting himself safely out of hot water. So no, he couldn't call Blair with his own phone, couldn't risk it. His story for running from this morning's horror on I-80 was that he had no juice left in his phone and that he had just decided to get to his final destination before making himself available for questioning.

In the part of his fevered mind that was still rational, he knew there was no legal reason to ever subpoena his phone records. He hadn't done anything. Nobody knew about the body in the toolbox, and he had been pulled over for an obscured license plate. And was leaving the scene of a vehicular homicide when you were only collaterally involved a crime? It certainly wasn't dutiful, but he didn't think it was a crime. Was he just being paranoid about all of this?

Affirmative, he thought, and suddenly he was laughing, laughing until tears were sprouting from his eyes and blurring the road ahead. You bet your ass. He had never felt so paranoid in his godforsaken life.

But he was here. He was safe. All he had to do was unload the body, give it to Sylvia and this whole nightmare would be over. Well, part of it. He would still owe the Mexican cartel who had fronted him the dope twenty grand, and another twenty to Sylvia.

That was fine. He would gladly trade his current predicament for that one. He had six figures coming to him, half of which would be his after taxes--plenty of cash to pay his debts with some left over to support his band.

But there was one other expense he had to keep in mind: finding another place to live, buying new furniture, new dishes, new everything. Those goons had really done a number on his last apartment. Just thinking about it made his stomach roil. He had come home to his Hollywood apartment building with a plastic bag of Thai food hanging from one hand and his keys in the other. The first thing he had noticed as he walked down the enclosed hallway to his door was that the door was ajar. The second thing he had noticed was that it was not ajar; it was off its hinges and just sitting in the door frame. Everything in his apartment had been fucked up in one way or another: the flat screen TV was shattered, all the cupboards had been emptied, his Peavy amp had a hole kicked through it and his bed had been stripped, overturned and pissed on by what appeared to be several people with prolific bladders.

How long ago had it been since that happened? Almost two weeks? It seemed like yesterday, and he certainly didn't want to go back to L.A. anytime soon and have to deal with that mess. God, he hoped Supernau would let him crash a couple of weeks, considering his father had died and all. Of course, Supernau didn't know yet that Foster "Hollywood is for Jackoffs and Why Don't You Get a Real Job" Briggle had officially bit the dust, but he would soon.

John Supernau was a good guy, and under any other circumstances Clayton would have been excited to see his old friend-- hell, best friend, he would say, even though they had been relegated to phone conversations over the last ten years.

Clayton hadn't been to Supernau's new house, but John had talked a lot about it. Evidently, it was a big ol' ranch house and it sounded like it had plenty of room, even with John's wife and teenage son in residence.

Clayton planned on helping around the house, keeping his head down and trying his damnedest to not be a nuisance. The Supernau clan was a Lutheran family, after all--well, Kat more than her husband--and they would probably be cool about helping a brother out for old time's sake. Clayton hoped that probating his father's will wouldn't take too long once the ball got rolling.

But Clayton knew the ball would never start rolling until he could somehow get Sylvia Blair to show up at her office. He pulled the truck off the road and around to the funeral home's loading bay. He had to call Blair and he had to call her now, even if later he would have to answer to why he had called a seemingly complete stranger who ran a funeral home before he had called the police after being the sole witness of a hit and run. He had to do it. What if there was a state trooper in the area that would swing by to ask questions while the body was still in the tool chest? That couldn't happen.

Clayton dialed Sylvia Blair as he watched the sky through the windshield of the truck. The morning sun had burned away most of the storm on the horizon, but the hood of his truck still glistened with a few rain drops. The air was thick. The humidity would be bad today, and like an old, familiar blanket its fever would soon swaddle him. He wanted to sleep. His vision swam. A mourning dove, sitting on a wire above the funeral home's gravel drive, watched him suspiciously.

The phone rang over and over in Clayton's ear before a voice snapped, "What now?"

It was Blair's voice, reedy and smoky. Funny, he had known a few women with such voices and they had seemed sexy to him, but Blair only sounded like a monster that was set to swallow him whole.

"I'm at your shop," Clayton said. He felt very far away, as if he was witnessing this conversation impassively, just as the bird on the wire above seemed to be.

A long pause followed, a pause that sank Clayton into a horrible realization: maybe her feet had gone cold. Maybe she had thought that he would never do it. Maybe she had changed her mind. She could back out. She could totally back out and he would be royally fucked. There was nothing really stopping her from doing just that.

He was sweating now. He was about to ask her if she was still there when she spoke.

"You around back?" she asked.

"Yes"

"Stay there," she said crisply. "I'll be there in ten."

The line went dead.

Clayton had been holding his breath and it now shuddered down the front of his shirt in a hot fan of relief.

All he could do now was wait. Ten minutes, she had said. He would use that time to review the story he and Blair had cooked up--just to keep it straight.

It went like this: some time ago, his father had hired an attorney, one Steven Rathbun Esq., to be executor of the old man's will. Mr. Rathbun Esq. had been the one who had called Clayton in Hollywood to inform him of the stroke, since Clayton was next of kin. When the semi-vegetative Foster "This Plan Better Be Airtight" Briggle had overstayed his welcome at the hospital in Colorado Springs and home care became a possibility, Mr. Rathbun Esq.--who had power of attorney--agreed to let Clayton be in charge of Mr. Briggle's convalescence. All of this was true.

What wasn't true was that Clayton had decided to transport dear ol' dad to Malcolm, Nebraska--a town thirteen miles from Dawson--so that his dad's sister Janine could oversee his father's care, allowing Clayton to return to his life in California. Trouble was, Aunt Janine had been dead for five years. No one knew that, though. Most importantly, the Dawson Sheriff's Department wouldn't know that. Malcolm was out of their jurisdiction, just over the border in Lancaster County. Aunt Janine had also kept to herself when she was alive. She did not frequent Dawson nor did she have any friends there, and nobody who would be involved in this story could possibly suspect that the altruistic Janine Foster had not been waiting with open arms to receive her brother.

If asked, Clayton would also maintain that from Colorado Springs to Malcolm, his father had coughed constantly, which was not unusual, as his coughing had been well-documented. At some point during the trip, the old man had fallen asleep. A few miles from Malcolm, Clayton had noticed--to his absolute shock and horror--that his father had not actually fallen asleep as he had thought, but had stopped breathing. In a panic, Clayton had pulled the car over, and had attempted cardiopulmonary resuscitation before realizing that the old man was quite dead, had been for some time, and was obviously unable to be revived.

When asked, Clayton would also maintain that he had been just outside of Dawson when it had happened and he had thought of Sylvia Blair first, since she had been a friend of the family growing up (definitely a lie), as well as his hometown's preeminent mortician. He called her for two reasons: first, because his father was to be buried in Dawson (this was true, according to what Foster had told Clayton, though he had yet to see the will that was in the possession of Mr. Steven Rathbun, Esq.), and second, that Clayton knew that calling 911 would have been completely useless.

Blair would say that she had chided Clayton for not calling 911 first, for that would have been the right thing to do, but seeing as how the body was "already stiff," as Clayton had put it, he could bring it to the funeral home, which wasn't far from his fictional position, and at that point, she would call the sheriff for assistance.

It had been at this point on the phone, while he and Sylvia had gone over the plan, that Clayton had learned who the current sheriff was.

"Bob Fucking Lutz?" Clayton had cried. "You're shittin' me!"

Clayton could remember when Lutz was a senior and he was a freshman at St. John, and when he stopped to think about it, he figured he always knew that guy would follow in his dad's footsteps and join the force.

I'll be damned, Clayton had thought, so Bob Lutz would be the one to decide his fate. He and Lutz had not been tight--seniors seldom hung out with freshmen--but there was zero bad blood between them. Lutz had been a good-natured, pudgy kid with mirthful slits for eyes and a waddle in his walk. Clayton remembered sitting next to Lutz when the Rivoli Theater had shown The Empire Strikes Back and how they had nudged each other when Darth Vader had told Luke that he was his father. Lutz had even invited the younger Clayton to join the seniors for pizza afterwards.

Yeah, Lutz was okay.

Of course, during those first phone conversations with Blair, Clayton had to go over and over the details of their plan. Blair did not, and her patience had waned. Her ghoulish confidence in the plan, while unsettling, should have inspired confidence in Clayton, but he had chalked up her insouciance to the fact that she didn't have as much to lose if it all went to shit. That had bothered him, and Clayton had almost scrapped the patricide idea all together.

There were three things that eventually calmed Clayton's nerves and made his mind up: first--and this according to Blair--a patient with a pre-existing condition as bad as a debilitating stroke would almost never trigger an autopsy, especially when the narrative included constant coughing which would point to pneumonia--the most common cause of death in such cases. Second, that Sylvia Blair and Lutz were tight. Not only were they tight, but Blair had claimed Lutz had "a thing for her," which Clayton couldn't imagine, but hey, whatever tickles your pickle. And lastly, that it would be Lutz that would order an autopsy if one were to happen and he would have no reason to do that.

Instead, this was what Lutz was likely to do: he would simply call the hospital in Colorado Springs and speak with the doctor who had treated Foster Briggle. He would hear confirmation of Clayton's assertion that his father had been on his deathbed for quite some time. Lutz would ask the doctor if he would be willing to sign the death certificate. The doctor wouldn't hesitate in a situation like this one, and the time of death would likely be estimated sometime between Colorado Springs and Dawson along Interstate 80.

Blair, in a flourish of creative thinking, also guaranteed that for the price she had quoted Clayton, she would mention that "Clayton was inconsolable," as long as Clayton felt he could back up such an embellishment with some convincing acting chops if need be.

And to answer the last of Clayton's questions: yes, Lutz would see the body.

"If your father is as skinny as you say he is," Blair had said, "his death will be no surprise to anyone. And if he looks a little beat up? Well, I'm damn good with makeup along with stuffin' and fluffin'. That's what I do. He won't have a mark on him. You can take that to the bank, honeybunch."

How many times had she done this? Clayton had wondered. Had she covered up real murders for people? Ones that were way more sinister than this one? Did she have a line she wouldn't cross?

Clayton suddenly knew the answer to that question and shuddered.

The only problem left, as far as Clayton could figure, was that if there had been a camera in that state patrolman's squad car, it would show that there had been only one person in the cab of his truck. If that were the case, he could do nothing about it now, other than maintain that his father had slumped out of view. Whether they would buy it was another question.

What he could do now is call the State Patrol and report the crash and offer himself as a witness and a concerned citizen before the delay became even more suspicious. Ideally, he should sound shaken up. Hell, that wouldn't be hard. He only hoped his lack of sleep wouldn't cause him to say something stupid and incriminating.

He stared at his phone as a man would stare over a ledge before a jump.

The sooner he called, the better. If they questioned him before he called, it would look so much worse. And they could find him, too. Even behind the tall grass and corn stalks of Dawson they could find him. There would be an all-points bulletin out for his license plate and...

Wait.

Out of nowhere, a realization struck him with the speed and clarity of a lightning strike: an obscured plate.

Clayton dared a smile. He had been pulled over for an obscured plate. In all of his panic he had not realized that there was no way to track him aside from the make and model of his truck or by running a partial plate.

You've got to get some sleep, he told his reflection in the visor mirror. You're thinking sideways.

Where was Blair? It had been ten minutes.

He figured he should still call Lincoln, but he felt a little better knowing that if he didn't, he could get away with it. Sure, the trucker could mention him, but the trucker couldn't deflect the blame no matter what story he came up with. That young cop's brains were still dripping out of the grill of his eighteen-wheeler.

Clayton had another idea: maybe he should just call 911? Yes, that was better. That's what someone would do. He braced himself and as he tried to work up a distressed voice, he found he had little trouble. When the operator answered, he told her everything that had happened that he had been pulled over because his plate hadn't been clearly visible because it had been caked with mud, and added that he was very sorry he couldn't have called sooner, but he had no working phone. He also said he probably shouldn't have left the scene, but he had to get help.

Then the dispatch girl asked where he was. In a cold sweat, he lied and said he was at the McDonalds on Highway 15, just outside of Dawson, and that an employee had let him plug in his phone. He offered his phone number if he could be of any help. The dispatch girl told him they already had it. That was freaky, but to be expected, he supposed, and then the dispatch girl told him that assistance was already on the scene. She ended by saying that a detective may contact him soon.

And that was it.

His hand shaking, Clayton hung up and took a deep breath. If the other shoe was to drop, at least it would drop much later, when he could think straight.

Minutes later, Sylvia Blair pulled up behind his truck in a black, 1994 Cadillac hearse, stepping out with a smoke hanging between her pink-painted lips.

Clayton had not laid eyes on Sylvia Blair since he was a kid. She looked old, but she always had. On her head she wore grey curls high and tight, a pair of gaudy pearl, clip-on earrings and a tight smile smeared across her wrinkled face. She wore white stretch pants with matching pumps and a red blouse printed with large yellow hibiscus flowers.

Clayton remembered something in school about how nature had a propensity to warn you of danger with bright colors, there was even a word for it: aposematism. He had only remembered the word because his biology teacher at St. Mark had brought in a coral snake coiled into a jar of formaldehyde to demonstrate the principle, which fascinated him. There had even been a rhyme that Mr. Ricket had taught the class to identify poisonous snakes.

("Red and black, venom lack...")

"Where's the body?" Sylvia asked, crunching toward Clayton through the gravel.

Clayton indicated the toolbox with his head.

("...red and yellow, kill a fellow.")

Sylvia's eyes trained on the toolbox and her smile widened, lips pulling back to show her yellow teeth. "Well, alrighty then," she said, dropping her smoke and crushing it into the gravel with a twist of her pump, "let's get him slabbed."

Chapter 9

The Writing on the Wall

Ruby Wegner, trowel in hand, was on her knees at the edge of her flower bed. Some of her posies hadn't taken this season. Sure, it was hot, but it always was this time of year. For some reason, one section of flowers had drooped in their beds, inconsolable, until Ruby had finally decided to replace them. She figured she could safely scratch that new nursery just outside of Goehner from her list of resources.

She stood with a grimace, shook out her legs, and wiped some black soil from her jeans. Hopefully, this new patch of marigolds and violets would be happy for a while.

The Wegner's house was on a double lot, and the backyard was expansive. There was a raised deck off of the sliding glass door at the back of the house--a must if she was to enjoy a shady lunch beneath the umbrella table without chiggers jumping up her legs. Beyond the deck, a crescent sward of lawn stretched to the woods at the perimeter. Just where the lawn and woods met, on the right side of the property, was the garden shed. It was a nice one, not one of those aluminum shacks, but a small wooden house with a peaked, shingled roof, and painted oxblood red.

The previous owner had built the shed. He had obviously been a skilled carpenter as the shed not only still stood, but had required little maintenance over the years aside from the occasional coat of paint. Allegedly, it was 150 square feet inside, and when Ruby and Scott were kids, it had too often served as a rather obvious hiding place for games of hide-and-seek. Later, during high school, Scotty had used the shed to host joints of the local ditchweed with his friends. Ruby wasn't supposed to know about that part of the shed's history, but she did. The smell of stale pot smoke had once mixed with that of fertilizer, snail killer and old bags of dirt.

Ruby gathered up the remains of her bag of soil, a wad of flower corpses, and her trowel. She began trudging across the grass which was still soggy from the morning sprinklers, heading for the shed.

She stopped cold. Her feet would take her no further. She gulped air, her heart beating like a jackhammer. She whipped her head around to look up at the second floor, hoping to see Scotty in the window. If he were watching her, it would calm her, give her some courage, but he wasn't. Ruby could feel the shed behind her, as if it were waiting there patiently for her to approach.

Ruby hadn't always been scared of the shed. Her fear of it started much later in life. When she had first moved to this house, she had been ten years old. Back then, she was still scared of the dark, but she could go into the shed with no problem. It was never that dark in there, even with the door closed. Sunlight always leaked in from between the door and the jamb, striping her face golden as she waited to be discovered during those long ago games. Sometimes being discovered could take a long time since Scotty often pretended he didn't know where she was. He had been good like that. Being three years older, he couldn't have given two shits about playing hide-and-seek, but he'd done it for her.

No, back then the shed had been fun. Back then, she never would have had nightmares about it like she did now.

She turned back to face it. The fear of it was not always this bad, but today it was. She should have torn it down. As much as she wanted to, she knew it would be a shame--a large, well-crafted structure like that? No, what had happened in the shed was not its fault, just like what happens in a house is not the house's fault, unless, of course, it was haunted. And she knew one thing for sure: the shed was not haunted.

She was.

Her phone was ringing back at the picnic table. Ruby looked at it from afar, her arms still full, and she blinked hard. Mercifully, the ring had broken her runaway thoughts, had broken the terrible spell, and her leaping heart calmed. With renewed purpose, she approached the shed, pulled open its door and quickly replaced her gardening supplies before turning her back on it and slamming its door with a wipe of her hands. Her cheeks puffed and she exhaled with relief.

Back at the patio table, the phone rang again.

Who could it be, she wondered.

She generally kept to herself, and not many people called her, but she was glad that someone had today. Her studies had not been keeping her mind from horrible things like they usually did, and she was beginning to worry about being overwhelmed. It would be nice to talk to someone other than Scotty. Supernau had not been at the Corner Café this morning like he usually was. She looked forward to a few words with him each morning before her jog. She had talked a little with Peggy Jones, but Peggy had been particularly busy behind the counter this morning. Besides, if a subject became too heavy--like Ruby's often did--Peggy was known to shrink away from the topic much like the uprooted violets at Ruby's feet. The Corner Café was never meant to be a psychiatrist's couch.

Ruby gained the deck and plucked her phone up from the umbrella table.

VANDERBOOM, LAURIE

She still kept in touch with a couple of friends, the ones that would tolerate her obsession with learning, her frequent and sudden mood swings, and her occasional need to isolate without warning. Laurie was one of them.

Before she had met Lance, Laurie had been Laurie Hessler, a quiet but wickedly funny girl who had sat beside Ruby in sixth grade. They had been friends ever since. Later, when Ruby lost her mother during senior year, Laurie had confided to her that she had no real parents either.

"I'm adopted," Laurie had said, "so in a way, my real parents are dead, too. At least, they're dead to me."

This new intelligence had shocked Ruby. She had never known this about Laurie. Obviously, it had been a subject that Laurie hadn't been keen to talk about, and divulging it to Ruby had been an offering of such trust and vulnerability that it had touched Ruby greatly, endearing Laurie to her at a time when she desperately wanted to pull away from everyone and everything. As a result, Laurie Hessler--now Laurie Vanderboom--was still one of the only people on earth allowed access to Ruby's private thoughts.

Ruby leaned back in the strapped chair beneath the umbrella's shade and returned the call without listening to the message. "Hey, it's me."

"Rubes, oh good," said Laurie, exasperated, "you got a minute?"

"Sure. What's up?"

"Actually," Laurie said, dropping her voice to a conspiratorial whisper, "I'd rather talk in person."

"Okay," Ruby said cautiously. That's fine, but let me just change clothes. I'm all filthy. What's up? Is something wrong?"

"Maybe, I don't know," said Laurie. "I'd rather come over there, if that's cool--just for a bit. I gotta grab Luke from school in about an hour. Then I need to run something by you, but Lance may come home for lunch. Sometimes he does."

"It's about Lance?" Ruby's interest was piqued.

"Yeah," Laurie conceded, a note of bewilderment simmering beneath her discretion.

"Come on by," Ruby assured her. "My class isn't until three. I got some of that good tuna salad from Pak N' Save. Have you had lunch?"

Laurie said she wasn't hungry, her stomach was upset, and that she would be there shortly.

After they hung up, Ruby sat in the wet heat and tried to think of what had gotten her friend so concerned. She wasn't crying, so it couldn't be too bad. As far as she knew, Laurie and Lance were relatively happy. Lance had never been violent so she doubted it was that. He was a drinker, but no more or less than a lot of guys in town. He was religious, too, almost overboard with it at times. That would hopefully rule out some of the major sins. Maybe it was about the kid? Doubtful, Luke was in good health and too young to be in any real trouble.

Then what was it?

Ruby looked up. Scotty was in the window now, looking down at her. She waved. Scotty waved back.

She would have to have a talk with Scotty, something along the lines of "us girls need some privacy for about an hour" and that meant he should stay upstairs. He usually did if anyone ever came over, but he was also shamelessly nosy.

Ruby looked up again, this time to the left of the house, at one of her hickory trees near the fence line. Like the sound of an orchestra tuning up, cicadas began to thrum somewhere in its boughs. Their season had come again.

Somehow time had passed. How many years had she planted flowers, heard the first chirps of the cicadas, mounted a Christmas wreath onto the same rusty nail on the front door--and all of it without a complete family? Sitting there under the umbrella, the meridian heat making her garden's perimeter hedgerow shimmer, a pair of white butterflies drifting above it like the last bit of confetti from a long ago party, she was amazed with herself. How she had ever put one foot in front of the other for so many years, she did not know.

Through the sliding glass door she went and then, once across the formal living room, she mounted the staircase leading to the second floor. It rose flush against the wall to an open balcony overlooking the fireplace and the room below. Down the hall to the left of this overlook was Ruby's room--formally her mother's--but Ruby cut right at the balcony, taking her past an extra bedroom--formally Ruby's--and then on to Scotty's.

Scotty liked his room, and he liked it the way it was: unaltered from how it had been growing up. His had been a hard struggle to accept the death of his parents, and being in this room, the way he remembered it, gave him peace.

Ruby found it annoying at times. Scotty didn't do much. He never left the house. Sometimes, Ruby would hear him crying softly late at night. She would console him as best as she could, but she felt her strength may be finite, and it was certainly tenuous. At her best, she would tell him what she had learned. She told him about chaos theory, about quantum physics, about how time and space were constructs and that everything--past and future alike--may be occurring all at once or maybe not at all. She also told him about how their family shared an energy that in principal could not die. It was against the laws of nature for energy to die. This helped him a little, just as it helped her a little.

Her resentment surrounding Scotty and how he was supposed to be the older and wiser one, the one who should help her get through everything, had been shelved long ago. If she could find the answers better than he could, well then she would do it.

Since they had both been students at St. Mark Lutheran, they had, at one time, considered going to church. But, as children of scientists, it had been particularly hard for either of them to derive any comfort from it. There was no basis for what religion claimed to know as certain, and worse, a lot of it had been disproven since it had been conceptualized, or at least supplanted by sound science. What Ruby realized now was that both she and Scotty could have benefited from the community of church all of these years, rather than remaining hung up on its fallacies. Instead, it had been knowledge without benefit of hope or faith that had become the family's chosen anesthetic. Sometimes it worked. Sometimes it certainly did not.

Ruby was relieved to see Scotty actually smiling when she came to his room. No such existential pep talk would be required of her today. There he stood, amidst all of his high school and college plaques and trophies. Though the most recent was almost twenty years old, Ruby knew that Scotty still drew inspiration from them, not necessarily because they were accolades, but because they provided a revision of history. For as long as they remained untouched, Scotty could live in that world again, back when such baubles had brought him and his family happiness, back when bad things hadn't happened yet.

Across the room, one of Scotty's walls was still clad in faux wood paneling--hideous by modern sensibilities, but de rigueur for a boy's room in the late 1970s. A faded Concordia Bulldogs pennant still hung there. Below, his bed was made and "Jimmy" the teddy bear sat in repose among a pile of fluffed pillows. The bear wore a Chicago Bears jersey with 80s quarterback Jim McMahon's number nine printed across its front. Scotty took a seat next to it.

"You look happy," said Ruby.

"I am," said Scotty. "You want to know why?"

"Uh...yeah."

"I learned how to paint," he said, his grin widening.

"Really? I didn't know you could do that."

"I didn't know I could either," he said, "and better yet, I'm pretty good at it, too. I need something to pass the time, y'know?"

"Yeah, you sure do," Ruby agreed, "and it's about time."

Ruby scanned her big brother's room looking for canvas and easel, realizing while she was doing it that Scotty had neither.

"Well," she insisted, "Where's the painting?"

"Behind you," he said.

Ruby turned around.

She yelped when she saw it, a hand flying to her mouth.

Scotty had drawn four stick figure people on the wall. The figures were bright red. They were all holding hands.

"What did you do?!" Ruby cried. "Is that...is that blood?"

Scotty laughed. The sound of it not only defused her fear, but it almost made her cry and want to reach out and hug him. It was so genuine, that laugh. It was mirthful, and Ruby had not heard it in a long, long time. Sitting there by his teddy bear, in his favorite brown shirt, his knuckles held up to his mouth to stifle his laugh, a flop of auburn hair on his brow above his twinkling green eyes, he looked so handsome, so young, so full of vitality.

"Blood?" Scotty spat. "No, it's not blood. Where am I going to get blood? I'm sure not getting it from me! And I didn't get if from you! And there's nobody else here! You're so funny, Rubes!"

"Then what did you use?"

Scotty nodded at the carpet at the base of the wall.

"My lipstick?" Ruby bent over and plucked up what was left of it from the carpet, twisting its telescopic base to reveal nothing but a nub of the mashed, crimson wax still left in the tube. "Why did you do that?"

"Well, you never wear your makeup anyway," Scotty protested, "It's just rotting in there."

"You shouldn't go in my room."

"Are you mad?" Scotty asked, his eyes wide.

"Did you have to write on the wall?"

"Paint," Scotty corrected. "I painted on the wall."

"Yeah, whatever. Did you have to paint on the wall?"

"You don't like it." Scotty deflated.

Ruby sighed. Agitated, she tapped the lipstick tube into her other palm and contemplated the painting of the stick figures joined hand in hand. "It's us, right? Mom, Dad, you and me. I get it."

Scotty nodded emphatically.

"I love it, Scooter," Ruby conceded.

All the guys used to call her brother Scooter back in high school: Lance, Clayton, Paul and John Supernau, who had come up with it when he returned to school one day after being numbed by the dentist and tried to say "Scotty." She knew her brother didn't care for the epithet, and that was why Ruby used it now. It was as punitive as she was going to get with him. He deserved that, at least.

"But do me a favor," Ruby added. "If I get you some canvas and paint at the craft store, could you try using that instead? How am I ever going to get that off the wall?"

"Never take it off the wall," Scotty said, darkening, his smile gone. "Never."

They looked at each other for a long moment, neither of them breathing. Ruby could hear nothing but her own blood in her ears and the cicadas thrumming in the trees beyond the window. A chill started to crawl down Ruby's spine. Scotty could scare her. He was scaring her now.

"Okay?" Scotty said finally, a faint smile curling his lips.

"Fine," she replied quietly, turning from him.

She began to leave, in danger of forgetting why she had come to see him in the first place until she heard the doorbell's chime downstairs.

"Listen," she told Scotty, regaining herself, "that's Laurie. Can you give us some privacy? No snooping around? She wants to talk about something."

"About what?"

"None of your bee's wax," Ruby snapped. "See? That's exactly what I mean."

"Sure," Scotty said. He lay back on his bed with his hands folded behind his head, resigned, "Whatever."

#

When Ruby pulled open the front door, Laurie was standing on the porch in burgundy shorts and a white blouse. She tugged off her gold-rimmed sunglasses and breezed past Ruby into the house, marched all the way across the living room to the sliding glass door, and then turned to face Ruby.

"Where do I start?" she said, collapsing heavily onto the couch.

"Alright, you're freaking me out now," said Ruby. "What's up?"

"Remember when I told you that Lance was thinking about buying Jimbo's power washer about a month ago?"

Ruby knew of Jimbo. He was John Neville's boy. He was in his early 20s and worked at Walker's. Allegedly, the kid had blown a disc on the job, but details weren't clear on exactly how. However, the rumor around the Corner Café was that Jimbo hadn't been hurt at all, that he was just lazy and sniffing around for worker's comp, and the theory would have held if Jimbo had not announced that he was putting his power washer up for sale. That had quashed the gossip in a hurry, shaming those who had given the kid short shrift. If he had actually sold his washer, he must have been in a lot of pain. Jimbo and his power washer had been inseparable.

"Anyway," Laurie continued, "Lance bought it. He said we could use a little extra cash. 'Why not,' he says. 'The kid sold it to me for a song,' he says. Then he tells me that sometimes the garage is slow, and he figures he could do a few odd jobs with it. 'I won't go out of my way,' he says, 'Only if the opportunities fall in my lap.'

"I thought it was a weird thing to buy. Don't you? The garage does well. I told him this, and he said that was true, but now that he has both Dan and Earl helping out, sometimes he finds himself with a little extra time and that he's pretty much just an owner now and not the grease monkey he was when his dad owned the place. 'Besides,' he says, 'getting out of the garage and into the fresh air wouldn't be so bad once in a while.'

"I figured 'whatever,' but I did remind him of one thing: 'It's almost July. Working outdoors is probably not what you want to do.'"

"Oh no," said Ruby, her hand at her mouth. "Did he hurt himself somehow?"

"No, nothing like that," said Laurie. "Really, I'm more worried about him at the garage, under the lift, than I am about him power washing. Actually, he hasn't used it much. Well, at first, he didn't know how to use it. He practiced on our place. Word got around town that he had the thing and Breck Schindler hired him to power wash the whole front driveway and sidewalks around the county courthouse. I don't think it really needed it, I just think Breck was being...well, you know how Breck is. He's just cool like that.

"Other than that job, there wasn't much work left in Dawson. Jimbo had pretty much cleaned the bejeezus out of the town. So Lance said he would put his feelers out in Lincoln. I told him to forget it. 'You're going to drive all the way to Lincoln and leave the garage to those guys?' I said. 'We don't need the money that bad.' He said he knew, but he would take it slow, see what happened.

"So we went back and forth on it, and since there weren't any jobs to be had with the thing anyway, I dropped it and just chalked it up to a bad purchase."

"So what happened?" Ruby urged.

"Well, the weirdest part is coming up," said Laurie. She was now sitting forward with her elbows on her knees, her knuckles under her chin, her stare into space getting further away."He finally found a job in Lincoln. In fact, he found several over a two week period. On one of them, he called me, but I think he called me by accident. It was late in the afternoon. Luke was home already, and Lance said he would be in Lincoln until just before dinner, so it was no surprise that he would call and give me an update. But when he called me, he couldn't hear me, and he went on talking, like, to someone else. I heard: 'If I have any problems, I'll call.' Of course, I just kept saying: 'Can you hear me? Lance?' He couldn't. Then he said: 'About fifteen minutes. I'm just gassing up.' At that point, I realized that he was talking on another phone in his truck and he had butt dialed me while he was doing it."

Laurie's eyes rose slowly to meet Ruby's. "He doesn't have another cell phone, Rubes. At least, I didn't think he did."

Neither of them said anything for a long while, Ruby chewing her lower lip in thought, and nothing but the whir of the cicada's song beyond the sliding door breaking the thick silence.

"There's more," Laurie went on. "Lance keeps the power washer at work. On a hunch, I put Luke in the car and drove by the garage. It was still there, covered up alongside the shop. I asked Lance about that later, saying I had just passed by to grab a lottery ticket at the Git N' Split and noticed it was there. His story was that they already had a power washer at the job he was going to, so he had decided to leave his. It would be easier." Laurie collapsed back into the folds of the couch. "Do you mind if I grab some water?"

"No, I'll get it." Ruby insisted. "I should have offered. Or how about a beer? If I need one, I'm sure you do."

"Yeah," said Laurie. "Maybe I should. What do you think all of this means?"

Ruby, her mouth screwed up in thought, returned with a can of beer for each of them, both stuffed into light blue, thermal koozies. "Well, I can't explain the double cell phone sitch," Ruby admitted, "but maybe they did have a power washer on site when he went to Lincoln."

"I don't know about that," said Laurie, cracking the beer and gulping down half of it. "Why would they have a power washer-- whoever 'they' are--and not use it themselves or get someone local to fire it up. There's more though," Laurie continued, her voice dropping ominously. "I have to tell you about the red backpack. Maybe it's nothing, but all of a sudden a lot of things are adding up. Things I didn't notice before, or really care about, are starting to make me wonder."

"What red backpack?" Ruby asked.

"The one in Lance's pick-up," Laurie said, "the one that's always in Lance's pick-up. I don't know where or when he bought it, but it's never been in the house. It sits between the two seats in the cab. I've only seen it through the window. I mean, who cares about a red backpack, right? It's small. It's not like a hiking backpack, so it might not even be called a backpack. Maybe you would call it a knapsack? Whatever, but I never saw it before last month.

"I never thought much about the fact that I never go anywhere in Lance's pick-up. Neither does Luke. Anytime either of us go anywhere with him, we just pile into the CR-V. I never thought much about it, but not only do we never go into his truck, he also never leaves his truck keys on the key pegs by the front door. He leaves the keys to the shop there, but not the keys to his truck.

"At first, I wasn't sure about this, so I paid attention for a week or so, and not once did I lay eyes on the keys to that truck. I thought I was making too much out of it at first, but then one day, Luke was throwing a tantrum because he wanted candy. I told him 'no' 'cause he'd gotten a time out at school and if he gets a time out at school then there's no video games or candy. He had a meltdown. He knows Lance always keeps a pack of gum or a roll of fruit chews in the pocket of his jeans since he stopped smoking, so Luke went into our bedroom and rooted around until he came up with a Jolly Rancher. He also had pulled Lance's truck keys out and he was walking through the house, sucking on his Jolly Rancher and pretending to lock and unlock doors with the keys.

"Lance flipped out. Not because Luke had stolen candy from his jeans and disobeyed us, but because Luke had the keys to his truck. You could tell. He didn't even mention the candy. He just grabbed the keys and shook them in front of Luke's face and said, 'Don't you ever touch these. These are not a toy!' It was weird. It's not like keys are fragile or anything. It was a strange response to a child playing with some stupid keys, don't you think?"

"So he's keeping something in the truck that he doesn't want you to know about," said Ruby.

"Yep," Laurie agreed, "and my hunch is that it's the phantom cell phone he butt dialed me with. I think of it as the Bat Phone. Remember the secret phone batman had? That's what I think is in the red knapsack, the knapsack that just appeared out of nowhere last month.

"But there's more," Laurie went on, "and I never told you this next part because, at the time, I think I just buried it. Do you remember when Lance and I went skiing in Colorado with the Schultzes in February? I got really motion sick on the way up. Tom Schultze was driving. We had all piled into his Suburban. Anyway, they pulled off the road to get something to eat, he and Lance. Marci took Luke and Dillon to the snow bank at the side of the road to burn off some of their energy. And I just sat in the truck, feeling woozy.

"Lance left his phone on the seat. His regular cell phone, I mean. I never snoop, and I've never looked at it. Why would I? But I was bored. They were taking a while in the diner. So I looked. Nothing to speak of in his inbox, but in his 'sent' file I found a message sent to blissmassage4you@yahoo.com, all one word. I never heard of Bliss massage. Have you?"

Ruby shook her head, her own beer poised at her lower lip, her eyes wide above its rim.

"There was no text in the message," Laurie continued, "but there was an attachment. I opened it. It was a picture of him, shirtless, with a socket wrench in his hand. He was making a kissy face at the camera."

"What?" Ruby cried. "You're kidding."

"I wish," Laurie said. "Later, when we got to the lodge, I confronted him on it. He laughed and said it was a joke. "You know Danny's mom?' he said. 'The kid who helps me out in the garage? His mom is a massage therapist in Lincoln,' he said. 'She wants me to come in because I complain about my back. I told her I was fine and that I appreciated the offer, but that kind of thing is not for me,' he said. Then he told me he sent her that pic as a joke. He said that she was always flirting with him and that he thought the picture would be good for a laugh. 'She's not close to being my type, honey,' he told me. 'Come on! Give me some credit!' he said."

"Did you believe him?" Ruby asked.

"Yeah, I did. If he was going to cheat on me it wouldn't be with Donna Martin. She's a big girl and I know for a fact that Lance isn't a chubby chaser in the least. But here's the thing: Donna's spa in Lincoln is called Serenity Spa. It has nothing to do with Bliss massage.

"So guess what I did? I came up with a fake email account and emailed blissmassage4you@yahoo.com and said, 'Hi! What's up?' or something like that. I never heard back. Whoever was at the other end must have been a suspicious sort. Either that, or Lance had tipped them off, told them that the heat was on."

Ruby whistled through her teeth. "This is unbelievable, Laurie. Oh my God. What are you going to do?"

"Nothing. What can I do? It sounds like a lot, but he hasn't done anything that I can put my finger on."

"Do you really think he's cheating?" Ruby asked. "Lance? You guys are in church every Sunday. You're like the perfect couple. Are you guys having sex? I know it can be hard sometimes with a kid around. I hear that a lot. Is everything, you know, up to snuff?"

"Not really," Laurie admitted.

"Why?" Ruby asked.

Laurie finished her beer and gazed up at the landing. Ruby hoped to hell that Scotty wasn't standing there, listening to every word. She wanted to crane her neck around and look, but Laurie looked away from the landing impassively and went on. "It's probably my fault. I'm not into it much."

"You're not attracted to him anymore?"

"That's not it," Laurie insisted, "I am. I just. I have problems with it. He's very aggressive. He likes to be kind of dirty--in a playful way-- but still. I get freaked out when I'm touched sometimes. It feels wrong to me. It always has, but lately it's getting worse. I rather just forget about sex altogether, but I can't or I know I would lose him forever. Look, I don't know if any of this worrying about Lance means a whole lot. I could be jumping at shadows. I just had to get it off my chest. I really should go. I have to grab Luke from St. Mark."

"It could all be sliding doors," Ruby conceded, "but the way you laid it out would make me wonder, too. I guess it depends if you really want to know the answer or not."

"That," said Laurie, "is what I'm most unsure of."

The two kissed on the cheek and Laurie headed for her car.

Halfway down the walk, she turned to look at Ruby standing in the door.

"I'm here if you need me," Ruby called out.

"I just might," said Laurie, her smile sad and crooked. "I hope I don't...but I just might."

Chapter 10

The Contaminant

Kat Larson first met John Supernau on her senior trip in high school. She had grown up in Kansas City, not far from Worlds of Fun Amusement Park, and even though John lived almost 300 miles away, Worlds of Fun was the nearest theme park and a popular day trip for Nebraskans. So he had his senior trip there, too, on the same day. And so it had been then that Kat first laid eyes on the blond boy with the great hair, the anachronistic-but-puzzlingly-sexy mustache, and the strange name.

They had spotted each other in line for the Orient Express roller coaster, making eyes at one another whenever the switchbacks would allow. With great serendipity, they ended up seated together, screaming and bonding with fear as the coaster looped its tortuous way back to the station. Ditching their friends, the two had grabbed an ice cream cone along the midway, John winning Kat a garishly colored snake stuffed with tiny Styrofoam balls. They knew its contents because a seam on its side had split within a half hour of their ownership, hemorrhaging the white beads onto the park grounds in a fine trail. The two had laughed at the thing, dubbing it "a rip-off" and "a piece of shit."

After carrying on a long distance relationship for years, John asked Kat to marry him. He then began the process of sweet talking Kat into moving to Dawson. She finally acquiesced under one condition: they had to visit her hometown of Kansas City often, as well as travel a lot, or she feared she "might lose her freakin' mind," as she liked to put it.

So Kat and John settled into married life just four years out of high school, and while Kat agreed with John that Dawson would be a great place to have a family, she had wanted to wait on that, wait until they had done the things they wanted to do. The wait ended up being over ten years when they had their first son, Flynn, now thirteen years old. Flynn was named for a character in Tron, one of Jon's favorite movies from the 80s.

Kat took to Dawson well enough, but her flair for high fashion quickly set her apart. Only Sylvia Blair could steal the title from Kat Supernau as the town's eccentric. But whereas Sylvia Blair's mysteriousness made people nervous and uncomfortable, Kat's indulgences inspired something akin to fascinated envy in those women faced with her diminutive frame, dark bobbed hair, and Parisian flapper style. And whereas Sylvia didn't care to socialize, dealt in death, and was rumored to have an obsession with taxidermy, Kat was the friendly proprietor of her own chic fabric store on Main Street.

Though Kat certainly thought life was slow in Dawson, once in a great while something extraordinary would happen, and this morning had proven to be one of those days.

She thumbed her cell phone on and called John at Pac N' Save.

"Hey, babe. Guess who showed up here this morning? Clayton Briggle," she said, shrinking into a corner of the kitchen as she talked to get out of earshot from Flynn who was in the family room and absorbed in a video game. "He got here just after you left for work--maybe around nine or so."

"No shit?" said John. "I thought he would call first. Where was he last night?"

"That's the thing," said Kat. "He drove all night from Colorado Springs. He looks like shit. He asked if he could crash somewhere and wait for you to get home. I told him you wouldn't be home until around five o'clock. He said he would wait and that he just wanted to sleep. His dad died."

"Oh crap," John sighed. "While he was there? Oh, man. That's too bad. Well, at least he was at his side. It's not going to be easy for him, but at least he was there."

"You should see his truck," said Kat. "It looks like it's been to Oz and back."

"What happened?"

"He said he was in a wreck, but he wasn't hurt. 'Looks worse than it was,' he says, and promised to tell us all about it later, but he could hardly keep his eyes open. He came in with a camouflage duffle bag and he smells like a dead rat. Is he staying with us? I mean, for a while or something?"

"For a little while," John said defensively, "maybe a few days. I told you he was coming, didn't I? He just lost his dad. Come on, babe, you like Clay."

"I don't know him that well anymore," said Kat. "Is he cool? I mean, he's been living in Hollywood since he was old enough to drink. You think he's into hard shit? How could you know him that well? You guys just talk on the phone. I don't want to sound like a prude, but the guy is in a death metal band and Flynn is out of school for the summer and hanging our around here. I don't want him to pick up any bad habits. I also don't want to find any needles in the bathroom wastebasket or find any jewelry missing a month from now."

"Ah shit, Kat. Come on. This is Clay Briggle we're talking about," said John. "He's the same old Clay. He had some problems with harder shit back when, but for all I know he just smokes weed like us. He would have told me if he parties harder than that. We talk a lot, we talk about everything. The guy's forty-seven, he has middle-aged problems now. He says he's trying to lose weight, so as far as I know, the only thing he's addicted to is pizza. So relax. Did he say how long he's staying?"

"No, that's why I asked. He's already snoring in the guest room. I can hear him from here."

"Maybe I can get off a bit early. Make him feel at home. The guy just lost his dad."

"Yeah, you're right." Kat conceded. "I like Clay. I guess I just didn't expect him out of the blue like that."

John was suddenly giddy. "Damn! Clay is in town! Wanna go to Misty's tonight and get a steak and a few beers? Talk about old times? No, better yet, maybe Flynn can go to one of his buddy's houses where they can play video games until their eyes bleed so we can have a barbecue. You know, roll a fatty in the backyard? Like old times? I can bring some steaks from the shop! Like a 4th of July dry run?"

"John, you'd sacrifice your only son to the video game gods to get high with Clay? I'll have you know that Flynn is already playing video games with his friends until his eyes bleed. They're connected online. Why would they ever need to see each other again?" Then Kat added with adolescent peevishness, "I mean, gawd! You're like, so old."

"Yeah, yeah, yeah. But talk to him anyway," said John. "Tell him Mom and Dad need some alone time tonight. Throw him a few bucks. Maybe he can call up Dillon and the two of them could go to Godfather's for pizza. Oh, and tell him to clean his bathroom. He's got to share it with Clay for a few days. It looks like a science experiment in there."

The two hung up and Kat leaned into the family room. "Flynn, I'm off to work. Clean your bathroom. Clay Briggle is going to hang out for a few days. If he wakes up, be nice. He just lost his father." She grabbed her keys and as she was heading out the door she turned and added, "Oh, and introduce yourself. The last time he was in town you were in diapers. He might think you're your father and that you dyed your hair and got zits."

"I only have one zit, Mom," came Flynn's voice from the other room, "and stop making fun of me!"

"Love you, bug." Kat said.

She paused for a moment, listening with her hand on the door. "Well?"

"Love you back" Flynn muttered.

Kat smiled and headed for her car.

#

"Mind if I take a shower?" said Clayton. He stood in the doorway of the family room, his eyelids still heavy with sleep. Flynn was on the phone, aimlessly channel surfing, and when he caught sight of Clayton, he jumped. Clayton was wearing one of his band's t-shirts. "Kribdëth" was written in red across its black front in a spiky, stylized font. The superfluous heavy metal umlaut over the "e" looked like drops of blood. Below the script, an evil baby with claw-like hands reached out for Flynn with blazing eyes.

"I'll call you back," said Flynn into the phone, keeping his eye on Clayton as he hung up. "You scared me. Wow. That's a pretty messed up shirt."

Clayton shrugged.

Flynn sized him up: bald head, salt and pepper goatee, beer belly, and decided that the new house guest looked a lot like a vampire's dad.

"I thought heavy metal guys were supposed to have long hair?" said Flynn.

"I shaved off what was left of mine at forty," said Clayton. "Better to burn out than fade away."

"Okay, I don't know exactly what that means," said Flynn, "but towels are in the linen closet, down the hall to the right."

Clayton cracked a smile. The kid was a bit of a smart ass and that was fine with Clayton.

"You don't remember me, huh? Nah, I suppose you wouldn't," Clayton said. "Man, you sure grew up fast. Last time I saw you..."

"Yeah, yeah, I know," Flynn cut him off and headed for the kitchen. "I was in diapers and super cute."

"I wasn't going to say that last part," said Clayton. "Actually, you were kind of ugly, cried a lot and smelled like old milk."

Now it was Flynn's turn to smile. "Hey, I was a baby. That's messed up."

"So you do remember me?"

"Maybe a little."

Flynn beckoned Clayton and he followed. In the kitchen, Flynn tugged open the fridge and pulled out an energy drink in an aluminum can.

"Here, drink this before you fall over. You still look, well...not good. Sorry about your dad. My mom told me. I was still in bed when you showed up so she texted me, told me not to freak out if there was some dude in the house with a beard."

"Thanks," said Clayton, popping open the proffered can, "and for the condolences, too."

The two lapsed into awkward silence.

"So you went to St. Mark with my dad, huh?" asked Flynn, "That's where I go now."

"Yep, we go way back. Partners in crime," said Clayton and immediately winced at his own words. What a stupid thing to say in front of a man's kid. He never knew real crime until he had left this town and none of it had anything to do with John. He also suddenly wished he wasn't wearing his band's shirt anymore. It didn't feel right here. It was okay for Hollywood Boulevard, but not here. He vowed he wouldn't wear it around Dawson. Main Street could probably do without a satanic baby reaching forth to rip out their very souls.

As he stood there in the domesticity of the Supernau family kitchen, everything about him was feeling dirtier by the moment. Not only did he need a shower, but his sense of decency could use a good scrubbing. What a boneheaded thing to say, looking the way he looked: "partners in crime."

He had never been more innocent then when he was in Dawson. Now that he had left, he actually was a criminal with actual partners in crime. He wished he could make clear to the boy that his father had never been, and never would be, the Briggle brand of loser. Being back in his hometown in his Kribdëth shirt with the murder of his own father under his belt, Clayton was beginning to feel like one giant, brazen profanity, or worse--a contaminant.

Clayton swigged his drink, studying Flynn from over the top of the can, looking at the boy for traces of his old friends, John and Kat, as Flynn opened the dishwasher and started putting away glasses in the cupboard.

Flynn had been a blond baby, but now had Kat's dark locks which were cut short in the perpetual-bed-head style. His eyes were close together, his brow heavy and his lips full. Coming from two rail-thin parents, Clayton couldn't understand how Flynn had turned into such a bruiser. He looked like a call from the Nebraska Cornhuskers wouldn't be out of the question. The Big Red farmed them early. Christ, he was an inch taller than Clayton and just as wide.

"You know a place where I can fix my truck?" said Clayton, polishing off his energy drink and crushing the can. "It's got a flat."

"It's got more than a flat," said Flynn, pausing as he put away the dishes to peer through the kitchen window to the truck parked in front. "Were you playing bumper cars on the way here?"

"Something like that."

"You live in Hollywood, right?"

"I do," said Clayton. He too looked out the window at his truck. It looked worse than he remembered. After five hours of sleep, things were beginning to come back to him and none of them were good. He had to get it off the street, get it serviced, or at least into a garage so he could stop looking over his shoulder.

Had he given his cell number to 911 dispatch this morning? He had. They could track him via GPS if they wanted to roll up and ask questions, and before that happened, Clayton had to make sure there was nothing about the truck that could royally fuck him. The body was safely in Sylvia Blair's hands, but there could be…

(residue?)

Clayton shuddered.

"Midwest Automotive," said Flynn.

"Huh?"

"Midwest Automotive, down Dawson Street, just past Amigo's"

"Oh," said Clayton. "Thanks. You mean Roger Vanderboom's place? He still owns it?"

"Nah," said Flynn, closing the dishwasher and leaning on the counter to face Clayton. "Roger died a couple of months ago. Drank too much, at least that's what I heard. His son runs it now."

Clayton's eyes widened. After so long without any good news, when a little finally came it felt unexpectedly euphoric, like that first line of blow he had as a teenager, the one that had kicked off a party that had lasted close to twenty years. Clayton had to lean on the refrigerator for support. "Lance?"

"Yeah," Flynn confirmed, "That's him. He was in your class, too, huh?"

"Yes, he was," said Clayton, closing his eyes and sighing deeply with relief. "He sure was."

#

John Supernau glanced up at the clock hanging on the wall of the Pak N' Save. It hung beneath a large cursive scrawl that read "The Only Thing Better Than Our Service Is Our Prices!"

2:00 PM

The day was dragging. John had just shaken off Mitzy Groener who had spent the last ten minutes in his face complaining about the price of produce. Patiently, John had told her that it was California's fault, that the state was in the middle of a drought, and that Pac N' Save kept prices as low as they could. But that explanation--nor any other, John figured--could never really slake her thirst for attention. John supposed Mitzy Groener would complain about her room number in heaven. If anyone ever had a perfect name...

He needed a break.

He ducked into his office. He would call Clayton; see if he was up and around. He was.

"Had a good nap?" John asked.

"Thanks, man," said Clayton, "It sure helped. I know I should have called, given you a head's up. Kat didn't know what to make of me this morning. Sorry, man, I was just a little...you know..."

"No worries," said John. "I'm sorry about your dad. At least you were able to say goodbye, and I'm sure he knew you were there, even if he didn't react exactly how you would expect. They always know you're there. That's what I've heard from other people."

Yeah, Clayton thought, he knew I was there alright.

For a brief moment when answering the phone Clayton had hoped that hearing John's familiar voice as he sat in the Supernau's sun-dappled breakfast nook might erase the horrors of last night along with the wasteland of his last twenty years and relegate them to the potency of a fading nightmare. But then he looked at his other hand, flexing it, the rope burn clearly visible, and then through the blinds at his mangled truck sitting at the curb, and it all became too real again.

He remembered his hallucination from last night, when his father had risen out of the toolbox to claw at the window of the cab, the yellow sheet cracking in the wind like a flag on a pole, the white hair tossing around the skull like a corona of snakes. Clayton also remembered the moment when he had squeezed his eyes shut, knowing that if that thing was still in the rearview mirror when he opened them again that he would go insane. He would go fucking insane.

"Are ya still there, Clay?" said John. "Can you hear me? Damn, I think I'm losing you."

Clayton gazed dreamily through the window of the breakfast nook at the row of simple clapboard houses across the street, shimmering in the heat of the day.

(contaminant)

"I'm here," Clayton managed.

"So, is there a funeral set?" said John. "I'd like to go."

Deep within himself, where it was hollow, but where he was sure it shouldn't be, Clayton laughed miserably. "There won't be a funeral. That's awesome of you though, Supe. It really is."

Of course there couldn't be a funeral. No one but Lutz and Blair was to know that the body was in town, much less the story of taking his father to convalesce with a nonexistent relative in Malcolm. Supernau knew that Clayton had no living relatives left in Nebraska. All of Clayton's old pals in Dawson knew that, but the story was a risk that had to be taken. Anyway, Blair wouldn't shoot her mouth off. She didn't pal around with anyone in town that Clayton knew of, and as for Lutz, he didn't see why the sheriff would ever bring up the story to anyone in such detail.

"I have an idea," said John, "let's barbecue tonight and knock a few back, like a wake. I'm sure you could use it. Just you, me and Kat."

"You know what Flynn told me this morning?" said Clayton. "He said that Lance inherited his old man's garage. That true? He owns Midwest Automotive now?"

"Not only that," said John, "but Linda died last weekend. I haven't had the chance to tell you that yet. You've been a little M.I.A."

"Linda? His stepmom? So both his parents are dead now?"

"What a kick in the nuts, huh?"

"It sure is," said Clayton. "Is he okay?"

"I think so," said John. "He and Linda weren't that close, but I think he's worried about the boy. That was Luke's grandma."

"I've got to see Lance soon," said Clayton. "My truck needs a little work. You think he's around?"

"Should be."

"And by the way, a barbecue sounds good," said Clayton, "Thanks, man. Can I get anything for it?"

"I work at a grocery store, dude."

"Oh, yeah."

"A couple more hours at the shop and then it's on."

"It's on," Clayton agreed and hung up.

#

Clayton showered, put on the only shirt in his duffle bag with a collar, and headed for Lance's auto garage.

The truck was a mess, but there had been no "residue" as he had feared, only the few ice packs that he had thrown on top of the body remained, now just warm bladders of water, and he tossed them into a rubber garbage bin at the side of the house. The binding ropes were gone. He had left those on the package that he had delivered to the Blair Funeral Home.

He didn't think the truck would start, but it did. He crept down back streets, riding on his rim and undoubtedly mangling the wheel even further. The side mirror was not only sheared off, but the front quarter panel was totaled, the left headlight shattered and the bumper torn off on one side, its opposing bolt the only thing holding the bumper aloft. The whole truck wiggled and creaked as he rolled along beneath the oaks, thin spears of sunlight managing to stab through their thick, summer leaves. Overhead, the song of the cicadas lulled cautiously as he passed beneath their symphony.

On his right, Clayton saw an older couple out for a stroll. He didn't recognize them. That was good. He would have to face people eventually, affix a smile to his face eventually, but he wasn't ready just yet.

The old couple stopped walking, faced Clayton's limping vehicle, and with the blatant, deadpan avidity for the abnormal that exists only in small towns, watched the battered truck roll by.

The first to receive Clayton when he rolled of off onto Main Street and up to the garage of Midwest Automotive was Dan Hicks, a kid in his early 20s, an overgrown towhead in coveralls who whistled in disbelief at the sight of the Dodge Ram, spat some chew into the dust at the side of the garage, and toweled off his hands with a greasy rag before waving the truck into the bay. "Come on up, sir. You're sure going to keep us busy for a while! Did you have a fight with a cow?"

From out of the shadows, Lance Vanderboom appeared in jeans and a denim work shirt with the company patch stitched to its breast. Through the windshield of his old friend's truck he recognized Clayton at once. Clayton hopped out of the cab and the two clapped each other on the back, pulled away, and hugged again.

"Well, fuck me," said Lance, "What are you doing in Dawson? Look at you!"

"I've looked better," said Clayton.

"I doubt that," Lance said. "Boys, get this thing fixed. Jesus, God, what happened? Clayton Freakin' Briggle? You didn't tell me you were coming to town." He cocked a thumb at Clayton and said, "Boys, this here is a genuine rock star! This is Clay Briggle. You can call him Mr. Hollywood!"

"Please don't," Clayton muttered.

Lance grinned.

Dan stared.

Earl, another kid in his early 20s with a ruddy face and a pug nose, slid out from beneath a Pontiac Firebird on a creeper and sat up to stare, too.

Clayton stood and took it, feeling like a giant asshole until Lance mercifully spoke again. "So what gives? What brings you to town?"

Clayton told him what he could.

"I'm sorry, man," said Lance. "My old man died, too. Just a couple of months ago. You remember Linda, my stepmom? She died a couple of days ago."

"Supernau told me," said Clayton. "Sorry, man. That's a lot of shit at once."

"Thanks. We weren't very close, but Luke thought the world of her and he's pretty bummed out. You haven't met my boy, have you? No, I guess you wouldn't have. He's six already, a good kid. How long has it been?"

"Ten years," Clayton offered, "Well, twenty since I moved, but ten since I came back for that reunion at St. Mark. Remember?"

"Of course I remember. That was quite a night. That was ten years ago? Shit. I guess it was. So what happened to the truck? You drove all the way from L.A.?"

Again, Clayton told him what he could.

Lance listened, screwing up his mouth. Then, with one brisk clap of his hands, he began showing Clayton around the garage. "It's mine now," he said, "free and clear. Linda didn't get squat. My dad told me as much before he died. To tell you the truth, I don't know why those two lived together for as long as they did. Makes no sense. They didn't even like each other."

"Not many couples do after a while," Clayton said, "Shit, my parents didn't last long, either. But then there's Supernau. What's with that? It looks like he and Laurie are still high school sweethearts--thick as thieves, huh?"

"Twenty-five years it's been for them," said Lance. "Makes you want to puke, doesn't it?"

The two laughed.

Dan and Earl were putting Clayton's truck on the lift. Lance grabbed a couple of beers from a squat fridge at the side of the shop, handed one to Clayton, and beckoned him outside with a flap of his arm. There the two stood in a cool rhombus of shade cast by the building's pitched roof.

"What's that?" Clayton asked, cracking his beer and pointing to a mound covered in a blue tarp. "A dirt bike or something?"

"Nope," said Lance. "Power washer. Just got it. Bought it used."

Clayton took a peek under the tarp.

"So you're still in the same house on Roberts, huh?" Clayton asked.

"Yep. Still there," said Lance.

"And Laurie?" Clayton asked, "How's she doing? You guys are still married, right? I didn't miss something, did I?"

Lance slugged the rest of his beer, "Fine. We're doing just fine." He tossed the empty into an open bin at the side of the garage, put his hands at the small of his back, and stretched with a yawn. "Well, I better get to work. Looks like I'm going to have to order parts for you. Hope you're not in a hurry. It could take the better part of a week. I'll put a rush on it for you. Of course, no extra charge for that."

"You rock, brother," said Clayton. "Hey, I'm staying with Supernau for a bit. He said we should get together tonight at his place. He's going to barbecue. You know, shoot the shit.

"I'll be there," said Lance. "You need a lift back?"

Clayton didn't. John wasn't home yet anyway, and Clayton was feeling a lot better about things. He would walk back to the Supernau place, directly down Main Street, and learn to face the world again. He could use the time to think, let the sun bake out the knot in the center of his head. Maybe then he could look around and see what had been lost, and what only might have been left behind.

Chapter 11

The Coals Heat Up

"You wanna do the honors?" said John, handing Clayton the joint.

John, Kat, Lance and Clayton sat out on the Supernau's deck around the patio table, the coals in the built-in barbecue only just starting to singe white on their edges, their cans of beer stuffed into the requisite thermal Styrofoam koozies. The sun was low, its light mellow, and the day's dying breaths were sultry whispers on the backs of their necks.

Clayton turned John's joint around in his hands, admiring a workmanship comparable to that of a Cuban Habano. Supernau always had rolled the best joints--just had a knack for it. His were fat, even and tight as a drumhead. Reflexively, Clayton looked over one shoulder at the house before sparking the sweet smelling spliff held between his lips, even though John and Kat had assured him that Flynn had been plied with cash and directed to make himself scarce. Clayton lit up, considered the tip of the joint, and pulled on it again, the paper crackling and burning evenly.

"How do you even get weed around here anymore?" Clayton asked, "Isn't it zero tolerance here still? I bet you have to be extra careful. Nerves of steel, huh, Supe? We used to get it from Brock. He was the man. Remember that dude?"

John looked at his wife and began to explain who John Brock had been. It was apparent to Kat that she was about to spend the evening as the group's sounding board. She settled back in her chair, resigning herself to the role.

It happened to everyone at some point, when old friends got together who shared a history that you didn't. And though Kat had been with John since the tail end of high school, it had been only the tail end. With a joint poised at Clayton's lips, she knew this evening was about to become a bout of reminiscing that pre-dated even her. She was up for the task. All she needed to do was listen and the guys would direct almost all of their tales, tall or otherwise, in her direction with the conceit of explaining things to her so she could follow along; but really, she would be incidental. Once they got on a tear, they might even forget to fill her in at all.

Clayton: "John Brock. Good ol' Kickstand. What happened to him?"

Clayton passed the joint to Kat.

Kat: "Kickstand?"

The three guys smiled at each other. John nodded slightly, giving permission to whoever wanted to stick their neck out on the subject.

Lance did: "The guy had a giant dong. We found that out in gym class in middle school. We gave him the name then."

John: "Down to his knee and I'm not kidding."

Clayton: "Tall dude, dumb as an ox. He grew weed on his grandmother's farm out by Utica. His grandfather died and left Brock and his grandma the farm and so Brock started growing weed out there right under her nose. Told her it was oregano. She didn't know. Is anyone going to smell this over the fence?"

John: "No. It's cool. The Meyers live on that side, and Tommy Down lives over there. Both Gus and Marlena Meyer are pretty old now and if they know what weed smells like I'll eat this table. Tommy Down knows what it is, but he doesn't care."

Clayton: "Tommy Down? No shit? He lives next door? Where the Schultzes used to live? How'd he pull that off?"

John: "He's a nurse practitioner at the hospital. He actually sees Flynn when Doc Lautner is too tied up. He's smart as hell now. I'm not the only one who would have lost money on that bet."

Lance took the joint from Kat and explained: "Has John ever told you about how Tommy grew up?"

John shook his head.

Lance went on: "Tommy comes from Grade-A white trash. I mean, bad. They lived in a shack in the old part of town that looked like it would blow over after a good fart. His mother lives in Bee now. You've seen her, Kat. She helps out at the fish fry once in a while. Red hair and fat? She's actually much thinner now--if you can believe it. Back in the day she was a real mudroller, and Tommy and his brother looked like Pig Pen from the Peanuts cartoons. Actual stripes of dirt across their face at all times. They had blond hair cut with a garden shears--I think they did it themselves when their hair got in their eyes. Their front yard was nothing but a wasteland of packed dirt."

Kat puffed her cheeks and blew out a breath in sympathy.

Clayton: "A freakin' nurse? Good for him. You talk about bucking the odds."

John hit the joint and passed it back to Clayton. "No doubt. Hey, you know who I ran into at the bowling alley?"

Clayton: "Who?"

John: "Frankie Schroeder."

Clayton laughed a trail of beer foam onto his chin: "Oh no. What was he doing in town? I thought he lived in Omaha."

John filled in his wife: "Frankie Schroeder was this kid in school who wore Underoos to school until sixth grade. You remember Underoos, babe? They were two piece underwear sets based on superheroes."

Lance: "Underwear that's fun to wear."

Kat looked confused.

John: "Guess girls didn't have them? Anyway, Frankie wore them to school on the outside of his clothes."

Clayton: "Didn't he announce that he was Wonder Woman or some shit once?"

Lance: "Oh yeah. He told us all that he was to be called Wonder Woman one day and we laughed our asses off for, like..."

Clayton: "...the next four years?"

Lance: "Yeah, pretty much."

Kat: "Oh, poor kid."

John: "He brought stuff like that on himself. Like during school dances..."

Lance knew what story was coming up. He clapped his hand over his forehead and pounded his feet rapidly on the deck: "Oh no! Here it comes!"

John: "He would clear the dance floor when "Footloose" would come on, and he would proceed to just flip out and start doing dance moves that had nothing to do with anything."

Clayton: "Oh, it was really bad."

Lance: "I mean really bad."

Clayton" "It actually made your soul hurt."

Kat looked horrified.

John offered more beer and they all took him up on it. He came back from the kitchen with four Budweiser tall boys still hanging from their yoke and passed them around. He peered at the coals and then sat down.

John: "I'll throw those steaks on in about five minutes. One of you stoners remind me."

Lance: "Don't hold your breath."

John to Clayton: "Oh, and guess who's working for me now at the Pak N' Save? Arnie Rothenburg!"

Clayton: "How's he look?"

This was the question that always followed when anyone mentioned Arnie. His disfigurement happened during Christmas of 1972, when snow covered Dawson like folds of cotton batting. Arnie was four years old at the time and, as he had done every year, his father had strung colored lights on the hedgerow in front of their house. They were fat, brightly colored incandescent bulbs and to Arnie they had evidently looked a lot like glowing, frosted gumdrops: lemon, grape, orange, blueberry and cherry. Arnie chose cherry.

With a crunch, Arnie bit down on one of those fat Christmas light bulbs. He said later that it had made a popping sound in his head, "like someone had clapped their hands once really hard by his ear." His mouth had been electrocuted, frying his upper lip so that it looked like a piece of crispy bacon hanging beneath his nose, consigning the boy to a lifetime of reconstructive surgeries.

"You can hardly tell anymore," said Kat. "It just looks like a slight harelip now."

"That's good news," said Clayton. "Arnie was always a good guy."

John rose and forked the steaks onto the grill.

"So what's up with you, Clay?" Lance asked, and then added in a parody of a mother's nagging, "When are you going to get married?"

"No one can tolerate me," said Clayton. "I can't even tolerate me."

Lance wondered which was worse: not having a family or having one. He loved Luke, and he loved Laurie, but when the sex dies and then your wife is caught finger-banging herself online with a guy she thinks is from New York City, it crushes you like nothing else can. Then again, the thought of not having her and Luke at all was unthinkable.

Six of one, a half-dozen of the other, Lance thought, quickly chalking up his cavalier assessment to the four beers already making their way to his bladder.

"He's got groupies," said John, "He doesn't need a wife. They're just a maintenance hassle."

Kat reached back to where John was tending the steaks, grabbed a spatula from the side of the grill, and started beating John's ass with it.

John: "Ouch!"

Lance: "You two need to take it inside."

Clayton laughed.

John: "I told a lot of people you were coming, Clay. You know who asked about you? Ruby Wegner. I usually see her at the Corner Café in the morning. She brightened right up when I mentioned you were coming to town."

Lance teased Clayton with a cat call and a sock in the arm.

Clayton: "Really? How is she?"

John: "Okay, I guess. She doesn't open up a whole lot. She goes to school all the time; it's about all she does. She still looks good, though, I'll tell ya' that. She runs every morning, a few miles I think."

Kat: "I always thought you two should have hooked up, Clay."

Clayton: "She was cute, no doubt, but she and Laurie were freshies when we were seniors, remember?"

Lance: "No, she doesn't mean you should have hooked up back in the days. She means now. Ruby doesn't have to be just Scotty's little sister anymore, you know. Remember when you came back to town for the tenth St. Mark reunion? You and Ruby danced all night together-- slow danced even--to Prince's "Purple Rain," if I'm not mistaken."

Clayton: "Oh, man. That was a long time ago. To "Purple Rain"? I must have been shit faced."

Kat: "Or sprung. I bet you think of that night every time your head hits the pillow."

Clayton: "Oh shut it, Kat. You guys are crazy. So who else asked about me?"

John: "Pastor Steitz."

Clayton: "Wow, he's still there, huh?"

John: "Still saving souls."

Clayton: "And you? Still going to church? Still trying to save yours, huh, Supe?"

John: "What else you gonna do? It's Dawson."

Clayton: "You, too, Lance?"

John: "You're asking Lance if he goes to church? You guys need to catch up. The Vanderbooms practically run St. Mark, so watch your step, Hollywood. Lance and I have talked religion a few times, and you don't want to mess with him. He takes it seriously."

Clayton: "You do, Lance?"

Lance only slugged the last of his beer in reply, his eyes narrowing and glittering with defiance above the can as he drank. Clayton smiled tightly and looked away, knowing he was a little drunk, but also knowing he loved busting balls on the subject of religion. He decided to avoid the minefield of Lance and go at Supernau for the win.

Clayton: "What about you, Supes? You serious about it?"

John: "Not as much as Lance."

Lance glowered comically, sat back in his patio chair and crossed his arms to watch the volley.

Kat: "I'll grab some more beers. That should help a conversation about religion go smoothly. Do we have more, babe?"

John: "Check the fridge in the garage. There's a cold twelver in there. So, yeah, Mr. Metal, I still go to church."

Clayton: "You know my band is all in good fun, right? It's not like I sacrifice goats to the Dark Lord."

John: "Tell Pastor Steitz that. He's more than a little concerned about your life out there."

Clayton: "So am I, brother. So am I."

That comment seemed to take the wind out of everyone. It was too loaded with import. Lance craned his neck to the garage entrance in the silence, hoping for Kat to appear with those beers.

Clayton backpedaled: "I'm still the same old guy; it's just that sometimes I feel very far away from that St. Mark kid who went to church and, well, you know. The older I get, the harder it is to believe in just about anything. I couldn't go to church now if I tried. Doesn't it just sound like a bunch of fairytales?"

John: "Of course it's a bunch of fairytales. No offense, Lance. You know where I'm at with the whole thing. Of course it is. The stories might be, but the morality behind them is timeless. You can't miss the forest for the trees. I also go for the community of it. Everyone I know is there, and what else am I going to do on Sunday morning? Plus, it makes you stop and think about how you can be a better person, how you can make your world better. What's so bad about that?"

Clayton: "That's not how it used to be. Remember that sermon about how Jews were going to Hell because they killed Christ, and that they would never get into heaven? It took me a long time to shake that one. Like the Jews needed more persecution, and like I needed to be fed a steaming pile of bullshit like that as a kid."

Kat returned with a fresh round, and Lance plucked one from her hand gratefully, cracked it, and with renewed energy said: "Supe is right. It's really not like that anymore. That was the old days. As conservative as Dawson is, it's still nowhere near as conservative as it was when we were coming up."

John: "That's true. When we were kids they actively condemned Jews and gays, and whoever else was on their shit list at the time. At least now, whatever the Missouri Synod might believe, they have the sense not to talk about it. These days a pastor might get shouted down. I don't buy any of that bigotry shit and I think they know it doesn't fly like it used to. Pastor Steitz is a good man."

Clayton: "So Flynn's going to St. Mark, too? I guess that's the best endorsement. Who all is still there?"

John flipped the steaks and came back to the table: "Mrs. Ragsdale is still there."

Clayton: "Holy shit! No way! She was old then!"

Lance: "She seemed old. She was probably only in her 30s."

Clayton laughed: "Do you remember when Supe made her cry?"

Kat: "John, you didn't!"

Kat reached for the spatula again, wielding it above John's ass.

John: "No! Don't hurt me! You tell it, Clay."

Clayton: "Mrs. Ragsdale was pretty meek. She was one of those women who seemed like she was always about to cry. She obviously didn't have much money. She dressed like shit. She had no husband--a real train wreck."

Lance: "Sad, really."

Kat: "You don't have to have a husband, guys."

Clayton: "Well, she was a train wreck anyway. So, John raises his hand in class one day and says, 'Hey, isn't that my mom's dress? I think it is! You got it at Second Hand City, right?' The whole class just died laughing."

Lance: "And Ragsdale hung her arms at her side and just started crying."

Kat: "On my God! That is the most horrible story I've ever heard! John, how could you do that? You guys are monsters!"

John: "I totally didn't mean to make her cry. I didn't! I just recognized the dress! I was excited! It turned out to be horrible, though."

Clayton: "It was really funny at the time."

The boys tried their best to stifle their laughs, but it only made it worse.

John: "You can't show that kind of vulnerability in front of middle school kids, babe. I mean, come on!"

Kat deflated and crossed her arms: "You guys are dicks."

John brought over a heaping plate of steaks and set them on the table, kissed Kat on the forehead and said, "We've gotten much better in our old age."

Lance slapped a mosquito into his fleshy arm and lit the yellow citronella candle at the center of the patio table.

The sky was now pale indigo, only the most diligent cicadas were still singing in the trees. As the sky darkened and the constellations brightened above them, the four ate, and they ate well: steak, potato salad, corn on the cob, and ending with a slice of apple pie topped with gooey cheddar cheese. Clayton had forgotten how good real Nebraska beef and corn could be.

"Oh!" said John, through a mouthful. "Speaking of who's still at St. Mark. They found Don Creech."

"I didn't know he was missing," said Clayton. "He's still the principal? Wow, he has to be old. Okay, maybe Mrs. Ragsdale hadn't been that old, but Creech? He had to have been in his late 40s. What's he now?"

"Late 60s, right?" Kat asked John.

"I'd say so," said Lance.

"But what do you mean 'found'? How was he missing?" Clayton asked again.

"I never told you about it?" John said, wrinkling his nose suspiciously at Clayton. He wiped his mustache with a napkin and settled back in his chair. "I guess you're right. I suppose it never came up the last few times we talked. Your dad was more important."

"That's right," said Kat, lifting her beer. "To Foster Briggle!"

"To Foster Briggle!" they all cheered, touching their beer koozies together.

"May he rest in peace," John added.

"Wait," said Clayton, "Another toast. To Lance's stepmom.""

"Here, here," said John, and they all touched their koozies together again.

"Lance is holding a memorial at St. Mark's this Sunday, right after the Fourth," said Kat. "Isn't that right, Lance?"

Lance nodded.

"I'll be there," said Clayton.

Lance got up, came to Clayton and hugged him from behind, growling like a bear through his gritted teeth. "We missed you, man."

"We have," said Kat. "When is your dad's funeral, Clay? John said your dad had been living in Colorado? We'll go there with you for the funeral. Not a problem."

"No, no," Clayton protested, "No funeral. He didn't really know that many people. That's awesome of you guys, but I'm just taking care of it privately."

That's one way to put it, Clayton thought, shame flushing him.

"Well, if you change your mind...you let us know, okay?" said Kat, her eyes bright above her forkful of apple pie.

Clayton's smile was wide and sincere. Suddenly, he had to look away, his eyes started to leak. These were good people, and he realized he hadn't had a real friend in years, only band mates who he partied with when they weren't desperately arguing about the minutia of a band that no one really cared about anymore.

He choked back the tears. John, Kat and Lance saw him do it and, satisfied their intentions had been received, John rescued him. "So, about Principal Creech…I haven't told you the story yet. It's a good one."

"You're not going to believe this," said Lance, leaning forward in his chair, champing at the bit.

John continued: "So it must have been, like, three weeks ago. I heard this from Bob Lutz. By the way, he's with the Dawson County Sheriff's Department now? Did you know that?"

Clayton sure did, and suddenly the heavy dinner in his stomach began to roil. "You're tight with Lutz?"

"Oh no," said John, "we don't hang out socially, he just told everyone in town to keep an eye out for Creech."

Every nerve in Clayton's body seemed to sigh in relief.

"But I've gotta tell this in order," John protested. "Okay, so, Lutz came up to our table at the bowling alley and told us that Creech's wife had reported him missing."

"This was three weeks ago," Kat put in.

"Yeah, about three weeks ago," John confirmed, "and we were, like, okay, that's weird. 'Missing how?' I asked him. 'Just missing,' Lutz says. 'Zelda doesn't know where he is.' You remember Zelda Creech? Granted, she couldn't find a chair if it was glued to her ass, but she swore she had no idea where her husband was.

"Keep in mind this was right about when graduation happened, right at the beginning of June. He didn't show up for graduation. The freakin' principal of St. Mark doesn't show up for graduation?! So, naturally, everyone is really confused. At the time, no one knew he was missing. At the time, we just thought he was sick or something. Still, we figured he would have to be pretty sick to miss graduation. It wasn't until a week after that when Lutz saw us at the bowling alley and told us what he knew. He went table to table and told us all to keep an eye peeled.

"A few days later, I ran into Lutz again when he came into Pak N' Save. We were standing in the produce section and I asked if he had any more details on Creech's disappearance. He said he did. He said

Creech's car was gone. It seems Creech took off in it and never made it back home."

"Tell him about the call," said Lance.

Kat returned from the garage with four more beers and the group took them gratefully. "Did you tell him about the call?" she said.

"Just about to," said John. "So, Lutz tells me one other thing while we're standing over by the potatoes, trying not to be overheard-- and, of course, everyone is trying to overhear. You know how it is. Lutz tells me that, according to Zelda, Don had been receiving some threatening phone calls. She never knew who was calling; she just knew Don was upset when he got off the phone. After this one call, I think it was kind of late at night, Don took off to go to the store. At least, that was Zelda's story, and that was the last time she ever saw him."

"Wait," said Lance, "it gets better. You're not going to believe this."

John raised a flat palm to Lance, wanting the punch line for himself. "Zelda finally clued in and looked at the caller ID. The calls had come from Florida."

"Florida?" asked Clayton. "Why would someone from Florida be messing with Creech?"

"No one knew," said John, "at least not for a while. Then one day, like a week ago, I ran into Lutz just around the bandshell. He was headed for the Corner Café. We talked small for a bit and then I asked him what was up with Don Creech. Lutz said they found him in Missouri."

"Missouri?" said Clayton, leaning forward. "What was he doing?"

"Just driving," said John. "There was a missing persons call out for his plate and a state 'P' just pulled him over."

"Where was he going?" Clayton asked.

"Nowhere," Lance said simply. "He was running."

"From what?" asked Clayton.

"That's the thing. No one knew," John said, "at least not then. But then Lutz told me who the Florida number belonged to, the person who was calling Creech's house."

John paused. Clayton held his breath. Kat and Lance knew the answer already, but they too held their breath. It was still unbelievable.

"Paul Neumann," said John. "Paul freakin' Neumann."

Clayton's jaw hung open. "As in our Paul Neumann? Like, sneaking a bottle of Yukon Jack into Worlds of Fun on our senior trip Paul Neumann? Fearsome Five Paul Neumann?"

"The very one," said John.

"Why was he calling Creech?" Clayton asked.

Everyone shook their heads.

Kat said, "That's the question: What did Paul say to Creech that made him head for the hills?"

"Wow," Clayton said and stood up. He paced to the fence line and came back and sat down hard. "Holy shit! That's really weird. So where's Creech now?"

"Home," Kat said simply, producing another joint seemingly from thin air. This time she did the honors and lit it with a crackle and a puff of smoke.

"We don't know much about Paul anymore," said Lance. "All we know is that he lives in Florida. Miami, I think. He does a drag show down there. He hasn't been back in a long, long time."

Clayton: "A drag show? So he's still gay then?"

Kat: "What do you mean still gay?"

Clayton took the proffered joint.

John: "I don't think you switch back and forth on that kind of thing all that much."

Clayton: "Okay, fine, that was a dumb thing to say. But what the fuck? As you say, he hasn't been back to Dawson forever. So what does he want with Creech?"

They all shook their heads again.

"Creech might be home," said Lance, "but he's not the same. He wasn't in church on Sunday. He's always in church. Something is definitely up."

"Maybe Zelda Creech is not telling the truth," Clayton said, "Maybe they just got in a fight or something and Creech took off. Maybe it had nothing to do with Paul Neumann calling."

"We thought of that," said Kat, "and I guess Sheriff Lutz did, too. But Don and Zelda Creech don't fight, not like that. Besides, Lutz didn't tell us outright, but I got the feeling from him that Creech admitted that the call had set him off. He didn't say why, though."

Clayton's pocket had been vibrating for some time. He had been ignoring it. He was stoned and drunk, and if it was the cops calling about the wreck out on I-80, answering the phone would be a very bad idea. On the other hand it could be good news, news he needed to hear. Maybe it was Sylvia Blair calling to tell him that all had gone well with Lutz, or maybe it was his dad's lawyer wanting to know where to send the inheritance check.

Clayton fished his phone out of his pocket and looked at it:

STEINER, RANDY

It was Randy, his bass player. Randy had been the last person Clayton had seen before he left Hollywood for the trailer park in Colorado. Of all his band mates, Clayton liked Randy best. He was generally low drama, didn't care much about most things one way or another, and had a big heart, letting Clayton crash at his apartment, even offering up his bedroom after Clayton's own place had been destroyed by "robbers," as Clayton had put it.

Clayton figured he could call Randy back later, but John, Kat, and Lance were now onto local politics and wondering how John's dad, Hal Supernau was getting on as mayor.

What if Randy had news on the band? Kribdëth had been fighting with their little record label to make another album, and it hadn't been going well. Maybe Randy had good news.

Clayton slinked away to the fence line and re-dialed the number. Randy answered after one ring.

"What's up?" said Clayton.

"You motherfucker," Randy spat. Aside from slurring his words-- which was strange since Randy wasn't a drinker--he was seething with such anger that Clayton unconsciously held the phone away from his ear for safety.

"Sheesh. What did I do?" said Clayton. "You sound blasted, dude."

"I'm not fucking blasted, asshole," said Randy. "I'm just out of the hospital. My jaw is wired shut!"

In an instant Clayton knew why.

He went cold.

Randy went on, "Thanks to you, motherfucker. You didn't tell me, did you? You didn't tell me what you were involved in when I put you up!"

Clayton was spinning now. He needed to sit or he was sure he would fall over. He crouched on his haunches, thrusting a palm at the nearby fence to brace himself. "What happened?"

"I'll tell you what fucking happened," Randy continued, his words racing. It was obvious that he was doing his best to remain angry and not to burst into tears. "I'm on fucking Oxy now. I have to be because the pain is fucking unreal. And if I get hooked on this shit like you did, I'll fucking kill you!"

"You won't get hooked, Randy. You're smarter than I am. What happened?"

"Oh shut the fuck up, Clay! Don't polish my ass! Not now! Do you know how fucked I am? They gave me an antibiotic I have to drink with a straw! It made me sick and I threw up and almost choked to death! Did you know you can't throw up when your fucking jaw is wired shut! I had to pull my cheeks out like a fucking chipmunk with my fingers until the barf could drain through my teeth!"

"Please tell me what happened."

"Some Mexican guys came looking for you! Three of them! I bet that piece of shit, Bear, who hangs out around the studio all the time has something to do with this, doesn't he?"

"No," Clayton said numbly. "He knew about what I did, but he wasn't involved. He told me not to."

"Knew about what? What did you do? You didn't bother to tell anyone shit about what you've been up to! You said you would, and then you just took off in the morning! These fucking Cholos, gangbangers, whatever they are, muscled their way into my apartment and asked where you went! I told them you went to Colorado to see your dad, that he was sick. They wanted an address. I didn't have it so they proceeded to beat me like a fucking piñata!"

Clayton now had a hand planted on the grass between his legs.

Kat called out, "You going to barf, Clay? Please don't do it on the lawn! Have mercy!"

Clayton was vaguely aware of laughter and jeering coming from the picnic table, but he only waved them away with the flap of a hand.

Randy went on in Clayton's ear, getting closer to the phone, his voice dropping to a slurring, menacing whisper, "They say I'll be wearing this thing for six weeks! And it'll take nine months to heal completely. So do you mind telling me what the fuck you did to these Mexicans? You crashed at my house! Before you took me up on my fucking hospitality, you maybe should have warned me I would be a target! Don't you think that would have been in order? You giant fucking prick!"

"I didn't know..."

"You didn't know," Randy parroted icily.

Clayton could hear him pull away from the phone to spit out the extra saliva that was building up in his mouth, then he was close to the mouthpiece of the phone again, speaking in a slow and seismic cadence.

"You owe me, all of us, an explanation. We've all waited long enough. What happened? Why are these people after you and why are they after me?"

"I told you," said Clayton. "It was a bad drug deal that I never should have been involved in. The band wasn't doing that hot and I thought I could make a little extra coin. I had no idea it would go as badly as it did."

"Did you steal dope from these maniacs?"

"No, I told you. I got jacked. Randy, I'm sorry."

"So why were you slinging it? Where did you get it?"

"Look, I can't talk about it right now. I'm with people."

"You're fucking kidding me," Randy said. "Then why don't you leave your fucking people and tell me in detail why my jaw is wired shut."

"I will, Randy," Clayton pleaded, "I'm so sorry. Did the Mexicans say they were going to Colorado? Wait...never mind...forget that. Look, I'm very, very sorry. I will, I'll call you back, okay? I promise. Then I'll tell you everything. I just can't right at this exact moment."

"Fuck you, Clayton," said Randy, "Find yourself a new bass player and a new friend. And a fucking clue while you're at it, you piece of shit!"

Clayton opened his mouth to speak again, but the line had gone dead.

Then he threw up on the lawn.

Chapter 12

The Red Backpack

A car passed below her bedroom window and Laurie peered through the curtains. It wasn't Lance.

12:35, the bedside clock read.

Laurie had been back from her shift at the Rivoli Theater for half an hour, the babysitter had just left, and, roused by the changing of the guard, a bleary-eyed Luke had come into his parents' bedroom to crawl in with his mother. Laurie figured he had seen another zombie in his closet even though Lance had just bought him a Sponge Bob night light that Luke was convinced would ward them off effectively. But it turned out that Luke had only been worried about his daddy. So was Laurie, who had been spending her last moments before bed peeking through the curtains at the only car to come down the street since she had been home.

Luke didn't last long. He was now conked out peacefully, tucked into a little ball at his mother's hip, and Laurie was stroking his hair with one hand. With the other, she was sipping on her second glass of blush wine. The barbecue at Supernau's place was going on awfully long, and though she wanted to call over there, she didn't want to be a nag. Lance had said Clayton Briggle was in town and she knew those two would probably talk all night, whether she called or not, so she tried her best to relax.

The wine was good. She hardly ever drank in bed, especially wine--it would totally ruin the sheets if she spilled any--but tonight had been busy at the theater. It had been one of those Fast and Furious movies, and the teenagers had come in droves with their exhausting energy flooding the theater's tiny lobby as they jostled for candy and popcorn, the noise level piquing every nerve she had.

Laurie figured she must have fallen asleep, the wine glass thankfully making it to the safety of the nightstand, when she opened her eyes at a sound coming from below the bedroom window. It was Lance getting out of the cab of his pickup and slamming the door.

The television was still running on the bedroom wall. Fumbling for the remote, she flicked it off. Was he singing? Yep, he was singing, but what she couldn't tell. He certainly wasn't singing well. He was drunk, obviously. She listened and heard him come into the entry hall downstairs; then came a thud, a pretty big thud, as he dropped something or knocked something over. She would have called out, but the odds were that she wouldn't have been heard and Luke would wake up for nothing.

She heard his footsteps on the hall tiles below. At least he was still on his feet. He was fine. Now she could tell what he was singing: "The Nebraska Fight Song": "There is no place like Nebraska! Dear old Nebraska U! Where the girls are the fairest, the boys are the squarest of any old place that I knew!"

Another thud; this one sounded like it came from the kitchen, but this thud wasn't as big as the last one. It was a dull thud at first, but then it repeated, increasing in tempo. He had dropped a plastic cup and it was hopping across the kitchen linoleum. She heard the water run as he sang, "There is no place like Nebraska. Where they're all true blue! We'll all stick together in all kinds of weather for..."

He was huffing his way up the stairs now, averaging about one word per step.

"...dear

...old

...Nebra

...ska"

"Hey, babe," said Lance, appearing in the threshold of the bedroom doorway, leaning on the jamb for dear life.

"Had enough to drink, I see," said Laurie, "and something involving cheddar cheese," she added, gesturing to his shirt front.

"Is that wine?" Lance asked, brightening.

Laurie tucked the glass demurely to her side.

"Give me some," said Lance.

"I think you've had quite enough," Laurie said tartly.

Luke stirred at his mother's side. He rolled over, his eyes fluttering open. "Daddy?"

"Hey, tiger," said Lance, shuffling forward. "Want me to put you to bed?"

Luke said nothing, staring groggily at his father as if the man were an apparition.

"I'll do it," said Laurie. In his present condition, Laurie was pretty sure Lance would drop the boy. She swallowed the last bit of wine in her glass, set it on her end table, and gathered Luke in her arms. With a grunt, she said, "Mommy isn't going to be able to deadlift you for too much longer. You're getting to be a big boy."

"I'm big," Luke agreed, still a little bleary from sleep. He wrapped his arms around her neck as she lifted him and together they went to his room. She tucked him in, kissed his forehead, and laid his stuffed rabbit beside him.

When she returned, Lance had his shirt off and was unbuckling his jeans, "The Nebraska Fight Song" now reduced to an indiscernible mutter. After battling for a moment with his button fly, he let the jeans hit the floor in a chink of keys and loose change. One leg was stuck in the denim and as he kicked himself free of its hold he fell sideways, sitting down hard on the bed. He didn't move after that, he only groaned. He lay in his tighty-whities, one leg still planted on the floor.

Standing in the doorway, Laurie just shook her head. "I can't believe you drove home like this. I hope you didn't take Main Street."

Lance's only answer to this was labored breathing into their mattress which sounded to Laurie a lot like Darth Vader might sound on a treadmill.

Laurie sighed, walked around to his side of the bed, hoisted his leg onto the mattress and assessed the situation. He was still partially on her side of the bed. She shoved him, trying her best to straighten him out.

Who was she kidding? Even if she could tug his 220 pounds into place, she knew he was going to snore like a chainsaw all night. She would never get any sleep. It was either the third bedroom for her tonight or a night of fruitlessly socking him in the arm for a blessed moment of silence. Aborting her efforts, she backed away from him and stumbled over his piled jeans. Peevishly, she reached for them and was about to throw them on the chair when she felt the bulge of keys in the front pocket.

She froze, her breath catching.

She squeezed the keys through the jean's fabric and looked at her husband. He was breathing hard and not moving.

Those were not the house keys she had her hand on. Even through the denim she could tell that much. The house keys had a bunch of keys on the ring. But beneath her fingers she could feel only two keys on a ring. They were the keys to his truck.

She figured one for the truck and one for the truck's toolbox, and they were right beneath her hand now, unattended.

(the red backpack)

She could get to it now.

When she had asked Lance what that red backpack was that he kept under the seat of his truck and where it had come from Lance had sounded convincing enough. He had told her that it was nothing. "Just some tools," he had said. But that didn't ring true for her. There was a tool box in the bed of the truck. Could it not fit whatever tools were in the red backpack? And where did the red backpack come from? She never asked him that specifically because it sounded like a paranoid and nosy question. Was he not allowed to buy a backpack if he needed one? After all, it wasn't an extravagant purchase that needed to go through committee. Still, there was something about it that had always struck her as odd. It had not been there and then it had been. One day she had just noticed it stuffed under the seat.

It wouldn't have alarmed her as much if Lance had not become obsessed with his truck keys. Never once had he left them on the pegged key holder by the front door. He kept them close at all times. For weeks after he had gone to bed Laurie had even checked the pockets of his clothes and could not find them. That meant he hid them. He actually hid the keys to his truck. It had started to make her feel crazy. Why would he do that? If she brought it up he would surely hit the roof.

One night, emboldened by wine, she had come very close to asking him about it. It had been the day of the butt dial, the day when he was talking on some other phone and obviously in his truck. But she had stopped herself. If she were to ask, and Lance was up to something, it would alert him to her interest in the matter and assure her that she would never get to the bottom of whatever it was that her intuition was screaming at her to solve.

Something bad was in the red backpack, something he was going to great lengths to make sure she never saw.

But Lance was passed out now and the only thing separating her from the keys to the truck was a thin, worn layer of denim.

Sure enough, Lance's heavy breathing had become long, grating snores.

Slowly, with thumb and forefinger, Laurie slid her hand into the pocket of Lance's jeans and pulled out the keys, being careful not to allow them to jingle. She stood, rounded the bed and slipped her feet into her slippers.

Was she really going to do this? Was she really going to spy on him?

The bedroom window was open. The truck was directly under the window. If she did go to the truck, as quiet as it was on the street below, she could probably hear Lance snoring from the driveway. She could monitor him.

She was forgetting to breathe. She let her breath out down the front of her night shirt, turned and walked out of the bedroom and down the stairs.

So that's what that thud had been. Lance had knocked over the umbrella stand. Laurie's adopted father had willed them the19th century umbrella stand which had come from London. Now Lance had knocked it over to the tile floor. With a grimace, she inspected it as she righted it. It looked fine.

She pricked up her ears. Had that been a creak from upstairs? She held her breath and waited. Like any old thing, the house was full of petulant little creaks, and Laurie knew that tonight they would give her heart more than a few squeezes.

She stepped over to the bottom of the stairwell and listened. Faintly, she could hear Lance snoring. She hurried to the front door and opened it softly, her heart racing.

She stepped onto the porch and pulled the door closed, leaving it unlatched. A June bug ricocheted off of her cheek. Laurie yelped, stifling herself with a hand across her mouth. The bug thumped off of the faux iron casing of the porch light, left its pale yellow glow, and buzzed away mindlessly into the night.

The temperature outside was surreal: it was like no temperature at all, like how it had been in that tornado's eye when she was a little girl, curled up in a bathtub with the wind howling like demons beyond the walls. She looked down the street both ways and saw nothing. No one was up, no one around. She figured it must be close to one o'clock in the morning now.

The cement walkway went out to the street, but it also doglegged to the right, to the garage. She had been right, she could hear Lance snoring from above--not as well as she thought she would have been able to--but enough. It was hard to hear anything with her heartbeat thudding in her ears and she was lightheaded from its runaway tattoo. She was also lightheaded from the wine, she supposed, but then again, there would be no way in hell she would be doing this without its convincing influence.

She looked up at the window. She had left the bedside lamp on. Its light cast a ghostly swatch of shadow across the popcorn face of the ceiling. She should have turned it off. If he awoke in the dark, he would have been less likely to move or call out. Though with all of that beer in him, he was going to have to pee eventually; it was only a matter of time.

She had to move quickly.

Laurie peered into the truck. There it was. The red backpack. As it always was, tucked under the seat, its vinyl surface crimson and as seemingly pernicious as the belly of a black widow. For good measure, she listened one more time for any movement upstairs, trying to still her runaway breath.

He was still snoring. It was faint, but she could hear it.

With a trembling hand, she slid the key into the lock of the driver's side door. It clicked open. To her ears, the tumbler had sounded as loud as a firecracker. She lunged for the bag. It was deeply wedged under the seat and it took her a moment to get it clear; one of the backpack's straps caught on part of the seat's metal undercarriage. Leaving the truck door open, she headed for the porch to unpack the bag.

As she made her way around the front of the truck she began to tremble even more. The backpack was not heavy. It had something in it, but it certainly didn't contain tools like Lance had told her. It weighed almost nothing.

She knelt beside the porch and pressed the button that easily allowed the backpack's binding drawstrings to pass through the eyelet of the clasp. When she expanded the opening with her hands she saw that there were only three items in the bottom of the bag, all clearly visible: a cell phone, a pair of binoculars and a single, white, lumpy tube sock.

She braced herself, blowing out her breath in a raspy shudder, as a flurry of prayers fluttered through her fevered mind. She picked up the sock first. It was stuffed with something. She fished her hand into it and inverted it onto the porch.

It was full of condoms.

Her mouth went dry. She had been crouched on her haunches before the porch step so as not to get her pajamas dirty, but now she just fell to the side and sat down hard on the warm cement walk before the step. Her breath now came quickly, as if she had just run up a flight of stairs, her legs stretched out before her, her slippered feet sawing at the ground in spasms of anguish.

As if in a dream, she took the binoculars out of the bag and, uncomprehendingly, turned them over in her hands. They were a small pair, the kind one might use for bird watching.

Next, she took out the cell phone. It was grey. It felt cheap in her hands. She had never seen it before. She had been right, there had been a phantom phone all along and this was it, the one she had described to Ruby Wegner as the Bat Phone. So she had not been crazy.

This was the phone Lance had been talking into when he had butt dialed her. She turned it on and the screen came to life:

ALERT! YOU HAVE 4 MINS. 33 SECONDS LEFT!

A pre-paid phone. Disposable.

Now she was shaking so badly she couldn't hold the screen steady enough to read it, and even if she could, the screen was refracting into a kaleidoscope of sickly green from her tears.

She brushed her hair from her wet and sticky eyes and scrolled to the phone's "inbox": there was only one message and it was from someone named Monica. As far as Laurie knew--and she knew just about everyone in town--there was no one named Monica in Dawson.

The message read:

"That was fun. Let's do it again soon."

It had been sent two days ago.

She scrolled to "Trash": there was nothing.

She scrolled to "Sent": there were several sent items. All of them were ads that appeared to have been placed on a website called Backpage.com. They were all very similar, but the most recent one featured two pictures, both of them thumbnails. The first was of a man with no shirt and no face. The second was of a woman Laurie had never seen before.

Unlike the man--who Laurie already knew to be Lance by his body and his hair--the woman's face had not been erased into an oval by some photo editor. She was a brunette with long hair and she smiled brazenly into the camera, recumbent on a brown couch and lit obliquely with seedy light. She was dressed in a pink, frilly teddy and wore black, six-inch heels, one foot kicked up over the couch's arm. There was a whorish, mischievous twinkle in her eyes above her coy pout.

The picture of Lance was from head to toe. His face had been erased to protect his identity, a white ghostly circle under his hair. He was shirtless, and his arms were crossed over his stomach. He wore tight jeans and light brown work boots.

"I gave you those boots for Christmas," Laurie whispered, tears streaming down her face. She began to rock herself as she sat there in her pajamas in the pool of pale yellow light from the porch's bulb.

He's covering his stomach in the picture, she thought, because he has a belly. I've been trying to get him to eat right. I make him turkey sandwiches to take to work with whole wheat bread and low-fat mayonnaise and I don't think he eats them. I make them for him...

"Because I love you," she told the faceless picture.

Her entire life seemed like a pantomime now, a perverse construct of lies. Her sobs turned to moans. Still rocking herself, she dared to look back at the phone. She knew the worst of it was yet to come. She still hadn't read the ad. She didn't want to read the ad. Why was there an ad? Why couldn't she walk away from this, why couldn't she have left this alone.

Gripping the phone with both hands between her knees to keep it steady, she read on:

Backpage.com>nebraska adult entertainment>nebraska escorts

Want to Watch a Sexy Couple? Want to Join? Fantasies come True! – 42

Posted June 25, 2015, 11:32 AM

We are a sexy next door type couple that is testing the waters of adult gigs. We are available to play out a voyeuristic fantasy for you. WE are both educated and pictures are 100% real! She is 38, 5'4", smooth, HOT. He is 42, 5'11" 195 muscular and hairy. We have a cozy place located in Lincoln near airport, but we can also come to you. Let's have an Adventure!

Serious Ladies and Gentlemen ONLY!

Available TODAY ONLY

IN & OUT Calls available

*82.402.555.9962

Poster's age: 42

Location: Lancaster County

Post ID: 6663247

"You're not 42," Laurie said. "You weigh more than 195 pounds."

She didn't know why it mattered that he lied on the ad. He lied about everything. He had been lying the whole time, probably through their entire marriage. She slapped a hand onto the warm cement walk, turned her head, and threw up into her row of ornamental bushes. It was the hot, acid sick of regurgitated wine and it burned her throat. Her eyes burned with tears. Her heart burned with anger and sadness and betrayal. The puke would probably kill her azaleas, but she didn't care. Her home was dead now anyway. Everything was dead now.

That's Monica, she thought, turning back to look at the screen, it has to be, and the phone number at the bottom of the ad? It's probably the number to this piece of shit phone she was holding in her hand, about to crush into powder.

She got to her knees, and then she got to her feet. Her legs shook. She was unsteady, but she gathered up the tube sock full of rubbers, the phone, and the binoculars.

A voyeuristic fantasy, she thought. Isn't that what the ad said? Was that what the binoculars were for? He passed them along to his trick so they could watch him and this Monica bitch fuck?

Laurie had known nothing about this kink. She never would have guessed it. Where had it come from, she wondered. He was an elder at the church, for chrissake. This would ruin him, ruin her.

She was about to stuff the binoculars back into the bag when she saw, at the bottom, a pair of white pills that caught the porch light. They were loose and had fallen into the deepest crevice of the bag's seam. She hadn't seen them before. She pulled one out and looked at it. She couldn't recognize it from her own medicine cabinet. There was something written on the pill, a word, or maybe it was numbers, she couldn't tell. She had needed reading glasses for a while, and the porch light wasn't very bright, and her vision was still swimming in tears.

She stumbled up the porch step, her legs still weak, and went inside. Then she remembered that she had left the truck open, wide open. She walked back to it and shut its door as gently as possible. She didn't bother to relock it. Although there was a part of her at this moment that didn't care if Lance ever woke up again, she didn't want him up just yet. She had to prove several things to herself first. If she was right, she wouldn't be here when he woke up.

Fuck no, she wouldn't be.

First, she set the backpack by her computer in the little office off of the kitchen, went back upstairs and entered her bedroom, their bedroom, and saw her husband still passed out in his underwear and snoring deeply. Fresh tears welled up in her eyes and tracked down her cheeks as she stood there in the glow of the bedside lamp. Her chest heaved, and she stood there and cried silently for some time before she could stop her mind from swirling. Finally, she pressed her lips tight, swept a blonde lock out of her face and, with a restorative sniff, she switched off the light on the end table. Then she replaced the keys in his jeans pocket before going back downstairs.

Back in her office, she pulled the cell phone out of the bag, turned it back on, and wrote down the phone number that appeared in the ad. She put the cell phone under the pillow of her office chair, knelt down beside it, and, using her land line beside her desk, called the number she had scratched onto her notepad.

The pre-paid phone rang.

She gritted her teeth. She was not going to cry again. She had work to do. Even though that ring had just heralded the destruction of her marriage, she would not cry again, goddammit, not now.

She looked through the eight other ads in the disposable phone's "sent" folder. They were all very similar, all using the same words only in a different order, words like "sexy couple" and "fantasy" and "voyeurism."

Laurie noticed that none of the ads went back more than a month; no more than three weeks to be exact.

Just about when Lance bought that power washer from that kid, Laurie thought.

She scanned the ads carefully, all business now, and noticed a discrepancy. It was on one of the earlier ads in the file, dated May 30th. The contact phone number was different: still a 402 area code, but different than that of Lance's disposable cell phone.

She looked at the clock on her desk.

1:22 a.m.

Like I give a shit what time it is, she thought.

She picked up her land line and dialed the number, knowing her caller ID would show as VANDERBOOM, but whoever was going to answer...

(Monica)

...probably wouldn't know who Lance Vanderboom was. Surely, Lance had given her a false name, but there was a good chance that the bitch would be asleep and caught off guard she might answer anyway.

Adrenaline jacked into Laurie's nerves as if she had touched a live wire. She gripped the phone with white knuckles. It rang. It rang four times.

And then...

"Hello?"

It was a woman's voice, a woman who had obviously been asleep seconds ago.

Laurie's tongue was thick, her mouth dry. She couldn't speak.

"Hello?" the woman at the other end said again, her tone now suspicious.

"Stay away from my husband, you fucking whore," Laurie hissed and hung up.

For a moment, Laurie just sat riding the rush of adrenaline, covered in sweat. She was out of breath and clutching the phone receiver as if she was holding on for her life, holding on while the mad world around her spun out of control.

Regaining herself, she rummaged for the pills at the bottom of the backpack. She opened the top drawer of her desk and found the little flip magnifier she kept there and trained it on the pill's face. It wasn't words, it wasn't a number. It was a symbol.

Laurie tilted the magnifier to let in the light from the desk lamp. Yep, it was a symbol. It appeared to be the sign for infinity, like a figure 8 crushed into elliptical loops.

Laurie fired up her computer and waited for it to boot up, the hard drive grinding away as she sat tensed, willing the old piece of crap to hurry up. After four minutes, she was finally able to start up her browser and begin a search, a search that turned out not to be an easy one. A pill with an infinity symbol didn't come up, at least not at first. Then, several pages deep, on one particular phrasing, she got a hit. It was an entry at Yahoo Answers.

The question had been posed a year ago:

"I need help identifying a yellow round pill," wrote the author, "with a symbol on it that kind of looks like an infinity sign, or a Pacman but it's skinnier. I have no idea what it is. If you could send me a picture that would be amazing. Thanks!"

Further down the page was the "Best Answer" as voted on by users:

"If you are unsure what the pill is, and you can read any type of imprinting on the pill, use the pill identification tool found at..."

Following was a URL, and Laurie clicked on the hyperlink provided to reveal a site featuring a search box that helped match key words to particular medications.

She typed: "infinity symbol."

Nothing.

She typed: "infinity."

One search result: MDMA, Ecstasy, place of origin: St. Louis, Missouri.

Laurie slumped back into her office chair.

"Who are you...?" she said to nobody, the words leaking from her as if from a hole in her heart. "Who are you...?"

She didn't want to cry again. She feared that if she did, she might just cry forever. She had to be strong; she had to be strong for Luke.

But as she tried to hold back her tears, they erupted from her in a seizure of sorrow and disillusionment, and in that wretched flush she was reduced to a slumping and inconsolable ragdoll of a woman, alone in her office, alone in the world.

"Who are you?" she said again, looking through the door of her little office to the foot of the darkened staircase that led to her husband. "I don't even know who you are anymore..."

Chapter 13

The Last Day of How It Used to Be

For more than a hundred years, since 1868, the town of Dawson has had the reputation for throwing a well-organized, folksy and wholly sincere Independence Day party. Before the automobile came into general use, special trains were run to bring people to the Fourth of July bash, and since then, the celebration's reputation has only grown.

In 1973, Governor J. James Exon issued a proclamation designating Dawson "Nebraska's Official 4th of July City"; in 1976, the city was chosen to host Nebraska's July 4 celebration for the United States Bicentennial, and in 1979, a resolution in the U.S. Congress named Dawson "America's Official Fourth of July City--Small Town USA," sealing its place on the Midwest tourist map so much so that recent attendance has been estimated at over 40,000--close to seven times the town's population,.

So, as John Supernau gazed out of the window of the Corner Café the morning of July 4th, he sipped his coffee and quailed at thoughts of the impending crowds.

It had been two days since the barbecue in his backyard. During the intervening time, John and his wife and Clayton caught up with each other even further. And when the hour drew John and Kat to work, Flynn took over as host, showing Clayton the gaming machine his parents referred to as "the time vampire" and what the boy just called his PlayStation. Reportedly, the two had burned hours in the dark with nothing but the click of their controllers and the occasional victory cry to punctuate their day.

"Here they come," said Peggy Jones from behind the counter of the Corner Café.

John watched the town square through the café curtains. The Rotary, the Kiwanis, the Chamber of Commerce, Eagle Club and nearly every other town delegation were erecting craft booths and rolling food carts into place in the shadow of the bandshell.

But John knew it wasn't only the crowds that would vex him this Independence Day. It was the phone call he had received this morning that was likely to consume him. Of all people to hear from on the morning of the 4th, John certainly hadn't expected it to be his estranged friend from high school, Paul Neumann.

"I always forget the time change," Paul had said. "I can call back."

"No, no," John had insisted, "I'm up. I went to the anvil firing this morning."

"They still do that at that ungodly hour?" Paul had asked. "I think all of the time growing up I only went to that once. Couldn't get up. Still, there's nothing like the 4th in Dawson. I don't miss a lot about that town, but that I miss.""

"I'm surprised to hear from you, Neumann. It's been a while. How is Miami treating you?"

"Hot," Paul had said, "and sticky! Just like Dawson. But the men are way hotter."

"And stickier?" John had ventured.

"Supes!" Paul had gasped chastely, adding with a Southern accent: "Well...I never!"

"Oh, I bet you have," John shot back.

Paul had giggled, put a hand over the phone and, with a flourish of misogynistic epithets, hushed a small dog yapping in the background.

"So, guess what?" John had said, "Clayton's in town. His dad died. You remember Foster Briggle, right? He took us all to the lake a few times."

"I remember. That's too bad. Were they close?"

"No, not really. But Clay drove to Colorado to be with him anyway, and when Foster died, Clay just decided to come by. He wishes you were here."

"He does?" Paul had said, farcically smitten. "An old queen like me? Isn't he a big ol' butch, heavy metal dude now? I doubt he would approve of me prancing around in gowns."

"Don't be a dumbass, Paul. You're Fearsome Five...always. He loves you. I showed him a pic of you at one of your drag shows and he thought you were really good. He was really impressed."

"Fearsome five..." Paul laughed, trailing off wistfully.

Paul Neumann had always had an effeminate and delicate voice, but when he spoke again, he dropped the campiness from his voice completely and changed to a tone of confidentiality. "John, I'm calling you because I have something to tell you. I wanted to tell you first, before you found out from someone else. I'm the one who called Principal Creech. I guess he was missing for a while? I didn't have anything to do with that. I just called him...well, threatened him."

"We heard," John said.

"You're kidding? I should have known. You can't keep anything a secret in that town."

"We know you called," said John, "but we don't know what you said that made Creech take off."

"Where did he take off to?" Paul asked.

"The cops picked him up in Missouri," said John, "just driving around in his car. They were looking for his plate since he had been reported missing. Bob Lutz told me that much, but he didn't tell me what you said that made him freak out. It must have been pretty bad, whatever it was you said, because Creech missed graduation at St. Mark."

There had been a long pause after that. At the time, John had figured it was due to Paul taking in the gravity of Don Creech being spooked enough by whatever Paul had said to actually leave town and miss graduation at the school he presided over. But in retrospect, and knowing what he knew now, John thought it had been more than that. He suspected that in that pause, Paul had been savoring a hard won catharsis.

"It's time this shit saw some light," Paul had gone on to say, "I'm going to nail that fucker to a wall, John. I'm suing him. And I'm not alone. I can't tell you who else is signing the complaint; she'll have to tell you if she wants to. 'Course, I'm sure everyone in Dawson will find out soon enough--the way things get around."

"For what?" John had asked. "Suing him for what?"

"He molested me, Supes," Paul had said, "when I was only a kid."

John remembered not being able to make sense of Paul's words, as if they had been spoken in a foreign tongue.

"And I'm not alone," Paul went on. "He molested a friend of mine, too. You knew her. And I'm pretty sure he molested a lot more of us."

"Paul...are you sure?"

"What do you mean 'am I sure'?"

"Sorry...I just..." John faltered as his mind spun.

Silence bloomed again and, looking back, John figured Paul must have been bracing for many things in the stillness that followed.

John knew Don Creech very well. Flynn went to Don Creech's school. John and Kat went to Don Creech's fundraising parties for the school. There was no way that Paul could have known just how tight John Supernau had become with the longtime principal of St. Mark through the many years since Paul had left. As a result, the ensuing moments of silence were as heavily charged as a pile of thunderclouds.

But eventually, John was able to take a deep breath and say, "Tell me what happened, Paul."

What Paul described made the coffee sitting in John's stomach turn to battery acid. And when Paul was done, John sat processing what he had heard. The details of Paul's story were horrible. But they were also so intricate and so plausible, that as much as John wanted to dismiss the allegation as a money grab by someone who no longer had a stake in life in Dawson, he couldn't.

He just couldn't.

"You mentioned someone else," said John, "someone else who was joining you in this suit. Who?"

"I shouldn't say," Paul had said. "It would be up to her to do that."

"Do you think..." John had ventured, "--and I'm just curious about this--that what happened to you has something to do with you being gay?"

"Of course not," Paul had snapped. "That's not how it works. I'm not gay because I'm mentally scarred. I was gay from as early as I could remember. No, if anything, he targeted me because I was gay. He figured I would be...receptive. That's how these predators work, John. Either that or they sniff around until they find the baby birds with broken wings. As for the other plaintiff, I think she was chosen because her parents were notorious alkies with zero influence in Dawson and even less credibility. Oh fuck it, it was Becky Krauss. Becky Krauss is the other plaintiff. You're going to find out anyway. Who cares at this point? The complaint is being filed after the holiday weekend. It will be public record then anyway."

"Becky Krauss?" In his mind, John had to do some considerable digging through time to match the name with a face. Yeah, he remembered her. Becky had been a meek, freckle-faced girl who always wore long-hemmed pale dresses and who, when sitting in class, would twist her hair in thought, using her pencil like a tourniquet. "Wow. Becky Krauss. Yeah, I remember her. She flew under the radar, that's for sure. God, I barely remember her. I do remember the Krausses were pretty poor. They lived over by the dike, right? They were very religious, too, I remember. They must have spent every cent they had to send Becky to St. Mark. Where is she now? She blew town before graduation. I think she left junior year."

Paul had told him that Becky had also ended up in Miami, and that he had run into her years ago at a club in South Beach, and that, yes, she had "blown town" after refusing to go to school anymore for reasons only she had known at the time but that would soon be clear to all.

Paul also said that he and Becky started comparing notes after Paul had a breakthrough with his psychologist after years of therapy. Their notes on Don Creech and what he had done had matched so well that they had both decided it was time to act.

"What about you, John?" Paul asked. "Did Creech ever touch you?"

"Never," John had replied. "Not a thing."

"Figures," Paul had said, "Even back then your dad was on the city council and your family was always a pretty big deal. He wouldn't have dared."

"Why now?" John asked. "Why bring this up now? Why not a long time ago?"

"You bury this stuff, Supe. You really do. You bury it because you have to, to move on, to go forward, you just do."

"Wow..." John had said aloud, his mind still flailing, and again, there was nothing left to say, both of them hundreds of miles away from each other, both quietly railing against the death of another piece of their innocence, fearing that as they silently took inventory of such, there might not be enough pieces left to spare.

Paul eventually went on to explain how he had called St. Mark's administrators and had been ignored, how he had called the Missouri Synod offices in St. Louis and had been ignored, and how he had finally gone after Creech himself, getting his home number through ingenuity and perseverance. But John had stopped listening. If this was all true, and if Paul's assumption that the abuse must have gone far beyond just he and Becky also turned out to be true, then what it meant for Dawson was nothing short of devastating.

"So did you go to the firing of the anvil this morning, John?"

It was Peggy Jones from behind the café's counter.

John blinked hard, realizing he had been lost in thought, playing that phone call over and over in his head while staring out of the cafe's window.

"Sure did," John managed, swiveling stiffly to face Peggy.

"What about Kat?" Peggy asked.

"Are you kidding? She wouldn't get up that early if Paul Revere himself was lighting the charge. Neither would Flynn."

John wondered why he always got up at 6:30 and went by himself. He always had. He hadn't missed the firing of the anvil in years.

He supposed he could just chalk it up to pride in his town, and in spite of his grumblings about the crowds that were just starting to show up through the window, he wouldn't want "America's Official Fourth of July City--Small Town USA" to be anywhere else but here.

So at a quarter to seven in the morning he had driven out to the staging field. The call from Paul Neumann had come in almost on cue; just a minute or so after the black powder charge had lifted the steel anvil into the air to a round of rousing applause by the circle of intrepid early birds. John had melted away from the crowd to the tall grass at the edge of the field to take the call in the shade of a stand of hickory trees.

After the call, he immediately rang Kat. There had been no answer. He called Clayton, though he figured he would still be asleep. He tried Lance, who also hadn't answered. Then, with a pang in his heart, he called his son, his son who had just finished seventh grade under Don Creech's watch.

Panic wormed into his guts as Flynn's phone rang and rang. John started walking briskly to his car, then he started running to it.

Flynn answered, "Dad? What do you want? I'm sleeping. Why are you blowing me up at seven in the morning?""

"Where's your mother?"

"In the shower. Why? What's going..."

"Listen to me, Flynn," John fumbled his keys from his pocket and started the car. "I'm on my way home, and when I get there, we need to have a talk."

"Oh no," said Flynn, "You're going to teach me about vaginas on the 4th of July? Can we put this off until, like, forever? I already know."

"It's not that talk, Flynn. I need you to be serious."

"Well, I'm not on drugs. Is it that talk? Because, if it is, then I should probably mention that I found a roach in the backyard and it wasn't mine. Guess you and mom had a pretty good time at that barbecue?"

"You think you're pretty smart, huh?" John had said, throwing the car into reverse with a small crunch from the transmission. "Well, it's not that talk either. I'll be there in three minutes. I'm not having this conversation over the phone."

Flynn was up, not looking very happy, and eating a bowl of Honey Nut Cheerios at the breakfast table in his boxers when John came in through the garage. Flynn dropped his spoon in the milk, "What's going on, Dad? You're kinda freaking me out."

"I don't want to freak you out," John had told the boy, "but I have to ask you something serious and I want you to give me an honest answer, even if it's hard for you, okay? It's very important."

Flynn had just stared at his father, all bed-head and red-rimmed eyes. He'd obviously been picking at the zit on his forehead.

"And don't pick at that zit anymore," his father said, "leave it alone."

"You rushed back home to talk about my zit?" Flynn had said, adding despondently, "Why does everyone want to talk about my zit so bad..."

"Flynn, has anyone ever touched you inappropriately at school? And what I mean by that is: has one of your teachers or anyone else in a position of authority at St. Mark ever touched you?"

John watched his son closely. He knew it was possible that Flynn would not admit to such a thing on the first try, and he looked for the slightest twitch from Flynn's eye, the slightest flush in his cheeks. But what had happened next John had not anticipated.

Flynn through back his head and laughed.

"I'm serious, Flynn."

"I can tell," Flynn said, his giggles percolating beneath every word. "You're like super, super serious about it."

"Listen," John tried again, "did Principal Creech do anything inappropriate with you, I mean, sexually. Did he touch you? Did he make you touch him?"

"Creech?!" Flynn cried, and he slapped the table, doubled over in his chair with a fresh gale of laughter. "That is so gross!"

"So, no?"

"Dad!" No! Oh my God!"

John kept watching his son, but Flynn's eyes only sparkled back at him with genuine mirth.

That was when Clayton had appeared in the kitchen doorway, "Looks like I missed a good joke. Is it for public consumption by any chance?"

John told Clayton that it certainly would be soon, but that it was no joke. And when Kat was finally dressed and in the kitchen, he told all of them everything he had just heard from Paul in graphic detail. He thought it would be best if they all found out now rather than later through bits and pieces of gossip.

"Paul said the complaint would be filed after the holiday was over," John had told them. "Today is Saturday, so Monday at the earliest. I wanted to tell you myself. I'm sick about it. I don't think Dawson is going to be the same after this, at least not for a long time."

At some point, as he sat in the Corner Café, recalling all of this, the square beyond the window had filled with tourists, and members of the VFW brass band were unloading their shiny instruments on the bandshell stage.

Looking down at his puddle of coffee, he knew his stomach would not accept any more of it. He stood to leave.

At the counter, Peggy Jones finished polishing the glass dome covering her lemon cake and said, "Going so soon?"

John said he was, and told her things were about to get crazy around here. He didn't know if she heard him. A crush of strangers had just approached the counter, but John supposed that was just as well. He wished more than anything, as the generators in the square beyond the café's glass began to hum to life beside the barbecue and funnel cake trucks, that he had simply been talking about Independence Day.

One thought kept looping through his mind as he left the café and entered the day's thickening air on Main Street, the little bell on the café's door tinkling behind him as it had since he was a child: Today was it. Today was the last day of how it used to be.

#

Ruby Wegner stood in her big brother's bedroom, staring at the image that had been drawn on Scotty's wall with her lipstick, the four stick figures holding hands. Scotty watched from the edge of his bed.

"I'm going out today," Ruby said, massaging her cheeks with one hand and evaluating the drawing like one might at an art gallery. She liked it. Ever since it had been drawn days ago, she had noticed its calming effect on her, as if it had been graven directly onto her wounded heart.

"I'm glad you like it," Scotty said. "When you first saw it I wasn't too sure. You got mad at me. So where are you going."

"Huh?"

"You said you were going out today. Where are you going?"

"Out," Ruby said. "I have no classes today. I skipped my morning run, too. I guess I'm just feeling like I need to be out." She turned to face Scotty. "I'm really going to try and enjoy the 4th of July for once. I wish you could, too."

"Yeah, but I can't."

Ruby turned back to the wall, her mind reaching for the image again, face slack and eyes glazed, until a new thought crowded her mind and she turned to her brother. "Your 48th birthday is only two weeks from now."

"I don't celebrate my birthdays anymore," Scotty said didactically. "You know that, Rubes."

"Of course I know that," Ruby said, turning on him, "Of course I know that. It doesn't mean I have to like it, does it?"

Scotty only turned his head to look out the window. He changed the subject. "The cicadas are starting up again. Is it hot out there?"

"Why don't you go see for yourself instead of moping around here all the time?"

Scotty skewered her with a reproachful glance.

Undaunted, Ruby waved the rolled-up flyer in her hand, "Well, just in case you're interested in what's going on outside of these walls..." She unrolled the flyer and read from it: "There's an exhibition baseball game at the St. Mark ball field between the Wahoo Plowboys and the

Dawson Locomotives. At the Civic Center there's an exhibit called 'Remembering Our Fallen,' including the photos of more than 100 men and women from Nebraska and Western Iowa who have been killed in Iraq or Afghanistan. Oh and there's a free aerobatics show at the municipal airport. And this sounds good: a strength competition for men and women that involves carrying railroad ties and lifting the back end of a car on the grounds of the Middle School. And of course, the big fireworks show."

Ruby rolled the flyer back up with finality and a raised eyebrow.

"I can see the fireworks from here," Scotty muttered.

"Barely," Ruby said, and left the room.

"Have fun, Ruby," Scotty called after her, "Have fun for me."

Ruby poked her head back into his room.

Scotty was smiling. It didn't happen often, but when he did smile, its radiance always stunned Ruby afresh. It was like fuel to her. She would do better with her classes. She would be chattier than usual each morning at the Corner Café. She would be happier in every way.

She sighed and smiled back at him, "Thank you," she said.

Light on her feet now, Ruby headed downstairs. Halfway down the staircase she heard a sound behind her. She turned. Scotty was following her.

"What? Did you change your mind" she asked hopefully. "Are you coming with me?"

"No. I just want to sit down here for a while," he replied.

As they reached the ground floor, Scotty rounded the living room couch and sat before the fireplace mantel with its picture of their mother and the solar-powered helicopter that their father once piloted among the trees in a far away garden in Chicago. "I want to sit right here," he said. "I like it here. I'd like to sit here forever."

"I know you do, Scotty," said Ruby, her hand on the handle of the front door. "I know."

Scotty craned his neck around. He was still smiling. "Don't worry about me so much, Ruby. Go have fun. I love you."

A single, plump tear tracked its way down Ruby's cheek. "I love you, too. Very much."

#

Clayton Briggle and the Supernau clan made their way through the gauntlet of craft booths along Dawson Street. At the bandshell, the public school junior high band was honking out patriotic tunes on their tubas and horns. Along the street, classic cars were lined up to be judged.

"There's Ruby Wegner," Clayton said to John, pointing at the woman with the ponytail browsing a jewelry booth, "I'm going to go say hello."

Clayton positioned himself on the other side of a row of hanging bead necklaces and spread them apart when Ruby browsed her way by. "Boo!"

"Clayton?" Ruby gasped. "John told me you were coming to town. Oh my god! How are you?"

"Okay," Clayton said, "I guess."

"Sorry about your father," Ruby said. "Was it expected?"

That was one way to put it, Clayton thought. He also thought that Ruby looked good. She looked even better than she had last time he had seen her at the reunion ten years ago. She was as fit as the girls back in L.A., and her skin seemed to glow, her eyes the green of an old-time soda bottle.

"You look good," said Clayton.

"So do you," Ruby said.

"What? Me?" Clayton asked, stabbing a finger into his chest. "This old horse has been ridden hard and put away wet."

"I like the beard," she said. "Oh, it's so good to see you. Are you staying with Supernau? Where are they?"

Clayton pointed. John and Kat were trying to pry Flynn away from a '63 split-window Corvette Stingray, but managed a distracted wave.

"You want to get some lunch?" Clayton asked. "The smell from all those barbecue booths is making me crazy. "

Ruby looked around, unsure.

"Come on," Clayton urged her, "I haven't been around for ten years. How am I supposed to know who has the good barbecue anymore?"

Ruby smiled, "Okay. Sure. I guess I'm pretty hungry, too."

They ate baby back ribs at a booth sponsored by the 4-H. When they were finished, they strolled away from the crowds to the head of Second Street.

"You still live in the same place?" Clayton asked, pointing up the street.

Ruby nodded, "Sure do."

"Man, we had some good times in that house, Scotty and I. We used to hang in the backyard and you used to flirt with me from the upstairs window."

"I was flirting with all of you," Ruby corrected.

"Yeah, but me especially."

"If you say so."

"Nah, actually," Clayton said, "I always thought you and Lance would have ended up together. I just saw him. He's working on my truck and he came over for a barbecue the other night at Supernau's. He says he's still with Laurie and they have a six-year-old boy. That's crazy. I can't believe I haven't talked to him for that long."

Ruby spared a thought for Laurie. She hoped she and Lance were still together. Laurie had sounded terrible when she had called the other day. She had gotten her hands on that backpack she had been talking about and it hadn't been good. Laurie hadn't wanted to talk about it just yet, but promised she would fill Ruby in soon.

"Second Street," Clayton mused, "Shit, we used to be scared to walk to your house. Does Sylvia Blair still live across the street in that big creepy house? Your brother and I used to dare each other to go knock on the front door."

Clayton hadn't heard from Blair. He knew no news was good news. Blair said she would only call if there were any complications between her and Lutz or with gaining a clean death certificate, and surely Blair would have known that by now.

"She still lives there," Ruby confirmed. "She still pretty much keeps to herself, but then again, so do I. We're both probably the most anti-social people in Dawson."

The two found a bench in the shade near the library.

"Oh, I wouldn't say that. You were pretty social at the St. Mark 10th reunion. Evidently, we were quite the item."

Ruby was wearing a white sleeveless blouse, jeans and crisp white tennis shoes, the latter of which she was now staring at and rubbing together like a cricket's legs.

"I remember," Ruby said. "Well...some of it at least."

"Yeah, I was pretty hammered," Clayton admitted. "I hope I was a gentleman."

"We just danced," Ruby reminded him.

"Yeah, but to 'Purple Rain,'" said Clayton, "I can't imagine doing that. I mean, not because of you. I mean, I liked dancing with you. I just don't dance..."

"I know what you mean," Ruby said.

They were silent for a while as they sat listening to the laughter rolling down Main Street and watching the crowds stroll by. In the distance, back at the bandshell, they could hear John's dad, Mayor Hal Supernau, whipping up the crowd for the annual pie eating contest, his distinctive, barking laugh echoing through the public address system and coming to their ears on a very slight and very muggy breeze: "Eat! Eat! Eat! Apple Pie on the 4th of July! What could be better? Where are my contestants?!"

"You know that barbecue I was talking about at Supernau's the other night?" Clayton said. "It was fun and all, but it was strange how incomplete it felt. It wasn't the Fearsome Five and we all knew it. We didn't say anything about it, but we all knew it. Without Paul and without Scotty, it just wasn't the same."

"The Fearsome Five," Ruby laughed. "I think Scotty came up with that."

"I think he did," said Clayton. "We sure did miss him. We wanted to talk about him, I could tell, but we all kind of avoided it. It was weird. None of us had to say anything, but we were all thinking the same thing. We were thinking about how much we wished he was sitting at that table with us--Paul, too, of course, but Scotty..."

Clayton trailed off. He tried to brace himself with a sigh that puffed out his cheeks, but he still hung his head.

For a long moment neither of them spoke.

Then Clayton said, "God, Ruby, how long has it been since Scotty died?"

"Twenty-four years," Ruby replied. "Almost twenty-five."

They both watched a lone, yellow balloon track across the cloudless sky.

Clayton wiped his eyes with the back of his hand.

"You've been through more than anyone should have to go through," he said.

"I talk to him sometimes," Ruby said softly to the folded hands in her lap. "I want him to be at rest, and I don't think he is."

"Of course he is," Clayton said. He fished for Ruby's hand, giving it a restorative shake and a pat. He wanted to hold it and not let go, but he didn't want it to be misinterpreted as making a move on her. That was the last thing he wanted. At this moment, there was no lust for her, only love.

Ruby and Scotty--along with the rest of the friends he had left behind--were everything good about his childhood. Those long ago days when the Fearsome Five were together and full of energy, potential and wonder had always been his paradigm of happiness, just as that horrible day when the news had come that Scotty had taken his own life had become the justification for his cynicism and disillusionment.

"Can we go see him?" Clayton asked. "I'd like to."

Ruby looked at him, "Really? Now?"

"Sure," said Clayton. "It's a perfect day for seeing old friends."

Chapter 14

Fireworks

Greenwood Cemetery sat in the shade of pin oaks between Second Street and Fifth. As Ruby and Clayton passed through its iron gates and between its welcoming sandstone columns, the carillon in the tower rising above the graves heralded the two o'clock hour by playing "The Yellow Rose of Texas."

Clayton laughed, "That thing still plays random shit, huh? It used to play 'Roll Out the Barrel' when we were kids. I thought that was pretty inappropriate, even back then. 'Roll out the barrel? We'll have a barrel of fun'?"

Ruby giggled, "Yeah, that's just wrong. You know, I jog through here every morning and I haven't heard that one. But I have heard 'Tea for Two'. That's also kind of a weird choice." Ruby cut across the lawn. "Over here."

As Clayton approached the grave, his face fell and he got to one knee before the marker.

SCOTT WILLIAM WEGNER

1968 – 1992

The marker was well brushed off, and beside it a single fresh lily listed in the built-in bud vase. Clayton supposed the flower was Ruby's doing.

Beside Scotty's grave was his mother's.

ALICE ANNE WEGNER

1942 – 1988

Although it didn't need it, Clayton brushed Scotty's marker with his hand, "Hey, Scooter. Love you, man. Happy Fourth of July."

Ruby stood beside Clayton's kneeling form, allowing him to have his moment. Clayton eventually sat down on the spongy grass, a hand splayed across Scotty's marker.

All was quiet. The crowds were far behind them, the distant strains of patriotic music in concert with the twittering of the birds overhead.

"I blame myself sometimes," Clayton said softly.

"What do you mean?" Ruby asked, getting to one knee beside him. "Why?"

"I smoked his first joint with him." Clayton looked up at Ruby, his face wet with tears. "I heard my whole life that pot was a gateway drug. I never believed it. I guess it was for him. He was a good kid, until you guys moved here, until he knew me. It seems everything I touch turns to shit. I wish I could take it back. I wish..."

"Ridiculous," Ruby said. She put her hand on his shoulder and squeezed. "Scotty didn't get hooked on drugs because you two smoked a doobie full of crappy ditchweed down by the Blue like everyone else in town did. You smoked out with John, Lance and Paul, too. They didn't throw their lives away. No, Scotty got hooked on drugs because he had to become my parent when he only wanted to be my brother. He had demons, Clayton. We all do. He just didn't want to live with them anymore. I'm still pissed at him about it. Sometimes I'm afraid I always will be."

Clayton said nothing. He looked back at the marker.

Ruby went on, "I can't stop going to school. I have hardly any friends. I'm fucked up, Clayton. Don't you think I blame myself, too? I should have seen the signs."

"You're right about having demons," said Clayton, picking at the grass. "I have a few of my own."

"We all do," said Ruby. "Why some of us can be happy in spite of them and why some of us can't, I don't know."

"Maybe this," said Clayton, rapping the grave marker with his knuckles, "is the only way they ever really go away."

Ruby didn't notice Scotty right away. At first, he had blended into the shadows beneath a far away oak tree on the edge of the cemetery, leaning on its trunk, arms crossed, his eternally 24-year-old face both solemn and contemplative. His blue suit was pressed, his tie knotted in a double Windsor, and his hair styled expertly into an auburn flop across his forehead, just as it always was, just as Sylvia Blair had fashioned it 23 years ago at the Blair Funeral Home.

"Are they gone now?" Ruby whispered to her brother across the lawn.

"What did you say?" Clayton looked up.

"Nothing," Ruby muttered. "We should go. The parade is gonna start soon."

Clayton stood, wiping the tears from his cheeks and the grass from his jeans.

"Do you want to watch the parade with me?" Ruby asked.

"I'd like that," said Clayton. "I'd like that a lot."

#

"Hello Clayton, hello Ruby."

It was Bob Lutz, in uniform, his hat shading his eyes. He was heavier than Clayton had expected, the eyes piggier, the eyebrows tinged with grey, but it was definitely the same guy with whom he'd seen The Empire Strikes Back on opening night at the Rivoli Theater, which seemed like a thousand years ago.

Clayton's breath caught. He knew he had only seconds to study Lutz, and to brace himself for what might happen next. But Lutz's face showed no sign of his intentions. Maybe there had been a problem and Blair had not warned Clayton like she had promised.

With Ruby by his side, Clayton was even more nervous. Anything that would lower her opinion of him would have devastated him. Would he be dragged away in cuffs in front of the entire town, in front of the thousands lining up to watch the parade? Is this how it was going to end?

"It's good to see you," said Lutz. "I wish it was under better circumstances."

The three of them were blocking traffic on the sidewalk and Lutz beckoned them to step into the street. The crowds were thick now, three deep on the sidewalks, most of them strangers and all of them jockeying for a good view.

"Is everything okay with my dad?" Clayton managed as breezily as possible, though his heart was hammering, his words clicking with dry mouth.

"You know," Lutz said, "your father helped me fix my Camaro when I was in high school. He was a pretty handy guy."

Then, for some reason, Lutz paused. It was a long, pregnant one, and under any other circumstanced Clayton would have just chalked it up to the Midwestern cadence of speech, but it had almost made Clayton cry out with anticipation.

(And you had to kill him. He helped me with my car and you had to kill him.)

"To answer your question," the sheriff went on, "I talked with Foster's attending physician in Colorado. He said Foster had been in pretty bad shape and that pneumonia was bound to happen eventually. There was not a whole lot you could have done. I hope you're not being too hard on yourself."

The relief made Clayton swoon. The day was hot, but he knew most of his sweat was not from the humidity. He could count the colder drops, the ones rolling down his back--five big ones. He thought it best to just nod solemnly and not risk opening his mouth.

Lutz said, "The Blair Funeral Home is taking care of the particulars, as you requested. Again, I'm sorry."

"I didn't know he died here," Ruby said, furrowing her brow.

"He didn't," Clayton said, a little too fast. "Not quite."

Did Ruby know if he had any living relatives nearby? Could he float the story that he was moving his father to his aunt's house where he could get better care and it had been than that the old man had died? He didn't think so and he sure didn't want to risk it. Even thinking about the horrors of last week with Ruby at his side seemed profane.

So instead, he said to her, "It's a long story," and turned his attention back to Lutz.

He had to shut down Lutz quick and make sure the sheriff didn't offer any more details.

"Thank you. Thanks for everything, Sheriff," Clayton said. "Oh, and congratulations on being the sheriff! Boy, I haven't seen you since you started, you know, law enforcement. You must be busy today. It looks like it's going to be quite a parade."

Clayton knew he was rambling, and it was lame rambling at that. Though he had to remind himself that in Dawson, talking small was not as out of place as it would be in L.A., no matter how lame it was, and mercifully Lutz thought nothing of it.

"We might break a record," Lutz agreed. "We're thinking about 43,000 people." His belt squawked. He plucked up his radio and thumbed a reply. "Copy that." He turned his attention back to Clayton. "Again, my condolences and great to see you again, but if you'll excuse me, I have to get back to work. They're starting."

As Lutz waddled off, Ruby said, "Come on, we can watch the parade from the Buellman's porch; it's on the parade route. Kathy Buellman was my lab partner last semester. She won't mind."

Clayton had heard about people having a spring in their step, but it hadn't happened to him in a very long time.

The two of them turned the corner at the end of the block and headed up Roberts Street to the Buellman house. The porch was already full, draped with red, white and blue bunting and crowded with old folks drinking beers. The two settled for a step.

"So, you said earlier that you never stop going to school," said Clayton. "So what have you learned?"

"I've learned that there's a lot to learn," Ruby replied, and the two of them laughed.

And so they watched the parade, Kathy Buellman thrusting a plastic glass of red beer into each of their hands. The beer and tomato juice combination had not appealed to Clayton in his youth, but today it tasted just fine. Kathy had even crusted celery salt on the rim of each glass.

"Fancy," said Ruby.

The volunteer fire department passed by, the crowd cheering, and then a small group of World War II vets performed their best recollection of a march in spite of their stiff limbs and wobbly gait. They carried Old Glory with them and everyone stood with hand on heart.

Next, a Pork Queen passed in a 1985 Buick Riviera convertible. Someone in the crowd squirted her with a water pistol, sending her blonde hairsprayed coif upwards in a flap and making her stop waving and grab her head. For many in the crowd, if it weren't for what happened next, this might have evoked JFK in Dealey Plaza. The Pork Queen swiftly produced her own formidable water weapon from beneath her seat and unloaded on the troublemaker with impressive accuracy.

"Let him have it, Your Highness!" Clayton hollered, getting a laugh from the crowd around him.

Ruby wasn't paying attention to the water gun fight. Her ear had locked into a conversation happening on the porch behind her. Taking a swift peek over her shoulder, she determined the conversation to be between Kathy Buellman's mother, Betty, and John Steiger, Chad Steiger's father and the proprietor of the hardware store in town. They were both sharing a porch glider.

Mrs. Buellman: "Did you hear that Don Creech was doing things that he shouldn't have been doing to the kids at St. Mark."

Mr. Steiger: "Yep, but I don't believe it."

Mrs. Buellman: "I guess a lot of people are coming forward with it."

Mr. Steiger: "I heard it was Ross Neumann's boy, Paul, who came up with all of this nonsense. And you know how messed up that boy is. I heard he dresses up like a woman in Florida, somewhere."

Mrs. Buellman: "Well, maybe that's why he's messed up."

Mr. Steiger: "Well, I think it's hogwash. Don Creech does a lot for the church and he doesn't strike me as some fairy."

Mrs. Buellman: "Oh, but he did things with girls, too. The Krausses are suing him as well. That's what I heard at the salon yesterday. Do you remember the Krausses? Used to live by the levee years ago? He worked as a foreman out at Hughes?"

Mr. Steiger: "Well, then they sure took their sweet time coming up with this nonsense...dragging a good man through the dirt."

And with that, John Steiger ended the exchange with a reproving click of his tongue.

Ruby meant to bring up what she had heard to Clayton, but she got distracted when a string of firecrackers went off in the driveway next to where they were sitting.

"God bless it!" Kathy Buellman cried, coming down the porch and squeezing her way past Ruby and Clayton and heading for her boy. "Don't set those off right next to grandma's ear, Jack! You want to give her a heart attack?"

But after this day had ended, Ruby would think about what she had heard. She would think about it a lot.

#

Back at the Supernau house, John was already manning the barbecue when Ruby and Clayton entered the backyard through the side gate.

"Ruby!" cried Kat.

"Hey, Ruby," John said, "Did Clay behave himself today?"

Chagrined, Clayton shot John a look.

"Mind if I stay?" Ruby asked.

"Don't be silly;" said Kat, "you're more than welcome."

Tonight, burgers were on the menu, along with the ubiquitous golden ears of sweet corn. The four of them, plus Flynn, gathered around the patio table in the dusk amidst the distant shrill whistles from Piccolo Petes and the popping of firecrackers.

"Haven't heard from Lance since the other night," John said, chewing. "I tried calling. Nothing."

Kat thwacked him with her napkin, "Don't talk with your mouth full."

Flynn laughed.

John thwacked her back and she recoiled with a yelp.

"They're in a fight," Ruby said, and as soon as she did, she flushed knowing she had just made a mistake. Laurie had sworn her to secrecy. Thankfully no one was in a nosy mood and no one followed up. They probably figured that if anyone could work out a disagreement, it was Lance and Laurie Vanderboom. But though Ruby didn't know everything yet about what had happened the other night, Laurie had told her enough to make Ruby not so sure things would work out that easily.

After dinner, John suggested that the five of them start walking to Plum Creek Park to get a good seat for the fireworks show.

"And this time put on some long socks, Flynn," Kat warned. "Last year the chiggers ate you alive."

They arrived at the park just as the first of the stars began to wink through the indigo sky. On a grassy slope toward the back of the park, John spread out a large, sunburst blanket and they all crowded onto it.

Clayton's phone chirped in his pocket. Not again, he thought. The last time he had answered the phone it had not gone well at all. The last thing he needed now was more of the same.

He never did call Randy back, but then again, what could he do about it now? What had happened to Randy made him sick, but all he could do now was wait until he got some money in his pocket, throw some at Randy and ask for forgiveness. He sure didn't need to hear yet again what a loser and an asshole he was.

Who else could it be? It wouldn't be the Nebraska State Patrol. That investigation was over a week old now. If they had meant to ask him questions, wasn't it safe to assume that it would have been done by now?

Clayton still had no intention of answering the phone.

As he watched the night gather above him, the children playing nearby and the gathering crowds of locals holding miniature American flags to wave, Clayton thought it surreal that Hollywood even existed somewhere down the endless horizon.

He thought of how he had told Ruby that he felt that everyone who knew him was the worse for it. It had been good of her to assuage his criticism of himself, but it was true--all she need do was ask Randy Johnson. But there was nothing that threw his life into stark contrast more than what he saw around him now: sincerity, community and peace.

"I think your phone is ringing," Ruby said. "Want a beer?"

"Have one," Kat said, fishing through the ice in her Igloo cooler and producing a can of Old Milwaukee. She turned around on the blanket with a grunt and a reach, "There you go. I didn't bring the koozies. Is that your phone?"

Clayton admitted that it was. It was supposed to have gone to message by now, but whoever had called had called back. Clayton sprung to his feet and looked at the caller ID. It was a 402 number, which was local. Maybe Lance is going to join us, Clayton thought.

He answered.

"Looks like you're right at home," came the smoky voice, and Clayton knew immediately who it was.

"Sylvia?"

"Happy Independence Day, honeybunch," Blair said. "Do you feel free?"

The chatter around him made it hard to hear and Clayton hunched, plugging his other ear with a finger. "Well, yeah. Thanks to you."

"Well that's what I'm calling about," said Blair, "There's been a little problem."

"What? What kind of problem?" Alarm flared in Clayton and he headed for the tree line. "What do you mean? I just saw Bob Lutz earlier today at the parade. He didn't say there was a problem. He was actually very nice, said everything went well."

"I wouldn't say that," Sylvia said, "I had to...do a little extra work on this one."

"What do you mean?"

"Oh, you don't want to know all the nasty details, honeybunch."

"But everything's fine, right?"

"You sure sound pretty relaxed for a guy who snuffed out his father only a week ago," said Blair.

"Where are you?"

"By Pastor Steitz's house. You remember where that is, don't you?"

Clayton scanned the backyards open to the park.

"A little to the left," Blair coaxed, "There you go."

There she stood, at the edge of Pastor Steitz's backyard, waving at him with her free hand, the one holding a fuming cigarette. She wore bright red pants and a blue blouse dotted with white stars. To Clayton, she looked like a hog caught in a flag.

Clayton treaded lightly, "What do you want?"

"I'm going to need double what I asked for," Blair said.

Clayton's vision tunneled. He could see her suck on the end of her smoke and he could hear it in his ear.

She exhaled and added, "Unfortunately."

"WHAT?" Clayton started walking toward her, stepping on someone's foot and stumbling as he went. He didn't look back. Powered by rage, he kept going, heading for the grinning pig at the edge of the park, the grinning pig in her ridiculous red, white and blue.

"You can stay right there," Blair warned. "Listen to me and listen good."

"Who the fuck do you think you are?" Clayton spat. He stopped walking, breathing heavily. A mother on a blanket below him pulled her child close, chastising him with large wet eyes.

Clayton lowered his voice and hissed into the phone, "What the fuck are you talking about? We agreed. We had a deal."

"You look like a murderer to everyone watching you right now," Blair said, taking another drag from her cigarette. "You really need to calm down and use what's left of your brain for once."

"What are you doing this for? Double? I don't have double."

"Liar!" Sylvia growled, the mocking sweetness gone from her voice.

Clayton's balls jumped into his stomach.

"You're a liar!" Sylvia repeated. "You may lie your way through life, but you're not going to do it to my face! Not to me!"

The two stared at each other from across the park.

When Blair spoke again, she reverted back to her usual tone, the one dripping with smoky syrup. "You told me you were due a hundred grand. I'm taking forty of it, so I'd shut your pie hole if I were you and consider yourself a lucky boy."

"It's your word against mine," Clayton said, shaking. "There's no proof I did anything. Lutz said it was pneumonia, and you can't do an autopsy on a pile of ashes, so you're getting what we agreed on, bitch."

Blair laughed her gravelly laugh, and Clayton's guts iced up as he waited for her to stop. When her laugh finally degenerated into a fit of coughing, Blair continued, "There is no pile of ashes. I never turned on the crisper, honeybunch."

The world around Clayton disappeared. "What...?"

"No. He's still around, preserved like a Twinkie. And you know what? From the blue in his face and the popped blood vessels in his eyes, it sure looks like he was strangled to death."

"You fucking bitch."

"You really should watch your mouth," Blair said, "What about the children? Its people like you that ruin wholesome events like this one. You should be ashamed."

It had gotten dark fast, and Clayton was vaguely aware of irritated mutterings coming from below where he stood. "If this guy would sit down..." said a man, and "I hope he doesn't stand there all night," said an old woman.

"Forty thousand," Sylvia said, "in cash, or the cat's out of the bag. You have one month. Probate shouldn't take longer than that."

She hung up.

Clayton saw her turn and disappear up a path that cut through the woods at the edge of the park.

The first reports of the city's fireworks echoed through the prairies and a few seconds later the shells hit the sky in brilliant splashes of red, white and blue. The crowd gasped. Children squealed with delight.

But to Clayton, it was as if his world was exploding above his head.

Chapter 15

The Letter

Ruby woke to the sound of cicadas. That was wrong. The insects never sang at night; only the crickets did.

As she lay in her bed, the moist blankets bunched around her, her heart pounding, she squeezed her eyes shut and willed the insects to stop. The bugs were screaming; it sounded like thousands of them, the shrill whine rising and falling to mix with the low rumble of blood in her ears.

The night was as warm and as thick as syrup, and there was a fever in the air, a sour one, one not of this world. And she knew what it was. It was Death breathing, it was what happened to the night when Death had come and was breathing somewhere close.

Terror shook Ruby as if she were a bone in its teeth.

As she lay on her back, against her will she began to slide from her bed. She clawed at the bedding, trying to hang on, but it couldn't tether her; the sheet ripped free from its tuck under the mattress, sending her falling to the floor. She landed softly, inches above the carpet, as she had many times before, as if cradled in the palm of a large, unseen hand.

She knew where she was being taken. She was to relive this again, as if by decree from Hell itself. She was being taken to the garden. She was being taken to the shed.

The cicadas beyond the window, the cicadas that had taken over the night, celebrated the horror of her revelation with an ear-splitting crescendo.

Ruby kicked at the carpet as she was dragged from her room, the bedclothes trailing behind her. She was able to flip around onto her stomach and grab for them, but her fingernails only found carpet, tearing and burning her grasping hands. She flipped onto her back again and then she was in the hallway, headed for the staircase.

Flailing and screaming, she was dragged down the hall to the landing. Not dragged exactly. She was lifted inches from the ground and pulled, as if some dark, unseen thing with huge hands was outside, fishing her out of the house, being careful not to knock a picture off the wall or to damage her as she turned corners; fishing her out as if she were a morsel in a dollhouse.

She was at the stairs now. She reached for the banister. She reached for the wall, but she knew it was no use. It wouldn't stop her. The dark, unseen hand she lay on would only tighten its grip, tug her until her arms ripped out of their sockets. It meant to take her to the shed, and it would take her in pieces if it had to.

Down each stair she went, her legs before her, scrambling, each step glancing just beneath her spine, her descent slow, methodical and all the more horrible for it.

It was so dark, unnaturally dark, as if all light had fled in the presence of the thing that gripped her. Only one spot shone through the inky blackness: the fireplace mantel. It smoldered with its own ultraviolet light, pulsing to the beating of Ruby's heart. Atop its marble sheen, she could see the whites of the eyes in her mother's portrait flash. The eyes were moving; they were watching something, rolling back and forth in their sockets, following something high above and out of view.

Still sliding down the staircase on her back, Ruby craned her neck and saw what her mother had seen. Just below the living room's vaulted ceiling, her father's solar-powered helicopter flew. In the darkness above, it glowed with its own ghostly light. It dipped toward Ruby, its rotors whirring so close she could feel the wind on her cheek. She reached for it, but it only jerked upwards and out of reach. Ruby cried out for it, but it didn't heed her cries. It only spun and looped mindlessly far above her.

"Daddy!" she screamed. "Help me! I don't want to go! I don't want to go again!"

The final step passed beneath her spine and, quick as a rocket, Ruby shot toward the sliding glass door. It was already open.

Of course it was, she thought, her mind squirming. This is where the monster's hand, the one she lay on, had begun fishing for her. This is where it had entered. Here, where the sweet smell of decayed flowers and death blew into the house on a hot, sickening wind.

The open sliding glass door framed the garden shed lying in wait for her far across the lawn, the shed's red paint oozing down its wooden frame like coagulating blood.

"No!" she cried, beating the floor with her fists. "I don't want to! I don't want to go again!"

The thrumming of the cicadas rose to drown out her voice. In that terrible din, she made one final attempt at wrenching herself free; she sat up and grabbed for the patio door jamb, her fingers fumbling for purchase on the aluminum frame as she passed. She got a hold and she kept it. With a cry of fury and fear she held on, her arms aching, her muscles straining, as the force pulling her showed no mercy. Her legs were straight out in front of her now, kicking the air, her arms splayed, holding the sliding door on one side and the jamb on the other. With a cry of frustration she was finally forced to let go, pain shooting up her arms and into her shoulders.

"NO!" she screamed.

On her back, she glided across the deck and onto the lawn. The cicadas watched her from the limbs of the trees, and somehow, she could see every one of them, thousands of points of red light watching her with bug-eyed malevolence.

The garden shed was twenty feet away from her now, light from within spilling out around its closed door, and as she screamed, the cicadas screamed with her in a crescendo that she thought might shatter the black and starless sky.

Then the force stopped pulling.

Ruby was thrown to her feet.

She stood and stumbled, and in the trees, the cicadas went silent. Reverently silent. Ruby, too, held her breath until all she could hear was the hammering of her own heart and the rush of blood in her ears.

The door of the shed slammed open, glaring light poured over her, and Ruby was face to face with her brother.

Scotty hung from the shed's crossbeam, a black leather belt cinched around his neck. His hair fell over his eyes; his tongue, blue and thick, lolled out of the side of his mouth. Ruby tried to back away, but the unseen palm that had fished her out of the house was now at the small of her back, pushing her forward.

Scotty's eyes popped open.

Ruby screamed.

Her brother's eyes, bulging and webbed with red veins, searched her. His thick, blue tongue began to move, licking around his cracked lips.

"Ruby..." he croaked. He reached out for her with one thin white arm, his body swinging a little as he did, the black leather belt creaking on the beam above.

"...the letter."

"Why did you do this?" Ruby sobbed. "Why did you do this?"

"The letter..." Scotty said again.

Suddenly, the force tugged Ruby backwards across the lawn, backwards so fast she couldn't find the air to scream, backwards toward the house. Before her, the shed's door slammed shut.

The solar powered helicopter banked and dipped into view, keeping pace with her as she was sucked back into her living room and thrown across the floor.

Free of the force's grip, Ruby rolled over onto all fours and stood up. Out of breath, shaking and covered in sweat, she stood in the middle of her living room, mouth agape, trying to take in what she saw.

Every light in the house was on now, upstairs and down, and Ruby had to shade her eyes against the glare. A single word was written all over the walls, written on the ceiling, written on the windows, written so that the word seemed to be crawling through every inch of her house, infesting it; one word written over and over hundreds of times in a bright red scrawl:

CREECH

#

Laurie Vanderboom was sitting at the dinette table in Ruby's breakfast nook when Ruby came downstairs.

"Good morning," said Laurie. "I made some coffee. Are you okay? It sounded like you had a pretty bad dream last night. I came to your door, but by the time I got there, I guess it was over."

Ruby's head was still thick with sleep, and for a moment she had forgotten that she had offered to put Laurie and Luke up for a couple of days until Laurie could figure out what to do about Lance.

Laurie had spent the 4th of July at her parent's farm in Utica, leaving a note for Lance informing him of where she was and asking him not to call. She said she needed time to think. She did promise she would attend Linda's memorial service at St. Mark on the morning of the fifth--for Luke's sake--and she had, sitting dutifully by her husband, knowing that her absence would have fueled unwanted gossip. But she had said nothing to him, and he had said nothing to her. When the service was over, Laurie had snuck out a side door with a confused Luke holding her hand, headed for Second Street to take up Ruby Wegner on her offer of sanctuary.

"It was a bad dream," Ruby admitted, "a very bad one. How long have you been up?"

"Oh, not long, maybe 20 minutes."

"And Luke?"

"Still sleeping," said Laurie. "It's hard for him to sleep away from home. Some kids can do it, but Luke isn't one of them. I forgot to pack him one of his fluffies...er, stuffed animals. That would have helped. He was up most of the night after he heard you scream."

"I'm sorry," Ruby said, shuffling toward the coffee pot.

"No, no," Laurie insisted. "Don't be silly. We are so thankful to be here. I don't know what I would do without you."

Ruby smiled as best as she could. She had a mean headache. "I'm going to grab the paper," she said.

When she returned from the porch, Laurie was pouring her coffee, "Do you take cream or sugar?"

"Black," said Ruby and sat down at the dinette, rubbing her temples. She pulled the rubber band off this week's Independent, spread it out and read the front page. Above the fold was an article reprinted from the Lincoln Journal Star:

LINCOLN, NE. - Two lawsuits were filed in Lancaster County District Court on Monday by unnamed plaintiffs who alleged they were sexually abused at a Lutheran school in Dawson. Named in the suit is St. Mark Lutheran school and its long-time principal, Donald R. Creech. Both lawsuits seek over $1 million in damages.

Herb Rosenthal, attorney for one of the unnamed plaintiffs, said his client has suffered from anorexia and post-traumatic stress disorder because of the abuse allegedly suffered from Creech.

"My client has had a very difficult life because of this," Rosenthal told the Lincoln Journal Star.

The lawsuit seeks unspecified general damages and $750,000 for medical costs related to the alleged abuse and lost wages in roughly 30 years since the incidents.

The alleged abuse took place in 1981 and 1982 when both plaintiffs were in the sixth and seventh grades, according to the lawsuit. Rosenthal declined to further identify his client.

Larry Marx, attorney for Mr. Creech, denies the claims, telling the Lincoln Journal Star that if the alleged abuse did occur, then the plaintiffs should have brought a claim within four years of discovering that Mr. Creech's abuse caused their injuries, consistent with the Nebraska statute of limitations."

Ruby was vaguely aware of Laurie chatting across the table from her, something about Luke being on the farm the other day, something about Luke milking the leaky cow, something about it being funny, but Ruby made no sense of her words. She was far, far away.

Principal Creech, her principal, Scotty's principal, the principal for half the town's population, a man they had known their entire lives, a man who had read the Gospel during church and had prayed for the souls of their departed, a man that most of them had entrusted with another generation of their family as students at a school that exalted the teachings of Christ, that man now smiled back at Ruby in black and white from the front page of her local newspaper.

In the picture, Creech was buttoned up in cerebral tweed, a shock of his thinning hair swept across his high forehead and glued into place with something greasy. His smile was slight, almost haughty, and his dark eyes behind his glasses now looked like shark's eyes to Ruby.

She flashed on the nightmare she had last night: "...the letter..." dead Scotty had said, reaching out for her with that thin, white arm, "the letter..."

And with dawning horror, Ruby knew what letter he meant. After all of these years she had almost forgotten about it. She still had it. She still kept it where Scotty had left it: in the top right drawer of his desk in his bedroom. The letter had never been sent, it had never been signed, and Ruby had no need to go get it because the letter was only one sentence long and she remembered quite clearly what it said. It had haunted her for years and she had never known exactly what Scotty had meant by it.

Until now. Her brother had written:

Mr. Creech,

You know what you did, and I'm going to make you pay for it.

Across the table, Laurie was still talking. She was saying something about Luke running from the barn screaming, something about thinking the cow would leak too much and drown him. "Isn't that funny?" Laurie said, "I thought he would run all the way to Canada. Ruby?"

Ruby looked up, "Huh?"

"Are you okay?"

Dazed, Ruby shook her head, and when Laurie's brow furrowed, she slid the newspaper across the table to Laurie with the tips of her fingers.

Confused, her smile dying on her face, Laurie read the headline:

TWO LAWSUITS FILED AGAINTS NEBRASKA CHURCH FOR ALLEGED SEXUAL ABUSE BY AN OFFICIAL

For a long time the two women sat at the dinette table, a bar of morning sunlight falling between them through the branches of the hickory trees beyond the window, a clock ticking somewhere nearby, but neither of them could speak.

Ruby thought of what she had overheard on Kathy Buellman's porch on the Fourth of July: "Did you hear that Don Creech was doing things to the kids at St. Mark that he shouldn't have been doing?"

The two of them had forgotten about their coffee, they had forgotten about everything else except for the picture of the man in the tweed jacket and one particular line from the article in the paper that now lay in the middle of the table, pushed between them as if neither woman wanted to be too close to it. It was the one line from Creech's lawyer that they kept turning over and over in their heads, turning it over with the hope it would alter with each reading, but it wouldn't, and in the silence of that absurdly golden morning, with birds chirping in the yard and cicadas just starting to thrum in the trees, they were lost in their emptiness.

"...the plaintiffs should have brought a claim within four years of discovering that Mr. Creech's abuse caused their injuries," Creech's lawyer had told the paper, "consistent with the Nebraska statute of limitations."

It was a smug statement, but a clear one. Regardless of fact, Creech would skate.

Luke padded into the kitchen in his footsie pajamas, eyes half open and hair tousled. He went straight to his mother and buried his face in her bosom.

"My little man," Laurie said distantly, hugging him tight.

"What's wrong, Mommy?"

Everything, Laurie wanted to say, everything is wrong, Lukas. Everything has been wrong for a long, long time.

Instead, she took a deep breath and said, "Are you hungry? Do you want some breakfast?"

Luke nodded. "I had a bad dream."

"You're okay now," Laurie said, patting his back, "Nothing can hurt you now…"

Laurie wanted to believe that more than anything.

Later that morning, Laurie and Ruby sat out on the porch, Ruby sometimes staring blankly at the garden shed across the lawn, and both of them occasionally staring up into the sky as if at any moment, God might deign to scrawl the answers to their questions across His endless blue canvas.

But Ruby's horror was a solitary one. She would share her thoughts with Laurie soon, but for now, it was too much to take in. If the conclusions she had drawn about that old letter she had found in Scotty's desk just after he had died were true, then everything was different now. It hadn't been just grief over the death of his parents that had killed her brother. It hadn't been just the pressure of being the only one left to assuage his little sister's fears and pain, and it hadn't just been the influence of drugs that had killed him. Now she knew who had really driven Scotty into the shed and had helped him cinch that belt around his neck. After all of these years, now she knew.

"I've got to tell you something, Laurie," said Ruby. "It's about my brother. It's about Mr. Creech."

#

When Lance called around eleven o'clock, Laurie answered for one reason alone: she wanted more than anything for something to be normal again. She thought she knew her church, her town, her school. She hadn't. She thought she had known her husband. She hadn't. Ruby had showed her the letter from Scotty's desk, and now nothing at all seemed real in her world. She was freefalling. She needed to reach out for something to hold on to before she landed hard, even if that something broke off in her hand, and that was why she rose calmly from the patio table, walked across the lawn, and after three days of avoiding him, accepted the call from her husband.

"Laurie, please. I am so sorry." Lance's voice was thin and shaking, his throat rattling like a broken reed. "Please Laurie, I'm lost without you. It isn't what it looks like. I mean, it is, but it isn't. I didn't do anything with her. I mean, I didn't sleep with her. I didn't." He stopped talking, trying to catch his breath as it came in rasps. "Oh God..." he moaned. "Laurie, are you there?"

"Yeah..." she said, the word no more than a sigh.

"I need help," Lance said, "and if you never want to see me again...I hope you do...someday, but I need help. I'm fucked up, Laurie."

"Yeah," Laurie said again, dreamily. It was all she could manage. None of this seemed real. All she could think of was her wedding day, her bridesmaids around her in their flouncy, lavender dresses, her own young face beaming back at her from her dressing room mirror, her blonde hair piled atop her head, her veil coming down over her eyes as St. Mark's organ began playing "Spring" from Vivaldi's Four Seasons, its sweet, lilting melody sighing through the church's heavy wooden doors and into her ears like the breath of angels. Then there had been Lance, waiting for her at the end of the aisle, her prince, looking lost in his formalwear, his hair shiny and overly styled, but as adorable as anyone she had ever seen. It had been the happiest day of her life.

"I want to tell you what happened," Lance said. "I don't want to do this over the phone. I know you're at Wegner's house, I saw your car..."

"Don't," Laurie said.

But her heart was softening, reaching to him as a flower reaches for the sun. And as it did, her mind chided her, reminding her of what a fool she would be if she ever thought that man who had waited for her at the end of the aisle could possibly exist again.

"Please," said Lance. "I want to see you. I want to tell you what happened. I want to get through this."

"I don't think we can," Laurie said.

"Don't say that," Lance said, choking on a fresh wave of tears. "You can't say that. You are everything to me. You're the only woman I've ever loved."

Laurie could say nothing.

"I'm coming by, okay?"

Somewhere deep inside herself, Laurie quaked, and she could almost feel the pieces of stone falling from her heart.

"Okay?"

"Don't come to the door," Laurie said, her tongue thick, her head light. "Just don't come to the door. I don't want Luke to know you're here. Text me and I'll come out front. I really don't know what the point is, Lance. This is bad, this is really bad."

"Five minutes," said Lance, "I'll be there in five minutes."

He made it in three.

Cautiously, Laurie emerged through the side gate to see her husband standing on the porch in jeans and a stained white t-shirt. He looked totally bereft, and to Laurie, he looked a lot like Luke at his most frightened and miserable, like Luke had been last night when Ruby had screamed in the middle of the night, sending their veins coursing with ice.

The impulse to run to him was strong, to hold him, to squeeze shut her eyes and will none of this to be so. But then she remembered the sock full of condoms, the woman in the ad, the pills at the bottom of the backpack, and again her heart began to harden to stone.

She hugged herself and sat, recalcitrant, on the steps of Ruby's porch. She looked up at Lance. He was backlit, the sun just short of the meridian. She shaded her eyes. Chivalrously, Lance moved to his left so his shadow fell over her.

Lance plunged his hands into the pockets of his jeans and stared at his feet like Luke might do when caught stealing candy. "I messed up. I know I did."

"Ads on a website?" Laurie said, "Drugs? You're a leader at our church."

Lance's foot had found an abandoned cicada shell, absently crushing it into powder with twists of his ankle. "I felt you didn't want me anymore, Laurie. I'd told you that over and over. You always said you would try and do better with sex, but you never really did."

"You cheated on me, Lance!" Laurie said, her voice now spiking with anger. "We took vows. Do you remember? You know, maybe I didn't put out like a 20-year-old..."

"Laurie, stop it."

"No, maybe I didn't put out like a 20-year-old, but I was a good wife and a good mother."

"I never said you weren't. I was just frustrated. You made me feel bad, bad about myself."

"So you sleep with some whore and ruin our marriage?"

Lance glanced from side to side. If any neighbor happened to be outside, Laurie's voice was now in danger of being heard. Suggesting a tone, he lowered his own voice to a stern and earnest whisper. "I didn't cheat. I came here to tell you what happened. I could lie to you over and over, and you would probably believe me eventually."

Laurie shook her head.

"Yeah, you would," Lance went on, "because you would want everything to be okay. That's how you are. You always want everything to be okay, but you never do anything to make it okay. But you know what? I'm not going to lie to you. I love you too much. I said I was fucked up, and I am, but not fucked up enough to not tell you the truth."

Her arms still crossed, Laurie looked away.

"That woman," Lance said, "the one in the ad, she's director of maintenance for Pinnacle Bank Arena in Lincoln. She gave me a power washing job, cleaning the outdoor concourse. She asked me if I wanted to grab a drink. I was flattered. I said yes. We've only met twice. Those ads you saw...they were her idea. They were wishful thinking. None of them ever panned out, so there was never a three-way. But I told you I would be honest, so here it goes. She did give me head both times we met. I didn't fuck her though. I swear on Luke's life."

Laurie started crying and got up to leave. "Don't you ever fucking swear on our son's life, you asshole..."

"Oh, sit down, Laurie," said Lance, "You're not above any of this. It's not like you haven't cheated on me. I admitted what I did. Now it's your turn."

Laurie spun to face him, "What are you talking about?" She wiped her nose with her sleeve, and with a resolute flip of her hair she added, "I never cheated on you."

"Maybe you don't think so," Lance said, "but I do. What you did hurts just as bad. I'm sure you're going to claim it doesn't, but it does. You can take my word for that."

They stared at each other. Laurie's face was hard, but as Lance held her with his eyes, Laurie began to wilt, her eyes widening.

"Yeah," said Lance, "I know about your little computer games, about you sending pics of you flicking your bean to anyone who asks. I know because I was one of them."

"What do you mean?" said Laurie, her bravura gone.

"New York Stud 007," Lance said, "Remember him? You had no problem flashing your beaver to that guy. Problem is, that guy was me."

"You fucking spied on me?" Laurie spat, turning white.

"You spied on me too, Laurie. You waited until I was home, drunk, and until I felt safe enough in my home to just pass out, and you went through my things."

"I didn't have anyone go down on me!" Laurie yelled. "It's not the same thing."

"It is to me, Laurie," Lance said, jabbing a finger into his own chest. "It is to me. You can tell yourself that it's different, that because some woman had her mouth on my cock that I couldn't possibly feel betrayed by you, rejected by you..." His eyes were streaming tears now. "Do you think I wanted some stranger to do that more than you? Do you? I've never wanted anything but you, and you wouldn't have me."

"I did..."

"No. You didn't and you know it."

They said nothing for a long time. Now it was Lance who took the porch step, his elbows on his knees, and his hands in his hair as the cicadas above pined away with their lustful noise.

Minutes passed before Laurie finally sat down on the porch step next to Lance.

"Did you see the paper this morning?" Lance said from behind his hands. "There was an article on the front page. It was about Principal Creech."

"I saw it."

"I...I don't know exactly why I never said this to you. I don't know why I never said it to anybody, and I don't mean for this to be an excuse for what I did. I never told you because I was ashamed and I didn't think anyone would believe me--not even you. Maybe you still won't. I really thought it would go away, but it never does. Maybe if I was normal I could have gone without sex completely. If I was normal, maybe it wouldn't have to be so dirty all the time. But I don't know what it's like to be normal about that kind of thing, Laurie, and sometimes I don't think I ever will be."

"What are you trying to say, Lance?" Laurie asked, turning to him. "What about Mr. Creech?"

Lance's mouth was pressed into a thin line. With a grunt of frustration, he buried his face in his hands and mumbled something.

"What?" Laurie asked. "What did you say?"

Lance tore his hands away from his face and looked at his wife. "He molested me. Mr. Creech molested me."

They stared at each other, and Laurie's eyes welled with tears. They streamed down her face as she looked into his eyes.

"You don't believe me, do you...?" Lance said, his own eyes wet and haunted.

"I do," Laurie sobbed. "I do because he did it to me, too."

Lance's mouth fell open. "No..."

She nodded, pressing her palms to her eyes, "...for almost two years."

Lance reached for her, laying his hand against her wet cheek and pulling her close. "Oh God..." he said, his voice barely a whisper. "My baby...oh...my baby..."

Together they sat on the porch in the warm shade of the pin oaks, holding each other's heads as the world around them faded away, and they cried in each other's arms.

Chapter 16

Black Tar

You have two messages. First message, sent Sunday, July 5th at 12:30 PM:

"...(click)..."

The caller ID had a 213 area code. Clayton recognized it. It was Randy Johnson, his bass player. He must have called again to chew him yet another brand new asshole, undoubtedly high on the painkillers that Clayton had sentenced him to by simple association. Clayton knew he would have deserved it, too, but mercifully, Randy must have changed his mind.

Second message, sent Monday, July 6th at 8:35 AM:

"Hi, Mr. Briggle, Steven Rathbun calling. I'm the attorney in charge of probate for your father's estate. Please give me a call when it's convenient at..."

Clayton's heart began to race. Excusing himself from the breakfast table where the Supernaus munched somnolently on breakfast cereals, he went to the patio to return the call.

A female assistant with a breathy voice and the ghost of a Southern accent told him that it would be "just one moment, please."

"Good morning, Mr. Briggle," said Rathbun, sounding to Clayton like he might be pushing 70. His voice had the silken purr and easy manner of old money. "I just wanted to touch base with you about your father's will. As you may know, I am the executor, and accountant for the estate, and I've sent you a copy of the will to your address in...Los Angeles. That address is current?"

"Yes," said Clayton, "but I'm not there right now. I haven't been there for a while. When did you send it?"

"Several days ago," said the lawyer, "Wednesday last, but maybe the holiday might have gummed up the mail a bit. Anyway, it was a simple estate and you are the sole beneficiary. Did you have any other family members that may have been disinherited?"

"No," said Clayton, "I'm it."

"Well then, I expect no one will come forward to contest the will--they haven't yet--so that should speed things up a bit."

"Can I ask you something?" Clayton said.

"Certainly. I hope I have an answer."

"Since I'm not home," Clayton said, "and I haven't actually seen the will...could you, I mean, is it possible..."

"You want to know what your father left you?" Rathbun said slyly. "Well that I can answer. Fifty thousand dollars."

"Fifty?"

"Five-oh," said the lawyer, "as I said you were the sole beneficiary. Of course, it is taxable, but I imagine you're looking at a solid forty thousand when all is said and done."

"Forty...?"

Clayton was going numb.

"Are you still there, Mr. Briggle?"

Clayton pressed him, "But I thought...I mean, I don't think that's right. He told me he had a hundred."

"That's true," Rathbun said, "he did. As a matter of fact he had about a hundred and a quarter, but he had some debts--the estate has to take care of those--and, of course, some legal fees. Also, there was a pretty substantial charitable contribution..."

"For who?" Clayton stammered, "To what? Charitable contribution?"

"To his church," the lawyer said.

"His church?" Clayton sat down hard on a patio chair. "What do you mean? He didn't go to church. What church?"

Clayton could hear the lawyer rustling some papers,

"Holy Cross something or other," Rathbun muttered. "Just a minute, here. Ah, here it is. Holy Cross Lutheran in Colorado Springs."

"How much?" Clayton said through his teeth.

"To the church? Forty thousand."

"Forty fuck--"

Clayton reached up and squeezed his temples so hard that later, on his way back into the kitchen, Flynn would ask him what he had done to his head. Slowly, as if any sudden movement might detonate a bomb between his ears, Clayton repeated it aloud: "Forty thousand dollars to a church?"

"That's not unusual," Rathbun said, his breezy manner tightening into one of caution, as if it were becoming clear to him that he was no longer dealing with a grieving or grateful man, but rather a desperate and craven one. "People leave money to their church quite frequently. I've seen it many times."

"When do I get the money?" Clayton said, dispensing with all pretense.

"Well, as I said, barring the unforeseen, I can probate the will by the end of the week. A check will be sent to you, to the address on file."

"I've got to go." Clayton hung up.

His head swimming, Clayton made his way back into the house. He was fucked, royally fucked. He wouldn't have enough cash to pay that greedy bitch, Sylvia Blair, and also pay back the Mexicans who were probably tracking him down right now. Whatever gang they were, they probably had connections in Omaha. Omaha was full of gangs. If they found out that the guy they think ripped them off was in Nebraska, then it was only an hour drive for one of their goons to break his legs...or worse. All Clayton could hope for was that in all of those years of playing together and drinking on the road, that he had never uttered the words "Dawson, Nebraska" to Randy Johnson.

There was no way out of this. No matter who he paid, he was going to be twenty grand short. Sylvia said she still had his father's body, and Clayton believed her. It was either deal with the results of the autopsy that Sylvia would call for and risk prison, or face a very bent-out-of-shape group of Mexicans with cartel connections who--according to the news--had a thing for putting car tires around your neck and setting them on fire.

Even if he could get hold of another twenty grand, he wouldn't have a dime left for himself. His apartment was trashed and uninhabitable, and though he had called the other band members to warn them of his problems and to lay low, he knew they were probably in the process of replacing him, if they hadn't already. No group of musicians needed the FBI or the DEA kicking down their door during a recording session.

Using his phone, he checked his bank balance:

Checking: $2,256.34

Savings: $5,854.00

If it was going to take $57,000 to ward off both Blair and the Mexicans, then he only needed ten grand. He would be penniless, but at least he would be safe--and alive.

#

"I need a favor, Supe," said Clayton, "not like you letting me stay here for the last seven days wasn't enough. I can never repay you for that..."

"Don't worry about it," John said.

John was home from work and the two were alone on the patio with beers in koozies, the summer sun low and golden at the treetops.

"But before I ask," Clayton said, "I have to tell you the whole story...where I've been for the twenty-something years since high school and what I've gotten myself into. I haven't told you any of this because I'm not proud of it, but I have to now. It's important that you know."

Clayton would certainly leave out killing his father along with the fact that he had entered into a monumentally naïve pact with Sylvia Blair who now had him by the short hairs. But if there was any chance of John helping him, he knew he had to tell him about the Mexicans and about the heroin. He had to at least tell him the truth about that. You couldn't just ask a friend for ten grand without it being a matter of life and death.

And it was certainly looking like that was the case.

Clayton chugged most of his beer and took a deep breath.

#

"When I first got to Hollywood, I knew no one," Clayton began, "I had nothing. My mother had taken off in high school--you remember that? She was cheating on my dad with some rich douchebag. She lives in Northern California now. I haven't spoken to her in years and I don't want to. She's fine with that. Christ, anything that would fuck up her meal ticket needed to take a hike. So I did.

"And my father? He was understandably upset about mom taking off and started hitting the bottle pretty hard. He turned on me, made me feel like it had been my fault. Instead of crying on each other's shoulders and calling my mom a selfish bitch like we should have done, he decided to isolate. He always had the tendency to be kind of a hard-ass prick, but after mom left he figured I was old enough to deal with it myself. So, I told him I was leaving, that I would try my luck drumming, maybe go to Hollywood. He didn't care. He didn't give two shits about where I ended up. He just pulled out a wad of money, peeled off a few hundreds and waved me on my way.

"Oh sure, he would bitch about my choices later, but he seemed to forget how he had done nothing to prep me for the world like a father is supposed to. So I figured I might as well head for the horizon. I thought I didn't have much to lose. I know now that I was very wrong about that.

"I had my first place just off Hollywood Boulevard and just blocks from the bus stop where Greyhound had dropped me off. I knew I was a good drummer and I knew I was going to make it in rock 'n' roll, but I had no band and no drum kit. Eventually, I scraped up enough cash, went down to Guitar Center on Sunset Boulevard, bought a Ludwig kit with some killer toms that sounded like H-bombs and crammed myself and that kit into an apartment the size of a roadhouse john.

Supernau laughed, "Not as glamorous as I pictured it."

"You're not kidding," said Clayton, "and I still had to look for a band. There was this rag sold on street corner newsstands called Music Connection where bands would advertise and post want ads. I auditioned for a couple of bands, but nothing would gel, so I kept looking, wandering the streets, trying to make friends, trying to make connections.

"Life was pretty seedy on Hollywood Boulevard in those days. It's a lot better there now--gentrified, they call it--but back then there were just drug dealers and gang bangers wandering around. I fell in with this group of punkers, mostly because a lot of them had come from the Midwest: Iowa, Indiana and even one guy from Grand Island. They were mostly harmless and they knew the streets. That was the upside. The downside? They were all tweakers, into meth, and mostly homeless. A lot of them camped under the Hollywood freeway, so everyone called them the Trolls. I got my first opportunity to sell drugs through their leader, a guy with green hair and a nose ring that everyone called Joker.

"I know what you're thinking: why fall in with a crowd like that? But in my defense, Hollywood is pretty overwhelming and I needed a leg up. Dealing was really the only thing I was qualified to do."

"What about retail?" Supernau asked, "Didn't you try that?"

"Sure," said Clayton, "I tried normal jobs. I worked at a record store for a week, a drugstore for a few days, but I just couldn't straighten up and fly right like a good Lutheran boy was supposed to. It was godless on the boulevard. That's one excuse, and I'm sure I could come up with a lot more of them, but it hardly matters now. The fact is, I ended up dealing methamphetamine for The Trolls--nothing big, just twenty bucks here, twenty bucks there, but I made enough money to feed myself and pay rent.

"I hated meth though, hated everything about it. You've heard my music. You would think a guy who ended up fronting a thrash metal band would like that sort of thing, but it's not often the case. No one likes tweakers. They're fiends. They have rotting teeth, they lie, and they steal. Most metal heads I know are drinkers. A lot are into heroin, and some, like me, are just stoners who love the power of music, so I wasn't cut out to deal with tweakers and my patience wore thin, fast.

"I moved into the weed business. Selling to stoners is a hell of a lot less stressful. I got into it by meeting a grower that everyone called

Bear for obvious reasons. This dude was huge. He looked like he should be throwing barrels at Super Mario. He was tall and fat, with a beard and long hair. He looked tough as hell, but actually, Bear was very soft-spoken--if he said anything at all, which he rarely did. He was connected with farmers up in Humboldt County, California, where the weed crops are legendary. A friend of mine made the introduction, and after I built a little trust with the guy, I started slinging some pretty sick weed all over SoCal.

"You'd be surprised who bought weed from me in those days. Remember, back then it was still illegal in all ways. This was long before the term medical marijuana was being thrown around, and even a longer time before anyone had voted to decriminalize it--which is still a miracle I never thought I'd live to see. I sold weed to actors, directors, and rock stars. I made some pretty good money, and more importantly, I met a lot of people who could do me some good.

"I met my guitarist, Tommy Riccola, by selling him a pound of herb that scared the shit out of even me. G-13, this shit was called. I wouldn't even smoke it. It made me retarded--or more retarded, I should say. He was one of the biggest guitar session players at the time and was looking for a new project. That's how I got in with him, and that's how Kribdëth began.

"So back to the friend who introduced me to Bear, because he plays an important part in what I'm about to tell you. Now when I say 'friend,' I don't actually mean friend. On the streets, a friend is just someone you tolerate and who doesn't actively try and fuck you every chance they get. Anyway, the friend who introduced me to Bear was one of the Trolls. We called him Jimmy the Spic because he was a quarter Hispanic--you know, just to break his balls.

"That nickname is funny as hell in several ways: first, who calls anyone a "spic"? That's, like, a racial slur from the 60s or something. It's just wrong. Second, you've never seen a whiter looking guy.

"The story went like this: his father was half Nicaraguan and half German. His mother was English and Irish. So, he became Jimmy the Spic. The funniest part is that he never even knew his Nicaraguan grandmother. She died when he was a little kid. Not to mention that Jimmy just may be the only guy in L.A. who knows zero Spanish.

"Don't get me wrong; my friend, my buddy, my pal Jimmy the Spic was still a fiend and a loser. He was the kind of guy who'd go to take a leak at your apartment and then later you would find that he had swiped every pill in your medicine cabinet and had drunk all of your cough syrup. Aside from that, he was mostly harmless. Besides, he had set up the intro with Bear, so fuck it; I let him have my Robitussin.

"Years went by and I lost track of Jimmy the Spic. I heard he had moved to San Bernardino. No surprise there. Rent was cheaper there and word on the street was that he was trying his hand at setting up a meth lab. I'd all but forgotten about the guy.

"The following years were good years for me, Supes, years I thought would never end. The band had taken off and I stopped dealing altogether. Money from the band wasn't stupid good, but it was good and it only got better. At our peak, we went on a nationwide tour. We couldn't sell out arenas or anything, but we sold out theaters, a few thousand people a night. It was awesome, and I really thought it would last, but it didn't.

"Tastes changed. We weathered the grunge movement better than most, but then came millennial pop crap. Our fans got a little older and the metal scene dried up. We still had gigs, but they were back in clubs, just like in the days when we started, and since we didn't exactly write hits, royalty checks weren't rolling in. We were a live band. We lived and died on our paid attendance and we were now drawing hundreds, not thousands.

"So, about a couple of years ago, I realized I was going to run out of money sooner than I thought. I needed a second job. I looked around and landed a construction gig--just some bone-headed, grunt work. Shit, my foreman was younger than I was. Worse, I was in such bad physical shape. I had no business fucking with manual labor. After about two months on the job, guess what? I blow out my back."

"Oh, shit, man," John said.

"Wait, it gets better," said Clayton. "After that, I get hooked on the painkillers they gave me. It took almost two years to shake that bastard of a monkey off my broken back. Of course, I was riding workers comp the whole time, and when those checks dried up, I was really up a creek.

"Then one day I was drinking at this dive bar on Hollywood Boulevard called the Frolic Room. It's a way station of street urchins, dealers, prostitutes and stray tourists. This place was like the fucking cantina from Star Wars, but the drinks were stiff and cheap, so I was a regular. And guess who I see at the end of the bar with a rusty nail in his hand? Jimmy the Spic--right out of the fucking blue. It had probably been five years since I'd seen the guy. So we have a few drinks and get to talking. He wants to know if I know where to get some H. He was looking for quantity.

"I told him I wasn't slinging and I hadn't been for years, and even when I was slinging, heroin wasn't my thing. Jimmy said he figured that. He said he figured I didn't need to deal anything anymore since I was a rock star and all.

"Looking back on that conversation, I realize now that Jimmy also knew I was drinking in The Frolic Room again and not exactly burning up the charts. He was sizing me up.

"'An obscure rock star,' I reminded him, 'and while we've been drinking, I've only gotten more obscure.' I told him that the only supplier I ever knew was Bear, and as far as I knew, he never touched H either.

"Of course, Jimmy knew that. He was the guy who had introduced me to Bear. But he wondered if I could ask Bear anyway. Jimmy said he couldn't. He had had a falling out with the guy. It was part of the reason he had moved out of town.

"I wanted to ask Jimmy what had happened between him and Bear, but then I realized I really didn't care. The more pressing question was why he was on the look for quantity. Was he really going to start slinging junk?

"Jimmy denied that he was. He said he simply knew a guy in the Valley--a guy who had the money to start up--who thought there was an untapped market around San Fernando and wanted in.

"'So, you're going into business with this guy?' I asked.

"'No.' Jimmy said. 'The deal is that if I can find him the goods, I get free junk.' Then he went on to tell me that he was hooked and that he had been for some time.

"So I asked Jimmy what I would get out of it if I found him what he needed.

"'Whatever you work out with your supplier,' Jimmy said. 'Honestly, you really wouldn't get much out of it unless you could go pretty far up the chain,' he tells me. 'That way you could turn a profit without jacking the price so much it spooks my guy in the Valley.'

"We ordered another drink and I thought about it for a while. 'My guy wants to start with a key,' Jimmy added, 'and after he finds a connection he can trust, he plans to go big and re-up often.'

"So I considered approaching Bear, seeing what he might think of all of this. I really didn't know what a kilo of heroin was worth at that time, so I had to do a little research on my own. I asked Jimmy where I could get a hold of him; he gave me a phone number and I just forgot about him for a while, deciding after I sobered up that I had no intention of going big with H. It was crazy and too high risk.

"A couple of months later, I still didn't have any prospects for making a decent living with the band. Our label didn't want to finance another release, and would only offer tour support. I figured they were going to drop us. In fact, we're still waiting to find out. We need another crack at an album. It's been tense lately, all of us afraid that we're going to be stuck in clubs until a miracle happens. So my thoughts turned back to Jimmy the Spic, and our conversation at The Frolic Room.

"So I met with Bear. He told me what I already knew: he didn't mess with H. 'No Class 1 narcotics, man. I'm not going to do that kind of time.'

"But Bear did have a lead for me under one condition: that he stayed out of the conversation entirely. He also confirmed the falling out with Jimmy the Spic, said it was personal, said he didn't want to talk about it, but that he realized I was my own man and could make my own decisions. If I trusted Jimmy, that was my business.

"'Fuck no, I don't,' I told him, 'but I'm not going to be the one doing business with Jimmy. It's some other guy who wants the shit. I'm just working the margin.'

"Bear advised against it, but that if I wanted him to, he would set up an intro.

"'But again,' he says, 'if my name ends up on anyone's tongue, then that tongue is going to end up in a fucking landfill.'

"I told him I understood. It was the first threat I had ever heard Bear make. I should have stopped there.

"And that was when Bear told me about the Mexicans.

"'These guys are straight-up cartel,' he said. 'These are the guys that the burros--or smugglers--bring the shit to directly. They don't have any white or brown stuff. They only deal in Black Tar. It's cheaper and it's easier to sling to low-class spikers. It just depends if your guy is looking for that kind of thing.'

"I told him I didn't know exactly what Jimmy's guy wanted, but I'd check. I called Jimmy back and yes, his guy was still interested, and yes, Mexican shit was fine. The only thing left for me to do was to meet with the Mexicans. Bear told me how to do it, and if I hadn't been smart enough to stop before this point, I really should have when he told me how this would all go down.

"I had to do the pick-up alone. Jimmy the Spic had told me on the phone that under no circumstances would his guy meet directly with the supplier. Jimmy's guy was well-respected, had a family, and had way too much to lose. Also, Jimmy's guy wasn't going to front Jimmy twenty grand to make the deal for him because nobody trusted Jimmy the Spic. Nobody. And Jimmy told me that he wouldn't have done it anyway. California has a three strikes felony law and Jimmy had two out of three. One more felony and he wouldn't see the sun again.

"'Somebody has to front you,' Jimmy said. 'Once you have it, then I'm willing to cruise to the Valley with you and act as your go-between and introduce you to my guy, then I'm out. I get free junk for as long as you two hit it off.'

"I laughed in Jimmy's face. 'Are you out of your fucking mind?' I said to him, as if that question had more than one answer. 'No one is going to front me a quantity of H. Nobody knows me in that world, man.'

"Jimmy was more optimistic. 'You only have to be fronted once,' he tells me. 'From then on, my guy will know you, and would have no choice but to trust you if he wants to set up shop.'

"So, I had to go back to Bear on this to tell him I had to be fronted the first time, that I knew that was impossible, that I should forget it, and that it had all been too good to be true.

"'I can make that happen,' Bear told me. 'I can get you fronted.'

"My jaw hit the floor. Evidently, while I had been gigging and doing my rock 'n' roll thing, Bear had climbed the ladder on the streets and had become even a bigger bad-ass than I thought.

"'If I vouch for you,' Bear says, 'you're golden. But, again, it's your deal,' he tells me. "I'm not on the hook for it. All I'm doing is vouching that I have worked with you in the past and that you're a stand-up guy. You are not working for me in any way. I will make that clear to the Mexicans and I'm making it clear to you now.'

"I told him that was fine, that I understood, and thanked him again.

"'You can make a lot of coin being a runner,' Bear added as he showed me to the door, 'But it takes balls, and if you get pinched, you go down hard. Keep that in mind.'

"I appreciated his advice, but I wasn't worried about going down. I was concentrating on the money I could make. For instance, Jimmy's guy wanted to start with a key, but was going to go bigger if it worked out. According to Bear, a key of Black Tar sold for about $17,000 wholesale. But the street price was $20,000. That meant three grand for me per kilo. Sure, it wouldn't be easy the first time, nothing ever is, and Bear was right, it would take balls or desperation, and is there ever really a difference? But you can see why I was tempted. It was only a half-hour drive from Hollywood to the North Valley and I'd be making three grand a key. It was good money for no work and God knew I needed it."

Supernau whistled through his teeth and slugged his beer, "Man..."

Clayton went on, "So, I met with the Mexicans at a place on Hollywood Boulevard and Western Avenue called Hollywood Billiards. The directions from Bear had me entering on the right side of the building at the ground floor fire escape at 2 PM sharp.

"The place was a shithole, and I stood outside of the brick building for a long time, staring at the graffiti and crumpled up newspapers and trash blowing down the sidewalk in front of it. I almost walked away. In fact, I actually did, but then I came back and just stared at the place some more, and then at my watch, and then up at the taped-up windows and then back at my watch. At two o'clock, I jerked open the ground floor fire escape door and went inside.

"I entered at a staircase landing, a flight of stairs going down into the dark and a flight going up into the dark. On the landing above me I saw three guys sitting on the top step, stone-faced, blue bandanas around their heads, one of them with a teardrop tattooed on his cheek, and then the heavy door slammed shut behind me and all was black.

"I blinked my eyes and tried to get them to adjust.

"'Stand right there, amigo. Keep your hands out of your pockets, it'll be better for you,' one of the guys on the top step said, his accent thick.

"I did what I was told.

"'Bear says we can trust you, that you're a rock star,' the gangbanger says. 'Times are tough, huh, amigo?' the guy says. 'So what are you really doing here? You look a little too much like a rock star to me. I think you're jump street, white boy. I think you're five-oh.'

"I must have turned white because one of the cholos on the landing hissed a little giggle through his teeth. I didn't really believe they thought I was a cop, but I was afraid that they were going to break my balls until they saw shit coming out of the leg of my pants just to make sure.

"So I looked up at them. I thought a little eye contact might help--you know, show them I had nothing to hide. Man, they were ugly mother-fuckers, I'll give 'em that. The one with the teardrop tattoo on his cheek looked like he'd had a fight with a chainsaw and lost, and he was the one who said: 'Slowly, with two fingers, reach into your pocket and throw up your wallet.'

"I hesitated.

"'You're not getting jacked, white boy,' he said, 'You want seventeen g's of smack for free today and you think twice about handing over your wallet? Now throw it up here.'

"I did, and one of the cholos caught it in the air, opened it and took out my driver's license. Another took out a phone and snapped a flash picture of the license before replacing it in the wallet and tossing it back down to me.

"'There's a shopping bag sitting on the landing below you,' Teardrop said, 'inside, there's a kilo of mud, and it will cost you $17,000. You have until eight tonight to bring the cash. If you are not here exactly at eight with our money, then you'll meet some of my homies from Juarez. Comprendes?'

"I did. I understood all too well.

"I went down the stairs. The paper bag was where they said it would be. The logo for Ralphs--a local grocery store chain—was on it. I reached in and felt what seemed to be about the weight and bulk of a small bag of flour. I said 'muchas gracias' to the Pirates of the Caribbean at the top of the stairs, hit the crash bar on the fire escape door and walked stiffly into the sunlight, shaking like a cheap dryer, and started breathing again. I got away from there as fast as I could.

"In the back of my truck I have a big toolbox, and that's where I locked up the bag. Then I went to pick up Jimmy. He said he would meet me out in front of The Frolic Room. I pulled up and he was standing there, hugging himself. The guy was probably junk sick, and this whole operation couldn't be over fast enough for him. That made two of us.

"'Where is it?' Jimmy asked, climbing into the truck. He was a beady-eyed, squirrely little guy at the best of times, but now that he was crashing, he looked a lot like a rabid ferret.

"'I got it,' is all that I said. 'We're good to go.'

"Jimmy looked around, even pretending to tie his shoe so he could peek under the seats before he finally fixated on the glove compartment, and then looked at me with a shit-eating grin. I smiled back, letting him think he was red hot. That seemed to make him relax a little, but I know he wanted to yank open the compartment, rip open the bag and rub it all over his face and into every orifice in his body. But that would have been bad form, even for a junkie, so instead he settled back in the seat.

"'Take freeways,' he said. 'There are more chances of getting popped on surface streets than there are on freeways. Take the 101 to the 170 and get off at San Fernando, and watch your speed.

"I told him to climb down off my ass and that this wasn't my first rodeo. He looked a little butt-hurt by that, and said nothing more. We rode the rest of the way to the North Valley in anxious silence.

"When we pulled off the freeway, he told me to take Pinecrest into the hills. The North Valley is ringed with hills and brand new subdivisions full of McMansions. Every fucking house looks alike. They're all nice, but identical. God help you if you were coming home drunk from a bar, you would walk right into the wrong house.

"So we keep climbing Pinecrest until we get to this little turn off called Bella Vista. We're pretty high up now on a narrow two-lane road, the kind where if I met someone coming the other way I would have to grease the side of my truck and slow to a crawl. To our right there's a drop off and a view of the whole Valley. To the left there are long, steep driveways that lead up to the houses. Some of them have gates. The one Jimmy told me to stop at had a gate, a gate and an intercom on the side of the driveway leading up to it.

"There was a dusty red 90s Mazda RX-7 parked on the street, but no one around. The driveway was one of the steeper ones and pretty narrow, so I coaxed the truck up the incline to the intercom, the branches of the trees and bushes along the driveway scraping the side of the truck. I've got a big truck, so it was like getting a cork back into a bottle going up that driveway. Looking ahead, you couldn't really see the house. The gate was iron and covered with black tarp in the middle.

"Jimmy told me to go ahead and let the guy know we were here, so I rolled down the window and reached for the intercom button. The guy with the gun must have been crouching in a bush below my window because he popped up like a fucking jack-in-the-box.

"'Hand it over,' the gunman said. He was wearing a black leather jacket and a black balaclava so I couldn't see his face.

"I froze.

"'Now!' the guy yelled. The gun was inches from my face. I could actually see down the barrel. I had heard about that--looking down the barrel of a gun--but it had never happened to me before. I couldn't take my eyes from it.

"The guy jerked the gun upwards and then back to pointing at my face. This seemed to break my spell. I turned to Jimmy. He was gone. The passenger side door was open and the glove compartment was hanging open, too, but no Jimmy. The fucker had been in on the jack the whole time.

"'Where is it?' the man with the gun said. 'Don't fuck with me. You have seconds to answer me, not minutes.' He jerks the gun toward the house and says, 'This place is a repo. A bank owns it. It's going to sit here for months, deserted. We throw your body over that gate and you'll be eaten by coyotes by the time they find your bones, so where's the shit?'

"I told him.

"The man in black stuck out his other hand for the keys and I gave them to him.

"Supes, I'm telling you, man, I was so scared. I wanted to cry but I was too fucking frozen to do it. I wanted to cry for being such an idiot, for getting in way over my head, for being so desperate, for having fallen so far. I was shaking so bad I almost dropped the keys when I handed them to the guy.

"The gunman grabbed them and tossed them to the side and out of view. I heard someone catch them and then the truck rocked as someone climbed into the truck's bed. It was Jimmy. I saw him in the rearview. He was unlocking the toolbox. He jumped out of the truck with the shopping bag full of heroin and ran back down the driveway to the street where I could just see the bumper of that red Mazda that had been parked at the curb. Then I heard the Mazda's engine.

"The man with the gun still covered me. He cocked the hammer and I flinched, looking away. I shut my eyes. My bladder cramped and I held my breath. He was going to shoot me anyway.

"It was only when I heard the Mazda take off that I opened my eyes. Both of them were gone.

"I just sat there, trying to catch my breath. I had no keys. I was wedged into a driveway, and I was now $17,000 in debt to a bunch of gang members that were never going to care how unfair this situation was. I didn't have enough money to pay them back or any way to make that kind of money before their patience ran out. They had told me I had until eight o'clock that night, and as of today, it's been just over a month.

"Supe, these guys are still looking for me and they're serious. They've already roughed up a guy in my band. I need help. I just got off the phone with my dad's lawyer and my old man stiffed me. He made me think I was getting all of his savings, but he only left me half of what he said he was going to. I just checked my account. I can show you if you want. Between my savings and my checking, I have about seven grand. I need ten more or else...I don't know what's going to happen to me. I don't know what."

#

John Supernau stared across the patio table at Clayton. "You need to leave here tonight."

"Huh?' was all Clayton could manage.

"Now, actually," John said, rising from his chair.

"No, you misunderstand, bro," Clayton pleaded, "No one knows I'm in Nebraska. They only know I went to Colorado...I don't..."

He was actually going to say "I don't think." He was going to say it because it was true. He really didn't know if Randy--with his life on the line--had managed to pull Dawson, Nebraska to the tip of his tongue. It was also clear from the flint in John's eyes that he did not begin to share Clayton's unwarranted optimism.

"Wait..." said Clayton.

John was walking toward the house. "You're not staying here anymore," he said, turning on Clayton, "I have a family. I have a son. And you thought it was okay to bring them into your shit?"

"I didn't mean..." Clayton said, "I didn't think..."

"And that's the problem," John snapped, "Maybe you should start. Now go pack your shit. You've been here a week. I've done my part. You need to get the fuck out now."

And with that, John went into the house, slamming the screen door behind him.

Chapter 17

Into the Tall Grass

Lance hung up his phone and turned to Laurie. "It was Clay Briggle. He just wanted to know if his truck was ready. He said he had to leave town tomorrow."

Laurie nodded. "It must have been good to see him,"

They were both home now, watching Luke through the sliding glass door as he ran through the backyard, puffing out his cheeks and making flying sounds as he held his Iron Man action figure aloft.

They sat side by side on the couch in the cool darkness of their living room. Laurie reached over and grabbed Lance's hand. "Therapy will be good for us," she said. "I just hope we can put it all behind us. I'm scared though. I'm scared we might not be able to."

"Of course we can," Lance said. "We only have one choice to make: can we forgive each other or not."

"The thought of you with another woman just kills me," Laurie said, reaching up to pinch the bridge of her nose.

"No more crying," Lance said, brushing her hair from her face and shushing her. He grabbed her and rocked her. "I thank God you let me stay with you after what I did, and I promise I will work hard to be a better husband. Like we both said, thinking we were both above what happened to us in school was understandable. It was a long time ago. But it shaped us. He shaped us, and now that we know that, we can do something about it. Maybe forgiving each other completely will take time, but I have faith it will happen. What worries me most is forgiving myself. I should have been stronger. I should have had more respect for myself, more respect for you. I pray to the Lord that we will be okay, but

I'm also scared, babe. I'm scared I will never feel like I deserve forgiveness."

"We can't let that monster destroy this family," Laurie said. "I just can't believe that it took until we were middle-aged to even admit it to ourselves. It makes you wonder what else we bury."

"I'm not surprised, I guess," said Lance. "Our parents didn't talk about things like this and we were brought up the same way. I can't imagine how much abuse went on back in the old days. But we're not alone; no one else brought up what happened until now either, and there has to be a lot of us out there who went through it. But I tell you one thing, they're sure going to start talking now. And it was all Paul Neumann. The guy who got picked last in sports turned out to be the only one with the courage to face what we've all had to go through."

"But are we going to be okay?"

"Yes," said Lance. "We will because I'm not blaming Creech for what I did entirely. Sure, he did mess me up, but I can't hide behind it. I made bad decisions and they were my bad decisions. Yours were your bad decisions, too. We have to make better ones. That's how we can get our power back. That's what the therapist said."

"It's like when you have a nightmare," said Laurie, "and there's that moment you realize you're having one. Isn't that when the nightmare dissolves? That's when you get your control back."

"I already feel like that's happening," said Lance, pulling her close.

They sat in silence for a while and just watched their son play.

"Ruby told me one thing before I left her place," said Laurie. "You know how smart she is, how many classes she has taken and stuff? She told me one thing that I kind of knew in my heart, but didn't want to believe."

"What's that?" said Lance.

"She said that it's probably likely that Creech will get away with it."

"How could he?"

"The statute of limitations," Laurie said, "Ruby admitted that she hadn't taken a lot of law courses, but she had taken enough to know that Creech's lawyers would have an easy time of it. She said that Paul and Becky's lawyer should have known not to bring the suit. It's not a winnable suit."

"But so many people...so many years of..."

"I know," said Laurie, "It makes me sick, but Ruby says--and she looked this up on her phone just to make sure--that in the state of Nebraska, you have six years to bring a sexual abuse suit once you've turned eighteen. So if you were molested as a kid, like we were around sixth grade, then the law allows that you become an adult first before the six years begin. So the six years would start at 18-years old."

"So we all had to sue him by the time we were 24?" said Lance. "But that's so young. That would have been..."

Laurie finished his sentence: "Impossible. For the way we were brought up? Impossible."

#

Clayton stood on Ruby's doorstep with his duffel bag hanging from his arm. "Thanks for letting me stay, Ruby."

"What happened with you and John?" she asked.

"I overstayed my welcome. We'll be fine. We just had a bit of an argument,"

"Come in," Ruby said, "It's good to see you."

"It's good to see you, too," said Clayton. "I was going to see you again before I left anyway...of course."

Ruby smiled and blushed. Her hair was down, spilling over her shoulders to frame her freckled face. She brushed a strand from her forehead, tucked it behind her ear, and closed the door behind Clayton. "I had a great time with you on the 4th."

"So did I," Clayton said, the duffle still hanging from his arm.

"Oh, just leave the bag here for now," said Ruby, "We'll figure it out later."

Clayton put the bag down and the two of them stood in the foyer, an awkward silence thickening.

"It's hot out there, huh?" Ruby said, "I bet you'll be glad to get back to California where it isn't so sticky. I just opened some wine. Can I get you some?"

"That sounds great," said Clayton.

Ruby showed him to the living room. She went to the kitchen and returned with the bottle of wine, joining him on the couch before the fireplace.

"Your mom was a beautiful woman," Clayton said, looking at the portrait smiling down on them from the mantel. "You look a lot like her."

"Thanks," Ruby said, handing Clayton a glass of wine.

"She was a good teacher," said Clayton, "My favorite. When did you guys move here? Wasn't it right around sixth grade?"

"Well Scotty started in sixth," said Ruby, "I was in third."

They settled back on the couch and looked at the portrait together, and Clayton said, "I'll never forget that day, you know, that assembly when they told us. Everyone loved her."

Ruby smiled.

"Everyone cried," Clayton went on, "I mean, everyone: jocks, burn-outs, grown men, everyone. She hadn't even been at St. Mark that long and she had that effect. That's...something."

"Thank you for saying that," Ruby said quietly.

"It's true," Clayton said, "and you're a lot like her. You're not only pretty, but you have her way about you...her gentleness."

"I hope I do."

"You do," said Clayton. "Hey, I remember that helicopter." Clayton brightened and pointed to the toy on the mantel. "Hasn't it always been there?"

"Pretty much," said Ruby.

"Wasn't it your father's? I think Scotty told me that once. He said you guys used to fly it with him when you were kids?"

"We did."

Clayton muttered something.

"What's that?" asked Ruby.

"I said it's not right."

"What's not right?"

"...what you've been through," Clayton said, "It's not right. No one should have to go through what you've gone through. Who have you had to lean on? No one, really. You lose both your parents and then your brother. I mean, Jesus, I remember when your mom died and when Scotty died, and I remember what a mess I was both times, and I can't even imagine how you felt. We were young, and I don't know if you ever got what you needed from all of us? Half of us were dumb-asses. Selfish. I know I was. I hate to think..."

"Everyone was very sweet," Ruby said, staring into her wine glass.

Clayton shook his head. "We all could have been there for you a lot more."

"It was my fault."

"What do you mean?"

"I mean, it was my fault that I didn't get what I needed," said Ruby. "Everyone tried, but I pulled away from everyone--Scotty and I both did. He really did his best to be a parent for those last few years, but he was hurting so much."

"I can't imagine," said Clayton.

For a while, neither of them spoke.

"I need to tell you something," Ruby said, "something I haven't told anyone."

"What?" Clayton coaxed, "What is it?"

"Have you heard about this whole thing with Mr. Creech?"

"Yeah, I know about it," said Clayton, "If it's true, it's pretty messed up. John told me about it and then I saw something in the paper about it and...wait. Hold on. You're not telling me that..."

"No," Ruby assured him. "He didn't do anything to me. What about you? Did he?"

"Uh-uh," said Clayton, "and you're telling me the truth, Ruby? Because I'll find him and..."

"No, I promise," said Ruby, smiling weakly. "But here's the thing, Clayton. I think he did stuff to Scotty."

Clayton's eyes blazed, his jaw clenching, and when he spoke, he spoke softly, deliberately, "How do you know? Did he tell you?"

"Not exactly," Ruby said, "but he wrote something. It was a letter, of sorts. Actually, it was only one sentence and I found it in his desk after he...well, you know. Anyway, I don't know exactly when he wrote it, if it was right before, or years before. I just don't know."

"A letter?"

Ruby took a deep breath. "I'll get it. I should have shown it to people a long time ago. I want to see what you think."

Ruby went upstairs and returned with a single sheet of folded paper. "Be careful with it."

Clayton unfolded it and saw his old friend's writing scrawled neatly and deliberately across the top of the page:

Mr. Creech,

You know what you did, and I'm going to make you pay for it.

"Holy shit," Clayton sighed, deflating. "Holy shit, Ruby." He looked up at her. She was stone-faced, biting her lower lip and staring at him with anticipation. Clayton folded the paper carefully and handed it back to her, his own face now a mask of anguish. "You think?"

Ruby nodded. "Do you?"

Clayton nodded, too. "And he carried that kind of shame with him? The whole time I knew him?"

Ruby nodded.

"And he never did make him pay, did he?"

Ruby shook her head, "Not that I know of. It looks like Scotty was the only one who ended up paying."

Clayton swallowed hard. "That son of a bitch," he said, his eyes welling with tears. "That son of a bitch..."

"And he's going to get away with it, too," said Ruby.

"How could he?"

"The statute of limitations," said Ruby and then she explained the Nebraska law to him.

"That's bullshit," Clayton said, standing up. He paced the room several times and then collapsed back onto the couch beside Ruby. "And now you have to deal with that shit, too? You have to watch Creech go free?"

"I'm only assuming that the letter meant what we think it meant," Ruby said, "Scotty never said a thing. Neither did Lance and Laurie."

"What do you mean Lance and Laurie?"

Ruby snapped her mouth shut and flushed. "I'm sorry, I shouldn't have said anything."

"Creech? Did things...to..."

"Both of them," Ruby said.

"Both of them? Are you kidding?"

"Both of them," said Ruby, "Years apart. It all just came out. They compared notes on it, and I guess all of the details were the same. Look, I'm sure they would tell you eventually. I wasn't sworn to confidence or anything, but try not to bring it up until they do."

"This is insane," said Clayton. "And they never reported anything, either?"

Ruby shook her head. "No, and their marriage is in danger because of it. That's really why it came out. The suit against Creech helped a whole lot, I'm sure, the fact that it showed up in the paper and all. They said they were going to call Paul and Becky's lawyer and tell their story, too."

"This is crazy," said Clayton, "Years apart? So Creech has been at this for..."

"Who knows how long," said Ruby.

"And you said Lance's marriage was in trouble? What happened?"

"Maybe they will tell you that part some day, but all I can say is that when someone molests you when you are young, it can make the duties of a marriage...more difficult."

"Sex, you mean?" Clayton leaned on his knees and grabbed the top of his head. "So who else? How many years has this been going on? How many people in this town has Creech messed up?"

Ruby could only shrug.

"You were in Laurie's class," said Clayton, "and you just promised me that he didn't touch you. But he went after Laurie?"

"He did," said Ruby. "And you were in Lance and Scotty's class and nothing happened to you or John, but three out of the Fearsome Five were molested: Lance, Scotty and Paul."

"Why not me or John?" Clayton asked. "Why would he pick just them? Not that I wanted to be diddled by Creech. Ugh...god. It's just so unbelievable."

"Because predators prey on easy prey," Ruby said, "Lance's mother left when he was young and that's when Linda, his stepmother, came into the picture. His dad was a blue-collar guy who ran the auto body shop. They didn't have much influence. They were a simple family. And Paul? Creech figured Paul was gay and wouldn't put up much of a fight. We all kind of knew that Paul was gay early on, even if we didn't come right out and say it. Plus, his parents were a little weird anyway. No one would believe anything coming from the Neumann's. And Scotty was the easiest. Scotty had nothing. He had no father; he was brand new in town, and the real kicker: Creech was his mother's boss during his sixth grade year. One comment from Scotty and she gets fired. It was perfect."

"But I was easy prey, too," Clayton said. "My parents were always fighting, my mom left, and let's face it, I was kind of a burn-out."

"Yeah, but she left when you were well into being a teenager. From what I've heard so far, it seemed like Creech preferred sixth-graders. And to be frank, but not to mean any disrespect, your father was a bit of an intimidating guy. It didn't seem like he would had a problem getting in Mr. Creech's face if he had to."

Clayton couldn't disagree with that.

Ruby went on: "And John was untouchable because of Hal. Even back then, Hal Supernau was already on the city council."

"So why didn't anyone come forward sooner?" Clayton asked. "Okay, fine, I doubt anyone would have had their shit together enough by 24-years-old enough to blow the whistle on the principal of their school and a pastor of their church, but why wait this long?"

Ruby was quiet for a moment. She sipped her wine, put down her glass, and said. "You know, I've spent a lot of time in school trying to figure out why things happen. I've taken courses in philosophy, psychology, physics, religion, and sociology. One thing I've figured out is this: human beings have a very strong need to ignore their weaknesses. We all like to think we're in command of our lives and that we're at the wheel. But a lot of the time, our demons are driving us. They may even drive us off the road a few times, but we are so used to having them around, and they've been in control for so long that we have forgotten how to drive ourselves. Essentially, our weaknesses become part of our identity. And let's say we did exorcise our demons. It would leave a big hole, a hole that we wouldn't begin to know how to fill. It's codependency, pure and simple. We live with our pain because it's part of who we are. Sometimes we're afraid it might be all we are."

"Man..." Clayton said, throwing back his head and draining the rest of his wine. "That rings true for me. More than you know."

Ruby poured them both more wine. "And when you live in a place like Dawson, where you know everyone and always have, and you know that you'll probably never leave and that you and the town will grow old as one, sharing all of life's moments with each other, then it becomes much harder to destroy your world by your own hand. And if you did smash your construct into millions of pieces, you'd destroy not only your world, but also the world of everyone around you. It's a big responsibility. So you just leave your demons alone and hope that they will show you just enough mercy to allow you to limp to the finish line.

But in the end, they'll take more than you would ever consent to give. Sometimes, they'll even take what you love most."

"Like Scotty," Clayton said under his breath.

"Like Scotty," said Ruby, turning away.

#

Ruby and Clayton drank the rest of the bottle of wine and the two of them ended up lying on Ruby's bed. The television was on at their feet, neither of them watching it.

"You remember when we were in school," said Ruby, "and you guys hung out in the backyard and I watched you from the window up here?"

"You were a flirt," Clayton laughed.

"Yeah, I guess I was."

"So who are you dating?" Clayton asked.

Ruby laughed hard and with enough surprise that spittle sprayed from her mouth, "Me?"

"Yeah, you!"

"Nobody."

"And why not?"

"Because..." Ruby trailed off, her smile sliding from her face, "because I'm not right."

"What do you mean you're not right?"

"I'm just not."

"Who is?" Clayton said, "Hey, I've got plenty of problems, too."

"Not like mine."

"If you only knew," Clayton muttered.

Ruby laughed, "This isn't exactly the best sales pitch for either one of us."

Clayton's grin widened.

"Oh, what the hell," said Ruby, hopping out of bed, grabbing Clayton's hand and tugging. "Come on."

"Where are we going?" asked Clayton, stumbling to his feet.

Over her shoulder, Ruby said, "To Scotty's room."

The door to Scotty's room was open, as it always was, and Ruby flicked on the overhead light, "See? It hasn't changed," Ruby said, "I like it just like this."

"Wow. I remember it this way, too. You know, I haven't been in this room for, I don't know, over twenty years." Something on a shelf caught Clayton's eye. "Oh! No way! Look at that! There's his boom box. I remember that was expensive at the time." He squatted before it on his haunches, "Sure, it has the cassette deck, but it also has..." He gently depressed a button on the face of the box and a lid on the top yawned open slowly. "Tah-dah! A CD player. Now, this was the shit back then. I think he bought this junior year. A CD player in 1986 was something else. He was the first guy I knew who had one. Man, we listened to a lot of hair bands on this thing: Mötley Crüe. Guns 'n' Roses. Actually, I made him listen is more like it. I have a feeling he was really a closet shit-kicker and more into country and..."

Glancing up at Ruby, Clayton trailed off, alarmed by something in her eyes, "What is it?"

"Behind you," Ruby said softly.

"Huh?" Clayton looked behind him. Painted directly on the wall, and lit only by the jaundiced glow of the overhead light, were four stick figures holding hands. They were all red, bright red, two big ones and two little ones, a couple of feet tall. They looked primitive, like a cave painting, and the sight of them sent a shiver of dread up Clayton's spine. "What's that?" he said thickly.

"My family," said Ruby, "It's my family...all four of us...together."

"Scotty did that?"

"No," said Ruby, "I think I did."

Knitting his brow, Clayton stood from his crouch. He walked up to the figures on the wall. His hand rose to run his fingers over them, but then he backed away. He turned to Ruby, but couldn't find the words.

"Crazy, huh?" Ruby said.

"It's a mural, that's all," said Clayton, "L.A. is full of 'em. Everyone writes on the walls around town. Hey, I'm no judge of art so I can't..."

"It's not supposed to be art, Clay," Ruby said sternly. "The problem is: I don't even remember doing it. I used my own lipstick. I found the empty tubes on the floor by the baseboards. I did it in the night. I don't do drugs. And I don't drink that much, so I have no excuse. I guess I must have been dreaming...or something."

"Huh..." Clayton grunted, and he turned to look at the image again. "You don't remember? Well...that's hardcore."

"It is," Ruby agreed. "It is...hardcore."

"Have you ever done anything like that before?"

"No."

"When did you do it?"

"Just over a week ago. I'm worried. I'm worried that I'm not right. I don't talk to people much--maybe John and Peggy when I see them at the Corner Café in the mornings--but other than that, I keep to myself, and I think it's made me pretty weird over the years."

"You don't seem weird to me," said Clayton.

"I talk to Scotty, Clay," said Ruby, "and I see him."

"Like a ghost?"

"Yeah, kind of like that. I don't know. Maybe I see him because I want to see him. So that's who I talk to most. Other than that, I just go to school. I've been going for years. All I do is distract myself with school. I've learned so much about so many things, but I still haven't learned to be...normal. Then I do something like this." She waved a hand at the painting on the wall, and then she looked at the floor, her arm falling to her side.

"I think it's beautiful," Clayton said. "Okay, I admit, I was a little shocked at first. I didn't know what to make of it, but now that I look at it. It's beautiful. You think you're crazy because you miss your brother, your mom, and your dad? That doesn't mean you're crazy, Ruby. It means you're sad. You should try not to be sad anymore. You've been sad for a long, long time."

Clayton wanted to reach out and hold Ruby. As she stood there, her creation on the wall behind her, she looked young and small, like the little girl Clayton remembered flirting with him from the upstairs window so many years ago. He reached out and touched her shoulder. "You and I, we've both been sad for a long time."

Ruby looked up at him, "You, too?"

"More than you know. I don't like who I've become, either."

"But you're a great guy," Ruby said.

"You don't know me anymore," said Clayton. "I think I used to be a good guy, and I think I can be again, but I'm not now."

Ruby looked back at her feet. Then she took a deep breath and took Clayton's hand. "Let's get out of here," she said.

She clicked off the light and closed the door to Scotty's room.

As the two of them walked down the hall, approaching the door to Ruby's room, Clayton said: "Maybe I should get some sleep. I'm leaving in the morning. It's going to be a long drive. I got to stop in Colorado Springs, clean up some stuff for my dad..."

Ruby looked away. She still had his hand in hers. "I understand," she said. She looked at him. "I like you."

"I like you, too," Clayton said, "but what? You say it like you've been sentenced."

"I just know that this can't happen. I mean...we can't happen. I can't love anyone again. I can't lose someone again. I can't."

"I'm not right for you, Ruby. I know that."

"That's not what I mean--"

"I know what you mean," Clayton said, "But I just had to say it."

They stood in the middle of the hall, the moment in stasis, both feeling as though they were standing on the edge of a cliff.

"So," said Clayton, "we both agree that we aren't right for each other. You realize that probably means that we are. But aside from that, do we really believe we don't deserve happiness anymore?"

"I think we do," said Ruby.

"Then, just for tonight, for just once, let's be happy again."

Clayton brushed her hair from her face and kissed her forehead. Then he kissed her lips. She fell into him, her hands on his waist, and kissed him back with all of her desire for the love she had been missing for so long.

Clayton, too, let go. He gave into her. He was gentle with her, as if she were the most precious thing he had ever held in his hands, because at the moment, she was.

#

Clayton opened his eyes when he heard the sound.

It stopped.

That's right, he thought, looking at four walls he didn't recognize, he was in Ruby's room, in her bed.

Whatever had been making the noise had stopped, but only because it knew it had been heard. How Clayton knew this, he didn't know, but he knew it.

He held his breath and listened, tense with anticipation. Yes, whatever was making that shuffling, scraping sound on the carpet in the hall on the other side of the door was listening, too. It was waiting for him to go back to sleep so it could keep creeping toward him, toward him and Ruby.

Clayton tried to stare a hole through the closed door, and he knew that whatever was out there was doing the same thing.

It was waiting him out.

Clayton looked at the crack at the bottom of the door where it met the carpet, but there was no light in the hall, there were no moving shadows, and there was still no sound. A minute passed before he dared take a breath, and when he finally did, he began to feel foolish.

Whatever he had heard could have been anything, and he had only heard it at the edge of sleep. It was likely that it had been the central air conditioning, the water in its compressor echoing through the ducts.

He was under a lot of pressure, he knew. Cracking up was a possibility that he needed to keep in check. He began to unwind, relaxing one nerve at a time.

Ruby was asleep beside him underneath the window and the pale, silver light of the moon. He thought of last night. It was wonderful, but it was wrong. He was wrong. He had profaned her, he had profaned something beautiful.

He watched her sleep for a moment. She slept peacefully, a thin smile on her face, and she looked to Clayton like a doll carefully tucked in by a doting child.

Clayton looked at the bedroom door a final time, sighed, fluffed his pillow and lay his head back down. That's when he heard the sound again.

(scritch...scritch...)

This time it was clear, and it was not on the edge of sleep, and he knew it was no air conditioner.

Someone or...something was in the hall.

He looked back at Ruby. He wanted to ask her if she heard it, too, but she wasn't even stirring, and he couldn't bear to awaken her. She was so peaceful lying there, and as white as alabaster under the moonlight streaming in from the window. At that moment, Clayton thought that she looked so much like her brother, so much like Scotty.

Gently, he put a hand on her shoulder and leaned over her.

She looked so much like Scotty.

It was Scotty. And he was peaceful and white because he was dead.

Clayton's blood iced over, and when Scotty's eyes popped open and fixed on Clayton's own, Scotty didn't look peaceful at all anymore. Far from it. Clayton knew from his old friend's horrible stare that he had been to the end of the universe, had been to the end of time, and had watched everything die a thousand times over.

Scotty sat up, the blankets falling to his waist, a black belt still cinched around his neck. He jabbed a trembling, white finger at the bedroom door. "There's something in the hall," he whispered.

Clayton screamed.

Scotty said it again and again, but his larynx had been so badly crushed by his own hanging weight that the words came out sounding like a venting steam engine.

Clayton scrambled backwards on the bed, still screaming.

A shiny black spider crawled from Scotty's open mouth. "Something...in the hall..." Scotty croaked, "There's something in the hall..."

Clayton fell backwards and onto the floor, dragging the bed sheets with him. He tried to get to his feet but he got tangled. He stumbled. He pawed at the air behind him and knocked a picture off the wall. It came crashing down within inches from his head; he deflected it with a convulsive swipe of his hand as he got to his feet.

Clayton found the handle of the bedroom door and yanked it open. He spilled into the hall, shouldering the opposite wall, turned, and groped for the bedroom door to slam it shut behind him.

He saw dead Scotty, on his knees in the center of the bed, still pointing at the hall, now pointing at him, still trying to talk through his shattered windpipe, his jaw bobbing up and down like a ventriloquist's dummy, the words coming in a raspy hiss: "The thing in the hall...the thing in the hall...now you're the thing in the hall..."

As the door slammed, Clayton spun around, his fists up. He could see nothing. He was in the dark. He couldn't find his bearings, and he was frozen, trying to run in all directions at once. His breath was out of control. He gasped for air, found the wall behind him, and pinned his back to it.

He flicked his eyes left, toward the open door of Scotty's room.

At the end of the hall, the four stick figures stood. They were life-sized. They were lit red from within by their own, unholy incandescence, swaying slowly back and forth, watching him with eyeless faces.

Clayton inched away from them, clawing his way down the hallway wall. He flicked his eyes right.

The way was clear. He could see the head of the staircase that led down and out. He wanted to run to it, but his legs weren't working. They seemed to be made of jelly.

Then he heard the sound again.

(scritch...scritch...)

It was slow and deliberate, and it was close.

(scritch...scritch...)

Clayton looked down.

About six feet away, crawling along the hall carpet, was what looked like a giant grub worm. It was white, over five feet long. It made its way toward him, inch by inch, by arching its back at its center and then scraping its way forward along the carpet.

(scritch...scritch...)

Clayton's mind slipped a gear. He pressed his back further into the wall and shrank away from the cocoon-like mass, going back the other way, away from the worm thing, and toward the stick figures that were still swaying at the end of the hall, watching him in silent judgment.

Looking back at the monster on the floor, he saw to his horror that the worm-thing was segmented. Or was it tied with ropes?

The front of the thing rose up a few inches and Clayton saw that it had a human face, an old man's face, and it was grinning up at him, its sunken eyes fixing on him, the tendons in its scrawny neck flexing, and its black hole of a mouth yawning wide with its effort as it gained another few inches on him.

It was his father, bundled in a sheet, tied with ropes, crawling his way down the carpet on his stomach toward Clayton's feet.

Clayton tried to scream again, but his throat had closed up, frozen with revulsion and fear. As he watched, Foster Briggle's prostrate form, the grinning face still looking up at him, it hunched again like an inch worm and managed a few more inches paces toward Clayton, gnashing its yellow teeth only a foot from Clayton's ankles.

With an explosion of terror-fueled energy, Clayton leaped past the slithering corpse at his feet and slammed into the opposite wall of the hallway, sprinting for the staircase. As he did, the man who used to be his father, in his cocoon of soiled sheets and ropes, reared up and gnashed at him like a breeching whale before crashing back to the floor with a hiss.

Clayton gained the handrail of the stairs and took them four at a time, flying toward the landing. When he got to the bottom, he chanced a look back up the stairs.

Scotty was there, standing naked on the top step, the black belt still dangling from around his blue neck. He was laughing, a gritty, panting laugh, and when Scotty began wobbling his way down the stairs, Clayton ran.

Pulling open the front door, he crossed the porch, stumbled, and ran down the cement walk for the street. The outside air was thick and hot, but Clayton gulped at it greedily. At the end of the walk he slowed and stopped. He was face to face with the Blair house.

Across the cement of Second Street, the crooked mortician's house, the Witch House of his youth, seemed to absorb the night like a sponge thirsting for darkness. The blackness around the mansion was so complete that Clayton couldn't discern its form from the oak and hickory trees that shrouded it. But he could feel that it was there. It was as if it were a living, palpable heart of evil, sucking up darkness with every pulse of its chambers.

Then, a light clicked on in its upper window, in the tower just below the widow's walk, and Sylvia Blair's face was looking down at him from the dormer window. She whispered to him, and somehow Clayton could hear:

"We will follow you," she said, "and we will always be behind you...forever."

In the sky, tendrils of gauzy cirrus clouds released the moon, and silver light poured onto Second Street.

Clayton could see everything now.

At the foot of the Blair house and at the edge of its weed-ravaged lawn, Mr. Creech stood surrounded by a throng of naked children, all of them with black, lifeless eyes, and all of them waving at him.

Clayton had no place to run.

Panicked, he looked for escape.

The houses that used to be beside the Blair house were not there anymore; they were all gone. The whole neighborhood was gone, save for the dark, breathing mass of Sylvia Blair's mansion. Now there was only tall grass where the road ended, and beyond that, fields of corn for as far as he could see.

Behind him, the front door was opening with a creak of hinges.

Clayton didn't look back. He sprinted for the tall grass and the cornstalks beyond. He ran until he couldn't run. He ran until his lungs burned and the sharp leaves on the cornstalks whipped and slashed his face into a stinging mask of pain.

Only then did he dare to look back, but as deep among the stalks as he was, he could see nothing. The corn was high, just above his head, and for a moment he felt like weeping with relief, but his face hurt too much, his legs hurt too much, and his lungs ached for air. He grabbed his knees, panting, and then stood.

Two hands parted the corn stalks in front of him and Clayton was face to face with the dead state patrolman.

"Tell my little boy that I loved him," the dead man croaked, his mouth just a dark, shapeless hole in the pile of bloody meat that had once been his face, "Would you do that for me? If you do, I'll tell Ruby that you loved her. I'll tell her right after I bury you."

The patrolman lunged for him. In a panic, Clayton tried to run backwards. He lost his balance and crashed through the cornstalks to the cold soil below, landing on his back. The cop was leaning over him now, hands like claws, the mangled face dripping gore into Clayton's screaming mouth.

"Wake up!" Ruby insisted, shaking him. "Clayton! My God, wake up!"

Clayton opened his eyes, shrinking from her touch. He was covered in sweat and shaking. "What?"

"You're having a nightmare," Ruby said.

"What time is it?"

"I...don't know," Ruby said, "almost ten."

"I should go." Clayton stood and pulled on his jeans. "I'm sorry. I shouldn't have, you know..."

"It's okay," she said softly, "You're okay."

"I have things I have to do back in L.A.," Clayton said. "I didn't want to..."

"Didn't want to what?" Ruby was on the edge of the bed now. "What is it? Just hold on. Relax a minute. You're shaking."

"I'll be okay." Clayton pulled on his shirt.

"Calm down," Ruby said, "and look at me."

Clayton did, and they stood there for a moment, the morning sun tilting into the bedroom window.

"Now..." said Ruby, "what are you thinking about?"

"You're amazing," Clayton said, the sun lighting Ruby's hair from behind like a Byzantine halo. "I don't know...I just hope you don't regret anything."

She shook her head. "Do you?"

"You are the only thing I don't regret, Ruby. I hope you believe me." He bent and kissed her forehead.

Ruby smiled.

Clayton stood and pawed his pockets for his phone and keys. He found his keys, but his phone was on the dresser. A new text had come in overnight. It was from a 402 number. It was from Sylvia Blair.

July 7th, 12:30 AM

You have one month

With a grimace, Clayton shoved the phone into the pocket of his jeans and looked at Ruby. "I've got to go."

"Well, let me make you some coffee at least," Ruby offered.

"No. I'll just grab something at the Git N' Split and hit the road."

"Are you sure?"

"Yeah, I'm sure," Clayton said. "I should go. It's a long drive."

He tried to take her in as she sat on the edge of the bed with the blankets gathered below her naked breasts, her hair falling to her shoulders in wild tangles. She looked to him like a goddess; a goddess that he thought might even give him salvation if he ever thought he could deserve it. With an effort, he peeled his eyes away.

"Goodbye, Ruby."

"Will you come back sooner this time?" she asked him.

"I will."

"Then goodbye, Clayton."

#

Lance told Clayton that his truck would be ready this morning and it was. It looked good as new. Lance refused payment for the labor and charged his friend only for parts.

"You really didn't have to do that, Lance."

"Fearsome Five," was all Lance said.

Clayton managed a smile, "And thanks, boys."

Lance's assistants stepped out of the shadows. Dan smiled. Earl doffed his cap.

"So when are we going to see you again?" Lance asked.

The two embraced, clapping each other hard on the back.

"Don't know," said Clayton, "Sooner than later. I really needed to come back here though, I really did." Clayton leaned into Lance and whispered in his ear, "Will you and Laurie be okay? Ruby told me just a little, but she wouldn't tell me much."

"I hope so," said Lance, his smile thin.

"I'm sure you will be," said Clayton.

They hugged one more time and then Clayton climbed into his truck, waved at Lance a final time, and to the shrill song of the cicadas in the trees above, Clayton headed through downtown Dawson to the highway that would lead him out of town.

ONE MONTH LATER

Chapter 18

The Red, White, and Blue Couch

You don't need to say anything. Just listen. You're the only one I'm ever going to say these things to. They're my deepest, darkest secrets, and I'm telling you because I know about you. You're no different from me. Do you want to know how I know that? Well, I'll tell you.

As principal of the school, I had my ear to the ground. All complaints ended up on my desk, so don't think for a moment that I don't know about your...proclivities.

What am I talking about? Oh please. Don't insult me with your claims of innocence. This doesn't need to be a two-way conversation, so save it. I have no interest in your false outrage or your pantomime of confusion. I'm only telling you that I know about you. I know because I fielded the complaints. I heard about what you've done in your art class. Don't worry. I can't do anything about it. I resigned before they had a chance to fire me, so I'm no longer the principal of St. Mark Lutheran. I'm no longer your boss.

Relax. Have a mint.

You may still get out of this unscathed. Not me. Everyone has it out for me, and everyone is going to think I deserve whatever happens to me. Well...everyone except you, because you've done the same things. So while it may be open season on ol' Don Creech, you may still be able to glide right under their radar. It all depends on what you do next.

I see your eyes flashing, and I would be worried if I were you. That would be wise. After all, there's blood in the water--my blood--and they might be looking for the fire behind the smoke. But as I tell you everything, remember that I'm your friend. I just may end up being the only one you're going to have left.

Sure you don't want one? They really are exceptional mints.

So you can trust me if I can trust you. How does that sound?

I have no need to implicate you. Really, if you think about it, it would be worse for me if I did. So don't make me.

As principal of the school, it was a dereliction of my duty to know that you had a thing for some of your students as well, and for me to have not done anything about it. Collusion, they would say. They would charge me with fostering a culture of abuse or some such nonsense when all we wanted to do was love those kids, love them in our own way.

There you go denying it again. That makes me angry. At least give me the dignity of your silence. I covered your ass for years. I told those parents that you were a stand-up guy, that their kids were liars, that their little imaginations were running wild, and that their devious minds would best be employed improving their grades rather than trying to deflect attention from their sorry test scores. Don't you dare try and squirm off the hook.

Don't you understand? You're the only one I can talk to because you're the only one I know of who shepherds their students the way that I do. So, you're going to be my confessor. Get used to the idea, and make yourself comfortable, because I'm going to tell you everything.

Did you hear that the Elders called for a special voter's meeting last week to deal with me? You might not follow all the machinations and intrigue in the church since you're one of our secular hires, so allow me to fill you in. There were two votes taken at that meeting: the first, to excommunicate me, and the second, to excommunicate anyone who knew about my supposed misconduct and failed to report it. The second motion didn't pass, but the first motion did, and it was approved by a unanimous vote from the congregation--my colleagues, my supposed friends. So, I've been officially excommunicated from the church I've attended my entire life, the church in which I was ordained.

I don't think I've ever seen that done before at St. Mark, and I've been a pastor here and a member of the school faculty in one way or another for thirty-six years. Later, I learned from a little cursory research, that it had actually been fifty-five years since the Missouri

Synod had excommunicated someone from any of their churches. That's how bad they think I am. That's how bad they would think you are.

So, that's that. I'm out. All of that counsel I've given as a pastor; all of my time I've given as a principal, improving test scores, courting the accreditation committees who would stroll blithely through Dawson ever so often wanting their asses polished. I delivered the stats. I kept academic standards high, and I did it for decades. Now, it's all come down to this, this bellyaching about nothing, about a little extra tenderness shown to a few kids when they needed it most.

Calling you here today, I had every intention of telling you how and when it all started, but I'm not sure I know myself. For me, it started slowly, I do know that. My wife and I were long past being interesting to one another physically, and our marriage became nothing more than a symbiosis predicated on necessity. Don't get me wrong, I love my wife, but I love her for her familiarity more than anything. Our time together has fashioned a cooperative ease of existence, rendering all alternatives too daunting to even begin to entertain. So, if that's love, then yes, I appreciate that security. She's an old shoe and you barely know you're wearing her.

Ah, but for passion? For excitement? That had to come from another source. So why do I like them young?

Why, why, why...

You know why, don't you? I did note that you liked them about the same age that I did. So you would agree that we have no interest in children. That's not our thing. Oh sure, society calls them children until they're eighteen, but no one believes that. Not really. It's just a lie that we all agree to perpetuate. Just like we tell our kids there's a Santa Claus, we tell ourselves that these newly formed adults are children, and we train our mock outrage on all who disagree with that faulty premise.

Every single student that I tried to love had been through puberty. I made sure of that. That was the first question I asked them. That was how I decided if they were off limits or not, and I had to be very specific about the questions I asked. I couldn't always tell from the sight of them, and if there was to come a time--like now-- when I would need to prove my innocence, in an unassailable way, then these standards had to be met.

I found that girls mature far earlier than boys, their first period happening as early as eight years old. Isn't that interesting? Some blame the hormones in our milk supply. Have you heard that one? But whatever the reason, I was pleasantly surprised.

As for the boys, it's easy to tell by the way they talk. They start talking about sex a lot, and they don't mind answering my questions. Did you know that throughout history, tribes determined the age of consent by the first appearance of pubic hair? Boys have no problem showing that off. I've seen boys start the change as early as nine, but to be safe, you can assume that they're pretty ripe at the end of their twelfth year.

You seem uncomfortable with me saying this stuff. Maybe hearing it out loud is making you squirm? Just sit still, will you? I have very good reasons for what I've done, and I need you to know what they are.

Have you ever asked yourself why we extend childhood past childhood's end? Why do we coddle these so-called children for so long? I have two theories: the first, that our fear of death, our fear of aging, motivates us to extend unnaturally what nature decided to abandon long ago. That way, we feel we have power over the very cycles of life that threaten our existence. We can bestow the gift of youth upon our offspring for as long as we choose. Second, I think we are intimidated by their vitality, their fearlessness, their hope. We make sure we don't let them out of the gate while they're cackling under that highly combustible fuel of puberty, not because we're afraid they will destroy our world, but because we are afraid they will own it.

You know about King Tut, who ruled at nine years old, but did you know about Cleopatra's brother, Ptolemy XIII? He, too, ruled before puberty. Jealous of his sister's celebrity, he banished her from Egypt, which, granted, you could argue was a result of youthful petulance, but I would argue that the oldest and supposedly wisest leaders in our world have not behaved much better.

This young pharaoh rubbed elbows with some of ancient history's most towering figures and held his own. He led an Egyptian army against the Romans--not just any Romans--against Julius Caesar. The kid lost, and the battle resulted in the burning of the famed Library of Alexandria, but it took balls, and balls that had probably only just dropped. Ptolemy XIII was twelve years old during that battle.

Oh, but he wasn't alone. King Baldwin IV not only saved Jerusalem from capture at the age of sixteen, but he did it while suffering from leprosy. If fact, he had the disease his whole life, but that didn't stop him from repeatedly defending his Christian kingdom against Saladin, the famed Muslim military tactician who ruled as sultan of Egypt and Syria. Would you have called him a child? I wouldn't have called him that to his face.

Then there's Mary Queen of Scots who ruled not one, but two countries, before she was eighteen. And King Louis XIII took the French throne in 1610 when he was nine years old, and he was quite successful. Mind you, these examples are just off the top of my head.

History contradicts our puritanical and absurd notion of what a child is, so I don't subscribe to this very modern, very recent notion that a young adult is a helpless child just because we say so. If they can reproduce, and they can rule a kingdom, then they can let me touch them if they decide to allow me to do so. It's their life, and their body, and to me, there is nothing more beautiful than the purity and the freshness of that transitional period of a human life. Why have its delicacies squandered by an unnatural and antithetical social construct formulated for the very purpose of preserving that precious awakening as if it were some museum piece trapped in amber? For that moment is a fleeting one, and it will never come again. The moment of that singular transition should be revered. It should be worshipped.

And by the way, all of this lofty philosophy on the subject and all my interest in it, started with the kid who is now trying to sue me, and I'll have you know that it was him who came on to me.

Let me pause here to remind you of something. Don't even think of repeating any of this to anyone, because if you do, you're going down with me. I know who complained about you. There were two of them. You preferred just girls, didn't you? Yes, you did. And those were just the ones who ventured to complain. I bet you dollars to doughnuts that there's more where that came from. So, remember that before you climb onto your high horse and think about heading for the door.

Paul Neumann is the name of the kid suing me, him and this little whore named Becky Krauss. As you may or may not know, Paul

Neumann ended up as a performing drag queen in Miami. So I'm not surprised that he wanted attention from me. He always wanted attention. And really, I don't even consider him my first boy. He was so feminine, so coquettish. He wanted me to see his body as much as he wanted to see mine.

Before Paul, I had never considered the idea of fraternizing with a student in that way. But Paul was beguiling and I was bored, and when you are in need of excitement there is nothing like the sweetness of forbidden fruit, as you well know. Let me be clear though. When I say Paul was beguiling, he was fascinating only for his anomalous nature. Others would come later who would truly mesmerize me, filling the hollow spaces I didn't know I had, and bringing heartbreak when they chose to move on.

Paul was the first only because he was the easiest. I figured he was a homosexual, and if I was ever going to touch someone so nubile and fresh, he was the perfect candidate, and he invited all of it.

At the time, I must have been in my late thirties and he was twelve. We were both repressed. We both needed an outlet. This was the early 80s--maybe 1981? There was no internet and there was no place in Dawson where one could buy a porno mag, so experimenting was the only option. I was curious about how he would look without clothes, and I think he was curious about how a grown man would look without clothes.

Paul had hips like a woman's. His lips were as soft as a woman's, too, and that spring he came of age with my help. Really, if you think about it, it was the only way it could have happened. He couldn't attempt to mess around with someone his own age because he would be called names, ostracized, and maybe worse.

They had what they called "fag drags" back in those days. They would beat up a little gay boy like Paul, tie his feet to one end of a rope, and the other to a trailer hitch, and take him for a spin along a gravel road. I don't remember it happening around Dawson, but I'd heard of it happening elsewhere. I'm sure Paul had heard about it, too. So, once he got the signal from me that I was intrigued...well, he was more willing than I was. I had more to lose, after all.

So where did this all happen? I won't ask where you conducted your sessions--that is, unless you would like to get it off your chest,

No? Fine.

For me, it was always the same place. In my office at St. Mark, I had a couch. I'm sure you've seen it. It's a love seat--red, white and blue. I had it ever since I started at the school in 1976. You're a little younger than I am, I know, but you remember the nation's bicentennial. Everything was red, white and blue: clothes, furniture...everything. We were all so patriotic, even when the result was as ghastly as this couch. It was a gift from the outgoing principal, so I kept it for the sake of graciousness. Believe me, I thought of getting rid of it many times, but since Dawson is America's Fourth of July City, well, it seemed only apropos that I be a trooper and keep it.

Most importantly, the kids loved it. They thought it was fun, and it went a long way to diffusing the tension that comes from being sent to the principal's office. They'd loosen right up, and I could get to the heart of the matter far easier when a student and I sat, side by side, on the red, white, and blue couch.

Paul was the first to sit on that couch with me. Before that, I sat behind my desk when a student came in, in the imposing manner befitting my station. Not so with Paul.

I remember it all started by me simply asking him why he was troubled and why his grades were taking a dive. So what answer did he give? I bet you can guess.

He blamed his parents. Have you noticed that they always blame their parents? Most of the time, the parents are not interested in raising their children as much as they would like to think. They drop them off with us, and they revert to indulging in the selfish behavior that they've sought to regain after long years of changing diapers and being awakened by their baby's constant crying. By late elementary school, and certainly by middle school, the parents are ready to reclaim their lives and what's left of their youth. That leaves me in charge of their kids, and I did my best to round their rough edges and make them shine...

I told Paul the same thing I told all of the students who needed such help: that a change was happening, that things would be difficult and confusing for a while, and that, together, we would get through it just fine. "Think of a caterpillar," I would say, "a caterpillar that is about to become a butterfly. It's dark and claustrophobic in that cocoon, but soon, you will be renewed. Soon you will be beautiful and free."

Paul told me that he had learned all about that in science class. "Isn't it called chrysalis," he said to me. I tousled his hair and told him how smart he was, and how proud I was of him. "Forget your parents," I told him. "They don't understand like I do. They are busy with other things." Then I told him that he and I would get through his chrysalis together. I asked him if he had started yet, if anything had changed down there. He said it had, and that's when I showed him what his future might look like, his future as a man.

Did you know the first recorded age-of-consent law dates to 1275 in England? A statute called Westminster 1 made it a misdemeanor to "ravish a maiden within age"--as they put it--whether with or without her consent. But how to determine what "within age" meant. That phrase was interpreted by a jurist, one Sir Edward Coke, as meaning the age of marriage, which at the time was twelve. Paul was twelve when he sat with me on the red, white, and blue couch.

My first girl was Becky Krauss. She's the other one suing me.

The Krausses lived in the poor part of town by the dike, and they couldn't have cared less about their daughter. They had no respect for themselves. They lived in squalor, and made Becky live in the same. Becky's father chose not to work. He knew Hughes Brothers was outside of town and always looking for a strong back, but did he care? No.

So Becky started acting out, and I gave her the love she was missing. I remember how thin her clothes were, how ill-fitting. I remember how much better she looked with them off.

So what do I get for helping her through the most difficult time of her life, when she had nothing, when she was nothing? I'll tell you what I get. She waits twenty-something years, waits until she's out of the state, and tries to ruin me.

Perhaps a drink of water? No?

I think I need one.

My first boy, my first real boy, I will never forget. I was nervous. It was a whole different feeling than what I'd experienced with Paul. Sure, technically Paul had the tools to qualify as a boy, but he was destined to be something in between. Not Scott Wegner. He was all man, and he was all man earlier than the other boys were.

I always wonder if you and I ever helped out the same students. Don't worry. I'm not asking for a confession--that wasn't part of the deal--I was just wondering.

If you didn't, you really should have tried Scott Wegner. He needed a lot of love.

Oh, but I forget, you stuck mainly to girls. Oh well, there's no accounting for taste.

Anyway, what can I say about Scott, or Scotty as I heard him called by his peers in the halls? I'll start by saying that I never thought of myself as gay. I still don't, but this kid would have made you think twice. He first came to my office when he was a new student. His mother, Alice Wegner, used to teach the seventh grade. Do you remember? This was...oh...1980, I believe. She died later, of course--very sad, such a tragedy--but this was before that. Anyway, he was acting out and was sent to my office. He was without a father. His father had died years earlier, and with his mother working, I don't think he had the guidance he needed.

Scott must have been eleven or twelve when he first came into my office, and I knew at that moment that he and I were going to hit it off. You should have seen him. He was gorgeous. He was an angel. His eyes were the bluest that I've ever seen. His hair was golden brown, and it was as if his cheekbones had been carved out of marble by Michelangelo himself. He was tall, his limbs muscular and developed, and you could tell by the way his jeans fit him that he was no child. He was like a big, beautiful present, begging to be unwrapped.

We sat on my red, white, and blue couch, and I remember how my heart beat. This was going to be risky, far riskier than Paul had been. Scott was not some confused gay boy. He was a real man, a real red-blooded, corn-fed, all American, Midwestern stud, and if I was going to experience his essence, the pure and unspoiled virility that he had only just come to know, then I would have to proceed with caution and humility. Such treasure I knew I didn't deserve, nor did I expect that it be handed over lightly. But he did eventually yield to me, and when he did, I felt as though I was alone in the garden with Adam, and it was then I knew just how generous God had been to that boy.

Don't worry. I'm not going to get explicit. Though part of you wants me to, doesn't it?

Scott and I had an agreement. I would see that his grades improved and that his performance in school would not disappoint his mother if he could agree to respect our privacy and not talk about the things I had done to help him transition. I told him that it would be very inappropriate of him to violate that trust, and that doing so would make his future very uncertain. He agreed.

Little did I know then that years later I would preside over his funeral. I suppose he committed suicide because he just couldn't get over the death of his mother--poor kid. But he was well out of school when that happened, and we had long since parted ways.

But he did leave me with one lasting gift: it was from our time together that I learned how to talk to the boys. After Scott, I had more confidence with them. I knew what they wanted. They didn't act as coy as the girls did. Almost to a one, they had no problem with taking my helping hand and showing me their newfound abilities. We would do it together, laughing and joking about it the whole time. It felt innocent to me. It made me feel alive and I made them feel good, too. I explained to them that no matter what was going on in their home life, they could always experience pleasure with me, and that such love and affection was good for them and that they deserved nothing less.

Girls, as I said before, were a bit tougher nuts to crack. You would think it would be the other way around, you would think that boys would be very uncomfortable with homoeroticism, but they love it, almost all of them do. Sure, I remember a few boys who didn't want anything to do with me, but my intuition gained in strength over the years, and I learned to avoid them. I had many takers though, all of them starved for attention. There was Paul, and Scott, and Lance, and Dustin, and Peter, and Stewart, and Jimmy, and Tim.

Though, I did sit on the couch with many girls over the years, too. I hadn't lost interest in the boys; I just needed something else, something more delicate. After Becky--who basically threw herself on me when given the chance--I took it slow. I wanted to find the right girl. I was far shyer around girls. Also, I didn't trust them as much.

With boys, once they had decided to partake in their awakening with me, I could sense that they were less likely than a girl might be to cause problems for me. Socially, it was not as acceptable for two men to help each other out, and the embarrassment of having consented to such a thing would not be worth it to them, regardless of what little catharsis would be gained by betraying me. For them, it was better to just refuse me if they changed their mind, and forget it ever happened. Boys don't whine so much about such things.

Ah, but girls require more than just joking around and playing "show me yours and I'll show you mine." They're a lot of work. They require coaxing, flattery and constant reassurances.

But Laurie didn't. Laurie was easy.

I'll forgo her last name--though you can probably guess to whom I refer. Maybe you helped her, too? Never mind. You don't have to tell me.

Laurie was cute, but not kid cute. She looked every bit a woman to me. And her eyes, they had a playfulness, a daring in them. She wanted to be bad. She wanted to be more adventurous than I had ever conceived of being. I've always had a thing for blondes, so how could I refuse?

I remember the first time she sat on my couch. She wore a white cotton blouse. She was eleven years old and her breasts were budding nicely, those perky little nubs pressing at the fabric, the nipples clearly visible. She was not yet in the habit of wearing a bra. She was sweet, and quiet, and her hair smelled like apples. She certainly had a woman's curves, but to be safe, I asked her if my supposition was right. She didn't know what I meant, so I was compelled to elaborate. Then her eyes lit up. "Do you mean...?" she asked me. "Yes," I reassured her, "When you bleed like that it means you're a woman." She considered for a moment and then said, "Well, then in that case, I am." And let me tell you, she certainly was.

As I said, I'm not into children, no matter what society says. What I did was playful, and I see no harm in it. I helped them all through that awkward, confusing time of their lives when their parents were too busy to care what their kids really wanted, what they yearned for. I made them feel good for a while, I made them feel like they had someone to talk to, a private outlet for all of that pent-up angst. A lot of those kids had alcoholic fathers who beat them, and what did I do? I blew on their wounds, and I lost my kingdom because of it. So it has been decreed by the Missouri Synod Lutheran Church and the Council of the Elders.

Do I have regrets? Of course I do. I'm sure you do, too. What I did might have been controversial, but I don't think it is as patently wrong as some might think. Sure, I realize now that I didn't really know what effect I would have on those students years later. But did our time together all of those years ago really impede their happiness now? Or are they just short on cash?

My wife doesn't believe a word of it. Zelda's not all there though. She has early dementia. It's a nasty business, but almost a blessing now. The slander that's been leveled at me would crush her if she could understand it. I've sent her away for a while to see her sister in Florida. That should shield her from this witch hunt.

So they will come at me, these students, and I'm sure more will pile on. They want to use me as an excuse for their failed lives. Funny thing is: I had all but forgotten about my private time with these people. Besides, I stopped helping students in that special way a long time ago. Times changed. Parents started getting obsessive about their kids, about everything they did, everything they ate, and everything they said. Every movement became accounted for. My services were no longer needed.

So before I let you go, know this: I've stopped. I stopped years ago. I've since put myself back into the hands of Jesus Christ and my conscience is clear, all impurities of my soul--perceived or otherwise-- expunged by His boundless mercy. Scripture ensures my forgiveness-- maybe not in this life--but certainly in the next, for I am reborn, and I am now without sin.

I have been absolved.

Chapter 19

The Museum of Death

On August 3rd at exactly 3:32 PM, the man entered the house on Second Street through the side door off the kitchen.

Perfect, he thought.

He didn't know exactly what hours Sylvia Blair worked, but it was a weekday, and it was before five o'clock, so he figured he wouldn't have long to wait before she returned home.

He was covered in sweat. Not only was he nervous, but it had been a long walk to the house from the highway and it was hot outside-- hotter than the devil's nut sack, as his father used to say. His shirt was stuck to his body and the leather of the shoulder holster carrying the nine millimeter Glock 19 was sticking to his ribs.

In the dark foyer of the house, he passed a mirror, the kind with a convex bubble of glass at its center, its frame an ornate tangle of Florentine woodwork, and he stopped to peer into it. He looked lost in its dusty, wide-angle reflection, like some hapless old man in a funhouse who was about to see his manner of death come up behind him in the form of a grinning clown holding an axe. But the glass revealed no murderous clown behind him, just the surreal kaleidoscope of Victorian flocked wallpaper striped with spires of shadow.

It was he who was the murderous clown, after all. He hoped it wouldn't come to that, but it could.

It most definitely could.

He pawed at his head and adjusted his wig. The thing was driving him crazy, but it was effective. Of course, that was the thing Hollywood was best at: deception. Good ol' Hollywood Toy & Costume. He had to admit, the wig's grey pile of locks, parted at the side, did a bang-up job of making him look like an innocuous retiree. The wire-rimmed glasses and the clean shaven face helped, too. With his bald head beneath the wig and his newly shaven face, he no longer had a hair on his head. That would help with forensics if things happened to get messy.

But it was the clothes that sealed the deal. They were the last thing Clayton Briggle would ever wear: a pair of tan chinos and a windowpane plaid, short-sleeved collared shirt.

Clayton leaned into his reflection. He looked gaunt. He'd lost a lot of weight. Stress, no doubt. It had been one hell of a month.

He never thought it would come to this. He never thought he would get his hands on a gun either, but now that he had, he couldn't quite forget about the weight of it under his shirt. He supposed if he had any experience with guns, or if he had ever carried a concealed firearm before, he would learn to forget about it, but weighing in at almost two pounds with its fully loaded fifteen round clip of nine millimeter full metal jacket American Eagles, the pistol demanded his attention.

It had been a week ago when Clayton had shown up with the Glock at Bear's cabin deep in the woods of Humboldt County with the story of how he had come by it, and of what had happened to the kilo of heroin.

"Everyone's talking about it," Bear had said. "You're up to your eyeballs in shit, brother, so if you got a good story, then let's hear it." With that, Bear had leaned back in his chair, fixing Clayton with a steely gaze, and crossing his arms.

Clayton had told him that he had staked out Jimmy the Spic for weeks to avenge that double-cross in San Fernando. He didn't know exactly what he meant to do if he found him, and there was no guarantee that Jimmy would ever show his face on the streets of Hollywood again. Most likely, the weasel had slithered back to San Bernardino to try and fire up a meth lab again or had simply left the state. But what the hell--Clayton had nothing to lose and nothing but time.

Then one day, as Clayton nursed a coffee at a tiny donut shop located across Hollywood Boulevard from The Frolic Room, he saw him. Jimmy was alone and heading into the bar. He was wearing a Dodgers baseball cap and sunglasses, but Clayton knew that build and that gait: a rail-thin wisp of a guy who swung his left arm too much when he walked. It was Jimmy. Clayton was sure of it.

Clayton figured Jimmy was heading into The Frolic to move some of the dope, so he sat back and waited. He didn't have to wait long. After ten minutes, Jimmy emerged from the bar; he looked both ways up and down the boulevard, his hands deep in his pockets.

Clayton tossed the Styrofoam cup of piss warm coffee into the gutter, jumped into a rented Mitsubishi Lancer parked two spots up the boulevard with its nose pointing east, and pulled into traffic. It was possible that Jimmy would remain on foot, but it wasn't likely. Unless he had taken an apartment close by, Jimmy was probably parked at the Hollywood and Highland garage and headed either out of town or to the east side where rents were cheap, neighbors kept their mouths shut, and the cops had their hands full.

Besides, following on foot wasn't an option. Clayton wasn't looking to take Jimmy down in public, on the boulevard where every costumed superhero begging for change in front of the Chinese Theater had a cell phone camera and delusions of grandeur. No, he was looking for the weasel's lair. That's where the dope would be--what was left of it--and maybe a pile of cash. He had to hang back and set up a tail.

Clayton was facing east and Jimmy was heading west, so Clayton had to loop around and come up Highland and pull up at Hollywood Boulevard where he hit a stale red light. Teeth gritted, he scanned the crowds for the Dodgers hat.

"If I lost Jimmy then, I knew I wouldn't get another chance before the Mexicans finally caught up to me," Clayton told Bear. "This was it."

There were tourists everywhere, throngs crossing the boulevard in every direction. Then he saw Jimmy bumming a smoke from a black guy on the corner before he suddenly broke right and high-tailed it up Highland toward Franklin. So he wasn't parked at the public garage under the mall. He was headed somewhere else. Still at the red light, Clayton was losing him.

The light turned green and Clayton gunned his six-cylinder shit box past a converted open-top tour van full of tourists with cheap shades and sunburned necks. He swerved right, cutting off a blonde in a Cadillac Escalade who laid on her horn and flipped him off. Clayton was just in time to see Jimmy yank open the door of a beat-to-shit 3-series BMW parked at the curb.

He was coming up on Jimmy too fast. He pumped the brakes and came to a stop, signaling as if he was waiting for Jimmy's parking space. He wasn't worried about being recognized. He had already adopted his new Old Golfer look, with the addition of some dime-store shades.

Jimmy finally pulled into traffic. Clayton allowed about a two-car buffer between him and the Beemer and followed it to Hollywood and Gramercy, where Jimmy signaled for a left turn. Clayton pulled behind him and did the same. Jimmy was no CIA operative, and hadn't given the Mitsubishi a second look back on Highland, so it was unlikely he would smell a tail.

"But while Jimmy was waiting for traffic to thin so he could turn left," Clayton had told Bear, "there was a moment when he caught my eye in the rear view and my heart stopped. But he didn't seem to recognize me."

Jimmy swung left down the residential street, slowing halfway down the block and signaling right to turn into the underground lot of a dingbat apartment building. It looked like a thousand other such courtyard apartments in L.A., probably six to eight units. On the stucco façade was drawn a turquoise, mid-century florette beside a scrawl of cursive font that proclaimed the building to be the Palm Palace.

Clayton breezed by, circled the block and cautiously rolled back up Gramercy. Craning his neck, he saw that the BMW was parked beneath the complex and that Jimmy was gone.

Clayton parked and got out. He was right. There were only six units, all of them with exterior entrances. He walked by each one looking at his phone, and pausing briefly by each door. Somewhere, someone was doing their laundry and it was venting the smell of a dryer sheet into the apartment's courtyard.

Finally, Clayton heard Jimmy's voice behind one of the doors; it sounded like he was on the phone. It was coming from Unit #4. Clayton walked back to the apartment's covered entrance with its ripped-up green indoor/outdoor carpet and row of metal mail slots. He smiled at the conceit that this was any kind of "palace." It was a shit hole and it was perfect for a double-crossing asshat like Jimmy the Spic.

Clayton checked the mail slot and the intercom button for Unit #4. Unlike the others, there was no paper tab slid into the provided slots proclaiming a surname for the tenant. Both were blank. This was all Clayton needed to know. These were definitely Jimmy's new digs.

What to do next was the hard part. Would he actually break and enter? He would have to.

Clayton told Bear that he had staked out the apartment for days, but Jimmy had no pattern, and that made it a lot harder. Drug dealers didn't keep regular hours, after all. Plus, they hardly ever left the house. Pizzas came, Chinese food came, shady characters with shifty eyes came and went, but Jimmy didn't leave. Clayton had given up on the notion that he could ever be an effective cat burglar if the mark never left the house. Then one afternoon, after three days of staking out the Palm Palace and dozing in and out of sleep, the Beemer finally pulled out of the garage. Clayton went for it.

Walking through the courtyard building a few times before, he had noted that nobody was home on weekdays--at least that he could tell. That meant he could make whatever noise he needed and there would be nobody around to hear. Now he just had to find the balls to break into Unit #4.

He knocked on the door just to make sure the way was clear and jumped a foot when someone answered.

Peering through the chain on the door was a bleached blond man in his early twenties who didn't look a day under forty. He had a tweaker's teeth--the kind of chops that looked liked the weathered picket fence from a haunted house--and a pair of glazed-over eyes that squinted like a lizard's.

"Can I help you?" said the loser.

Startled, and without knowing what to say, Clayton said, "Um...I'm here to see...is this where Jimmy lives?"

"Who are you?" said the kid.

"A friend," said Clayton.

"Yeah, this is Jimmy's place."

"I guess he's not home?"

"No, he's home. But he's busy."

This Clayton didn't understand. He had seen the car leave.

"I thought I saw him leave," Clayton said, "But I wasn't sure. I thought I'd stop by anyway."

"Oh that," said the kid, "you must be talking about Frodo. He took the car to Venice Beach. You want to wait for Jimmy? He's a little busy right now."

"No, I'll come back."

"It's no problem," said the kid. "I'm waiting."

"You scoring?" Clayton asked.

"Yeah," said the kid. "You?"

"I'd like to, yeah."

"You don't look like the type," the kid said suspiciously. "You're not five-oh, are you?"

"Fuck no," Clayton said. "I knew Jimmy when your twin brother was running down your mother's leg."

"Easy, bro," the kid said. "No need to get jumpy. Just making sure."

"I couldn't believe it," Clayton told Bear. "Was this guy going to actually invite me in with Jimmy in the fucking apartment? I wasn't ready for this. This hadn't been part of the plan. This was not stealth. I would have to kick Jimmy's ass the old-fashioned way."

The kid unchained the door.

"The question was," Clayton told Bear, "whether this kid would step in if I attacked Jimmy. That was what I had to figure out quick. I decided that he wouldn't. He was just there to re-up. The last thing he wanted was to get dragged into something. The kid was a bottom feeder. If anything, he would fight me for scraps. But I also had to remember that I was in disguise. Jimmy would see through me eventually, but not before I could get the drop on him."

As he entered the apartment, Clayton asked where Jimmy was.

"In the bedroom," said the kid. "He's fucking some chick."

The apartment was as expected. To Clayton's right was a darkened kitchen that smelled like a dead animal. There was a Hefty bag of garbage on the carpet near its entrance. To his left was a dining nook that had no furniture but held a built-in mini chandelier hung with glass jewels and burning with low-watt bulbs. Before him was a living room with a blue velour couch parked before a wooden coffee table with all manner of shit carved into it: a flaming skull, a pot leaf, a snake wrapped around a sword. Across the room, a television muttered a baseball game.

"Just hang out," said the kid. "I'm going to bounce. He's taking too fucking long. I gotta take my mom to chemo."

Clayton had watched in disbelief as the blond kid marched to the front door and left. Clayton remembered how his mouth had hung open as he sat in the dark.

"Just like that," Clayton told Bear, "I was left alone in Jimmy the Spics apartment while the dude was dipping his wick, naked and defenseless, in the other room. I was floored."

Across the living room was a door to the hall and the bedroom beyond, and all Clayton could hear was the squeaking of springs and a girl moaning.

Thinking quickly, Clayton got up and rummaged through everything he could find, even going through the refrigerator and freezer--the oldest trick in the book for hiding dope or money--but found nothing. There was a hall closet with one winter jacket hanging in it and Clayton slammed himself into it when Jimmy's voice, suddenly just on the other side of the bedroom door said, "I need a beer after that. What about you?"

Clayton waited in that closet for another fifteen minutes before Jimmy and the girl finally came out of the bedroom, Jimmy saying. "What the fuck? Brian must have bounced," before suggesting to the girl, who Clayton could not see, that the two of them get a pizza at Little Caesar's.

"But didn't Frodo take the car?" came her reply.

"It's two blocks away," said Jimmy, "you have legs, don't you?"

"Yeah, but they're not working right now," the girl said, and Jimmy giggled like a moron.

"And that was it," Clayton told Bear. "I didn't even have to break a hand on the guy's face. Just like that, I was totally alone. Not only that, but I knew about how long I had. I figured a good half hour. And holy shit, did I find the mother lode."

"What did you get?" Bear asked.

"Almost everything," Clayton told him. "I got about half of the kilo back, a five thousand dollar wad, and something else, something you have to come out to the truck to see."

Bear followed Clayton through the woods and down the gravel driveway to the truck. Clayton popped the glove compartment, took out the gun and handed it to Bear. "What do you think?"

Bear turned it over in his hands, letting out a straw-dry whistle between his teeth. "It's a drop," said Bear. "You found it in the apartment? Where?"

"Under the bed," said Clayton, "shoved into a hole punched into the box spring. What's a drop?"

"See this?" Bear said, pointing to a scratched part of the gun's frame. "The serial numbers have been filed off. And notice how the grip is all taped up. I can bet you this is already a murder weapon. It's a common model, perfect for a drop gun. You can plug anyone with this, get rid of it, and the cops will have a hell of a time. It's no get out of jail free card--CSI will still pinch you for hair, skin or for breathing wrong at a crime scene--but the ballistics guys will be scratching their head. This gun is not traceable to you."

Clayton smiled wide at this.

"Ah, no," said Bear. "Don't tell me you're going to go after the Mexicans? Remember, I can't let you do that. I'm the one who hooked you up, remember?"

"No, nothing like that," Clayton had assured him. "I'm not that crazy. Plus, I already paid them back."

"Yeah?"

"Yeah," said Clayton. "I walked right into that pool hall, right into that stairwell where I met them the first time. They stared at me like a cow would stare at a passing train. It was like I was a fucking ghost. I threw a half key of heroin on the steps and $12,000 cash on top of it."

Bear smiled at this.

Clayton went on, "You see, my inheritance check came through, and with the five grand I stole from Jimmy, it was only seven grand out of pocket. I told them the story of how I got jacked and by whom. I also told them that I figured I owed them a point for their troubles. That's what the extra two grand was for. Then I asked them if we were good. They said yes. And then I turned around and calmly got the fuck out of there. And that was it."

Bear nodded reverently. "And you're sure they're cool with you now?"

"Yep," said Clayton. "Wouldn't you be?"

"I would."

"That left me about thirty-four grand," said Clayton, "but I owe forty on another matter. It's some greedy bitch who changed the terms of a handshake deal and thinks she can strong arm me. So, no, this gun is leaving the state and so am I. I have some unfinished business."

#

So here it was, a week after his good fortune at the Palm Palace apartment complex in Hollywood, and Clayton Briggle was standing in the hallway of Sylvia Blair's mansion on Second Street in Dawson, Nebraska, staring into an antique mirror to meet the eyes of a man he didn't recognize.

Nobody knew he was back in town. He left his truck in Lincoln, and a cab dropped him off at the Walmart out on Highway 15. He was a ghost.

He pulled the gun from its holster and headed deeper into the house. He would wait for her, and when she got home, he would spring. He would make her wait until night fell, and then she would escort him to the Blair funeral home and finally burn his father's body, ending their relationship once and for all. There was no way in hell she was taking his money as long as he was holding a drop gun. Sylvia Blair wouldn't know what a drop gun was, but Clayton would explain it to her.

Oh, yes, he would.

Crazy spires of shadows cast by the antlers of a mounted eight-point buck striped the Victorian wallpaper of the darkened hallway as a knife of sunlight stabbed through the side door's fan window. Nobody ever locked their doors in Dawson. Lucky him.

The buck turned out to be one of three heads in the narrow hall. A black bear and gazelle with glassy eyes watched Clayton pass.

It was true what the townsfolk had said, Clayton thought. This really was a museum of death.

A chill shot up Clayton's spine when he entered the living room. There were dead things everywhere: a fox grinned at him from around a bookcase, while atop it, ravens with their wings spread looked ready to take flight. A dray of dead-eyed squirrels holding nuts stared at him at the foot of the grand staircase, as if frozen in mid chew to assess the coming danger. There was a woodchuck, a coyote, a pair of prairie dogs, and a huge black bear bearing its fangs in the corner beside a mahogany grandfather clock which struck the hour, shattering the silence.

Clayton jumped. "What a freak," he muttered, turning in a circle to meet the eyes of the long-dead menagerie surrounding him, sweeping the gun from side to side, and stepping gingerly into the center of the room. He cocked his head and listened, but he heard nothing but the ticking of the grandfather clock.

He cringed his way past a motionless spiny iguana on an end table. The creature looked past him with two yellow, reptilian slits. Suddenly, Clayton didn't want to be in the center of the room surrounded by impassive, doll-like eyes stuffed into carcasses staring at him through the dark, and so he headed for another massive, pillared bookcase along the far wall. A plump, hairy tarantula squatted on a shelf at eye-level. Clayton yelped and took a step back. But it too was dead and dried.

He nudged it with the barrel of his gun and the spider skated sideways unnaturally, all eight legs fixed in place.

A stuffed bald eagle with wings spread looked down at him with a haughty stare from the top of the bookshelf, its talons gripping the arabesque scrollwork of its capital.

"You've got to be illegal," Clayton muttered at the bird.

His eyes drifted across the bookshelves, glowing dimly with the pale light from an adjacent floor-to-ceiling window hung with burgundy velvet drapes tied back with golden tassels, its ivory sheers drawn tight. None of the titles on the shelves were putting Clayton at ease: several books on human anatomy, both the Tibetan and Egyptian Book of the Dead, one of the Eternity books, The Complete Book of Witchcraft, and a dog-eared copy of The Necronomicon.

Clayton blew out his breath and looked at the clock as if in doing so he could speed it up and get this over with. He was officially done with being in this room.

4:10

To his right, and through a much bigger foyer, was the front door, paneled and carved with rosettes, a rectangular window at its upper half, the glass etched and wavy with time. Through the foyer toward the right was a floor to ceiling wooden pocket door half slid open and leading to a darkened parlor. Through the foyer to the left, the carved staircase--guarded by the dray of squirrels and a hedgehog that he hadn't noticed before--began its tortuous way upwards. On the landing above, a square stained glass window shot prisms of blood red and cobalt blue across the high ceiling.

Clayton looked behind him where he had come from. The side door off of the kitchen wasn't visible but it was still well within hearing. Whether he liked it or not, he would have to stay in this room, his gun poised between the two doors, and wait.

He sat on a Chippendale loveseat done in a florid petit point, its arms draped with lace. The Queen Anne coffee table before him was littered with tools and brushes. A small, stuffed white rabbit acted as a centerpiece, and an album full of mounted butterflies sat beside a box of pins.

Clayton heard voices. He stood and spun around. There were two people coming. One was definitely Blair, but the other was male.

They were at the side door. Clayton's blood pumped through his neck. This was all wrong.

He had planned to sit on the couch, in the dark, pointing the gun at Blair when she walked in, and when she popped on the lights, she would scream. He would be the man in control, with a confident, insouciant smile on his face, just like he had seen in the movies, but that wasn't going to work now. She wasn't alone.

Some man was with her.

He ran to the wall closest to the hallway leading to the side door to see if he could hear better and caught a toe on a side table, the one with the spiny iguana, knocking over a lamp.

"Shit," he hissed through his teeth.

As he turned to right the lamp, he heard Sylvia say something at the side door. The man barked out a laugh, and with wide-eyed dawning horror, Clayton suddenly knew who the man was.

It was Sheriff Bob Lutz.

Clayton could hear the handle on the side door turning. He had seconds. He sprinted for the staircase.

"...just for a moment," Blair said. "Then we'll get you back on the mean streets."

"Well...I don't see why not," Lutz said, giggling like a school boy.

"We can talk about Steinhart's death certificate later," said Blair, "but first we need to release some of that steam."

Lutz groaned mischievously, "Oh, you're bad."

Clayton was on the landing above, his back pressed to the flocked wallpaper and the light from the stained glass window overlooking the front porch dappling his face with shards of crimson light. He stilled his hammering heart and with a hand slippery with sweat shoved his gun back into his shoulder holster. Lutz would be gone soon. Clayton would just have to wait him out.

"Let me show you just how bad I am, honeybunch," Blair cooed.

Lutz made a yummy sound and then chugged out a knowing laugh.

Gross, Clayton thought. Is Lutz banging Sylvia Blair? That's just wrong. That settles it. She is a fucking witch. It would take all of the spells in the world to make a man want to hit that shit.

"Let's go upstairs," Blair said.

Clayton froze like he had been hit with an ice bath. Then he peeled himself off of the landing wall and scrambled up to the second floor on jellied legs.

The two were coming after him.

The hall above was dark and lined with doors on each side. All of them were closed. Behind him, he heard the tick of Blair's heels on the tiles of the foyer below.

Clayton had no idea where Blair was headed. Choosing a door could trap him in the same room, which might work if he could find a good hiding place. But what if he couldn't?

Maybe a bathroom, he thought. But that might not work either. If these two were going to fuck each other's brains out, then both of them were going to end up in the bathroom at some point. For all he knew, Blair had a glass shower and no curtain to hide behind.

Shit, he thought, pick something, anything. Behind him, two sets of footfalls were coming up the stairs.

Clayton ran to a door that capped the end of the hall. It was a little smaller than the others. He hoped it might be a closet.

He yanked open the door, threw himself inside and as he looked down the hall to see Blair's grey curls just bobbing into view as she ascended the staircase, he pulled closed the door with a click and blew out a shuddering breath.

Backing away from the door, he almost fell on his ass. A flight of stairs were behind him, a steep and narrow staircase leading upwards into the dark.

The attic stairs, Clayton thought. Oh thank God, he thought, closing his eyes and calming himself. Thank God.

Pressing his ear to the door, he could hear the two lovebirds goofing off, their voices fading into some other room down the hall, and Clayton spared a moment to be grateful that he hadn't inadvertently locked himself into the same room with them. His nightmares were bad enough.

He took a deep breath. Christ, he thought. It was freezing in here.

He looked up the staircase. He could see nothing. Somewhere above him, he could hear the hum of air conditioner units laboring, a draft pouring down from the darkness above. It had to be thirty degrees cooler in this stairwell than it was anywhere else in the house. He was covered in nervous sweat, and as it began to dry down his back, he shivered violently, wrapping his arms around himself.

Blair and Lutz, he thought. Unbelievable. He wondered how long they had been doing each other and wondered if that little morsel of gossip had made it to the Corner Café.

With a flash of recollection, he thought of something Blair had said the day she suddenly upped the agreed price to dispose of dad: "I had to do a little extra work with Lutz," she had said.

It looked to Clayton like Sylvia had been doing a lot of extra work with Lutz.

Damn, he thought, it was cold. Hopefully they wouldn't be long, but he didn't know. He might as well head upstairs. Every attic has a blanket somewhere--maybe in a trunk? He had nothing but time to find one.

At the top of the stairs, he pawed at the wall for a light switch, finally found one, and flicked it on.

He went numb.

He wasn't alone.

In the center of the attic, and below the beams of the peaked roof, a group of people were gathered around what looked like a card table, in the middle of a poker game.

"Sorry," was all Clayton could think to say, and then he turned to run back down the stairs before anyone could get a good look at him.

But then he froze as the corner of his eye turned him back around and he stared in horror at what he saw. His heart iced over, and a sound escaped him, a sound he had never made before and would never make again. It was the sound of something deep in his head shattering.

His father was at the card table.

"No..." Clayton moaned. "What the fuck...no!"

Foster Briggle sat looking at the cards in his hand with dead eyes, a pile of poker chips beside him on the table's green felt. He was dressed like an Old West gambler: a dark suit, ruffled shirt and string tie. His wisps of white hair combed over and styled, a circle of rouge on each cheek.

Slowly, Clayton walked toward the table, each foot creaking on the floorboards, his neck long and his eyes wide.

Beside his father was a woman in a flouncy red dress and black lace shawl, with a pearl necklace hanging around her turkey neck. She was also dead. She had no cards or chips. She was only watching, a rictus grin frozen between her red painted lips.

Clayton swallowed hard, circling the table, the air conditioner units in the corner of the room roaring with the blood pumping through his ears.

Across from his father, also in a western suit and also holding cards in one white hand, was Lance's dad, Roger Vanderboom.

His mouth hanging open, Clayton leaned toward the old proprietor of Midwest Automotive and then recoiled, clapping a hand over his mouth, fighting the urge to vomit. The skin along each side of the man's face was stippled and torn, and right along the hairline, just above the glazed, lifeless eyes was the glint of what looked like a staple.

"What do you think?" came the raspy voice of Sylvia Blair.

Clayton spun around.

Chapter 20

The Witch's Oven

Sylvia Blair was at the top of the stairs, a cigarette fuming in one wrinkled hand, dressed in a hot pink dressing gown bedazzled with silver starbursts. "And who the fuck are you?" she growled.

Clayton drew his gun.

Sylvia threw back her head and laughed her smoker's laugh. She narrowed her eyes at Clayton. "Nice piece," she said.

Clayton flicked his eyes to his gun.

"Not that one," Blair said, "the one on the top of your head. It's a little sideways."

Clayton ignored this. "Where's Lutz?"

"Gone."

"That was quick."

"Always is," Blair said simply, taking a long drag from her cigarette, her feral eyes still keen and fixed on Clayton's. "So what do you think of my tableau?'"

"It's fucked up," said Clayton, "that's what I think."

"You ever heard of Madame Tussaud?" said Blair.

Clayton said nothing, his gun still trained on her. He wanted to pull the trigger. He wanted to see her explode and crumple to the ground like an old, pink casino, but he couldn't. He needed her, at least for a while.

"She did wax figures," Blair continued, "and everyone gave her the keys to their city for it, but this is much harder." Blair took a step into the room. "For starters I have to work in a fucking refrigerator. Then, the bodies all have to be put into position before I embalm them."

Clayton chanced a sideways glance at the corpses at the table. There were five: his father, Lance's father, the woman in the red dress and two other old men Clayton didn't recognize.

Horror wormed its way through his guts when he realized there were more bodies in the darkness beyond the poker table. Two young spectators were sitting on a couch watching the card game from the shadows, watching with their dead eyes. They couldn't have been older than teenagers. They were dressed identically in white, short-sleeved shirts, black pants and ties.

"It's not easy," said Blair proudly, "but I do it all myself. All of it."

Clayton scanned the other corners of the attic. The walls were lined with shelves holding plastic jugs, lengths of tubing, and syringes. In one corner of the attic, tucked beneath the eaves, were several opened crates.

"Those crates," Blair said, following Clayton's eyes and taking another step into the room, "are how I bring the bodies up here..."

"Stay where you are," Clayton warned, glancing at Blair's slowly shuffling feet.

Her feet stopped moving. They were clad in white bunny slippers: black, stony eyes fixed above little pink noses and a spray of whiskers. With a lurch of his stomach, Clayton realized they were real. She had slid her feet into real, hollowed out rabbits.

"Of course, I can't lift crates with bodies in them," Blair went on. "I pay high school kids to do that. Once I get the body out of the crate, I usually start with a pre-injection into the carotid artery. I use a fluid that helps break up clots and about a half gallon of water to build up pressure in the circulatory system before I open the vein for drainage. As I said, the bodies have to be in position before the embalming fluid goes in. It hardens them right up. You need a strong back for this kind of work, you know?

"In this scene," Blair continued, waving a hand at the card table, "they happen to be sitting, but I've also done standing, crouching--all sorts of scenes over the years. The features of the face also need to be set prior to injecting fluid. Take ol' Foster Briggle here, for instance. He was skinny--just a wisp of a thing, really--and he had dentures. That makes it more difficult to get the mouth right. I had to suture his mouth closed. A little extra work, but it was worth it, don't you think? Just look at that poker face. I bet you can't tell what cards he's holding."

Blair took another step into the room, "And what about you? What cards are you holding?"

"I said stay there!" Clayton shouted.

Blair stopped and frowned, but kept talking, though now with frustrated patience, "For this scene, getting the cards into their hands was the challenge, but I pride myself on my detail work. I used tape prior to embalming. Then once the hands hardened up, well, then they gripped the cards by themselves."

Blair took another step toward Clayton.

"I told you not to move, bitch," Clayton said icily, "and why don't you stop flapping your gums while you're at it." He could feel himself turning white. His mouth was filling up with spit, his stomach churning.

Blair stopped, lifted her hands with mock submissiveness, and with a limp wrist took the last drag from her cigarette as she watched Clayton, her eyes glittering. She let the butt drop to the wooden floor and crushed it out with one of the rabbit carcasses on her feet.

"You got to massage your bodies while you embalm them," Blair said. "By applying nice, even pressure on the arteries and veins, you make sure fluid is getting to all parts of the body. Then, when the arterial injection is complete, I use a trocar--a long hollow spear that has suction--to puncture the abdominal organs. This is done through one hole made just to the side of the belly button. Excess fluid is sucked out while puncturing each organ. Cavity fluid is then added to the abdominal area by removing the trocar from the vacuum and then adding a gravity attached tube to the bottle of fluid to flow it into the area..."

"Okay, it's high time you shut the fuck up," Clayton snapped. "You are one sick bitch, you know that?"

"I'm an artist," Blair said with a pout. "Some people have no taste." She smiled wolfishly, her teeth smeared with pink lipstick. "And I know who you are now. It took me a while, but I figured it out. What are you going to do, Clayton? Shoot me?"

In spite of the freezing cold, Clayton's nausea had glazed him with a blanket of thick sweat.

"Cat got your tongue?" Blair teased.

Clayton wanted out of this room and fast. He swallowed hard and said, "This is how this is going to work. You and I are loading my dad into one of these crates and we're taking him to the crisper. Now."

Clayton straightened his arm and aimed the gun afresh, pointing it right between her eyes.

Her smile still stretched across her face, Blair said didactically, "I can't lift one side of a coffin by my lonesome, honeybunch. I'm an old lady."

"Then you're going to die trying," said Clayton. "Now grab him and drag him to that corner of the attic." Clayton waved the gun, indicating where the crates were, and circled behind Blair, blocking the staircase. "Move!"

Blair shot him a hurt look as she headed for the card table. "Laszlo Toth," she said.

"What?"

"You're just like Laszlo Toth, that guy who went into the Vatican and chipped up Michelangelo's Pieta with a hammer."

Blair hesitated as she approached the body of Foster Briggle and looked back at Clayton.

"Do it," he said.

"Laszlo Toth," Blair spat and grabbed Foster Briggle by the shoulders. With a raspy grunt, she heaved him off the chair, the body crashing to the floor, the cards fluttering out of the dead man's hand. She started dragging the body across the wooden floor of the attic. "Laszlo...fucking...Toth," she muttered breathlessly.

Clayton had to look away. "And what's with the costumes?" he asked. "What the fuck?"

Sylvia paused to catch her breath. "Dawson Arts Council," she panted. "From last year's production of Oklahoma! I saw them at Kim Steiger's thrift store. I get a lot of ideas shopping there."

"Jee-zus..." Clayton said, wiping cold sweat from his brow with the back of his hand.

"Well, you asked," Blair panted, shuffling backwards, still dragging the body.

"What did you do to Lance's dad?" Clayton asked.

Blair dropped the body with a thump, and turned around to stare at Clayton.

"What happened to his face? Did you do that? Tear it up like that?"

"That's a long story," Blair said, her chest heaving. "Linda and I were just having a little fun. She was my best friend. Did you know that? And Roger treated her like utter shit. I need a fucking cigarette. A body gets heavy when you fill it. You should try this."

"Get him in the box." Clayton was doing everything he could not to throw up, but the spit in his mouth was thick and his stomach was doing back flips. He grabbed a crate and lid from the corner of the attic and dragged it toward the body. He holstered his gun. "Do not try running for it, or I'll plug you where you stand. Don't think that I won't. Now you grab his feet."

If he was going to throw up, this would be the time. At his feet, his father lay on his back, staring up at him with milky eyes. The body was still in a sitting position, the arms and legs cocked and braced like he was a dead beetle that had just been sprayed with poison.

They lifted the body and dropped it into the crate with a thump.

"Put the fucking lid on, for chrissake," Clayton said thickly, turning away.

Now they had to get it downstairs. It turned out to be easier than Clayton thought. Since he had no regard for Blair's house, he simply waited at the landing of each flight so that Blair couldn't run away, and ordered her to push the crate down each flight, using the stairs like a log flume. Sure, it took chunks out of the wall, the banister, and marred up the floors, but he couldn't have given two shits about how her house of horrors would look later for the appraiser.

As he waited below the attic stairs, he wiped off the door handle with the tail of his shirt, and Blair pushed the crate along the waxed hardwood floor of the upstairs hall. They passed an open bedroom where clothes were strewn across the poster bed and across the floor.

"Grab that shirt," Clayton commanded, "and both of those socks and throw them over the rail."

"What are you up to?" Blair said under what was left of her breath. She looked exhausted. She grabbed the clothes.

"You can leave the pants," Clayton said.

Blair shrugged and grabbed the rest: a yellow tank top with a brightly colored macaw embroidered across the breast, and two white bobby socks with pom-poms on their heels. She dangled them over the railing above the entry hall and let them go. They fluttered down to the first floor.

Clayton went downstairs and waited for the crate. With undue force--evidently hoping it would bowl Clayton over--Sylvia Blair pushed the crate down the final flight of stairs. It came barreling toward Clayton, taking a sizeable chunk of the entry hall's peg and groove floor with it, before it skidded to a stop in front of the parlor door.

"Leave the crate here," Clayton said. "Go get me two plastic garbage bags and double bag them and put the clothes inside."

"But you left the pants," Blair protested. "How are you going to cover up your tiny dick when you play dress up?"

Clayton smirked and waved her toward the kitchen with the gun.

Blair went, her freakish bunny slippers slapping on the hardwood floor, and plucked two white plastic trash bags from a roll in the cupboard. Returning to the living room, she put the clothes in the bags. "There you go, cowboy. You gonna beat off with them?"

"Sit down," Clayton said.

She did.

"Now what?" Blair asked disinterestedly, reaching for her skull lighter and touching it to the tip of an American Spirit 100.

"We wait for dark."

And they did, in that living room full of dead things, with the day's pale light slowly extinguishing beyond the window's ivory sheers. The grandfather clock ticked. Clayton watched shadows slowly swallow the crate in the front hall.

He was strangely calm. Sitting in Blair's great room again, surrounded by her stiff menagerie with their wiry hair and stony eyes wasn't as bad as it had been before, because the bogeyman--or bogeywoman, as it were--wasn't waiting to come up behind him. She was sitting across from him in plain sight, chain-smoking with a scowl on her face, beaten. If all those years at St. Mark would have stuck, and he had become a religious man, he would have praised God.

#

The grandfather clock voiced a single chime to mark 8:30.

It wasn't completely dark, but 8:30 in Dawson was the equivalent of midnight in L.A. Nobody would be out.

"Get up," said Clayton. "Let's do this."

Blair was half asleep. The two had said nothing to each other for over three hours.

"I said, get up," Clayton repeated, standing with a crack of his joints. "We're going to your car. We're going to end this and give my father a proper burial. He was a dick, but he didn't deserve this. I was going to pay you the twenty grand, but you got greedy. That was your mistake. My mistake was trusting you; but that's not going to happen again. Now, if you're smart, you'll do what I tell you, and then I'll go away, and you'll be free to play your sick little games, and fuck Lutz, and do whatever it is that monsters like you do."

Blair stood. She said nothing.

"And I'm not holding a gun on you the whole time, either," Clayton said. "I've had a lot of time to think sitting here. You're in far more trouble than I ever was. If you try anything, I won't tell Lutz. I'll tell the feds. They'll be the first to know about your little museum. But if you cooperate, I'll go back to California and forget any of this ever happened."

Blair, still in her ridiculous pink gown and taxidermy shoes, her eyes beady and still glaring malevolently at Clayton, sized up his offer with a gravelly, "Hmmm..."

"So do we have a deal?" said Clayton

"Sure," said Blair crisply, slowly exhaling a cloud of smoke.

"Those things are going to kill you," said Clayton, "Hopefully soon. Choke it down, freak show. We need to get a move on."

Clayton didn't need to ask where the car was. Sylvia Blair's hearse had always been indelibly parked in the same place. It was a fixture of the neighborhood, like the bandshell downtown, or the Corner Café. The entire time he and his friends were growing up, the hearse had always been backed into the driveway at the side of the mansion, its nose sniffing the street as if it could smell children and gun its engine and pounce on them at will.

This made Clayton think. Just how many years had Blair been unloading bodies into her attic to feed her hobby? No reason to ask her really, for as he watched her snuff out her umpteenth cigarette, he knew a lifelong addict when he saw one.

After they loaded the crate into the hearse, Clayton paused to look across Second Street at the Wegner house. There were lights on in the upstairs windows. The proximity of the Wegners to Sylvia Blair had always been unsettling, but tonight it was perverse.

He longed to see Ruby again, to forget what he had to do and to spend another night in her arms, far away from this madness. The glow from the upstairs windows transfixed him and for a brief moment he forgot about all that still haunted this town. Instead, he thought of her quiet strength, her kindness, and the warmth that radiated from her bashful, crooked smile like a heat lamp.

She was the opposite of him in every way, he knew. Yet, with her, he didn't feel like a contaminant, like he had felt when he had first entered Dawson in his beat-up truck. Her beauty and her strength were pure, and their potency would know no dilution, even from the likes of him. On the contrary, she had infused him, had healed him, and he had carried the moments he had with her in his heart the long month he had been away. Now, staring up at that lit window burning through the young night was like staring into the candle at the altar where he had learned to pray, and where he had finally known the embrace of forgiveness.

"Are we going to do this or do you plan on peeping in windows until the sun comes up?" said Blair, her cigarette bouncing between her wrinkled lips as she spoke. With a petulant puff of her cheeks she blew out a plume of thick smoke, her hand falling limply away from her face at the wrist. She cocked a hip and waited for an answer.

"Get in the car, you ghoul," Clayton said. "You're driving."

#

The Blair Funeral Home was at the far edge of Columbus Avenue, set apart, and at the end of a gravel drive. It was where a bleary-eyed and haunted Clayton had first met Sylvia Blair on his way into town last month to deliver his father's body. He had thought that would have been the end of it, but like many things in his life, he had been wrong.

Clayton sat in the backseat of the hearse, directly behind Blair, the double-bagged plastic garbage bag containing the few items of Blair's clothes on the seat beside him. When the wheels crunched to a stop beside the loading bay, Clayton told Blair to unlock the doors, to clear a path, and to take him to where they were going.

Blair was still dressed in her pink negligee and dead rabbit slippers, and Clayton wondered if he shouldn't have had her change clothes before they left her house. It was nine o'clock at night, and though he doubted anyone would come by, this couldn't look more suspicious. Granted, Blair dressed like a tropical fish on the best of days, but explaining her current getup to Lutz or one of his deputies would take more creativity than Clayton could ever begin to shit at the drop of a hat. The sooner they got inside, the better.

Blair had gone surly and quiet, and Clayton wondered if she had something up her pink sleeve. He couldn't think what, but he had to keep himself sharp once they got inside the funeral home. This was her stomping ground. If she was the shark, then the Blair Funeral Home was the deep water, and Clayton could almost feel his bare limbs dangling above her open jaws.

Blair took him down what looked like a service hallway. The rooms off to the sides were dark, but the silver moonlight coming through their high windows was enough to see what the rooms contained. In one, there were coffins stored on racks. In another he saw the glint of a metal table, a gurney, surrounded by bottles, tubes and beakers. He couldn't help but think of how these were scenes from every haunted house slapped up in mini-malls every October, a place to dare your friends to walk through at night.

Blair stopped at a door on the left. It opened with a creak of hinges, and she flipped on the overhead florescent panel lights. They sputtered to life with a hum to reveal the crematorium.

Clayton always supposed a crematorium would be a large, vaulted and foreboding place. Maybe that was because "crematorium" sounded a lot like "auditorium" to him. But this wasn't a large room at all. It was rather plain. Missing were the gargoyles crouched voyeuristically in the eaves, the stone floor that echoed your footfalls, the arched stained glass windows, and the rows of belching furnaces straight out of a World War II allied newsreel.

Instead, in the center of the long, narrow and brightly lit room was a single, metal unit. It reminded Clayton of the industrial dish sterilizer he ran at Village Inn restaurant in Lincoln just before he moved out to California long, long ago. It was eight feet tall, eight feet wide, and looked to be close to twenty feet long. Out of the top of this machine there was one large exhaust pipe, two feet in diameter, rising to the ceiling. A series of gauges and several large buttons were clustered on one side of the machine's gleaming metal face.

At the side of the room, there were shelves. One shelf displayed urns of several sizes and styles. On the bottom shelf were large, neatly stacked cardboard boxes. On the wall opposite these shelves was a series of pegs holding little metal disks stamped with numbers. Below that, was a table supporting another, much smaller metal machine about the size of a three-gallon bucket, sitting beside a pair of thermal gloves, a cluster of rakes, a couple of thick brooms and a large metal dust pan.

Clayton looked at Blair. Her wrinkled face was sour and her eyes glittered with malice. He couldn't wait to get this over with. After his tour through her museum of death, he knew she was capable of anything, and hanging out with the Witch of Dawson in a crematorium while she was dressed in a sparkly pink negligee with her feet slipped into the carcasses of dead animals was far from his ideal evening.

Do not, he thought, turn your back on her for a second.

"After you," he said with mock cordiality, and waved her back into the hallway and toward the hearse.

The night was quiet and thick with heat. The day's cicadas had stilled and no cars moved on the street. Nobody was likely to pass by this part of Columbus Avenue at night. Still, as they dragged the crate out of the hearse and the pine scraped the trunk's metal runners, a jolt of anxiety shot up Clayton's spine. Only a few more minutes, and the evidence of his awful deed would be gone forever.

The two shuffled the crate down the funeral home's darkened hallways, their feet whispering on the low nap carpet. With a grunt, they set it down on the crematorium's sealed cement floor.

"Now what?" Clayton asked. "How does this work?"

Blair said nothing. She was still in a mood. She went to the face of the machine and pressed a large red button. The oven's metal door shuddered and then began to open slowly with a whine of gears, revealing a large cavity lined with red fire bricks.

"We put him in there," said Blair, "that's what we do. We can leave him in the crate. It will burn up, too. But you need to grab a few of those cardboard rollers on that shelf and put them in the retort or we'll never get this thing in. There's too much friction."

"What's a retort?" asked Clayton.

"The oven," said Blair. "Put them in the oven."

Clayton flicked his eyes to the shelf. He saw the thick, cardboard dowels and grabbed a few, never taking his eyes from Blair.

"You won," said Blair.

"Huh?"

"I said, you won," Blair repeated. "You keep looking at me like I'm going to jump you. You don't have to be scared of little old me. What can I do to a big, strong man like you?"

She said this in a sweet, little girl's voice that both chilled Clayton and made him sick to his stomach. They stood looking at each other. Her face, with its traces of smeared lipstick, looked like a shrunken apple, and the glitter in her eyes had extinguished. They were dead eyes now, dead and as cold as the eyes in her bunny carcass slippers.

Shark's eyes, Clayton thought, and he could feel himself drowning in them, drowning into their numbing abyss.

"I notice you're done calling me honeybunch," Clayton said dispassionately, peeling his gaze from hers, though he was far from calm.

Blair only stared at him.

"Whatever," Clayton muttered, and handed her the dowels.

She snatched them and said, "You realize it will take about an hour and a half for him to burn. I'll start it, but I'm not going to sit here with you the whole time. I need my beauty sleep."

"I would say you need a lot of it," Clayton said, "and yes, you and I are going to sit here until it's done."

"I can clean out the retort in the morning," Blair said with an exaggerated pout. "We don't have to sit here. You're off the hook. So let me off mine."

"We are staying until it's all done," Clayton said wearily, "so you can stop bitching about it. I'm not having any more fun than you are. So, go lock the doors."

He followed her into the hall and as soon as she had locked up and had tossed the keys onto the metal table next to the big blender looking thing, he yanked the wig off of his head and shoved it into his back pocket. "Now let's do this."

The two lifted the crate to the mouth of the oven and slid it down the cardboard rollers into the tomb of red fire bricks. Clayton squeezed shut his eyes with the effort and with the thought of his father inside the crate, still dressed in a community theater's idea of an Old West card sharp, still frozen in a squat with his hands pinching the air at his chest as if he were a martial artist killed at the moment of exacting some ancient finishing move.

A lot of strange things had happened in his life, Clayton thought, but this certainly took the fucking cake.

Blair pushed the big red button again and the metal door whined closed. She pushed another big red button and the machine came to life with a hiss. The gauges trembled and began to spike.

"What's going on now?" he asked.

"Your pops is being licked by a 1600 degree flame coming straight down from the ceiling of the oven," Blair replied. "It will incinerate everything in there, but as I already said, it's going to take between an hour and a half to two hours."

"And that's it?"

"Pretty much," said Blair.

"Then we collect the ashes?"

"Yep."

"Then what's that machine for?" Clayton asked, cocking a thumb at the large blender looking thing on the metal table.

"Bone fragment pulverizer," she said. "Normally, when we rake out the ashes, they're chunky with bone fragments. You can't give a customer an urn full of chunky ashes, now can you? So we run the ashes through that machine to make them all powdery and nice. Do you see that?" Blair pointed at a garbage can full of what looked like metal nuts and bolts. "You also get pins, replacement joints, and titanium dental implants...all sorts of metal goodies end up on the floor of that oven. But you don't care about bone fragments do you? That will just take extra time."

Clayton said nothing. He watched the gauge on the oven waver between 1600 and 1700 degrees. He watched the large exhaust pipe rising to the ceiling, and he waited.

There was one chair in the room and Blair was on it. Clayton slid down the wall and sat on the floor. Together they waited, saying nothing.

Blair had been right. It took just over an hour and a half.

"It has to cool down now," Blair mumbled, "another half hour at least."

They waited forty-five minutes.

"It's still going to be hot in there," Blair warned, and pushed one of the big red buttons. The gears whined, and the metal door of the oven slid up to reveal a deep pile of white ash, some of it still smoking.

Clayton's eyes widened. He peered into the oven. She was right. There were chunks.

"Put him in one of those urns," Clayton said, "but get rid of the chunks first."

"For chrissake," Blair snapped. "What do you care? You killed him and stuffed him into the toolbox of your truck and drove him here on I-80 with a few ice packs thrown on top of him. I doubt a few chunks of bone are going to offend your fragile sensibilities."

Clayton only glared his reply.

With a petulant sigh Blair raked the ashes into the collection tray and took them to the pulverizer.

The machine worked a lot like a blender, or a large coffee grinder. Bone fragments went in, and fine white powder came out. The machine was loud. Clayton had to yell to be heard above the din.

"Let me ask you something," he said. "I mean, since the last thing I want to do is to ever see you again and don't care what shit you pull in Dawson once I'm gone. So you can answer me this: when you take these bodies for your little museum, set them up and play with them like dolls, does that mean you've been burying empty coffins?"

Blair turned from the pulverizer and cut the power. Her eyes narrowed, and her lips bent into the slightest of smiles. "Maybe," she said. "Usually I stick to customers who want to be cremated. Everyone always thinks you don't get the right ashes back when you're cremated anyway, so who cares? If they're all going to assume the worst, than why can't I have a little fun?"

"I saw Roger Vanderboom in your attic," said Clayton. "That's the father of one of my best friends. I've known that family my whole life."

"My condolences," said Blair sarcastically, returning to the mouth of the oven with her rake for another batch of ashes.

"What did you do to his face? It looked like it had been ripped up."

"He owed his wife money," Blair said, raking ashes into the collection pan. "It's none of your business."

"So what did you do to his face?"

Blair didn't answer.

"Oh, so you're not going to tell me?" Clayton said. "Fine, but what about his wife? What about Linda? I went to her funeral with Lance last month. Was she even in the coffin?"

"Of course," Blair snapped. "She was a friend of mine."

"What about Scotty Wegner?" Clayton asked stepping toward her. "Over twenty years ago? Do you remember him? What about him? Tell me if he's in the ground. That I need to know. Tell me if he's in the ground, Sylvia."

Blair said something, but she was leaning into the oven with her rake and Clayton couldn't hear.

"What was that?" Clayton asked. "What did you say?"

"I said maybe, maybe not. It's none of your business. Therefore," Blair said, reaching to rake the back corner of the furnace with a grunt, "you are cordially invited...to fuck off."

Clayton brought the gun down hard on the base of Sylvia Blair's skull. The rake she was holding clattered to the fire bricks.

Her body crumpled. Clayton rushed forward, and with all of his weight, pinned the falling body to the machine. He reached down and grabbed her thighs and heaved her upwards and into the mouth of the oven. His back popped, the old, familiar pain from his construction site injury, shooting through his vertebrae and legs in white hot spasms, but he kept lifting. She was halfway into the oven. He gritted his teeth and shoved at her ass.

Blair's night gown ripped a little as Clayton pushed her across the firebricks, the gauzy fabric bunching at the mouth of the oven like pink tissue paper on the top of a boutique's gift bag. Clayton grabbed her ankles and pushed, one of her bunny slippers clattering to the cement floor. Clayton tossed it back in, and as soon as Blair's feet had cleared the oven's mouth, he hit the big red button. The metal door shuttered, whined and closed.

Clayton's mind reeled. He stepped back, half expecting her to pound on the metal door, or shoot through it like a missile and come for his throat.

Wasn't it the witch who was supposed to put you in the oven? he thought, laughing breathlessly. *Not today, kiddies.*

Clayton hit the other big red button on the panel; the machine hissed and he backed away. He was shaking and covered in sweat. His back felt as though a hot iron was being driven into his spine.

Please don't let her scream, Clayton thought. *When the jet of fire hits her, please don't let her scream.*

But Clayton heard nothing but the hammering of his heart.

He backed up, staring at the machine until the wall came up behind him. With a wince of pain, he slid down to the floor and grabbed his knees.

On the roof of the Blair Funeral Home, the smokestack began billowing tendrils of Sylvia Blair into the warm August night.

Chapter 21

Creech

Dawson had but one big box store, and the Walmart out on Highway 34 was it. Surrounded by an expansive belt of freshly paved, jet black parking lot, it sat alone, the last stand of commerce before tall grass and endless farmland reclaimed the land all the way to the curve of the earth.

Don Creech pulled up to the store in his blue Toyota 4 Runner. Nautical Blue, the dealer had called it. He had planned on grabbing a pair of them when he went car shopping in Lincoln last spring--both he and his wife, Zelda, desperately needing new wheels--but thought twice about it and returned from the capital with only one. With her dementia getting worse, Zelda hardly drove anymore anyway.

In fact, it had been such a long time since Zelda had started up her car that the battery on her '92 Olds Toronado was shot. Creech knew this, because he had just tried to start it. If it had turned over, he wouldn't have needed to come to Walmart at all. He also knew that the 4-Runner wouldn't produce the kind of exhaust that an old shit box like Zelda's Toronado could spew out in short order. No, modern emission standards weren't great for what he had planned, and anyway, such a thing was not what he had in mind when he had gone to the car lot last year. Back then, he never would have entertained such a notion.

Last year, his job as principal of St. Mark Lutheran School had been secure, even garnering him a nice bonus at Christmas. Enrollment in the school had been on a steady increase. The children of the so-called Generation X were legion and were now grade school age. It seemed all of them had their noses pressed against St. Mark's stained glass windows, trying to get into a good school and away from the plebian prospects of a public school education. St. Mark had even been able to jack up tuition a bit, not enough to spook any parents into considering public school, but just enough to gild the old lily. Supply and demand, that's how it worked everywhere else, so why not in Dawson?

But then The Scandal had come along. When it ignited in late June, it had spread like a brush fire, and Creech couldn't keep in front of it. Accusations flew at him from every quarter, subpoenas piling up on his desk. He knew he would be fired, guilty or not. The Damoclean sword that had long trembled above him had finally snapped its tether and the race to assassinate his character had begun.

And it hadn't stopped since.

But it would stop tonight.

The vast blacktop in front of the Walmart was never close to being full, but at this time of night, save for a dozen cars peppered throughout the lot, it was almost deserted. With a deep breath, Don Creech got out of his car, shoulders hunched, hands shoved into the pockets of his trousers, and headed for the entrance.

He wondered if his disguise would work, but he wouldn't have put money on it. He wore a red baseball cap and a shoddy shirt the principal of a Lutheran School would never wear: a long-sleeved, olive-green t-shirt with the word "Hollister" across its front. He didn't know what "Hollister" meant, but he assumed it was the brand of shirt or some rock band. Whatever it was, it had cost him five dollars at Steiger's thrift store, and it would become apparent within minutes that neither it nor his baseball cap was going to fool anyone.

He approached the store's electric doors and they hissed open dutifully to receive him. As they did, they disgorged an older couple wrestling with several plastic bags. It was Bob Hoagan and his wife June.

Bob, a local farmer in his trucker hat and thick glasses, a VFW pin displayed prominently on the suspenders that bound his plaid shirt around his belly, visibly recoiled when he looked up at Creech, almost running into him.

"Wasn't that Don Creech?" June Hoagan whispered when she thought she was well out of earshot.

She hadn't been out of earshot at all.

Creech double-timed it into the store. The villagers had their torches lit, and those bloodhounds would have recognized him even if he had stuffed his shirt with fake titties and painted his face like a Vegas showgirl. Did any of them care that he had been a pillar of the community? Well, he had been; for most of their lives, he had been. He had helped them through their most trying times, and had congratulated them on their greatest triumphs. Still, they had banished him, relegating him to the trash heap of historic villains to rot alongside the likes of Hitler and Charles Manson.

"Look, there's Mr. Creech," they would say in the produce section of the Pak N' Save. "Let's get out of here." Or snot-nosed teenagers hanging out by the Git N' Split would say, "There's the guy who diddled those kids." Again, they always said such things when they thought they were out of earshot, but just like June Hoagan, they never quite were.

A month ago, just after The Scandal had become common knowledge all across town, he had foolishly attempted to have a nice, quiet breakfast at the Corner Café. And who had given him the old stink eye? Peggy Jones herself. Peggy, whose husband's funeral he had presided over, whose granddaughter's baptism he had performed in the church he was now excommunicated from.

Well, all of it ended tonight. They could say what they wanted after tonight.

All of them would be well out of earshot tonight.

"Can I help you find something?" said a squeaky voiced teenage boy in a blue Walmart vest.

"Where are the barbecues?" Creech asked. "They're usually out front."

"Oh, they're in back now," said the kid apologetically, "by the patio furniture. Just over there under that picnic sign with the..."

The kid visibly deflated. He recognized who he was talking to, but Creech didn't wait for the familiar pallor of recognition to fully set on the kid's face like hardening plaster. He kept moving. Maybe the kid had been one of the boys he had helped come of age, maybe he wasn't. It didn't really matter either way. Everyone in this town knew who he was and what he was presumed to have done. The verdict was in. They would all hate him whether they had any personal reason to do so or not. It was a litmus test in Dawson now. Are you a Lutheran? Are you a Republican? Do you despise Don Creech?

He found the barbecue grills and lifted the lid on a Weber 22-inch Kettle charcoal grill and peered inside.

"That's a good size. Perfect for two, I think."

Creech looked up. It was a girl with streaked blond hair, also in a Walmart vest. Creech didn't know her. He thought she might be from a neighboring town, maybe Milford.

Was this co-ed really going to hard sell him on a charcoal grill at midnight? These kids were bored out of their minds, he thought.

"I can get you one from the back," the girl offered.

"Give me two of them," said Creech.

"Two?"

Creech only stared at her.

The girl frowned self-consciously, but then bucked up in a matter of seconds, her smile re-stretching across her face as if it had been on springs. "You got it," she said. "You can keep shopping and I'll bring them out to the loading dock around back. How does that sound?"

"Where's your electrical tape?" Creech asked.

"Electrical tape? Aisle eight, across from the scissors."

Creech grabbed three rolls of silver duct tape, thought better of it and grabbed a fourth roll before heading to the row of checkout counters.

The store was a morgue, nobody in line, only two young employees flirting with one another at one of the registers. When they saw Creech coming, they peeled away from each other guiltily.

A short, plump girl with red hair tied back into a ponytail started to ring him up. Between scanning the rolls of tape, she was sneaking glances at him, the way someone might keep an eye on a poisonous spider until they could inch their way toward a broom.

Creech noticed how uncomfortable she was. Her mouth wouldn't quite close and when her eyes weren't flicking up at him, they were darting to the sides, probably hoping that the boy who had been chatting her up would rescue her from her undeserved sentence.

She was more nervous than most, Creech thought. Had he trained her? Had they gone through her change together? Was that why she looked like a cow in a squeeze chute?

So why didn't he recognize her?

The girl with the streaky blond hair who had helped him with the barbecues flitted by and dropped off the invoice for the two grills to the red haired checker with a brief instruction before she was off to something else. The red haired girl looked relieved; for the moment she had company. But once she was alone again with Creech, she darkened.

Creech recognized her now. It was Lisa Valecheck, of course. He remembered her as a quiet girl. He hadn't seen her much in school over the last several years because she laid low, she wasn't involved in sports or theater, and she had managed to stay out of the principal's office all during high school. That was why he hadn't recognized her. Not to mention that she had become unrecognizable from the waif of a sixth-grader that Creech remembered. She had plumped up like a state fair mudroller. She looked primed to be a baby factory for some dim-witted farmer. Undoubtedly, she would end up working at this Walmart--in between her water breaking--until box wine glued her to a couch.

And yes, she had been one of his trainees.

And who knows? Maybe she had even piled onto the lawsuits against him; the lawsuits that his lawyer had correctly surmised would go nowhere. The first two suits to be filed had already been decided--or more like it, been thrown out of court.

Lisa kept looking at the rolls of duct tape and kept stealing her distrustful glances like a beaten dog. Sure, he could have explained what the tape was for, that it wasn't for binding his victims in his basement like she supposed, but he didn't owe her an explanation. He didn't owe her anything but...

"Three hundred and eighty-five dollars," Lisa Valecheck mumbled, "including the two barbecues."

Creech handed her four one hundred dollar bills and left the store without waiting for change. He pulled the 4-Runner around to the loading dock and declined help getting the two barbecue grills into the back of his car.

The two young Walmart employees in their blue vests and khaki pants stood in the loading dock and watched Don Creech disappear down Highway 15 toward Dawson.

#

When Creech returned home, he threw his car keys on the console in the hallway, pausing when he saw his wedding picture. Like many old things in his home, the silver framed portrait had stood at the same place on the mahogany veneered side table for so many years he had stopped noticing it.

He picked it up and stared at the two young faces in their dated wedding costumes. It had been the spring of 1967. His powder blue suit had a bowtie the size of a helicopter rotor, and Zelda's dress looked like she had fallen through a doily, but they both looked happy. Soon after this photo had been taken they had headed for Niagara Falls to consummate their marriage, which they did at the Red Coach Inn amidst the rumbling of the falls, and he had never regretted his choice. They had been happy for a few months shy of 50 years, and though Zelda wasn't all there as of late, he would miss her, miss the idea of her if nothing else. She would be the only thing he missed.

For the first time, he was thankful for her dementia. It would finally benefit them both. She hadn't been quite sure what the fuss was all about in Dawson lately and why court papers had been piling up on his desk, so she wouldn't be too shocked when she eventually found out about what was going to happen tonight. She would be spared that, at least, and it would all be cleaned up by the time she returned from her sister's farm.

The barbecue grills were easy to get through the house. Each of them had nice rubber wheels that whispered over the deep pile carpet. Now it was a question of where to put them. Should he go through the trouble of taking them upstairs or just use the guest bathroom downstairs?

He decided to take them upstairs. The master bath had a deep Jacuzzi tub. That tub could probably just accommodate both of these grills if he set them just so, side by side.

Now where had he put that box of stick matches?

He entered his den, clicked on the light, and pulled open the large bottom drawer on his desk, his junk drawer, and pulled out a box of EZ Strike matches.

He was arrested by the sight of the court papers that littered his desk blotter. With a tight grin, he plucked one of them from the pile:

In 2015, Neumann discussed the abuse with a licensed professional counselor, Donna Vancini. Her treatment notes indicate that Neumann told her he had sought counseling about the sexual abuse in 2012. Vancini advised Neumann that there was a strong possibility that the sexual abuse he had suffered as a child was contributing to his current problems.

Neumann hired an attorney who wrote a letter to the school on May 5, 2014, in an attempt to have Creech removed from his position at the school. The letter states that Neumann "is now emotionally able to publicly reveal the nature and circumstances of these acts and to pursue the appropriate redress for the conduct, if necessary." (R. at 52.) On May, 24, 2014 Neumann's attorney wrote to the school board again, stating in part that "Neumann is seeking compensation for injuries suffered by him as a result of acts committed by [Creech]." (R. at 57.)

On May 16, 2014, Neumann's attorney referred Neumann for an evaluation with Dr. Fisch, a clinical psychologist. Dr. Fisch diagnosed Neumann with moderate to severe posttraumatic distress disorder, moderate to severe dysthymic reaction, moderate to severe fulminating somataform disorder, complex trauma reaction, and chronic fulminating dissociative disorder.   Dr. Fisch's affidavit states that Neumann did not make a connection between the abuse and his mental disorders until after he had started his treatment with Dr. Fisch.

"Uh huh," said Creech sardonically. "You didn't make the connection until the shrink told you to." Creech plucked another sheet from the pile of papers.

Vanderboom filed this lawsuit on July 6, 2015, seeking damages against the church, the congregation, the school, and the principal, Donald Creech. The district court granted summary judgment in favor of the defendants, concluding that Vanderboom's complaint was not timely filed. Vanderboom appeals.

Vanderboom reached the age of 21 on April 13, 1989, but he did not file this lawsuit until July 2015, some sixteen years later. The district court dismissed his suit as untimely, finding no basis for tolling the limitations period. On appeal, Vanderboom asserts that factual disputes preclude entry of summary judgment. Namely, he contends that the limitations period should be equitably tolled on the ground that he did not discover a connection between the abuse and his problems until sometime within four years of the filing of the complaint, and that his mental disorders prevented him from pursuing legal action.

While an action in tort generally accrues as soon as the act occurs, Nebraska applies an equitable tolling doctrine referred to as the discovery rule in certain categories of cases where "the injury is not obvious and the individual is wholly unaware that he or she has suffered an injury or damage."

"Blah, blah, blah," said Creech aloud. "You lose. How many words does that take?" He skipped to the bottom of the page:

Accordingly, we affirm the district's court's grant of summary judgment dismissing Vanderboom's lawsuit as barred by the statute of limitations.

Creech smiled.

He removed one of the EZ Strikes and tested one by striking it on the edge of his wooden desk. It sputtered and lit. He shoved the box into his pants pocket.

"You all lost fair and square," he muttered. "You're all sore losers. All of you."

One at a time, he dragged the charcoal grills up the carpeted staircase to the master bath, their laminated price tags still dangling from their wooden handles. He had been right, the two grills fit side by side in the Jacuzzi tub though one was cramped, one of its tripod legs floating in the air at one side of the tub, the grill listing toward the other.

No matter, Creech thought. It would do just fine.

In the garage he grabbed the almost full bag of Kingsford charcoal briquettes that had been the impetus for this idea in the first place. He had eyed the wadded-up bag of briquettes after failing to turn over the engine in Zelda's dusty old Toronado.

He whistled as he left the garage.

Why? Was he looking forward to checking out? He supposed maybe he was. Maybe the idea of a dirt nap was putting a spring in his step. This town could find some other whipping boy. He was checking out. He was soon going to be well out of earshot.

Back in the master bathroom he started ripping long lengths from the silver rolls of duct tape. He started with the double hung window that looked over the backyard, taping up the frames and smoothing the strips into place with the palm of his hand.

Next, he would tape the door closed. He would start by sealing the space between the door and the jamb and then making sure to fill the gap beneath the door with plenty of tape.

But an idea struck him. He should get a pillow from the bed. Yes, there was no reason to just lie on the floor without being comfortable. Besides, he didn't know how long any of this was supposed to take. Was it quick? Or did it take a long time? Would he cough a lot? Or would he just pass out?

He returned to the bathroom with a feather pillow clad in a silk pillow case and laid it in the center of the tile floor before returning to his work. Maybe he should put the briquettes in the grills first before he taped himself into the room for good? And did he bring the matches? Yes, he had. They were in his pants pocket. He started dumping charcoal into the grills. The briquettes were louder than he expected when they careened into the enameled bowl, echoing off the bathroom's tiles as if off the walls of a mausoleum.

Creech noticed he was breathing heavy now, and it wasn't just from his exertions. It was terror. The grills were full. The windows were taped up. There was only one task left.

He turned to face the bathroom door. With a resonant rip he produced a length of tape from one of the silver rolls. He could hear his heart now. It was in his ears, and his stomach was in his throat. He crouched and with a trembling hand placed the strip of tape down one side of the door jamb where it met the wall.

With the roll of tape in his hand, he turned to look at his garishly lit tomb: the pillow where he would take his final breath on the floor. The tottering grills in the sunken bathtub--his funeral pyre. They were waiting for a kiss from the tip of a match.

He was dizzy.

Dizzy.

He threw down the roll of tape and sat on the toilet, his hands gripping tufts of his hair. Why should he have to do this? Why did he have to run from all of them? He had won. The courts had said so. Their claims were baseless. Their problems had nothing to do with him. He was not theirs to sacrifice. Sure, if he went through with this, they would rejoice for awhile, but they would also forget about him within months, and they would know no real solace. Their failings would still persevere. Their demons would still breathe.

He stumbled to his feet and ripped open the bathroom door.

He was shaking. He needed a drink. On wobbly legs he teetered down the stairs to the kitchen, flipped on the overhead lights, and took a rocks glass out of the cupboard.

When had he drunk hard alcohol last? He couldn't remember. He had no idea if he had any left in the house. Didn't Zelda keep a bottle or two for guests?

Oh, he hoped to God she did.

He rifled through the pantry. Behind some sauterne cooking wine and a sticky bottle of sherry, he found a fifth of Jim Beam. There was a quarter of a bottle left.

With a sigh, he jammed the rocks glass into the ice maker on the door of the fridge, his hand shaking, and after a couple of cubes had tumbled into the glass, he filled it with whiskey and took a deep gulp.

That's when Clayton Briggle shot him three times.

Like the boom of steel girders felled in a parking garage, the sound of the gunshots filled the kitchen, ricocheting between the tile floor, the metal appliances and the plastic of the panel lights with a hellish roar.

The first bullet spun Creech around, sloshing the bourbon out of his glass in a golden spray, entering his shoulder and shattering the scapula, separating the clavicle and humerus bones as it shredded the connective deltoid and trapezius muscles, exiting cleanly and nicking a chunk of plaster out of the wall in the darkened dining room.

The second bullet hit the glass in Creech's hand before he could drop it, sending shards of glass spraying into the air in a phenomenon of light. It then entered through the pectoral muscle, grazing the upper lobe of the lung and splintering the first rib. Fine shards of glass tinkled to the floor like diamond snow.

Wide-eyed , and with his mouth hanging open, Don Creech had half a second to look his assailant in the eyes before the third bullet hit him. Standing at the edge of the living room was a man he had never seen before. The man had grey hair, almost white, and he was wearing glasses.

It's one of their fathers, his mind screamed, and it would have been his last thought had it not been for the utter confusion of what he noticed just before he died.

The man with the gun was wearing what looked like white bobby socks for gloves. With an almost farcical look of shock and confusion spread across his face, the last thing Donald Creech's eyes focused on before his brain was swallowed by white stars were the torn pieces of plastic bag tied around the stranger's shoes.

The third bullet struck Don Creech in the throat, tearing a hole in his trachea the size of a nickel, puncturing his larynx, and exiting through the back of the neck in a pink mist of blood and spinal fluid, the slug lodging in one of the kitchen's country oak cabinets where later Sheriff Bob Lutz would pry it out with an army knife.

Creech tried to scream, clawing at his throat, but no sound came; pink bubbles boiled through his splayed fingers.

"That's for Scotty Wegner, motherfucker," said Clayton.

Creech made one attempt to walk forward, stumbled, then fell straight backwards, landing hard on the tile floor. The dishes jumped in their cupboards.

Then, all was quiet.

Clayton walked slowly forward, the plastic on his shoes crinkling, and craned his neck to look down at the body. Creech stared back at him with eyes as empty and as foggy as the glass on a shower door. The little pink bubbles percolating through the hole in his throat had stopped.

Clayton stood motionless for a moment, every nerve in him tingling, every sense heightened. His ears were ringing. Fine tendrils of gun smoke had turned the kitchen into a hazy dream world. Clayton had to shake his head to wake from it. He turned and went upstairs.

There were no secrets in Dawson. Through regular phone calls with Ruby he had learned what everyone in the Corner Café already knew: Zelda Creech had dementia and she was out of town for safe keeping. She would be for a couple of weeks. The house would be empty.

The bed in the master bedroom was made. With Blair's white bobby socks still on his hands, Clayton pulled down the bedclothes, throwing the comforter off of the bed and mixing up the bed sheets into a tangled pile. He grabbed Blair's yellow tank top with the brightly colored Macaw embroidered on its front from where it hung out of his back pocket, and rubbed it onto the pillows, denting them with his fists. Then he threw the tank top on the floor near the bed.

Retracing his steps downstairs, Clayton exited the house the way he had entered it, through the sliding glass door and into the backyard.

Even though Creech's kitchen was situated in the center of the house, and even though the lots in this part of town were generous and far apart, there was certainly a chance the shots had been heard. He cocked an ear, but no dog barked and no car whispered on the street. This town was asleep, dead to the world.

Clayton crept down the side of the house and out of the side gate. He slipped the white bobby socks from his sweaty palms, but he chanced walking a full block before he dared remove the plastic bags from around his shoes, wadding them up with the socks and shoving them deep into his pockets.

All was dark. All was quiet.

Peaceful, he thought, the way Dawson should be.

The gun was still hot where it hung in its shoulder holster against his bare skin. Walking briskly, he turned off of Columbus Avenue and disappeared into the shadows.

Chapter 22

The Last Kiss

Clayton arrived in the parking lot of the Walmart on Highway 15 just after midnight. Dispatch assured him that his taxi was on the way, but they cautioned that the meter would have to run from Lincoln in order to pick him up in Dawson. Clayton said it was no problem, that his name was Paul, and that they should call him when the taxi arrived as he would be inside the store at the coffee shop. "Look for the guy with the grey hair and glasses," Clayton had said.

Then he grabbed a real estate circular from a wire rack at the side of the coffee shop and ordered a large cuppa joe. It was going to be another long drive tonight, but this time he would be just another traveler forced to traverse the great emptiness of the Nebraska panhandle on his way to somewhere--or on his way to nowhere at all.

It was a good half hour before the taxi arrived. Clayton didn't say much to the driver, only enough to be friendly and forgettable.

"Car broke down?" the driver asked. "You really should look into that Triple A. It's a life saver."

Clayton agreed that he really should, and then stared out of the window for the rest of the trip. As subterfuge, he told the driver to drop him off at a Red Roof Inn outside of Lincoln. From there, he walked the quarter mile to his truck, parked in a long term public lot just off of O Street where the chatter of frat boys and local barflies was still pouring out of a row of brick drinking holes. He passed an alley that connected two of the bars and went around back. He took the white bobby socks and the pieces of plastic kitchen bag from his pants pockets, wadded them into a ball, and shoved them down the side of one of three overstuffed dumpsters. It appeared that trash day might be tomorrow.

Sometimes things just went your way, Clayton thought.

Tonight he planned on finding a cheap motel in Denver, paying them in cash and getting some sleep before heading for California in the morning.

#

The Corner Café was buzzing on Thursday morning, August 10th. It had been two days since the murder and the scene at the Blair house, but Lutz had only managed to keep it quiet for about a day before details started spilling into the streets from all quarters. The town crawled with a team of investigators from throughout the county, and rumor had it that Blair's disappearance had garnered response from the FBI.

It was standing room only in the café, Peggy Jones hunched and spinning in frenzied circles trying to fill orders for coffee and Danish. John Supernau had managed to secure a table with Kat, and Ruby--fresh from her morning run--had squeezed in to join them.

Lance Vanderboom was standing over Supernau's table, speculations between them flying, when the phone in his pocket buzzed. It was Laurie.

"Hi honey," said Laurie, "What did Bob Lutz want this morning?"

"Hold on," said Lance, making his way to the door sideways, "it's very crowded in here. I can't hear a thing."

Lance squeezed out the front door of the café and walked across the square toward the bandshell, caught his breath and said, "Now what?"

"What did Bob Lutz want this morning?"

"To question us," said Lance.

"About the murder?" said Laurie. "About Blair? He thinks we have something to do with it?"

"I guess," said Lance. "I don't blame him. We did have a motive. He wants to talk to both of us tonight at the station."

"But that's silly," said Laurie. "On Tuesday night we were in couple's therapy in Lincoln until...I don't know..."

"Until 9 o'clock," offered Lance, "and then a half-hour drive home puts us both here at 9:30. From what everyone is saying, they think the murder took place around midnight. That rules us in."

"But we were in bed," Laurie protested.

"Only Luke knows that," said Lance, "and he's a toddler who was dead asleep at the time. He's not much of an alibi. Look, we're going to be fine, it's just going to be a little stressful, that's all. Just answer his questions honestly and he'll know we're telling the truth. That's all we can do."

Laurie was quiet.

"Okay?" Lance asked. "We didn't do anything. We'll be fine."

"I guess," said Laurie softly. "Well, then who do you think did it then?"

"Could have been anyone," said Lance, "anyone that Creech...you know, took advantage of."

"That's half the town," said Laurie.

"I just heard from Supernau that Paul Neumann and Becky Krauss are the leading suspects," said Lance. "They were the first ones to file suits and the first ones to be rejected by the courts."

"But they live in Florida. Someone would have seen them in town if they came here."

"I don't know," Lance admitted. "You're right. It seems pretty unlikely, but that's what people are saying."

"You think Paul could shoot someone?"

Lance laughed. "I don't think he would know which way to hold a gun."

Laurie laughed too, although without humor, and the two fell into silence.

"There's something else," said Lance. "Lutz wants to talk to me about the funeral arrangements I made with the Blair Funeral Home for both my dad and Linda."

"Why is that?"

"Not sure," said Lance. "The rumor right now is that Sylvia Blair was somehow crooked, like she didn't cremate people when she was supposed to or didn't bury them where they were supposed to be buried or something like that. It's all kind of fuzzy right now. Ruby says Blair's house is all cordoned off. You can't get near it. She has to show her ID just to get down Second Street. She saw a coroner's van there. I don't think Dawson even has a coroner's van. So the feds must have found something in there, something bad. Lutz said he would tell us what he knew tonight when we came down to the sheriff's station."

"This is crazy, Lance."

"Yeah, it sure is." Lance's voice was distant as he watched two strangers in expensive suits--probably G-men--huddled in conversation in the shade at the other end of the bandshell.

"I hope everything's going to be okay," said Laurie. "Nothing like this has ever happened here. I hope whatever is going on doesn't change anything."

"I hope it doesn't either," said Lance.

#

That sure was one hell of a head scratcher he had left for Bob Lutz back in Dawson, Clayton thought, turning on his computer.

As he waited for the boot-up, he gazed through the blinds. His new L.A. apartment was just south of Wilshire Boulevard at the edge of Koreatown, the small second bedroom he used as an office looked onto a portion of MacArthur Park.

Yep, it was going to be the biggest shitstorm that town, or any town in Nebraska, would ever see.

He almost felt sorry for Lutz. Not only would the sheriff have to sort it all out, but at some point, another salacious detail would surface: Lutz had been banging Sylvia Blair. Not only that, but he had done so on the night of her disappearance and the night of Don Creech's murder. Lutz's DNA had to be all over the Blair house. Clayton assumed there was still a crispy cum towel on the floor of Blair's bedroom upstairs, or surely something else with Lutz's goo on it. Who would discover that? Lutz himself? Would he try and cover it up? Or would one of his deputies stumble on it first and not give him the opportunity?

However it happened to come to light, it would certainly gum up the investigation.

There was another factor, too. Did Lutz have any emotional attachment to Blair? Would he be jealous or enraged that the resident child molester and all-around creepazoid, Don Creech, also appeared to be helping himself to sloppy seconds on the same night? It sure would look that way. After all, one of Blair's shirts would be found at the foot of Creech's bed with her DNA all over it, and probably a bit of Lutz's, too.

Of course, that shirt would lead the investigation back to the Blair house, and that's when the shit would really hit the proverbial fan. Clayton had seen a lot in his life, but even he still couldn't believe what had been going on in Blair's attic. Wait until Dawson got a load of that kind of crazy. It would hurt everyone's brain like a ten-penny nail in the skull.

And where was Blair? Oh where, oh where could she be?

Clayton had re-parked her hearse where it always was, where everyone in town always knew it to be: backed into the drive at the side of her house, its nose facing Second Street. Of course, Clayton had driven it from the Blair Funeral Home with Blair's socks on his hands and with one of the plastic bags under his ass. Even then, he had still wiped down the car twice with wads of paper towel he had swiped from the funeral home bathroom.

The other of the two plastic bags had briefly held a combination of Foster Briggle and Sylvia Blair's powdered remains just long enough for Clayton to pour them down a storm drain about a quarter-mile from the funeral home on his long walk to Don Creech's house. There had been summer rain since that day—twice, in fact. Clayton knew this as he had always subscribed to the local paper and it was now delivered by mail to his new digs.

Of course, someone could have heard the hearse pull into Blair's that night at an untimely hour, and of course someone could have seen the stranger with the grey hair and glasses carrying what looked like a bag of garbage down Columbus Avenue in the dead of night, but according to the Dawson Independent, nobody had.

But the one thing the Independent had pointed out that even Clayton hadn't known about was that on the night of his murder, Creech had been poised to commit suicide in the upstairs master bathroom. Two Weber kettle grills were found in the tub, loaded with charcoal, along with a box of matches. The windows had already been taped shut and so had most of the door, which had been ripped open after having been taped.

Clayton's jaw hit the floor when he read that little morsel. He must have passed right by that bathroom when he had placed Blair's shirt and messed up the bed, but he hadn't noticed. He seemed to remember the light being on in the bathroom that night, but had thought nothing of it. This new intelligence baffled even him. Had killing Creech been unnecessary? Had the principal been minutes away from taking his own life anyway and had simply chickened out?

Maybe, and Clayton would have to live with that. But more pressing was what Lutz would be compelled to consider given the circumstances: that Creech had briefly escaped from the gunman and the bathroom, thwarting the gunman's attempt to make Creech's death look like a suicide? And would Lutz assume that it had been Blair? That she had been overpowered and the fight had moved downstairs to the kitchen where Creech was eventually blown away?

It was a mess, but it was a mess that would not point to Clayton, and that was all he cared about. He hadn't been in town for over a month, he lived over a thousand miles away, and he was one of the few Dawsonians around his age that hadn't been diddled by Creech. For the finger to point at him, there would have to have been one hell of a foolish oversight. And Clayton couldn't think of one.

He didn't regret ridding the town of its monsters, but he did regret one thing: not being able to break the news to Lance about Roger Vanderboom. Knowing that his father's body had never been buried, and that it had remained Blair's plaything, would devastate Lance. The next several months were not going to be easy on his old friend.

On the one hand, Lance and Laurie would both feel a guilty relief in knowing that Don Creech couldn't harm any more kids, but on the other hand, Blair's secret was out. Lance would be left wondering why in hell his father had been embalmed and kept in her attic, his face torn up on the sides and staples in his skull (Clayton still wanted to know the answer to that one), dressed in a costume from the town's production of Oklahoma!

That was going to be one weird ass police report.

Then there would be the question of Sylvia Blair. She had disappeared into thin air—literally, as only Clayton knew. This would point to her guilt as Creech's executioner, but where she had gone and how she had gotten there would leave the town speculating for a long time to come--maybe for generations.

The legends had already begun. It had already been weeks since the murder and the grisly revelations at the Blair house. According to Ruby, screams had been heard rolling down Second Street from those children who had taken up the dare to stand before the now-haunted mansion. It was said that if one was to look up at the dormer window, high above at the rooftop, and if one was unlucky enough to catch the eye of the Witch of Dawson looking down at them, then they would end up in her attic stuffed like a teddy bear, where they would remain forever.

Outside Clayton's window an ice cream cart's bell tinkled. The Mexican pushing it, his skin like rutted clay, his wide-brimmed hat tilted back on his head, whistled as he coaxed the cart onto the grass and into MacArthur Park.

Clayton wouldn't be in this apartment for long if all went well. He didn't belong here anymore. He would go home, home to Dawson, but before he could he had some patching up to do and some emails to write.

#

From: <Clayton Briggle> cbgb@krbdeth.com

To: <John Supernau> jsupe@gmail.com

Subject: Hey...

Message: I wanted to thank you again for letting me stay with you guys in July. It was really cool of you, and I hope you can forgive me for subjecting you to my bullshit. I never meant to jeopardize your family. I love Kat and Flynn, and you all were so good to me. The last thing I would ever want would be to make you all feel unsafe in any way.

I just want you to know that the situation I told you about has been resolved. Again, it isn't who I really am, and getting involved in such things was a moment of weakness and desperation that I don't plan on repeating. Anyway, I've paid off the people who I thought might be chasing me, and they understand now what happened. Everything is fine.

As far as Dawson, I know you all have had your hands full. I've heard about what happened to Creech. I subscribe to the Independent and get it delivered here in L.A. I've been following everything, but I'm sure you know more than the paper does just by hearing things around town. From what I gather, I guess they can't find Sylvia Blair? And there's some connection between her and Creech? Weird. Anyway, I know this might not be the most tasteful thing to say (not like I've ever been tasteful) but I'm glad for you guys. I'm glad that Dawson is rid of such monsters. They have no place in our town.

This is turning into a really long email, I know, but I am just writing to ask for forgiveness. I'm also writing to tell you that I'm thinking about coming back, maybe for good.

As you may or may not know, Ruby Wegner and I kind of hit it off. She made me realize that there is still amazing people in the world who can weather far greater things than I have. Yet she is still courageous and has never given up. She amazes me. She is everything good, everything pure. She deserves someone far better than me, but I hope to become that person. Maybe together, we can find something new to live for. That's my hope.

I really look forward to seeing you again, Supe. Hopefully you can find it in your heart to forgive me and we can have another barbecue soon.

Lots of love,

Clayton

#

To: <Randy Johnson> rj68@mac.com

From: <Clayton Briggle> cbgb@krbdeth.com

Subject: I'm sorry.

Message: Randy, I am so sorry for what happened. I never thought it would ever involve you. Please tell the band that I resign. I'm sure you will all find someone new who will inspire you. I wish you all the best. I think it's time for me to move on to the next chapter of my life.

Please find attached a receipt for a deposit into your PayPal account. I hope the money helps with your medical expenses, but more than that, I hope it can be just a small symbol of my sincere apologies. I've always valued you as a friend and I think you're an incredible musician. I wish you and all the guys the best.

I have some business back in Nebraska. That's where I'm from and that's where I should return. My old town needs me, and more than that, I need my old town.

I know you probably don't care why I'm leaving, and you probably still hate me--though I hope you won't someday--but I need to say this to somebody, need to tell you why I'm probably not coming back.

I just think there has to be a place where evil can't be allowed to live. There needs to be a place where innocence isn't murdered, where idealism can still have a chance at being reality. There needs to be a place that is immune from the sins of this world. My hometown will be that place. I will see to that.

I will be its guardian. While I live it will not be profaned. No harm will come to it. It will remain simple and pure. We can have heaven on earth. I know we can. I think that Dawson, Nebraska can be that place.

As long as I have an ounce of strength in my body, or a thread of goodness still woven through this black soul, and as long as my bones remain above its soil, I'll defend my hometown with all the fury and righteousness of angels.

I have found my purpose.

Until we meet again,

Clayton

#

"You're back?" Ruby cried. "I didn't know you were coming back to Dawson! Why didn't you tell me?"

Clayton smiled. "I wasn't sure myself. Are you busy?"

"No," said Ruby, hanging onto the knob of her front door, her face still slack with shock, "not at all."

"You aren't going to school today?"

"I'm...well..." Ruby bit her lower lip, searching for words, "taking a break from all that."

"Then come down to the river with me," said Clayton. "I got a blanket and some sandwiches." He held up a plastic bag. "Some Cokes, too."

"A picnic?"

"Yeah," said Clayton, "why not?"

It was the last day of September, and a breeze came across the Big Blue River with the first hint of fall on its breath. Above them, the leaves on the pin oaks were just starting to bruise.

"It's been crazy around here," said Ruby as they walked through the park to the riverbank.

"Yeah, you've been keeping me up to speed, you and the paper."

"But we haven't talked in a couple of weeks. Did you hear about the bodies in Blair's attic?"

"I did."

"All that went on right across the street from me," said Ruby. "Crazy, huh?"

"It is."

"You wouldn't think those kind of things would happen in this town."

"No, you wouldn't." said Clayton, and he produced two sandwiches from the plastic bag. "Italian or roast beef, or half and half?"

They split both sandwiches and threw crusts of bread to a pair of yellow rails who were hopping across the glassy surface of the Big Blue.

"Flashback," Clayton said. "Did your class ever take a field trip to see the cranes on the Platte River in the spring?"

"Yes!" Ruby cried. "I remember that. I loved it!"

"I never saw them again," said Clayton. "I don't know why I didn't go back year after year. Where else can you see thousands of cranes dancing around like that? It was pretty amazing."

Ruby smiled with the recollection. "I never went back either. I guess I never thought about it."

Silence bloomed between them.

"I'm thinking of hanging up the rock n' roll thing," said Clayton, standing up, cocking his arm and skipping a stone across the surface of the river. "I think I might move back here, back to Dawson."

"Why would you want to do that?" Ruby winced.

Clayton sat back down. "Well, you're here."

Ruby blushed.

"I know you're not into, y'know, having a relationship," said Clayton, "and I don't know what I could give you that you don't already have. But I know I want to give you all that I've got. I've never even thought of saying that to a girl until now. I guess you have to be willing to be more than you thought you were to say something like that, but I feel like something more than I thought I was when I'm around you. Does that make any sense?"

Ruby laughed. "Kind of," she said. That's sweet, but…"

"But what?"

"I'd be a terrible companion," said Ruby. "I think I might always be a pessimist. I've always hoped for the best, and expected the worst."

"That's fine with me, Ruby," said Clayton and, as the sun dipped low, igniting the Big Blue River into a sheet of gold leaf, he kissed her.

"Hoping for the best and expecting the worst is all I've ever done."

October 2014 – May 2015

www.ingramcontent.com/pod-product-compliance
Lightning Source LLC
Chambersburg PA
CBHW050519110726
47899CB00005B/1513